I0788722

THE GOLDEN DESIRES

~~~

The Golden Desires
The Golden Supremacy
The Golden Unity

ANN M PRATLEY
~~~

BY ANN M PRATLEY

Power Moore Investigation Tales
Hoonigan
Resolution of Happiness
Home by the Sea
Tiger in Our House

Forbidden Conflicts Series
Amethyst of Youth
Ruby of Law
Diamond of War
Sapphire of Prejudice
Emerald of Wisdom

Freedom of Flight Series
Christian
Brandon
Trinity

Painful Deliverance Series
Painful Deliverance
Darkness of Heart
Friendship of Desire

Chisholm Manor Series
Alessandra

CONTENTS

THE GOLDEN DESIRES

~~ Golden Desires Series: Book 1~~

ANN M PRATLEY

CHAPTER 1

From a great distance, it could be seen as a silhouette that should have immediately commanded attention. It was vast and high, located and stretching across the broad horizon line of a long mountain range.

The shape of the structure looked like it might be a castle built hundreds or even thousands of years ago. Perhaps it had been constructed to house reigning monarchs and their hoards of higher and lower class minions. For this reason, it might have been regarded as somewhere that attracted people from far and wide, but to this place, nobody ever came. No-one from outside, that was.

If anyone had ever seen and become curious about the structure, the closer they got, the more the grey brick would have become visible. Also evident would have been the height and strength of its walls, and an indication of the many hundreds of years they had stood.

In truth, it was far too cold for outsiders to venture near. With the mountain range for its protection, it was a place where no-one ever endeavored to go. For the most part, the structure was long ago forgotten and now unheard of to the known world. It was nestled in an area that people of the modern world saw no need to go near.

To the people of our time, it was a wasteland and a wilderness. There could be nothing of value there. It could not be habitable in such extreme temperatures. It must have been built in a vastly different time that had a completely different climate.

No-one of the present world gave it a thought. The people who'd built it must have been long dead. The story of the structure must have died with them.

After all, if they had still been alive, they would have been *ancient*.

CHAPTER 2

Isabella set off for her morning chore of taking a large basket to gather eggs from the chickens and deliver them safely to the kitchen. Being a kitchen that served more than 2,000 people, it was a place that bustled all day and all night. Its workers came and went throughout all hours in a well-oiled gear of order that had worked for hundreds of years. It was the heart of the sanctuary - the place that kept the inhabitants fed and healthy.

No sickness had come to the small township for as long as anyone could remember. No-one ever questioned why they did not get sick. It had always been the way for the people who currently resided there. They did not question why no-one ever got ill simply because they had no idea what illness *was*.

All around her, Isabella saw the many faces that she had known since the day she'd been born. They were always the same faces, day after day. Some were her age, some were younger, and many were older. They were a constancy in her life, as was the daily routine of every one of them.

She had a restlessness inside of her. She had always felt like there must be more for her than what she lived each day, but she knew the rules. It was forbidden to go near the great outer walls that stood high against the sky backdrop.

No-one had ever told her why she must never go near the great outer walls. Sometimes she wondered if anyone did actually know why it was forbidden at all, or if generation after generation had just accepted the rules and never questioned them.

Being twenty-one years of age, Isabella had grown into a similar young woman like any other twenty-one-year-old in the township's population. Her only real exception was the color of her hair. It wasn't as light as half of the residents, nor as dark as the other half of the residents. She didn't even know what the color *was*. She'd heard others refer to it as the color of a dark flame. That description she'd never understood since all of the flames she'd seen were more like a yellow than the reddish tone of her hair. She could only assume that perhaps the elders and the ancients knew of a dark flame that was different.

In everything, the elders and ancients knew most and knew best. How many years they'd lived, no-one knew, but they were old enough to live separately from the rest of the community. They resided in the large temple that stood majestically in the center of the village. Constructed of stone with writing and messages on the front of it, Isabella often stopped and looked at it on her daily rounds. Nothing about it ever changed but now and then she felt drawn to it as if it were calling to her.

Just her.

~~~~~

"Good morning, Miss Isabella!" she heard Cook Joan call out to her as she entered the broad kitchen area. Isabella immediately smiled at the vision before her.

Every single morning, Cook Joan was a sight to see. Always she seemed to have flour through her hair, which in turn was in a mess around her face. The graying hair looked sometimes more like a nest the chickens built for themselves, rather than how Isabella was sure it should look. It was also a daily pleasure to see which colors and shapes she would see on the cook's apron.

"Hmm ... you are cooking something with tomatoes today, I am guessing?" Isabella teased the older woman. The judgment was made purely by the red color and scattering of small yellow seeds that seemed to be ground into the apron in front of her.

Cook Joan laughed heartily and out loud, throwing her head back as she did so. Isabella could see the cook's whole body shaking with laughter.

"Oh, Miss Isabella, how well you know me by now! Yes, today, for our evening meal, we shall have a slow-roasted tomato rice pie. Oh, it is going to be..." Cook Joan said before delivering a wide gesture with her hands to indicate an impression of magnificence. "Make sure you get some early because it will disappear quickly today!"

Isabella laughed at the cook. Every day she came up with new and adventurous ways to use the spoils of the fields and orchard within the village. Even though it appeared to be some kind of magic on her part, every day she did produce something delicious. Never were there any complaints about the meals that were cooked by Cook Joan, or any of the many other cooks that worked as hard as she did.

"Here are your eggs, Cook Joan," Isabella said. "Is there anything else you would like me to gather for you this morning?"

"Oh, now let me think..." Cook Joan replied, going into her thoughtful pose. Her chin rested on her hand, which in turn belonged to the arm that connected the elbow that rested on her other hand. "Oh, yes! Please, Miss Isabella, if you would be so kind. Could you go and harvest for me some basil? Just a large handful will be sufficient. Oh, and a small amount of oregano. Only two or three sprigs of that will do."
~~~~~

Isabella waited a few moments longer in anticipation. She knew that with Cook Joan, there was usually an afterthought coming.

"Oh! Wait," the cook said finally. "Also, if there are any ripe, half a dozen apples. Only if they are red, mind you. The green ones are not as sweet. If there are no red ones, then do not worry. Just leave them on the tree. I shall use those ones another day."

Isabella nodded and smiled at the older woman.

"Very well, Cook Joan. I shall return shortly with your gifts," she said with a teasing sound in her voice, making the cook laugh at her once again.

~~~~~

Once out of the kitchen, Isabella quietly walked toward the garden and orchard area. On the way, she heard the voice of her friend, Adrian.

"Isabella! Wait!" she heard him call out. When she turned, she saw him running toward her. As always, a broad smile graced his face.

Isabella watched him, smiling as he caught his breath.

"You know you never have to run after me, Adrian. Even on these days where you have slept in and missed the morning meal, you know that I would gladly wait for you," she teased, making him slightly blush as they began their routine walk together.

"I know you keep saying that, but if I did not run, you might *not* stop and wait for me, and then where would I be? My morning would be ruined. For it is seeing your beauty that puts such a smile on my face first thing, and stays in the forefront of my mind all day long until I can go to bed at night, dreaming of your lovely face," he ran off in long dialogue to her, making her laugh out loud.

"Oh, Adrian, please stop!" she said, laughing hard with and at him. "You do talk such nonsense!"

"Ahh, but see how successful I am in putting such a smile on your face," Adrian said. "That is rewarding enough to me for delivering such creative poetry to you each and every morning, my beautiful Isabella."

As she looked at him, she saw the all too familiar cheeky grin that he sported. The two of them had grown up together, as had everyone their age. In such a close-knit and guarded community, everyone was familiar with everyone. As far as they knew, it was as it always had been for centuries, and seemed to work in keeping everyone tranquil and easy with one another.

"Now then, how are your mother and father this morning?" she asked him, knowing he always had something fun to report to her. "And your sisters?"

"Mary this morning fell and hurt her little knees, causing great mayhem and noise in our home. I am not sure why she keeps tripping over her own feet, but she does do it a great deal!" he said, watching
~~~~~

Isabella's face break out into a further smile. "Other than that, nothing has changed from yesterday or the day before…"

Isabella looked closely at her friend, hearing melancholy in his voice.

"Would you prefer your family was always in vexation?" she asked.

"No! Oh, no, of course not," replied Adrian. "But, Isabella, do you never wish that there was change? That *something* would change?"

The two of them had talked about the same topic of conversation many times. Each time they did, Isabella felt a slight concern for him when he brought the subject up. She, too, felt the yearnings for something different to happen, but she would never be verbal about it, even to the good friend standing before her. She had been raised to appreciate everything she had. No matter what level of turmoil she occasionally felt inside, she was committed to *keeping* it inside.

"Adrian, I am happy. I love being here," she replied as she waved one hand around to indicate she meant the entire village. "I love my family. I love all the people I come in contact with every day. And I love…" She paused, making him look closer at her. "I love having you as my friend. I am happy enough. I do not need anything more."

Adrian was quiet for a few minutes. It wasn't necessarily normal for him. More and more, he was finding that on occasion, he needed to silence his mind, and the best way to do that was to consider every word he spoke.

"Very well, Isabella. We shall not talk of this again today. So tell me, what things are you seeking today in the gardens?" he asked, veering the conversation to a much safer subject.

"Cook Joan wishes for me to get some basil and some red apples - not green! - and something else," Isabella said, her voice tapering off in an attempt to recall the entire list she'd been given by the cook. "I shall remember when I get there…"

Adrian laughed at her. Almost every day, Isabella forgot one thing that was asked of her. Adrian saw it as an ongoing joke that made him feel both greatly affectionate toward her, and exasperated with her. Her determination to try and remember things was admirable, but she never quite seemed able to do so completely.

Finally, they approached the fork in the path. The path leading to the right would take Adrian down to his workstation for the day at the grain mill. Isabella would head down the path to the left to visit the garden and orchard.

"Can I see you later?" he asked as he faced her.

"Of course," Isabella replied, surprised by the question. "I will see you at dinner…"

"No. I mean after dinner," Adrian said. "Can we spend some time together … tonight?"

Isabella smiled at him with her usual friendly and relaxed smile while nodding at him in reassurance.

"Of course," she said. "Have dinner with me, and we can go on from there."

Adrian smiled broadly at her. After he'd turned and started to walk away, she saw him turn once more to give her another smile and a wave.

As Isabella began walking down her chosen path, she found herself in deep thought about Adrian. She saw many people every day and knew the names of so many in the village. Adrian seemed to be the only one who ever questioned their existence in the way that he did. He was generally happy-natured, but on occasion, he did seem extremely discontent. Isabella didn't know how he'd come to be like that. It was the one aspect that made him so different from everyone else. Even though Isabella also felt like that at times, she had long ago recognized that there was a different degree of it deep inside of Adrian.

~~~~~

After her thoughtful walk, Isabella reached her destination. As she entered the small iron gate, she immediately was greeted by a wide plethora of sights and scents. In the first section of the wide-open space in front of her, vegetables were laid out in strict rows that from a distance looked perfectly straight. Whenever she got closer, she was reminded that there was a far more relaxed imperfection about the garden.

The vegetable and herb growing area was vast, as it needed to be to feed so many people. Every time she entered the area, she could see a healthy amount of people working away. Laboriously, some were weeding, some were planting, and some were watering.

"Good morning, Isabella," someone or other would yell out to her. Always she would cordially greet them in return with a smile on her face.

She was always envious of the people who worked in the gardens. They were there because they truly loved it and gained a high degree of satisfaction from it. Just like Cook Joan gained so much joy from working in the village kitchen. Just like the tailor found so much happiness in making his creations. Just like the blacksmith loved working with metal in repairing and making things for others.

People around her seemed to know what they wanted to do for their whole lives, and then they started doing it. They learned from the elders of their trade and then later became elders of the trade themselves.

At twenty-one years old, she too should have already established herself into some trade or other. Instead, she seemed to have fallen into the role of assistant to a great number of people of different trades and stations. It wasn't the way things were meant to be, and yet she did love it. It often meant that she drifted all day long, fetching this for this person and that for that person. It was a nice way to spend her time even though
~~~~~

she knew her mother wished for her to pair with someone and start a family. That was the responsibility of all villagers. It was needed to help contribute to the ongoing survival of the community.

Even in the prospect of pairing, Isabella was uncertain. She knew everyone so well that all the men her age were her friends. It made it difficult to determine who would be the best pairing partner or the best father for her children. How was one to make such a choice?

After the gardener had listened to her request for what she'd been asked to gather, Isabella continued to consider the question. It wouldn't be long before her mother and father pushed a little harder for her to choose who she would pair with. She could only see two possibilities before her. She could choose someone she hardly knew, or she could choose Adrian. Was he the person she wanted to make a family with and live in the same home with for as long as they both lived? He was her friend. She valued his friendship deeply. She just wasn't sure if that made him the right person to live with.

Pairing was forever. That was the harsh reality of the ways of the ancient village. She didn't know how she would choose who to pair with. She *did* know that before she did, she would make sure she was certain she was making the right choice.

CHAPTER 3

"Adrian," Isabella said, smiling as her friend sat beside her at her dinner table that evening. "How was the mill today?"

Adrian appeared less than his usual cheerful self. He looked at her intently and then grabbed a bread roll from the basket set before them on the long wooden table.

"The mill has not been so good today, Isabella," Adrian replied. "It is the time of year when there is less water flowing from the mountain. That causes the water wheel to slow down, which in turn slows down the milling of the grains. It is still working well enough. We have a good store of grain to see us through times like this, but it is hard at this time of year. It always makes for a long day with everything moving so much slower."

Having already eaten as much as she could, Isabella watched him as he indulged in his food. He was always so open about his work. She loved hearing him talk about it. She got on with everyone, but having no trade of her own, she enjoyed hearing about all the workings of the village through everyone else.

Adrian felt her staring and turned to face her. He stopped his chewing when he saw how attentive she was being.

"Do I have food on my face?" he finally asked her once he had swallowed. "Or perhaps I have grown a third eye? A second nose?"

Isabella couldn't miss the very distinct glint of amusement in his eyes. She laughed at him and shook her head.

"Silly boy."

They laughed together softly as two companions would. They were so comfortable with each other. Everyone in the village was comfortable with each other, but she knew that her friendship with Adrian was closer than some.

"How was your day?" he asked her. "Did you find the perfect apple? One that was only red, but not green?"

"I did find some perfect apples for the cook…" she said, her voice tapering off slightly.

The change in volume made Adrian almost anticipate what she was going to say next since he'd heard it so many times before.

"I did forget the oregano, and Cook Joan did tell me off for that,"

Isabella continued.

Adrian laughed out loud at her. It was the same thing, day after day, but it was one thing he never did tire of - hearing which item Isabella had forgotten on any given day. It amused him immensely. He had almost come to look forward to dinner times so he could hear the latest episode of 'the forgotten'.

Isabella watched him as he finished up his meal. The two of them automatically stood and went to the wash station to wash, rinse, dry off, and put away their dishes on the large table set up for the purpose.

Walking outside again, she saw and heard him speak to her quietly, as if not wanting anyone else to hear.

"Can we go somewhere quiet, Isabella? Alone?" Adrian asked.

The request startled Isabella as it was something new from Adrian. Seeing no reason to fear him or worry about his intentions, she nodded.

"Of … of course, Adrian," Isabella replied. "Where did you have in mind?"

"Come. Walk with me," he said. "I want to show you something."

They walked down the same path they had that morning. He led her further down the path that he took each morning to get to the mill. Before the mill came into view, he stopped and looked at her.

"I want to show you a place that I found a few days ago," he said. "I haven't told anyone else about it because, to be honest, it is quite nice to have somewhere that is just mine for the moment, but I do want to share it with you."

Isabella found herself rather intrigued. She nodded but said nothing. She then found her hand taken in his as he started to walk with her beside him. They veered off the path and into an area of open ground where only grass and a handful of low growing bushes grew.

After a while, Adrian stopped walking and turned to her.

"Here we are," he said, smiling as if he were showing her a great secret. Straight away, he could see Isabella's look of confusion. "Sit down," he instructed. "Here."

Isabella followed his direction, and the two of them sat on the grass. It was not something that she'd normally do so immediately she felt different just from doing that. Regardless, the look on his face confounded her. She could not guess what had him so excited.

"Do you feel it?" Adrian asked, desperate for her to confirm that he wasn't imagining things.

"Adrian, I do not understand. Do I feel what?" Isabella asked, her confusion growing.

"Place your hands flat on the ground like this," he said, demonstrating by putting both palms flat down on the grass. He saw her do the same before he continued. "Do you feel it?"

Finally, he saw a look of realization on her face.

"Adrian, the ground is warm - *very* warm," Isabella said in surprise. "How … how can it be as warm as this so late in the day with the sun starting to go down?"

"I do not know," Adrian replied, feeling even more excited. "I am uncertain of how or why it is happening, but it *is* happening."

"Is it always like this?" Isabella asked.

"I do not know!" Adrian exclaimed. "That is just it. We never come out here after the sun goes down, so we always assume the ground is warm from the sun, do we not?" he asked and saw her nod slowly. "What if that is not the truth, Isabella? What if the sun is *not* what makes our ground so warm all the time?"

Isabella was stunned. She'd been brought up to believe that warmth came from the sun. The very reason they never went out at night was that it would be far too cold without the sun above in the sky. There had never been any reason to even think about the possibility that the warmth didn't come from above.

"You think that this warmth is coming … from below?" she asked, pointing one finger down toward the soil. She saw him nod while maintaining the large smile of excitement on his face. "But how, Adrian? How could that be?"

"I know not, but I want to find out!" Adrian replied. He paused for a long time before continuing. "Isabella, I do not want other people to know about this. I would not like to get either of us into trouble by asking questions. I will try and figure this out, but with much discretion so that no-one knows I am asking about it. I do not know who knows about this. I want to be careful."

He saw Isabella slowly nod her head again.

"Alright, but please be careful Adrian," she replied. "If someone knows the answer to this mystery and has not been honest with everyone all of these years…"

"Yes, I agree," Adrian said, nodding. "I am unsure who to trust about it. It could be that generations have been telling each next generation the same thing, and no-one knows about whatever it is that is generating the heat. I would not want to risk the wrong person knowing I am asking questions. Do you promise to keep it to yourself?"

"Yes!" Isabella exclaimed. "Of course I shall keep it to myself. I would not do anything that could result in you getting into trouble, Adrian. You know that."

"Thank you," he replied before building up the courage to present a second question to her. "There is something else I wish to talk to you about…"

Isabella saw his face take on a serious unease all of a sudden. It made him seem more morose than she'd ever seen him before.

"Yes?" she asked him, nudging him to keep speaking even though he did seem extremely awkward at that moment.

"I..." Adrian started to say before feeling a sliver of panic. He wondered if he should say something or if there was a chance that he would spoil things for them. It was such a long term friendship, did he want to risk upsetting her and ruining it?

As he continued to hesitate in asking whatever he was going to ask, Isabella sat patiently. She knew him. Instead of pressuring him to continue, she patiently watched him struggle to find the right words he needed for whatever he needed to say.

"Isabella, have you ... wondered ... thought about ... finding someone to ..." Adrian knew he was stumbling, but kept going regardless. "Finding someone to ... pair with?"

Isabella was surprised. He had never brought up such a topic before. It was one thing that they'd never covered in their conversations as friends. As a result, she found herself as tongue-tied as he'd just been. She knew she had to respond in some way. She could see that he was eager and waiting for an answer.

"No," she replied.

"Just like that?" Adrian asked, his voice revealing his surprise at her answer. "You answer so easily..."

"Adrian, you asked if I had thought about it, and I have not," Isabella said. "How were you hoping I would answer?"

"I wished you would answer yes, and that you would consider me ... you and I ... to be suitable for it," he said, his voice full of emotion.

Isabella should have been surprised, but she wasn't. Nothing physical had ever happened between her and Adrian but hearing such a declaration - such a *question* - somehow did not surprise her. As he spoke of it, she realized she'd just been put in a position where she could truly hurt her close friend if she did not find the right answer to give him.

"I esteem you greatly, Adrian," she said. "You know that. If I were thinking about that yet, I do believe that you *would* be someone I would be considering, but I am not thinking about that yet."

"Isabella, we are 21 years of age!" Adrian said. "Do you not think it is time?"

"Yes, my mother and father do wish for me to pair soon," Isabella replied. "They are eager for me to provide them with another generation of our family."

"Well, then!"

"It is still not something I yet feel that I am ready for," Isabella said. "I am sorry, Adrian. I can see that you wanted me to say yes, and perhaps you wanted me to choose you. Maybe, when the time is right, if you are still free to pair then..."

Adrian looked at her sharply.

"I am not going anywhere!" he exclaimed. "I want to set up a life with you. I have no desire to pair with anyone else!"

"How do you know?" she asked and saw him appear confused by the question. "How do you *know* that I am who you want to pair with? We are such good friends..."

"Yes! We are good long-term friends," Adrian said. "We know everything about each other. We know what each other likes and what each other dislikes. What could be a better grounding for a pairing than that if we are to share the rest of our lives as partners?"

Isabella listened to his justification and could not find any fault with it. There was no real reason why the two of them could not go through the pairing and share their lives so closely entwined. Knowing that didn't instill in her a desire to do it.

She found herself concerned about how she could talk to him about the subject. She had no wish to hurt him or make him feel neglected or rejected in some way. She was considering what the best thing to do was when she saw him shake his head and stand up.

"Do not answer, Isabella," he said. "Your lack of ... *enthusiasm* ... shows me how you feel. There is no need for you to say anything more."

Isabella stood up and faced him before doing something she hadn't done before. Moving closer to him, she wrapped her arms around him, desperate to not let him be upset by her words. As she held him close, she found that it wasn't at all an uncomfortable thing to do.

Adrian was stunned. Despite his surprise, he welcomed her arms around him, and in return, wrapped his around her. With their heads resting on each other's shoulders, he closed his eyes and breathed in the scent of her. Silently, he desperately wished that she could look at him the same way that he looked at her.

"We should get back to our families," he said. "I will walk you to your home."

Walking beside each other, they remained quiet until they stood outside the house where Isabella lived with her parents. Before Adrian could move away, Isabella moved closer to him.

"I love having you as my friend, Adrian," she said. "I know that is not what you want to hear, but it is all that I can offer you for now."

Adrian nodded at her, resigned to wait for however long he'd have to in the hope that she would change her mind.

CHAPTER 4

Trent Solace stood on the summit of the mountain and stared out in all directions that he could see. From where he stood, he was amazed at the feeling of intoxication that came from the freshness of the air and the views from such height above sea level.

There were things he'd wanted to escape from in his home city. He hadn't meant to fall in love with a married woman. Despite his best efforts, he had. At thirty years of age, he knew it was a stupid thing to have done, but how could he help it? She'd made herself available so easily. She'd appeared wherever he'd been located for his work. She had followed him to wherever he'd been for his pleasure. She'd gone out of her way to lure him after the first time she'd seen him, and he'd too easily and desperately succumbed to her advances.

Her suggestion to leave her husband for Trent had been what had tipped Trent over the edge. At that moment, he'd realized that it wasn't love he felt for her at all. Spending time with her like they had been was one thing, but marriage had never been on his agenda. He'd watched his mother and father endure hating each other for too many years when he was a child. He would never consider marriage a true path for him. It was something that others were meant to do; not him. He was a bachelor. He would happily stay that way.

He could still remember the conversation so clearly.

"I'm going to leave him, Trent. I'll get my lawyer to draw up the divorce papers tomorrow and then it won't be long before you and I can finally get married," she'd said as if he hadn't been required for any part of the decision making process. "We'll have a large wedding with lots of guests. You don't need to worry about the cost. I'll have enough money from the divorce to be able to pay for it all. It'll be so big that society page journalists will pay us for the exclusive coverage of it…"

He'd listened to her go on and on, completely oblivious to the fact that he hadn't even asked her to marry him. It hadn't seemed to occur to her that he equally hadn't even said anything about her declaration that she was going to get divorced.

"Stop!" he had finally said when he knew he couldn't bear to hear anymore. "For God's sake, please just stop!"

When she'd looked at him at that moment, her confusion had been painfully evident.

"Stop … what?" she had asked.

"Just stop … *talking*," he'd said, trying to get his breathing, thoughts and speaking under control. "And don't get a divorce because I'm not going to marry you."

"What?" she'd asked, her head shaking from side to side as if she thought he'd been speaking an entirely different language.

"You heard me. I'm not going to marry you. I'm not going to marry anyone *ever*. So don't worry about getting a divorce because there is absolutely no need for it. Stay with your husband. We are done," he had said before walking away from her.

Whatever he'd felt for her had, at that moment, instantaneously evaporated. He knew that was a final judgment on his feelings. The feeling of being in love with her was gone. He equally knew that when those kinds of feelings disappeared, they never came back.

As he'd expected, she had then increased her efforts to be close to him. No matter where he went or who he was with, she kept turning up. Finally, desperate to be free of her, he had done something he'd always dreamed of doing but had never before gotten around to. He'd packed up an extensive list of small essentials into a tramping pack and left with the full intention of getting as far away as possible from her, and society in general.

He was tired of crowds, he was tired of technology, and he was tired of screens everywhere. Big or small, sometimes he felt like they had taken over the world. He wanted to be away from it all and touch base with fresh air and nature again. As a result, he'd driven as close to a nearby mountain as he could before getting out, laden with supplies and essentials, and just walking away.

He'd tramped over that first mountain, only to find that once he reached a decent height, on the other side of it - hidden from his initial public view - he could then see another mountain. The sight drove him on to tramp down the far side of the initial one and pass through a valley that provided him with the enjoyment of water. It was refreshing for bathing, clothes washing, hydrating, and replenishing his drinking water supply.

Then he'd started to walk up another mountain.

~~~~~~

Three mountains over, it seemed like months that he'd been away. Having tallied the nighttimes in the small notebook he carried with him, he knew it wasn't as long as it appeared.

When he'd set out, he'd wanted solitude. He had certainly found that. Even animals seemed to be in short supply where he walked. Sometimes it seemed like he wasn't only the sole person on the planet, but also the
~~~~~~

only living thing. Initially, it had been invigorating. Then it had been lonely.

After the excitement and loneliness came peace. Trent felt inside of him a beautiful calm. That was something he'd never had in the populated world. Once away from the stresses of daily life, it had been easy for him to realize just how many stresses there had been. They hadn't been things that *should* have contributed to stress - sourcing food, keeping warm, keeping sheltered, talking to people. There were so many things that should have been easy but always had other conditions attached to them. To eat, he had to have money - stress. To have money, he had to earn - stress. To earn money, he had to have a job - stress. To have a job he had to deal with far too many people - stress. It went on and on and on, day after day. No matter how many things he found to distract him - the many women to share pleasure with, including that married woman - the core stresses never went away.

While in the concrete and steel jungle, it had been impossible to be away from it, so leave the concrete and steel jungle, he had. After all the walking he'd done since that moment, he had no regret. In no way did his life before compare with how he felt enjoying the fresh air that he could lay claim to all by himself.

~~~~~

As always when he reached the heights of each mountain, he looked through his binoculars from up on the summit. So much could be seen from such height. It invigorated him, no matter which direction he looked in. While pondering his luck to be experiencing what he was, in the distance he saw something different.

At first, as he looked through the binoculars, his eyes passed over it. He then found his sight returning to the line of horizon meeting the mountain line. He had to look again for a third time.

It wasn't a mountain range at all - not at the very top. It was a structure, like something man-made. He guessed that to have been able to see it from as far away as he was, it must have been extremely immense in size.

He stood for a long time, trying to focus better on it, but the zoom focus of the binoculars was already at its maximum setting. He knew he wouldn't be able to see any clearer from where he currently stood.

He shifted his gaze, looking at the distance between where he currently stood and where the structure appeared to be. He would have to climb down the mountain he was currently on and then over another two. If he could do that, he would then be at the base of what he was certain would be the mountain that the structure was sitting on top of.

Trent felt his heart racing, and a sense of excitement come over him. Looking up at the sky, he hoped for good weather. He knew he'd been
~~~~~

lucky so far in that regard. Apart from three nights when it had lightly rained, there generally hadn't been a drop in sight. He'd been able to keep dry. That, in turn, had meant he'd been easily able to stay warm in his cold-weather gear.

Considering he wasn't a tramper, his body appeared to be holding up remarkably well. He guessed it was his lifelong dedication to physical fitness that had helped. Although it did surprise him that he seemed able to walk extremely long distances without feeling like he was too exerted, he conceded it was likely because he was in no hurry. He had left his job and let a friend move into his apartment. He could take as long as he wanted to.

He didn't need money and he didn't need any material things from the city. Except for a good meal, which he did think about fairly regularly while walking, there was nothing else he desired or needed other than what he readily had access to. He wasn't a hunter. Even if he had been, he hadn't seen any animals at all on his trek.

He'd learned enough to be able to locate and sufficiently prepare the right flora to see him through. He also had extensive bundles of dried goods in his pack. He'd rationed them out and only consumed small amounts on days when he absolutely couldn't find anything else to eat. It probably wasn't a wise plan - it probably wasn't a *right* plan - but it was a plan that so far was working for him regardless.

~~~~~

After sitting down on the summit and basking in the warmth of the sunlight, he stood and prepared to leave. In the middle of the day, with the sun out, there was warmth to be had with as many layers that he had on. But it was still a freezing climate on the upper half of each of the mountains he'd made his way over and around since he'd begun on his journey. He was no expert, but he had learned through trial and error. It seemed best to enjoy the top views in the heat of the middle of the day, and then edge down the other side of the mountain before late afternoon. There, he'd set himself up with a small camp for the night in the protection of the mountainside.

~~~~~

As he lay in his sleeping blanket and tiny pup tent, Trent thought about the structure he'd seen. Being the realist that he was, he had to allow for the possibility that he might have been seeing things. It very well could have been a mirage. At those altitudes, he expected the mind could play extreme tricks on anyone. Regardless, even thinking to himself that it could have been a trick of his mind or his eyes, he still felt excitement at the prospect of something being out there.

That night he dreamed of a woman - a young woman with vibrant red hair. She was absolutely beautiful. She approached him, walking toward him with a smile on her face, and her hands outstretched to him. Trent was mesmerized as he walked toward her and looked down to see what she was holding. He was surprised to see that in her hands was an entire handful of gold. At first, he thought it was normal gold - the same metal that his ring would have been made of if he'd given in and let himself be taken away on the recent offer of matrimony. When the girl in his dream reached out and indicated with her facial expressions that she wanted him to cup his hands for her to put the gold into, he realized it wasn't normal gold at all. It *looked* like gold, but when it was placed in his hand it was *hot*. He was surprised that it could have so much heat. As he looked around to see what was heating it, the girl in his dream laughed at him, seeing his disbelief that it could just be hot in its natural state. It required nothing to heat it at all.

Looking back at her face, he was in awe of the intensely warm feeling in his hand and the natural beauty of her. In the world that he'd come from, women hardly ever showed their true selves, hiding behind makeup and accessories. To see the woman so natural and not trying look different, he felt like she was someone of incredible confidence - and power.

~~~~~

The next morning Trent ate and then packed up his gear once again. Only a shadow of the dream remained in his head. He filed it away in his mind as just another dream that didn't in any way associate with reality.

~~~~~

That day he made even faster progress but at the same time had to keep stopping himself from rushing too much. He knew that if he had an accident out where he was, he'd never be found by anyone. Even without an accident, he knew there was an increasing chance that he wouldn't survive and get back to civilization safely. Despite that consideration, he still wanted to take care, do his best, and go the furthest that he could.

His daydreaming helped him to pass time. Seeing the structure - or *thinking* he had seen it, as the case would probably turn out to be - had caused his mind to wander. He wondered what could have been built so far away from the rest of the world. It must be in the middle of nowhere, as far as he could tell. Who built it? How long had it been there? And what was its purpose?

The question that his mind kept taking him back to was, was it even real? And if not, did it really matter?

CHAPTER 5

After breakfast, Adrian walked to the place where he usually met up with Isabella. There he waited. He felt strangely nervous at the prospect of simply meeting his lifelong friend, even though he'd done that thousands of times. He hoped that by having spoken to her the night before he hadn't frightened her or made her so uncomfortable by his words that she would avoid him.

He needn't have worried. When he saw Isabella approaching him, she did so with a smile on her face once again. It wasn't the same smile as usual, but it was a smile nonetheless, and it was definitely directed at him.

"You have beaten me here this morning, Adrian. This is so unlike you," she said, instantly teasing him upon her approach to where he was standing. "What mischief have you been up to, to have you standing here before I have arrived here this fine morning? And if you *are* so early today, why did you not come and dine with me for breakfast?"

Adrian smiled at her. Simultaneously he felt his body relax and his breath ease out slowly and deeply. Late into the night, he had been worried about the possibility of having overstepped a friendship boundary and her being inaccessible to him today. He knew he should have known better. Isabella had never acted in such a way, even when they were children and she would think he wasn't being nice to her. No matter what, she was - and had always been - there for him as a trustworthy friend.

"I did not want to miss you," he said.

The sheepish grin on his face made Isabella laugh.

"I keep telling you that I will wait for you! When will you ever believe me about that?" she asked, the two of them laughing together softly. "Come. I must go and get apples for Cook Mary - *green* apples!" she said vaguely. Adrian knew what was next. "And something else ... hmm, I cannot quite remember what it was, but I am sure it will come to me when I get down to the garden."

Adrian laughed out loud at her again. So many things about where they lived and the *way* they lived never changed, and made him almost desperate for *something* to change. Each morning, as he got to meet and listen to Isabella not remember what she was supposed to get for the cook, he knew that was something he would never tire of. It was one of the things that set him up in a good mood for the rest of every day. That and looking at her beautiful face that almost always had the happiest smile on it.

"Have you asked or said anything to anyone about what we talked about last night?" he asked her after they'd both relaxed from their laughter.

"Which aspect are you speaking of, Adrian?" Isabella asked. "I seem to recall we talked about two equally important things last night."

"Just the first one. I shall not pressure you for the second," Adrian replied. "If you reach a place where you want to talk to me about the possibility of you and I pairing, I will be here for you. For now, let us not talk of it again. Your friendship is too important to me," he said and saw her look intently at him while nodding her head. "So, the other - the warmth of the ground."

"No, I did not and will not speak of it to anyone," Isabella said, glancing at him. "Did you?"

Adrian shook his head and spoke noticeably quieter and closer to her.

"No, but I want to go out again and walk further tonight," he said. "Will you join me? After dinner?"

"Oh, Adrian. I do not know that we should," replied Isabella. "You know we are not supposed to go out at night. And two nights in a row? What if we put it off till tomorrow?"

"No!" Adrian exclaimed, his tone more serious than usual. "I want to explore now, but I can explore alone. You do not have to come with me. It is quite alright."

As they reached the fork in the path where they would go their separate ways, Adrian moved closer to her and reached out to touch her arm lightly. It was a move of friendship and did not startle or concern her.

"I will see you at dinner?" he asked.

Isabella nodded and smiled at him before turning away and beginning her daily trek to the large garden and orchard.

As she walked, she thought about what had intrigued Adrian so much. When he'd introduced her to the idea that the warmth of their village came from under the ground, she'd also been curious about the finding. That was where her interest ended.

Thinking about Adrian's level of interest in his finding, she wondered if it was driven more by his overall dissatisfaction. Sometimes it saddened her that someone as alive and friendly as he was could also be morose at times. He was a naturally cheerful person. She knew from their years as friends that even when he was doing an incredible job of presenting that happy face, he had his moments when he was unhappy underneath.

That was something that he'd been right about in his speech the night before. The two of them did know each other extremely well. After so many hours of talking closely, they knew almost everything about one another. There was comfort in that.

For a moment, she considered the possibility of them pairing. There were many reasons for it to happen. She wasn't sure what exactly was holding her back, but she felt she wasn't to move forward in that. Not yet.

CHAPTER 6

Trent had crossed another mountain and knew he was growing weaker. Although he was eating enough to sustain himself in his usual stationary life in the city, the lesser amount of food combined with the excessive walking was resulting in a negative equation in energy levels. He could easily feel his clothes getting looser.

Finally, he reached the top of the mountain that stood directly before the one he wanted to get to. As he reached the summit, he eagerly took out his binoculars and looked in the direction of where he thought the structure must be.

At first, he didn't see it. He felt a thud in his heart at the discovery that he must have been seeing things previously. There was nothing there after all.

Looking again after a few minutes, he was excited to realize that it *was* there. It was so high that some light cloud had been sitting in front of it, hiding it from view. Now that the cloud had passed, the structure was visible once again - *very* visible.

He sat down on a large rock with force, his legs trying to give way as his brain tried to argue with him that he was still seeing an optical illusion of some kind. Through the binoculars, he still couldn't make out exactly what it was, but as he was getting nearer, it was starting to look like a castle. It was large, high, and broad with incredibly sturdy-looking walls that appeared to be made of grey brick.

What he was seeing made no sense. Castles were from the days of medieval kings and queens. They were in England, France, and other parts of Europe.

He quickly considered leaving his present location immediately and trying to go straight to the valley and up the other side without stopping anymore. He knew he couldn't do that. It was already possibly a mission that he'd likely not survive, now being so far away from civilization. To try and walk at night when he couldn't see his footing properly would be more than irresponsible.

He resisted the urge to rush. Instead, he made his way down to the sheltered side of the mountain he was on and set up camp. It would only be a few more days. Then he would finally be there. But what then? Did the grandeur of claiming an unknown and unheard of castle seem in any way appealing to him? It was a useless thing to seek. Regardless, his curiosity about the structure was already piqued. He couldn't just give up. If nothing else, it might provide him with some shelter for a few nights. From that, at least he might regain his strength before attempting to head home again.

Home.

Where was that, anyway? Where did he belong in the entire scheme of the whole world? If he really loved his 'home' so much, why had he felt so suffocated and desperate to leave?

As he climbed into his sleeping bag, his mind was active. There were still options open to him. He could move forward without any expectation of returning. He could retreat and try and make his way back to civilization and his home.

The more he considered what could lie ahead for him, the more his mind took him in circles in his thinking. Neither option proved more attractive than the other.

Finally, when his mind focused more on how his body was feeling, he fell into a deep sleep.

CHAPTER 7

Isabella woke abruptly from a night vision she'd been having. She didn't often have visions of the night. This one was far more vivid than she'd ever experienced before. She took a moment to think about it before it disappeared from her mind. So often, she woke with something she was visualizing, but then as the day wore on the memory of it dissipated until she couldn't remember what she'd seen in her night vision at all.

She considered how different the night vision had been. In it, there had been a man. He'd walked toward her. Isabella could see that he was not of her people. She could tell that from the clothing he wore and the things he carried. He was the first person she had ever met - had ever *seen* - who was unfamiliar and new to her.

In her dream, she walked toward him and saw him walk straight up to her. His hair was dark and short. Unlike the men in her village, his facial hair was short, like he cut it as the people of her village occasionally cut the hair on their heads.

He held out his hands to her. When she looked down, she saw yellow in her hands. Although she did not know what it was, she could feel it warming her. The warmth made her smile. She felt a need to give it to him to warm him, sensing how cold he seemed.

Why had he seemed so cold? They were never cold in the village. That was what was going through her mind when she awoke suddenly, experiencing her very first feeling of an extreme chill running through her body.

CHAPTER 8

Trent stood before the massive walls. It was while standing before such a structure that he finally comprehended just how big it was. As he stood at the base of one grey brick wall and looked upward, he had to crane his neck back a long way to be able to follow the line of sight upward and see the sky.

He reached forward and touched the brick. Starting to feel the effect of the air lessening, he expected the wall to be frozen at such height.

He was surprised that the wall was not only not frozen to the touch but almost warm. He looked upward again. The sun was out. That must have been the provider of the warmth. Of course, it was. Sun beating down on a brick structure would always enable the brick to absorb the heat and hold it for probably the whole day. He knew that was a perfectly sound and reasonable explanation.

He placed a marker where he initially stood and then started to walk along the edge of the wall. Remaining close to it, he continued to feel the warmth it emanated. After so many cold nights, it was as refreshing as his discovery of the structure. He felt a new level of energy flow through his body.

From where he was, he couldn't see any gate or doorway, but there had to be one. If there wasn't, how would it have been built? He guessed it could have been built from the outside in. If that were the case, and the builders never left, those men would be long perished, given how old the structure looked.

"What mysteries do you hold?" he asked out loud. The question, he'd presented to nobody. There was no-one around and nobody listening.

Unknown to him, although he hadn't intended it, someone, in their subconscious, *had* heard.

~~~~~

He seemed to walk alongside the tall heated walls for hours. As the sun began its downward journey again, Trent found himself feeling considerably colder. When he'd started walking around the structure's perimeter, he had purposely tied a marker to a nearby tree so that he would know when he was at the right point to start heading back again. As yet, he didn't think he'd even begun to make an indentation on the entire perimeter.
~~~~~

The question now was what to do. He could walk partway down the mountain to find some shelter for the night and then come back the next day. The other option was to huddle against one of the tall walls in the hope that it would shelter him somewhat. He didn't know how long the sun's warming would still emanate from the brick walls, but it was certainly nice standing up against them at that moment.

Looking up at the sun, he assessed which would be the most sheltered side of the mountain to rest on for the night. He then continued his skimming of the perimeter for a bit further before tying a second marker. From there, he walked down the mountain a short way until he found a more sheltered spot to rest up.

From where he camped, he could see the enormous structure through the flora. He felt invigorated by having found it. It put his mind at rest that he hadn't been seeing things. He could now rest in the certainty that it was real.

Now he just had to find a way *into* it.

CHAPTER 9

Very early the next morning, with the sun only just starting to rise in the sky, Trent woke with the knowledge that he felt warm. Wrapped in his sleeping bag inside the tiny pup tent, night after night, he'd not had any nights where he felt too cold, but the warmth he was currently subjected to was different. It almost felt like a man-made heat. It felt like it was reaching him from a heater or a heating appliance such as an electric blanket.

Enjoying the warmth, he moved so he could view the structure again. He feared for a moment that it might not be there. He worried that it might have been a vision of his imagination after all. When he looked, he was relieved to see that not only was it still there, but it was also unavoidable in being seen by him from the close distance he was from the walls.

He climbed out and quickly ate, noticing he was now on the last dregs of the dried food he had brought with him. It was an expectation that he wouldn't - *couldn't* - endure a return trip to his home city without finding sustenance. He equally knew the likelihood of that was grim. It was now a well-accepted expectation that he wouldn't survive much longer. He was at peace with that thought. He had set out from civilization wanting to simply find peace and quiet. He had succeeded in finding plenty of that.

Despite his resolve that his time on Earth was coming to an end, he maintained a determination and excitement to explore where he was. He was desperate to try and learn as much as he could about the structure before him. Even if he didn't live to tell one other living soul about it, he just had to know.

He packed up his things into his tramping pack once more and walked up to the point of the wall where he'd set the marker the evening before. From there, he continued his walk along the wall perimeter, desperate to find the entry point.

After a good hour or so, he leaned on a portion of the wall bathed in sunlight. It wasn't the first part of the wall he'd leaned on. The warmth coming from the brick was soothing. He found himself more and more frequently desiring to let its emanating heat engulf him to help him feel recharged and able to continue.

At the next particular point, as he leaned in to once again enjoy the heat, something different happened. All of a sudden, without any expectation of it being possible, he found himself on the *other* side of the wall.

At first, he didn't realize what had happened. He felt the fall, but it wasn't until he refocused that he could see that he wasn't in the same place.

He looked around him. For as far as he could see were the remnants of buildings. They were broken as if they'd gone through a war and had suffered the horror of bombing.

Trent staggered to his feet, feeling a combination of excitement and fear as he looked around. So many questions came into his mind about the strange place, but the one that called out to him most loudly was, 'what happened here?'

Before he walked forward, he placed a third marker at the point where he'd come through. Even looking at the spot on the wall that he'd come through, he couldn't see any doorway. He tentatively placed his hand on it. In doing so, he felt the absence of the solid wall that he could see. It was like some kind of magic, covering the entry point. A hologram? A portal?

He turned, excited to begin his further exploration. Although he could see that there must have been many buildings at some point, the sight of rubble far outweighed the success of any one building having survived.

The massive space that he could see seemed to go on for miles. He realized the extent of which it must have been more than just a castle, as he had originally guessed it would be. It was more like an entire township - an entire land within a land.

His curiosity piqued, he felt alert and full of excitement. He began walking around all of the distinct outlines where individual buildings must have once stood in a long past period of time.

The other thing he was aware of was that he was warm. He knew at a logical level how high he was currently on top of a mountain, and yet his body and the air around him seemed truly warm. With it still being early in the morning and the sun hardly up, he couldn't account for it being the result of the sun. No, there was something more going on. Something magical.

He walked further, trying to visualize what the layout of the buildings must have been like. After a while, he found himself standing in front of what appeared to be a pile of rubble far greater in size than any other he had yet passed.

As he stood in front of it, he studied large pieces of stone. He tried in his mind to put them back together like a jigsaw puzzle, so he could imagine what the structure had been.

As he stood there, he became aware of a new feeling start to come over him. His senses told him that not only was he not alone, but he was also … being … watched.

He stood where he was, facing the same direction, excited and yet fearful of what he would see when he turned around.

CHAPTER 10

Isabella awoke, once again startled by a vision of the night. The same man was in it, but the vision itself was different. This time she could see him sleeping. He was in strange clothes, and even though he had many layers over and around him, he was so very, very cold. She could feel the cold come to her through the vision of the night. Once again, it distressed her.

When she could see what he was seeing, she realized he must be looking at the outer walls of her village. There was no mistaking what walls they were, but they looked different from his view. She knew that within their outer layer of the village, the walls were covered with roses of a deep lavender color. That was what she saw whenever she went anywhere, every day of her life.

The point of view she got from the man in the night vision was not that of a wall covered in roses. It was grey, dark, blank, and so *bleak*. She'd never seen that view of the walls, but she had no doubt that it *was* those walls that she was seeing.

All of a sudden, a deep male voice echoed into her head, stunning her as she could not make out where it had come from.

"What mysteries do you hold?" the voice asked. What was he asking about? The walls? The village? Or her?

Her vision changed so that she was no longer seeing from his point of view anymore. Instead, she felt like she was looking *at* him again.

In her vision, she walked toward him and watched him sleeping in the odd layers of cloth he seemed to be using to keep himself warm. He looked so cold. How could he be so cold? The village was always warm.

In her vision, she knelt close to him and reached out her hand. Upon touching his cheek, she saw him wake up, confused, before settling his eyes on her. They did nothing more. They did not smile. They did not speak. They just looked at each other with such a knowing.

Isabella sat upright in her warm bed, holding onto the night vision as tightly as she could. The visions were different from others she'd had. They were so real.

Immediately she jumped out of bed and dressed. She had to get to breakfast and find Adrian.

<div style="text-align: center">~~~~~</div>

"These night visions are different, Adrian! Something is different!" she said to him, showing him exactly how much the night visions were affecting her.

"Isabella, all of us have them at some time or other," Adrian replied. "They do not mean anything."

"Yes, but that is where something is different. I know it is. Something is not right. I think I need to go and speak to an elder - perhaps Elder Rhys," she said and saw Adrian's eyes go wide. "What do you think?"

"Elder Rhys?! He is … an ancient!" Adrian exclaimed. "You cannot just go and talk to him about something trivial…"

"These visions of the night are not trivial! I know they are something else," she said to him with a volume much louder than her usual voice. The unexpected tone caused people to turn and look at her. Instantly, she lowered her voice as she spoke again. "I must go to see him. Straight away. I shall see you at dinner time."

As Isabella stood to leave, she saw him do the same.

"Wait, Isabella," said Adrian. "I will walk over to the temple with you. I may not be able to go inside, but I will escort you as far as I can."

"Thank you," she said in gratitude.

CHAPTER 11

Isabella tentatively stood in the temple entrance. It was a commanding structure that had always seemed to call to her as if it were silently but consistently extending a private invitation to her. She didn't know if everyone else felt the same way about the building. She didn't even know if the feeling was real or just a figment of her imagination.

As she approached to enter, she felt a sense of homeliness come over her, like the structure was where she was always meant to be. It seemed as if the spirits of her ancestors still resided there, calling out to her, telling her she was special and that she had a purpose - a calling.

She stepped further into the temple, aware that it wasn't a public space that people went to for trivial purposes. For a long while, she wondered if she should really be there after all. Visions of the night weren't rare. As far she knew, they never meant anything. But something about her recent visions felt different to her. She was sure they were not something to be overlooked or ignored.

Isabella stood for a moment and closed her eyes, taking a deep breath as she felt … something … flow over her. She couldn't define what it was, but it stirred her blood while at the same time, made her feel incredibly at peace.

"Isabella," she heard a voice call out to her. For an instant, it alarmed her and forced her to open her eyes and look around.

Her eyes settled on Elder Rhys. In addition to being an elder, he was also an ancient - one of the oldest persons of the village. She did not understand yet why some elders were ancients and some were not. She only knew that they were old and wise. The people of the village put full trust in them on the rare occasion when any decision had to be made. At other times they were never seen, keeping themselves hidden away behind the façade of the large temple.

"Elder Rhys," she whispered, in awe of the power of the man in front of her. She wasn't sure what etiquette she should follow by greeting him in the temple.

Elder Rhys saw her start to smile, then seem to change her mind as if she were uncertain if she were welcome to do that. He watched further as she then started to bow, nod, and once again seemed confused. Suddenly she heard him quietly laugh.

"Isabella, you are welcome here. Come. I can see that you have something to discuss," he said to her, helping her to relax. She smiled at him and began to walk alongside him until they were in a small room.

After he'd guided her to sit in a hard wooden seat in the room, he sat down opposite her then looked at her with an expression of anticipation and patience. In front of him, he saw the young woman looking around her, full of curiosity and extreme inquisitiveness.

"What do you wish to talk about?" he asked her.

Finally, she turned her head to look right at him.

"I … I have seen things in my visions of the night, and they are … confusing me," she said. "I know night visions are unimportant…"

"On the contrary, Isabella," the ancient replied. "Visions of the night sometimes tell us things that we need to know. They can provide us with the right direction for us to go on our path of life. I sense that you have been experiencing something more than a standard vision of the night, though," he said. Isabella saw him lean forward, as if hungry to hear what she was going to say. "Tell me."

"A man…" Isabella started to say. "There is a man who appears. He is not from here. He looks different, and he is so cold. When I wake, I can feel the cold that he is feeling. He has a different face, but how can I have a vision of someone I have never seen and do not know? My visions of the night are about Adrian, or my mother or father, or … other people. The people in my night visions are people that I *know*. I do not know this man. I have now seen him in more than one vision of the night. How can that be?"

Elder Rhys sat quietly. He already knew of her vision of the night. He had seen it too, but he did not share that with her. She was startled by the night vision. Her knowing that the vision had been seen by him as well would not serve any purpose or put her more at ease.

He kept quiet, his mind also curious about the discovery that he had witnessed a vision of the night that had belonged to someone else. When he had woken from that vision of the night, he'd wondered if she might have seen him in the vision too. As he listened to her, he realized that she must not have. She had seen the vision just as he had, except to her it was only the man and herself in it. To him, he had been watching from a third-person viewpoint, as if seeing it happen from a distance.

"How many visions of the night has he been in, Isabella?" he asked her, curious since it had only been the one that he had been somehow made a party to.

"Two," Isabella replied.

Elder Rhys was surprised further by her answer. Why had he seen one but not the other? He was 600 years old. He had been through one similar experience before, but not quite the same. In his extremely long lifetime, the rarity of anything new happening made the discovery intriguing to him.

Isabella watched his face, expecting him to laugh at her and tell her she was being silly. She thought he would tell her there was nothing to worry about or even think about concerning her visions of the night. He did none of those things.

"Sometimes, Isabella, things happen that we cannot explain," Elder Rhys said. "Perhaps it is your mind creating this person as a way to indicate to you that you should be moving forward in some part of your life."

"You do not think it is in any way real?" Isabella asked. "You do not think that the *man* in my visions of the night is real?"

"I think … I think that you should keep remembering your night visions if you can, but do not worry about them," Elder Rhys said. "In time, if there is something you are to learn from them, it will be revealed. It is always the way."

Isabella looked at him in the hope that he would continue speaking. She soon realized that those words had been his closing of the conversation. She stood up and smiled at him before quietly leaving the room, having not learned anything more about the odd instances that were happening to her in the night than she had known before.

Walking out into the sunlight, she was no wiser about what had been happening. The ancient had said she shouldn't worry about them. In truth, she hadn't been. They felt real, but they did not feel dangerous.

Determined to push the matter from her mind, she began to walk toward the village pool. She didn't often bathe at that time of day, but she knew she needed to relax. The feelings that the visions of the night had produced in her weren't bad feelings, but they were strong. It would take some effort to just forget them.

CHAPTER 12

The following morning Isabella awoke again with yet another night vision fresh in her mind. In it, she saw the same man again. The vision showed that he was inside the village, near the temple.

After taking a moment to make sure she was properly awake, she quickly dressed and began running from her home. She knew it was a ten-minute dash to the temple, with it being at the far end of the village.

As the temple came into view, she slowed. She saw a figure standing directly in front of it, staring at it. As if sensing her there, the person turned and looked at her. Isabella saw him drop the bag he'd been holding over his shoulder. She then saw his face go white.

Slowly they walked toward each other. It was still early. No-one in the village was roused yet apart from the cooks in the kitchen. Isabella knew they would not come outside.

Trent saw her walking toward him. His heart began beating heavily in his chest.

Finally, they stood facing one another, each accurately identifying the look of intense curiosity on the other's face.

"You have been in my visions of the night," Isabella finally said, not sure if it was a statement or a question that she was trying to portray. Regardless, of her intention, the man looked confused.

"Visions of the night?" Trent asked. He played the words over in his mind and then smiles softly. "Oh, perhaps you mean dreams."

"Dreams," he heard her repeat as if she'd never heard the word before.

"You were also in mine, although you are far more beautiful now that I see you in person," he said, instantly hearing himself as if he were a player from the life he had just left.

Isabella was enraptured. Automatically drawn to him, she moved closer.

Trent didn't step away from her. He also felt they were meant to be much, much closer. He brought his hands up to gently touch each side of her face. His palms and fingers were warmed by the feeling of her skin. To him, it felt as if she were emanating warmth from deep within her. He saw her lean into his hands as she continued to look directly into his eyes. He was instantly drawn to want to kiss her.

Isabella saw his lips coming down toward hers but felt no fear. When they touched, she felt something she had never felt before. It was as if it was the moment she had been working toward - waiting for - all of her life. She did not dare pull away. She had no *wish* to pull away. She was twenty-one. It was her first kiss. She wanted it to be, and to remain, the most special kiss - the most special *moment* - that she would ever experience.

At thirty years of age, Trent had kissed a great many women - far *too* many, he knew - but he'd never before felt what he felt at that moment. In his dreams, he had felt an incredible pull toward her. Those feelings were only intensified now that she was so close to him and her lips were on his.

When they separated, they stood back from one another. Looking closely at each other, both were uncertain about how the situation had come to be.

"I don't understand any of this," he said, shaking his head as if he expected to wake up from a dream. "Who are you?"

Isabella looked closely at him, scared and yet at the same time excited by what it all meant.

"I am Isabella," she said simply.

Trent laughed softly at her. It was clear she did not understand the full extent to which he was asking.

"Who are you?" Isabella went on to ask.

"My name is Trent. Trent Solace," he said and held out his hand in a greeting that was natural and often expected in his world.

Not familiar with the greeting, Isabella immediately stepped back and stared at his hand. She looked up into his eyes, suddenly remembering another part of one of the night visions she'd had.

"There was something else … something yellow. I handed it to you," she said.

On hearing her words, Trent remembered that part of the dream also. He had forgotten, but he could clearly see it in his mind now that she had mentioned it.

"Yes! You handed it to me," he said, letting his mind remember. "It was…"

"Warm," they both said at the same time.

"What was it?" he asked her.

Isabella could not answer.

"I do not know," she said. "When I saw it in my night vision - my *dream* - I did not recognize it."

Trent looked around, suddenly remembering what had seemed so odd to him when he'd first arrived within the interior of the large walls. He was warm, but outside, at a distance from the walls, it had been extremely cold.

"How can it be so warm here?" he asked her.

Isabella was alarmed. The question was almost identical to the one that Adrian had so recently asked. As she did not want to betray her friend, she felt it best to pretend to be unsure of the question.

"What do you mean?" she asked. "It is always this temperature here."

"But you are on top of a mountain, and it is very, *very* cold out there," he said, pointing in such a way as to indicate he meant outside of the walls.

"Yes," she replied, remembering the other aspects of her night visions. "When I had my night visions of you, I could feel the cold, but it does not get cold here. It is always like this. It is our home."

He looked at her, for the first time wondering about who the structure had been built for.

"Our? Are there other people here?" he asked.

At that moment, Isabella saw a stray mill worker come outside and make his way toward the eating area. She laughed softly and quietly at the strange man before her.

"Yes, there is one right there!" she said, pointing. Trent's face revealed that he didn't see anyone. "You cannot see him?" Isabella asked.

Trent was confused at what she was saying - what she was *seeing*. He began wondering once more if he was inside a dream.

"All I see are a lot of broken buildings and rubble … and you," he said.

Isabella looked around her but could not see the broken buildings he referred to.

"Nothing is broken here. What looks broken to you?" she asked, curious.

Trent pointed behind him to the temple.

"That, for starters," he said. "It looks like a bomb went off and flattened it."

Isabella walked past him and up to the temple door. To her, it felt normal as she passed through it.

"What is this 'bomb' you speak of?" she asked. "There is nothing wrong here. This is our temple. It stands as it always has."

To Trent, it looked like she was magically walking through rubble.

"Wait! Don't go there!" he yelled at her. To him, it seemed that she would surely bring down some of the random beams that were standing upwards but which looked completely unsecured in any way.

Isabella turned to him and saw the concern on his face. She stopped and came back to him.

"I do not understand," she said. "Do you see different from what I see? How could that be?"

"I..." he stammered, feeling well out of his depth. "I don't know, but

Isabella, please don't go there. It doesn't look safe. Is there an open area nearby? Somewhere where there are no buildings or any other things that might fall?"

Isabella smiled at him, wondering if he was jesting her as Adrian did sometimes. Already she'd noticed the strange way that he spoke. It wasn't the same as the way the villagers talked. She wondered if that was also some kind of joke. All she saw on his face were fear and seriousness. She held out her hand to him.

"Come," she said. "I know a great open space that we can go to sit and talk."

Trent looked at her extended hand. He found himself surprised at how at ease he was with her, and how at ease she seemed to be with him. Taking her hand in his, he let her lead him. They walked past the broken down buildings and rubble that he could see must have been a great township at some time - a very, very long time ago.

They walked in silence, looking at each other while continuing to hold hands. Neither was sure what was happening with or between them. At a logical level, it seemed wrong that they should be walking together so companionably when they did not know each other. Even for Trent - a man well versed in meeting strangers and even taking some of them home with him for sexual pleasure - he felt that they might be crossing a boundary by holding hands. Despite his reservations about etiquette, he didn't stop it. As much as he had wanted to be away from human contact on his quest, he found that in the present moment, he was very glad of it.

When they reached the area where Isabella had felt the land warm when she was with Adrian, she sat down on the ground and invited him to do the same.

Sitting down on the dirt, Trent was again surprised that he felt no cold there. When she told him to put both of his hands flat on the ground, as Adrian had done, something surged through him. It was warmth, but it was more than that. He closed his eyes and let the feeling rush through him. It was unlike anything he had experienced before. His veins felt like they had something new and exciting rushing through them. At that moment, he felt incredibly healthy and alive.

While he was absorbed in his experience, Isabella took time to look closely at his face. He was unlike anyone she already knew, but she found she liked looking at his face. She felt close to him, not only like she was meant to be close to him, but also like she was meant to be even *closer* to him. As she watched, Trent opened his eyes and initially looked directly into hers. Then she saw him jump up and backward, looking confused again.

"What is it?" she asked, alarmed at his response and standing up with him.

"What? I just saw things … differently…" Trent said, confused.

Neither knew what that meant, but with the softness of her voice, Isabella coaxed him to sit down again.

When he did, he put his hands on the ground once more. This time he kept his eyes open. Things instantly changed. Before him, she still sat, unchanged, but the dirt had been replaced by green grass. Beyond, in the distance, he could see buildings - upright, intact and well-formed buildings.

When he removed his hands a short way, just lifting them clear of the grass, everything grew dark again. Instead of the lush grass that he'd just seen, it was once more dirt they were sitting on. Regardless of the changes he'd seen, Isabella remained sitting before him, looking just the same. She was in his view, no matter what he did. "What is happening? What do you see?" she asked him, full of curiosity and intrigue at what new and exciting things appeared to all of a sudden be happening in her home village.

Trent refocused on her as he lowered his hands down again. Once more he could see a completely different landscape.

"It's all changing. When I have my hands down like this, I can see what I think you see. This is green grass we are sitting on," he said and saw her nod. "And I can see buildings that look intact, over that way."

Isabella smiled at him.

"Yes," she said. "You are seeing my home, but why do you not see it when your hands are not down? Who is seeing real? Me? Or you?"

Trent focused his eyes on hers.

"You are the constant here, Isabella. You, I can see either way. Do you have a power that is making me see you?" he asked.

Isabella shook her head.

"No, I have no power," she replied, smiling. "I am just me. No-one in my village has powers, I do not think."

In the otherwise silence, Trent's stomach growled loudly. He knew he was well overdue for food but did not know how he could get to any. Isabella heard the sound and laughed softly.

"You must eat," she said.

"Yes, but how?" asked Trent.

Isabella was thoughtful for a while, wondering how she could help him with the current dilemma. When she'd considered an idea, she stood up and held out her hand once more.

"Come with me," she said. Trent took her hand as they began to walk. "I do not know if this will work as I do not know if this will happen on all of our land, but our orchard is this way."

She held his hand as she walked him through what now looked like dry dirt and overgrown areas of growth. Eventually, he could see what must have once been healthy trees. Now, they were just dried and dead stumps.

"Sit down here. Let us see if it works here," she said and watched as he obeyed.

As soon as Trent's hands touched the ground, he could see he was in an orchard with a large vegetable garden nearby.

"Oh!" he exclaimed, unintentionally indicating to her that he could indeed see what was around them.

He watched as she reached up and picked a red apple off one of the trees that he could now clearly see was a fruit tree. She went to hand it to him, but as he reached out to take it, even with just one hand, the image died - and so did the fruit. He was suddenly looking at nothing.

Isabella was thoughtful enough to comprehend what had happened. She instructed him to put his hand down once more.

Trent watched as she reached up and picked another apple. This time she came to him and pulled out a small knife from the side pocket of her dress. He watched as she cut off a slice and leaned in to place it in his open mouth. It wasn't the most gracious way to eat, but he let her feed him like that. He did not want to think about what would happen to the food inside of him once he moved his hands.

As he sat cross-legged, she remained close to him, almost leaning over him. He was very aware of her as the beautiful woman that she was. It had been so long since he'd had a woman's company - since he'd had *any* company. But it was more than that. Because of the dreams, he felt like he knew her - like they were meant to not only know one another but completely be together.

Perhaps the fruit would end up being real. Perhaps it wouldn't. No matter what would come from it, at that moment, it felt like his stomach was getting nourishment. He also appreciated that the fruit was far fresher than any he'd ever had before in his life.

He let her feed him, partly because he knew his body needed it, but also because he wanted to be that close to her. He had dreamed about her. Now she was real - seemingly in either reality. He had no idea which vision *was* the reality. That was the ongoing question to which the answer was completely and utterly unknown.

When the apple was finished she threw the apple core away onto what appeared to be a compost heap, then remained kneeling in front of him.

"Isabella," he whispered, wanting to be closer to her but knowing he could not.

The pull to her was great, like the universe wanted them to be closer. He had slept with many women but had never felt anything like he was at that moment.

Isabella surprised him by leaning in and kissing him. Trent groaned in response, moving his hands off the ground as he did so. They remained kissing until she heard a voice getting closer. He saw her head turn before she stood up quickly with the look of embarrassment. She knew that the outlook had changed for him again when he'd removed his hands from the ground, but she couldn't leave him there for the gardeners to unknowingly walk through if they were to go near the trees. If he *was* there.

Trent could see her talking to people but he couldn't see them. He could only see her talking as if she were talking to no-one. When she began walking, he saw her indicate subtly with her hand behind her to follow her so he did. As he followed her, he couldn't see the people, but he could tell from watching her where they were. He had no way of knowing if they could see him. He guessed not as she seemed to act as if he weren't there, even though she now and then would look back at him.

He couldn't even tell where they were, so had no idea if people were walking through him. Were they ghosts? Was *she* a ghost? She certainly hadn't felt like a ghost when she'd kissed him.

Or perhaps *he* was a ghost. Suddenly he considered that maybe he had actually died and was now haunting the place. Perhaps the people there were real and Isabella was some kind of medium.

The thought caused a shudder to pass down Trent's spine. He forced himself to dismiss it quickly. Whatever was happening, he couldn't change it or stop it. Trying to analyze it would do him no good. He opted instead to enjoy the feeling of food in his stomach. To his surprise, the apple did feel like it was staying put, even though everything else had changed and disappeared around him.

Isabella had to think of where to lead him. She wanted him to be able to sit down and enjoy her village as she did, but without him being seen.

Trent saw her leading him once more into the pile of rubble she had tried to earlier. This time he let her, but while she seemed to walk freely among it, he had to climb over broken debris.

"This won't work, Isabella," he called out to her only a meter or two into what looked to him to be a war zone. "I can't go that way."

She looked thoughtful and nodded in acknowledgment. Looking around first, she then looked at him and said quietly, "You lead me to where you can go, where you think you can sit and be safe."

He understood her logic immediately. He looked around, grabbed his backpack, and eventually led her to where they had first sat. Seeing no-one nearby, she leaned in close to him and whispered into his ear so no-one else could hear.

"I must get on with my day as usual," she said and saw him nod in full understanding. "I am going to go into the temple and talk to one of our ancients, Elder Rhys. I will bring him here. Will you stay here?" she asked and saw him nod again. "Are you warm here?"

"Yes, I will stay right here. No-one will walk through me?" he asked, feeling giddy at the thought.

Isabella laughed softly.

"No, I do not think that they can see you, nor you them," she said. "You are not on a path. No-one should walk here."

Trent saw her look around once more before moving right up to him, pressing her chest into his, and leaning forward to kiss him fully on the lips. He felt hungry with passion for her. He didn't know if it was a real passion - a real desire - or if it were driven by a hunger for human touch that he had been without for what seemed like so long. He didn't even know if *she* was real. Certainly, at that moment, she *seemed* real. Whether or not she was, Trent was ready to indulge in the feelings that were passing between them.

He put his arms around her and pulled her tighter to him. As he kissed her hungrily, he heard her moan slightly at the passion they both seemed to feel.

Isabella felt desperation she had never felt before. She wanted - *needed* - to be closer to him. Letting herself go with the feeling, she kissed him back as hard as she could. Soon the sound of people starting to emerge from their homes made her pull away.

"People are waking up," she said. "I must go. Please stay here. Do not leave."

Hearing the pleading in her voice, Trent nodded and smiled at her.

"I will be here," he replied. "I promise."

He watched her wander off before he lay down on the grass. He did not want to risk being seen so kept his hands off it, choosing instead to lie on his back and keep his hands on his chest. He didn't yet know if when he was able to see what she saw, other people in her view might be able to see him, even though she had said it didn't appear that they could.

Through the day, he saw her from a distance a few times, often chatting and laughing as if she were having a conversation. Never seeing anyone with her as she talked and smiled, the sight brought out in Trent a combination of amusement and intrigue.

When he got hungry, he reached into his pack and ate a few of the last tiny morsels he had left in the form of dry food. He could still remember the taste of the apple. The memory made him salivate. Although he couldn't be sure, it felt like even though that apple perhaps should have disappeared from his stomach as soon as he removed himself from the time and place that he ate it, it hadn't. His stomach had continued to feel the same as it had when he had first eaten it. It was a good sign. If he could get more food from her, he might survive his journey after all.

Later on, when he'd had some sleep, he heard her voice coming toward him. Opening his eyes, he saw her striding in his direction. She was looking around her, but she also had someone beside her. Trent noticed immediately that not only could he see the man, but the elderly man was looking straight back at him.

The older man guided Isabella to sit down on the ground, cross-legged, facing him so that to others it would look like they were meditating and having a serious conversation. He instructed her to not look at the third person in their seating arrangement, now that other people were seemingly moving around the village.

"You are a traveler, I see," the elderly man said.

"Can you ... see me?" Trent asked, uncertain what was happening.

"I can indeed," Elder Rhys replied. "You are not the first traveler I have encountered, but it has been almost 300 years since the last one came through here."

Both Isabella and Trent asked at the same time, "300 years??"

Elder Rhys laughed softly.

"Yes, 300 years," he said. "The last time someone came here, it did not end well. Your name is Trent, yes?" he asked and saw Trent nod. "What you see, Trent, I think, is the result of what happened when the last traveler was here. When he first came here, he merged with our people, fitting in as a welcome guest. Then he went away. Not long after he had left, he came back, this time with many people. They did not want to just visit us. They wanted to take what was sustaining us - the power and heat source that sits under the earth that we sit on now. We would not let them take it. They fought us to try and take it by force."

"And that is how your village became destroyed?" Trent asked, feeling quite ill at the story being told to him.

"Yes," the ancient replied.

Isabella was disbelieving of what she was hearing.

"But Elder Rhys, we are here, and the village is not destroyed..."

The ancient looked at her.

"You have much to learn, Isabella," he said. "You and I are in a different time to what Trent is. What we see is hundreds of years behind what he sees. The ground here is the only link he can have to our time."

"But then how can I see Isabella? And you?" Trent asked, still open to the possibility that he had died and was a ghost.

The ancient nodded.

"It is a complex thing indeed. I have lived for 600 years and I have always had the gift to see and talk to people from different times. I was not aware that you had it too, Isabella. I fear that we are the only two, although if Trent remains here, it may come to light that some others may see him also."

"But how can he survive here, Elder Rhys? He cannot eat or drink..."

Isabella began to say.

"He can change," the ancient said as if it were the most obvious answer in the world. "We can bring him back into our time, Isabella," he continued, looking at her first and then more intently at Trent. "But if we do that, Trent, you will be in our time securely. Your time will not exist. Do you understand?"

Trent nodded his head.

"We can only do this once," Elder Rhys said. "I do not have any ability to send you back to your time if you are unhappy in ours. Therefore I wish to advise you to take a day or two to think about it first. You are safe here. I believe that Isabella will be able to help you to eat and drink, even though she will have to do it discretely. At night would be better, Isabella," he said.

Isabella nodded in agreement. She'd already planned in her mind to find Trent that evening and bring at least some bread with her to give to him.

Trent saw the ancient look at him closely.

"I sense you are a good man, even though I equally sense turmoil in your soul," said Elder Rhys. "You must take the time needed to make the right decision. I can see your journey here has taken a toll on your body. We will be able to amend that for you so you will be able to journey home again if you wish. If you do that, there will be no advantage to bringing people here in the future - in your time. As you can see, there is nothing here anymore," he said. "Do you understand what I am saying, young traveler?"

"Yes," Trent replied quietly.

"Good. Now I must stand up and move. Joints do not work well when you reach the ripe old age of 600!" Elder Rhys said, slowly raising himself off the ground with the help of both Isabella and Trent. "Take your time in thinking about what I have said, Trent. It is a one-way trip, what I offer you, so be sure. Isabella here will come to me when you have made your decision."

"Thank you, Sir," Trent said, in awe of the ancient as he moved away from them.

"I must go to dinner, but I will bring some food for you afterward," Isabella said quietly and watched him sit down again. As soon as she was on the path, she heard Adrian call out to her.

"Isabella! Are you coming to dinner?" he asked.

Isabella nodded, quickly putting on the mask she knew she needed to.

"Yes, of course," she said to her friend. "Let us go."

~~~~~

Left alone again, Trent pondered what he'd been told were now his options. Stay, eat, recuperate, and then tramp home, but to what? Noise?
~~~~~

Pollution? People? Screens? Oh, how he had come to loathe screens!

But what of the other option? He didn't know how the villagers lived, so how could he make that judgment? He couldn't see them. He couldn't even see the landscape unless he placed his hands to the ground beneath him. But if he did that, would they then see him? It wasn't a risk he was willing to take yet. First, he had to focus most of all on whether he even wanted to go home … ever.

He considered all that had happened since he'd fallen through the wall earlier that day. He'd met two people who seemed to be in the past. It was difficult to dispute that being the case, given the state of the buildings Trent had seen in both times.

There were big things to consider. Should he try and return to his previous life?

There were also little things to consider. If he converted to be back in time with Isabella and Elder Rhys, how would his life change? He'd already noticed their different use of language. They weren't lazy in their words. That was one small thing he could consciously work on, even if in the village for only a short time.

CHAPTER 13

Isabella and Adrian sat close together, as they always did during their meals.

"You are very quiet, Isabella. What is troubling you?" Adrian asked her, not able to even imagine where her mind was taking her. She had always been such a fluent person, doing the same things day after day, and never having any different thoughts at all. Over the past week, she had begun to change before his eyes.

Isabella looked at him intently, wanting so much to share her discovery with him but not knowing if he could be trusted. On the one hand, he was Adrian - her lifelong friend and confidant. That Adrian would never betray anything that she told him, and would always support her in whatever she said or did.

On the other hand, he had, only days before, offered her a pairing with him, and she had not said yes to that. He seemed to have accepted her decision not to rush into that. She wasn't sure he would be so accepting if he knew about the strange man who had not only appeared and come into her life, but she had also kissed.

"You can talk to me about anything, Isabella. You do know that?" he asked and saw her smile and nod at him.

"Of course I know that, Adrian! You are my closest friend," Isabella said. "You have proven to me over and over how much I can trust you."

Adrian looked at her with an expression of curiosity on his face.

"Trust me?" he asked. "Oh, that sounds intriguing. What have you done, Isabella? Let the chickens out again when you gathered their eggs this morning?" he teased her. "Did you forget which herb you should have gathered for the cook again? Did you grab a green apple this morning when you should have grabbed a red one?"

Isabella knew he was trying to lighten the mood, but in the depths of his eyes, she could see that he was concerned about her. When he mentioned apples, the memory of feeding Trent made Isabella's face grow warm. She could see on Adrian's face that he had seen the blush.

"What is it?" he finally asked, his voice now more serious, lower and quieter. He suddenly felt concerned they were about to talk about something that no-one else must hear.

"I..." she started to say before becoming tongue-tied. She lowered her eyes from his before she spoke again. "Adrian, something is happening, and I do not know how to talk about it."

Adrian raised his arm and slowly stroked her forearm, trying to soothe her.

"It is alright," he replied, his voice revealing his concern for her. "You can tell me - or not tell me - whichever you wish. Do not worry yourself so, Isabella. You are starting to worry me."

"No, I trust you, and I do need to share this with someone other than Elder Rhys," Isabella said as she met his gaze.

"Elder Rhys?" Adrian asked. "What has he to do with this?"

Isabella felt confused and conflicted, not sure what was the right thing to do. She looked at the plates before her and Adrian, resolved to include him in her discovery.

"Let us eat, and then I wish to show you something," she said. "It might be difficult to understand. It is impossible for *me* to understand, but it *is* real."

Adrian looked at her and accepted her words as being sincere. Turning to his food, he began to eat quickly. All the while, his mind churned over many possibilities about what could be happening that had his friend's interest so captured.

~~~~~

When they had both finished eating, Isabella took another two bread rolls and stood to leave. Adrian quietly followed her, not asking what the bread was for.

After washing, drying, and putting away their dishes, they walked out of the dining area together, initially saying nothing while walking.

"Adrian, I am unsure if you will be able to see what I see, so please be patient with me and just trust that I believe in what I am seeing," Isabella said.

Her words intrigued him further. On a regular day, he would tease her about such words and the drama of them. On this evening, he sensed he was best to remain silent.
~~~~~

CHAPTER 14

Trent was lying down on his back with his head on his backpack, enjoying the feeling of warmth coming from underneath him. He still didn't know how it could be so warm, but he could certainly appreciate it regardless.

Hearing Isabella's footsteps coming across the dirt, he quickly sat up to look at her. He was not oblivious to the fact that she appeared to be looking at someone right beside her, even though Trent could see no-one.

He watched as she sat down on the ground before him and indicated to the invisible person to sit with her before she turned her eyes to Trent.

"Put your hands down," she said, looking directly at him.

Adrian had no idea who Isabella thought she was talking to. He remained silent, hoping something would be revealed to him soon enough.

Trent lowered his hands, nervous as he could tell that someone else was there, but for the moment, both were completely oblivious and invisible to each other. As he lowered his hands down, he closed his eyes and once again felt the power surge through him. When he opened his eyes, he found he was once again immersed in color. Before him was the green of the grass and the trees, and the orangey terracotta color of some of the buildings around them.

Of greater note was that he could see a young man sitting next to Isabella, and the man was looking right back at him.

~~~~~

Adrian jumped up in shock.

"What is this magic, Isabella?" he asked, the sound of fear rich in his voice.

"Adrian, please sit down," she said quietly, trying to indicate to him to keep calm and not draw attention to them.

"Well, I guess that answers my curiosity about whether other people would be able to see me when I did this," Trent said, smiling as if he'd told a great joke. No-one was laughing.

Isabella pulled the bread out as Adrian sat down and watched her, not knowing what to say.

"Adrian, this is Trent," Isabella said. "He is not … of our time. You were curious the other day about the warmth coming from the ground…"
~~~~~

she started to explain and saw him nod in recognition of her words. "This seems to be another … gift … of it. When Trent touches it like this with two hands, he is here, with us. When he does not touch it with his two hands, he is not in our time at all. He is in … our future."

"Isabella, I believe you must be jesting me," said Adrian. "You know that is not possible."

Isabella nodded and looked into his eyes.

Trent could see how close they were. As friends? As lovers? While pondering that question, he felt a strong unease at the possibility of the latter. His thoughts were interrupted when he saw Isabella nod at him.

"Show him," she said with a fair degree of force.

Trent immediately followed her instruction and raised his hand. The next moment he appeared to be alone with her.

With a nod of her head, she guided him to put his hands down once more. The result was he and Adrian once again being able to see one another.

"I cannot watch any more of this … madness. Isabella, come with me. I shall walk you home. This is some kind of … trick. Please come with me," he said to her, standing up.

Isabella heard pleading in his voice, but shook her head at him.

"No, Adrian, I shall stay here," she replied. "Trent needs sustenance and I brought this bread for him. Do not worry about me. I shall see you at the morning meal."

Adrian looked at her, scared for her, but knew how strong-willed she could be. He turned and walked away without looking back.

Trent looked at her. He could see the distress on her face.

"You care about each other," he said.

Isabella nodded. "Yes, very much."

"But you let me kiss you."

Isabella blushed at the thought.

"He and I are friends … good friends. We are nothing more," she said as she started to break off a small piece of the bread that she held in her hands.

"But one of you wishes it were something more," Trent said, sharing his observation.

He saw her nod again, softly and with a look of affection mixed in with dismay at the observation.

"The other night he asked me about pairing…"

"Pairing?" asked Trent.

Isabella blushed profusely, making Trent consider what it could mean. He suspected he understood but waited for her to explain.

"In our village, a man and a woman pair … and then produce offspring so that the village can maintain our population," Isabella explained.

Trent nodded at her, not wanting to make her any more uncomfortable. He was surprised but pleased when she continued to speak.

"He asked me, but I did not feel I was ready. I … I told him I was not ready and he accepted that," she continued and then paused. She looked him directly in the eye while she raised one piece of bread and eased it toward his mouth, allowing him to take it in. "I did think then that I was not ready, but … when you kissed me … when I kissed you … I felt … different."

Trent watched her as he enjoyed and savored the flavor in his mouth. Now that he was 30 years old, it seemed an eternity ago that he'd lost his virginity. Sex had seemed so easy where he'd come from, like it was hardly worth anything at all.

"Different to … how it felt when you kissed others?" Trent boldly asked her.

He was curious because she was like an enigma to him. She had invaded his dreams and then appeared as a reality before him.

"Oh, no. I have never kissed anyone before," she said and saw the surprise on Trent's face. "No, I would only kiss someone I was paired with."

Isabella saw Trent's eyes go wide, as if he was worried he had been committed to pairing with her.

He saw her laugh softly at him. He was mesmerized by the sound of it.

"Oh, do not look so scared," she said with humor in her voice that made him even more captivated. "I am not saying you are now paired with me. I do not know why I enjoyed you kissing me, but it did not come from knowing each other over a long time, knowing what we each like and dislike..." she continued, remembering the way Adrian had explained things to her when he had suggested the two of them pair.

She tore off another piece of bread and again offered it to Trent's mouth. He was desperate to move his hands, but at the same time, he knew he needed the food so would not risk losing that opportunity. His body needed so many things, but the feeling most able to be felt inside of him was that he needed *her*. He could feel the pull he had toward her and believed it was mutual. It was something unknown that had pulled them to be near to one another.

For now, he would eat. He knew Isabella only had limited food with her. That was good as he would have to slowly build up the quantities he could eat, letting his body gradually adjust to proper food once again.

They looked at each other as she slowly fed him. Once the food was gone, Trent took a moment to enjoy the fullness in his stomach.

"I would like to kiss you again, Isabella," he said.

Isabella nodded. "Yes."

"I want to stand and put my arms around you, but although people will not see me, they will see *you*," Trent said.

Isabella realized the predicament and nodded again.

"Yes, we must go somewhere where no-one else will see. I cannot see the dangers you can, so point me in a direction and I will tell you if I can go there," she said.

She stood up and watched him as he lifted his backpack in preparation to follow her. The sight made her quietly laugh.

"You can leave that here if you wish to," she said. "No-one else can see it so it will not be taken."

Trent laughed in agreement with the point she made. It was an easy moment for them before she moved closer to him and stood before him.

He was desperate to kiss her, so quickly looked around and started walking toward the outer wall. Between him saying when he could not walk over or through something, and her doing the same, finally they reached a discrete corner behind a building.

"Are you safe here?" he asked her to be sure. He was hungry for her and didn't want to deal with the two-hands-on-the-ground saga.

"Yes, no-one can see me here," she said and stepped forward to him.

After their arms wrapped around each other, Trent plunged his mouth onto hers. He was hungrier than he had been before. He could tell she was finding her way in kissing, but the desire and passion emanating from her were overpowering. He felt like he should break away from her but at the same time, that was the last thing he could do.

He pulled back only slightly so that he could look at her. The brilliant red hair was like a wild mane. He couldn't help but slip his fingers into it, feeling it run across his palm like it was silk.

"Isabella, you are so beautiful. I don't know where you have come from, but I am drawn to you. I have been drawn to you since before I was even here, with you in my dreams," he whispered to her before kissing her again, this time more softly.

Isabella reveled in the feelings flowing through her body. Never had she felt such emotion. She had never even dreamed of such things. Being able to touch him and hold him invigorated her even more.

When Trent pulled back again to look at her once more, Isabella moved one of her hands to his cheek. Under her fingertips, she could feel the short hair over his chin and face.

Trent naturally tilted his head to move his face against her hand. It had been so long since he'd experienced any human interaction at all, let alone touch.

In a fleeting moment, he thought back to life as it had been before. He had been seeing a married woman for many months. They'd often had sex, but it had felt different. It hadn't meant anything. Just the touch of Isabella's hands on him was enough to make him crave more.

"I shall need to go home soon, Trent. My mother and father will be worried about me," she said. "I cannot help you to find somewhere safe to sleep…"

Suddenly she seemed so young and innocent, even though he could tell she had a great passion inside of her, waiting to be set free. Not wanting to focus on her passion, Trent looked around. As far as he could see, there wasn't one building standing.

"I have a small tent in my bag…" he began to say.

"A … tent?" Isabella asked with obvious curiosity.

Trent smiled at her. Of course, she wouldn't know what a tent was.

"It is a small shelter that I carry with me. I will set it up where we were sitting earlier. I will sleep there for the night," he said and saw her nod as she looked down. "I can walk you to your house now though. I mean, no-one is going to see me, right?" he said.

Isabella could hear the amusement in his voice, making her laugh lightly in return.

"Yes, of course," she said, smiling and nodding. "Thank you."

She held out her hand to him and once more they negotiated the way to her home, both of them pointing out the obstacles they could see that the other one could not. Finally, she stopped and leaned in close to him, but not touching him.

"I am here," she whispered.

"Will you come and find me tomorrow?" he asked and saw her nod in response. He sensed she was worried someone might see her. "I can see that you cannot move toward me, or kiss me, or say anything right now, but I can lean in and kiss you," he said, leaning in and just lightly kissing her lips, ever so softly. "Goodnight, Isabella. Thank you for a remarkable day."

After watching him walk away, Isabella turned and entered her family home, wondering what adventures could possibly come her way next.

CHAPTER 15

Throughout the night, Trent felt incredibly warm and safe in his small pup tent and sleeping bag, even though he could hear the wind gusting around the outside of the tall village walls. It was a strange sensation, knowing that people were nearby, sleeping, and yet they didn't appear to be there at all.

With his mind working so much, he found sleep difficult. Nothing made any sense. He kept returning, over and over, to the possibility that perhaps he had perished on one of the mountains. Maybe he was now drifting as a spirit without a body. He didn't know if he believed in ghosts. After such a day, he had to acknowledge that *anything* could be possible.

He thought about Isabella. That morning, when he'd walked into the interior of the large grey walls, he'd been sure no-one could be around, and yet he could feel her before he saw her. Not only had he known there was a presence, but he could feel it was *her* - the woman from his recent dreams.

Over the course of the day, so much had happened to keep his mind busy and thoughtful. Now that he lay in the quiet and calm of his sleeping bag, he found his mind drifting specifically to her. When he thought about her - her flowing red hair; her flawless skin; and her plump, full lips - he felt himself become aroused. Sex hadn't been on his mind for a long time. Even during the day that was now finishing, it hadn't been something that he'd thought about. When they'd kissed, there had been something so different about the kisses - about kissing *her*. They seemed to have a different effect on him than kissing and being so close to a woman would normally have on him.

He instinctively knew - *believed* - that she was a virgin. It was quite possible that she was unaware yet even of what sex entailed. She had told him she'd never kissed anyone before he kissed her. He guessed she must be in her twenties. By that age, many women had already succumbed to the temptation of passion in his world. It was common. It had become *too* common, he supposed. That was why sometimes it had never felt special to him. He was attractive, and he had his share of women approaching him whenever he went out to bars. Sometimes he would use them for sex. Sometimes he would end up dating them. Even then, he would still have sex with them. He couldn't remember when he'd spent quiet time with a woman without them having sex relatively shortly after meeting.

The trek across the mountains had taken its toll on his body. Regardless, he had to admit that even having eaten only one apple and a small amount of bread, he could feel his body rejuvenating.

He had so much to think about, but finally, he found himself start to relax and become sleepy. There was no need to keep thinking. More thinking could be done in the morning, he thought to himself as he quietly drifted off into dreams once again.

~~~~~

The dream had begun but it was different. In it, Trent was back where he'd met Isabella that morning, but he no longer saw rubble. Instead, he could see a large building with symbols carved into its stone frontage, either side of the doorway and over the top of it.

He turned as he felt her approaching. When he looked at her, he was overwhelmed by the beauty before him. Suddenly, instead of just her porcelain skin and long flowing hair being what attracted him, he could see a glow emanating from her. He stepped forward as they walked toward each other. As he stopped still, facing her and within arm's length of her, she moved closer and kissed him.

Even in his dream, Trent could feel the depth of passion that resulted deep within him as she touched her lips to his. He didn't move, keeping his hands by his side. Eventually, she pulled back from the kiss, smiled at him, and placed her hand on his heart. As she did, he felt incredible heat and power coming through from her and into him. It was like ecstasy to him, as if they were making love. It felt like she was taking him into an extremely deep and long-built-up climax. He had never felt anything like it. In the depth of his dreaming, the thought made him smile…
~~~~~

CHAPTER 16

As Isabella prepared for her night of sleep, her mind wandered to the stranger she had met during the day. It seemed as if nothing that had happened could be real, and yet it felt as if it were *very* real. Even the things Elder Rhys had told her did not seem like they could be real. Perhaps she was dreaming. Maybe even now, climbing into her bed, she was already *in* bed, dreaming about everything that had happened since that morning.

She lay down, pulled the covers over her, and remembered the kisses she'd shared with Trent. Her first kisses. She had never anticipated that kissing would feel like that, but kissing him had touched her in places she'd never felt before. She shouldn't have kissed him. It was not right to do so. And yet, at the same time, it *was* right. She had never been more certain of anything in her life.

<center>~~~~~</center>

In her vision of the night, she saw him again. This time he was different. There was an aura around him, shimmering like a wave. It was alternating between a light blue and a deep orange, like he was changing back and forth, over and over, from cold to warm. They stared at each other until she could not bear to see him like that anymore.

She moved closer to him and placed her lips on his. The feeling from that kiss was overpowering to her. In her head, she could only see brilliant yellow. When she pulled away to look at the man who was driving her forward in her need for passion, he was still changing, cold to warm, cold to warm. She reached forward and placed her hand on his heart. The changing stopped as she saw him become engulfed in a steady, warm color of flame.

He opened his eyes and reached out to her, pulling her close to him and taking her mouth with his, before his hand reached down and touched her...

Suddenly, Isabella jolted awake. She had never seen anything like that in a vision of the night before. Where had that come from? And why did she feel so heated, as if she had enjoyed such a vision?

CHAPTER 17

The following morning Trent woke up feeling more refreshed and relaxed than he had in a long while. His body ached in desperate longing to not have to walk anymore - at least for a while. He happily lay still and chose to not move at all. The ground underneath him was so warm, it almost felt like he was indulging in a warm bath.

Suddenly he found himself wondering if there was water in the area and, if so, if it was heated. He could only imagine how good a warm bath would feel after so long walking most of every day and only washing in cold rivers when he'd been in the valley areas.

As parts of the dream from the night of sleep came to him, he found himself focused on Isabella once more. He was sure she was real, but how could she be? How could *anything* currently happening be real?

He pulled his water bottle from his bag and noticed it would need filling soon. Having not yet looked further around the ruins of the village, he hoped he would find a water source eventually. He couldn't think of any real reason why water would have stopped flowing to wherever the past residents had gathered their water from.

He was deep in thought when he heard footsteps approaching, and Isabella's soft voice call out to him from outside the tent.

"Trent," Isabella whispered as loudly as she dared, with it being so early in the morning.

Even the sound of her voice was intoxicating, Trent realized as his body instantly jumped to attention. In silence, he cursed that part of him as he did not want there to be awake right now. Clutching his sleeping bag tightly around him, he leaned forward and unzipped the small entry point of the tent.

"Oh!" Isabella exclaimed, intrigued by the zip itself.

Trent laughed softly at her as she took the zip in her fingers and moved it upwards and then downwards, then upwards and then downwards. While she was intrigued by that, he took the moment to lie back again. Resting his head on one arm crooked behind his head, he smiled at her.

After a few minutes, Isabella looked at him with a sheepish look on her face.

"Sorry, Trent. I have never seen such a thing," she whispered and saw him smile at her. "May I ... come in here with you?"

The question was an innocent one, but Trent's body immediately jumped to even greater attention.

"Yes, of course," he said.

He watched her slowly find her way in climbing into the tiny space and eventually lying alongside him, her face close to his.

"Did you sleep well?" she asked.

She was so close to him that he found himself enchanted by the beauty of her eyes, and the movement of her lips.

"I did, thank you. I had the best sleep I have had in a very long while," he responded, unintentionally raising his free hand to touch her cheek and jawline. "Did you?"

Isabella closed her eyes and indulged in the sensation passing through her.

"Yes," she seemed to breathe out.

Trent knew that sound. Even though she might have been inexperienced in sex, she still had a great depth of passion inside of her. Not only that, but she was waking up to it, seemingly right before his eyes.

Isabella leaned in to kiss him, enjoying the new feelings the stranger was invoking in her.

Trent welcomed the kiss as they lay together, his body's wakefulness fortunately contained within the thick sleeping bag. He felt like he was transported. The feelings were incredible. He had been with some amazing and very memorable lovers in his adult life. None of them had ever had quite the same effect on him as she was.

He moved so he was facing her, and pulled her close to him. He felt her body naturally move so that she aligned herself perfectly, raising one knee so it rested on his hip through the protective layer he had around him.

Both of them sunk into the feelings, not wanting them to stop until Trent pulled away.

"Oh, Isabella," he heard himself groan as he fought to find words. "I ... I think we should not get too close here and now."

"Have I done something wrong?" she asked.

"No!" he said, reassuring her. "Oh, no. Kissing you is the most exquisite thing I have ever experienced. You have no idea how it feels to kiss you..."

"Yes I do," she argued back softly. "I *do* know how it feels, and it feels wonderful."

Trent closed his eyes and shook his head, desperate to keep control of what was happening. He forced himself to focus on anything other than the desire he felt. Her presence was intoxicating, but there were other aspects of her that held his interest.

He let his focus move to the way she spoke. He had never been a great scholar, but he couldn't help but notice she'd never used any contractions in her speech. That seemed a perfect skill he could focus on in her presence to keep his mind off more pleasurable pursuits.

When he opened them again, he saw her still staring at him with an intense look on her face. It seemed the perfect time for him to begin his new experience in language.

"Other people will see you, will they not? They will see you lying on the ground here, looking like you are ... kissing someone," he said.

Once Isabella comprehended his words, Trent heard a slight giggle come from her.

"Yes, you are right, Trent. I imagine it would be quite an image to others who can see me but cannot see you," she said, nodding and smiling broadly. "I shall leave you now."

"Oh, you don't - do not - have to go..." he said, reaching out and stopping her progress that had begun to move toward the zip once more. "I just meant that perhaps you should not be *kissing* me..."

She smiled such a beautiful, intense smile at him that he felt a natural urge to grab her and pull her back. In truth, he felt a desperate need to pull her into his sleeping bag with him. That need, he fought, forcing himself to instead think of the day to come.

"Isabella, do you have water here somewhere?" he asked and saw her lack of understanding. "Water for drinking, and water for bathing?"

"Ahh, yes, of course. I shall go to the morning meal now while you rest and then get ready. When I have eaten, I shall bring you some more bread?" she asked and saw him nod. "After that, I shall go with you to where our water supply is. I did not bathe yesterday so I will do so today," she said.

As she said the words and looked at him in such a way, Trent could only imagine her naked body. Once again, he was very pleased to have such a thick sleeping bag wrapped around him.

CHAPTER 18

At the morning meal, Isabella met up with Adrian. Although he was usually happy and energetic in his enthusiasm to see her, he appeared particularly eager to talk to her.

"Isabella, I am still confused by yesterday," he said. "How did we see that man? Who is he and where did he come from? I just do not understand…"

Isabella looked at her friend and understood his confusion.

"I know, Adrian," Isabella said as she placed her hand on his arm. "It is beyond me also how anything like this could be. I thought I might be seeing things because he was the man from my visions of the night, but…"

"He is who you saw in your visions of the night?" Adrian asked, an intense depth of concern growing in his heart. "I do not understand…"

"It is beyond belief," replied Isabella as she nodded. "Elder Rhys said it was real. He told me that he had seen someone like Trent before. A traveler, he called him."

Adrian listened and wanted to focus on the words that she spoke. Instead, he found his thoughts returning to her statement that the man had been seen in her visions of the night.

"What happened in your night visions? When you saw him?" he asked.

Immediately he saw Isabella's face fall into a deep blush. Adrian was instantly angered. He knew that look and the significance behind it. He had not seen it on her before, but he had seen it on others after they had gone through the pairing.

"No! Isabella?" he asked with tentativeness and horror in his voice. "You did not … *join* with him…"

"No! Adrian, no!" Isabella exclaimed, horrified at the suggestion. "I have not joined with him!"

Isabella could feel her face burning. She did not want to lie to him. She'd never lied to him in their many years as close friends. She equally didn't want to hurt him by telling him the truth.

"What then?" Adrian asked. "There is something that you are not telling me."

"Please. No more about this, Adrian. I do not wish to talk about him anymore." Isabella paused before turning to him more fully. She spoke again as she tried to force a smile onto her face. "I want to talk about you. Please ... how was the mill yesterday? Is the water running more freely now?"

Adrian knew it was a diversion but conceded that perhaps it was best that he play along with it. He didn't want to argue with her, and he certainly didn't want there to be vexation between them. For now, he would let it go.

Isabella saw him take a deep breath as if trying to realign his thinking and ready his words. She was relieved he'd accepted the change of subject without argument.

"The mill was busier yesterday," Adrian said. "There was enough warmth yesterday, we think, to create more water flowing. That enabled the water wheel to flow more freely. It was a good day of milling all round."

"I am glad," Isabella said, smiling. "I know how you get when your days are not busy."

When she smiled at him with the deepest look of affection, Adrian felt his heart pound in his chest. For a moment, he just looked at her, enjoying the look of her eyes, her mouth, her hair. He knew they were friends, and he knew they were lifelong companions. At times he wished so much that they could be more, that he found it physically hurt inside.

"Come, let us wash up and then leave," Isabella said all of a sudden. While she did so, she took more bread, including one slice with some mushroom spread on it.

Adrian knew who it was for but said nothing. Despite how the man seemed to be affecting Isabella, he was a man nonetheless. Even Adrian had to concede how little food Trent must have had in recent times. No matter how the two men might not wish to know each other, Adrian would at least help her to keep the strange man alive.

As they walked out of the dining area, both were silent. Despite their combined effort to move on from the seriousness of their conversation, things felt strained between them. It wasn't the first time that had been the case, but it affected each of them.

When they'd walked down the path together to the point where they'd part, Isabella stopped.

"Adrian," she said, prompting him to turn toward her. "You are my closest friend."

Adrian nodded. "As you are mine."

"Please trust me in how I am helping this man," Isabella continued. "He needs help that only I can provide to him. Please understand."

"I do," Adrian said, delivering her a smile that comprised a sliver of sadness. "Please do be careful, Isabella. You do not know him. I am only concerned for your wellbeing."

Isabella moved forward and hugged him.

"Thank you," she said before pulling away. "I shall see you for the evening meal."

Adrian turned and began walking to the mill. He didn't like knowing that she was going to be spending the day with the man who was a stranger to them, but what could he do? Resolved to accept it, he pushed his friend and the stranger from his mind.

CHAPTER 19

"Trent," Isabella said as she approached him. "I have food for you, but come with me and let us find somewhere quieter and less open."

Trent absorbed the look of her, thinking about their earlier kisses. He became aware at that moment that since arriving in the impossible place, he had become completely obsessed with her - enamored. The uncertainty for him was not knowing if that was real or not. He wasn't even sure if *she* was real, so how could he begin to be sure if any of his feelings were real?

He grabbed his packed up gear, stood, and began following her. Ease had grown in their having to work together to avoid the different obstacles that each other could see in their path.

Isabella led him to an area where the people of the village bathed. She knew no-one was ever there in the mornings. It was a place people tended to go late in the afternoon after a day's work was done.

Trent heard the sound of water. When he focused, he could see that she was leading him to a small pool with a waterfall flowing into it. It was the first moving thing - apart from her, her friend, and the ancient he'd met - that he had seen in the grey landscape that was his constant view.

Isabella sensed his attention and questioned him with a look of curiosity on her face.

"Do you see the water?" she asked.

Trent smiled broadly.

"Yes!" he exclaimed. The word came out almost like a laugh, he was so overjoyed. He wondered why he hadn't been able to hear the water running from within the main part of the village. He quickly dispelled the question in his mind. It was far more enjoyable to focus on the water he could drink and bathe in.

Isabella watched him edge closer to the side of the pool, crouch down, and touch the water with his fingers. Instantly, he looked back at her and smiled.

"It is warm," he said and saw her laugh at him.

"Yes," replied Isabella. "It is where we bathe."

"And drink?"

"No, do not drink that," she replied. "There is water running through it constantly, so it is safe to bathe in, but we gather our drinking water further up from here. I can take you there now if you wish…"

"No!" he said, too intrigued by the warm water pool before him. "No. Thank you, Isabella, but I would like to just stop here for a while and take my time to enjoy this, if alright with you."

Isabella nodded at him and stood to leave.

"Where are you going?" Trent asked.

"You wish to bathe," she replied. "Do you not wish to do so in private?"

Trent stood and walked to her. Wrapping his arms around her, he indulged in kissing her on her lips. He smiled as he felt her melt against his chest and her arms enclose him.

"Are there any other people here now?" he asked. "From your time?"

Isabella shook her head.

"No. No-one comes here in the morning," she replied. "It is usually later in the day when anyone bathes."

Trent kissed her again, deeply, and heard a groan escape from her throat.

"Stay with me. I have so much to ask about your life here," he said and saw her nod as she smiled at him.

Trent edged closer to the water.

"I am going to undress, Isabella," he said, wondering what she would do.

Instantly, she turned away and presented her back to him, but not before Trent saw a distinct level of redness on her face. He undressed quickly and tentatively crept into the water. Under his feet, he felt a soft and silky texture on the ground in the water. It was like sinking into a hot bath. He relaxed down, eventually putting his head under and vigorously rubbing his hair to loosen what he knew must be layers of dirt on his scalp.

When he turned around to face her, he saw that Isabella had turned back again. She was watching him with a vast smile on her face and intense amusement in her eyes.

Trent trod water as their eyes locked.

"Are you going to come in?" he asked and saw her blush again.

"I should bathe today, but no, I do not think so, Trent. It would not be right," she replied, all the while looking longingly at the water … and him.

Although he was mostly covered by water, Isabella could see his arms and his shoulders. She liked the shape of them. She knew he had told her he'd reduced in size since starting his journey, but she liked his shoulders. She was curious about what his body would look like once she helped him to begin regularly eating again.

As she watched, she saw him smile brilliantly at her and then dive under the water. When he came up, she laughed at him.

"Do you do such things in water, where you are from?" she asked, full of curiosity.

"Yes, where I have lived, we have large pools, but the ones I have been in were mostly man-made," Trent said. "I have never seen anything natural like this. Not natural and so warm, although I know there are such places around still."

He watched her as she sat, continuing to look at him with her intense curiosity.

"I should wash those clothes in here, too," he said, nodding his head to indicate the pile of clothing he had just removed. "Could you pass them to me, Isabella?"

Isabella stood, walked forward, and crouched down. One piece at a time, she passed his items into the water for him to catch. She couldn't stop watching as he washed each item in the water, squeezed it out, and then passed it back to her to put on the ground before doing the same to the next item.

"Thank you. I shall get out now," he said. Seeing her continue to watch him, seemingly not comprehending what he had meant, Trent laughed softly at her. "Isabella, can you please turn around for a few minutes?"

Finally, he saw her face realize what he was implying. She turned and walked back to his backpack. After bringing it forward for him, she turned and walked a short distance away, keeping her back to him.

"I dreamed about … touching … your body," he heard her say softly. They were few words, but the result was that he was instantly aroused. He dreaded she would turn around at that moment.

"I did, too," he replied. "Touching you and … kissing you."

He pulled from his pack the cleanest clothing he had - not that anything was really clean anymore - and quickly put them on.

"Okay, I am dressed," he said. "It is safe for you to turn around now."

Isabella turned and saw that he was in different clothing. She watched him as he gathered up his wet clothing and haphazardly threw them over various rocks to let the sun and warmth from the ground under them dissolve the moisture from the fabrics.

"This part of your village must still be intact then?" he asked her and saw her nod.

"It seems so, does it not?" Isabella replied. "I do not know what happened here, but I believe Elder Rhys has more to tell us."

Trent moved to sit beside her. He still only saw dirt around them, even though he knew what she saw was greenery and color.

"No-one is here?" he asked her. He felt desperate to see what she saw and wondered if the same action of placing both of his hands down on the earth would provide him with that view.

She nodded at him. "It is safe."

Trent lowered his hands one at a time. When both came in contact with the ground, he felt the same energy surge through him, once again forcing him to close his eyes and indulge in the feeling.

When he opened them, he was astounded by the color around him. The green of the trees, bushes, and grass before him was vibrant and lush. Nearby, he could see and smell the lavender-colored roses climbing up one of the walls. The scent emanating from them was heavenly.

Isabella watched his facial expressions as he moved from one time to another. Studying him, she saw something new. A small tear began appearing in his eyes. It was just enough to show moistness where a moment ago there had been none.

"What moves you so?" she asked and saw him shift his focus to her.

"Everything," Trent said, feeling the emotion that he believed must have been evident for her to see.

He moved his eyes away from her for a moment, once again looking all around him.

"Your land is so beautiful," he said. "It should never have changed..."

He felt overwhelmed by emotions and needed to be closer to her. Knowing - weighing up - that he would lose the views around them when he moved his hands, he made the judgment to stand up. As he did so, he saw the landscape change back to the brown and grey it naturally was to him.

Isabella saw him reach out his hands toward her. She stood and walked into his arms, once again feeling the pull toward him.

Trent focused on the intense need to kiss her. The hunger had come and gone since he'd first seen her. Its strength was intense and highly invigorating to him.

They clung to each other, kissing with mutual desire. At that moment, Trent found no arousal in his body. It was her lips touching his lips that drove his hunger, but at the same time, it felt as if his body knew she was not his ... yet.

Isabella pulled away from him suddenly.

"You must be hungry," she said, remembering the bread she had carried with her.

Trent laughed out loud, for a moment confusing her.

"You have no idea," he said.

Seeing she did not understand his play on words, he didn't say anything more. He sat down on the ground and watched her sit before him. Happily, he placed his hands down and saw the vista change once again.

Isabella broke up the plain bread first and fed him piece after piece, neither of them saying anything.

"I also brought a piece with a small amount of special mushroom spread that Cook Nina prepared," Isabella said after a long while as she grinned. "I like it, but not everyone does. Would you like to try?"

The thought of tasting fresh mushrooms made Trent salivate as he nodded. He was eager to try a different flavor from the bread, which perfectly served to fill his tummy but left a gap of taste on his tongue.

Slowly, he saw her present to his mouth a small piece of bread with brownish spread over it. Without hesitation, he pulled it in.

Trent felt like he was in food heaven. It tasted similar to mushrooms he had eaten in the city, but the depth of the flavor was incredible. Without thinking, he let out a groan of contentment at the effect it had on his taste buds. He then closed his eyes to savor the flavor.

The delightful sound of Isabella giggling at him woke him from his enjoyment. He couldn't help but present her with a sheepish grin.

"I have not tasted anything that good for a very long time," he said.

Isabella happily broke off another piece to present to him.

~~~~~

"I must not stay here much longer, or others will notice my absence," Isabella said to him later as they both relaxed on the ground, lying down but facing each other. "But I shall come and find you after the evening meal. Will you stay here now?"

Trent nodded. While he couldn't keep seeing the grass and greenery, it was still a peaceful place to be. He also looked forward to washing more of his clothing while happily listening to the waterfall.

"I will," he replied. "I do not think I can sleep here at night due to the sound of the water but I certainly could sit here all day. I might even venture back into there," he said, pointing to the pool once more.

Isabella sat up to begin her move toward getting on with other things she should already have been doing.

"Now that I know you like mushrooms, I shall be able to bring you more flavors to try," she said. "I can see that your appetite is already mending. It will be good for your body to have better sustenance."

"Thank you," replied Trent, unable to shift his sight from her smile.

She leaned into him and kissed him softly. Feeling the passion for him so strong, she pulled away quickly.

"I shall never get anything done if I keep kissing you," she said. "That would not do at all."
~~~~~

CHAPTER 20

Left alone, Trent pulled everything from his backpack and laid it out in the sun. The warmth of the ground appeared to be a naturally perfect heat for water evaporation from clothing. All of the items he had washed earlier were already close to dry. It was a small thing to excite him, but it made him surprisingly eager to wash more items.

His thoughts turned to the uncertainty about what lay ahead for him. The ancient had presented him with two options. He could stay in the village and change the time he lived in, or he could return to his previous life. He took some time, sitting in the warm water, to consider those options.

After much contemplation, he decided he would move ahead as if he would leave again when he found the strength. In the meantime, he could ensure he was prepared for the journey back to the life he'd left behind. That life already seemed far behind him, but it was *his* life. That was where his friends and family were, and everything he had ever known.

He knew inside of him that the odds were great that he would not - *could* not - survive a return journey, but he had to move through the day with something to do. A part of him yearned to be in another time - in *her* time. As he couldn't see people of that time unless he made himself visible, he opted to remain hidden in his own time when she wasn't around. At least he was in a place where he could bathe and be clean, and completely relax.

CHAPTER 21

"Miss Isabella, where have you been this morning?" Cook Joan asked, having witnessed Isabella running off that morning after breakfast rather than asking for requests from the workers in the kitchen. "I am in need of carrots. Could you go and get some for me? Take that basket over there and fill it to the brim if you can. I am going to cook a carrot and barley stew, and it will be magnificent!"

Isabella laughed at the cook as she obligingly took the basket.

"Of course I shall do that for you, Cook Joan," she said. "I shall return shortly."

As she left the kitchen area, Isabella saw Elder Rhys in the distance. The ancient rarely left the temple. Upon seeing him, Isabella veered off her path and moved toward him.

"Young Isabella," Elder Rhys said as he saw her approach. "I wish to talk to you. Can we walk together?"

"Yes, Elder Rhys," Isabella replied. "I must gather carrots from the garden for Cook Joan. Can you walk with me, or would you like me to come to the temple?"

"Oh no!" the ancient exclaimed. "I gladly shall walk to the garden with you. It has been so long since I was there. I am sure there is a heavenly scent there at this time."

They began walking together at a slower pace than she usually would walk at, out of her respect for him. It was some time before he spoke.

"Where is our new friend today? The traveler?"

"He is near the waterfall, Elder Rhys," Isabella said. "It appears to be one part of the village that is much unchanged. This morning he was enjoying our warm water to bathe in."

The ancient saw a smile pass over her face at the memory of it.

"Isabella, you are now 21, are you not?" he asked and saw her nod, not saying anything. "Have your parents talked to you about you going through the pairing?"

Isabella looked down, blushing and flustered at the thought of having such a conversation with him.

"I … yes," she replied, stuttering. "It has come up in conversation, but I have not felt ready."

"And do you still not feel ready?" Elder Rhys asked. "Or has something perhaps changed in recent days for you?"

"I do not know what you mean, Elder Rhys," Isabella said before seeing him look closely at her.

"I think you do, Isabella," the ancient said. "We have all believed you would pair with Adrian, but I believe now that someone else - another - is meant to be your mate. Do you not feel it too?"

He watched her and saw conflict on her face.

"I know that I *should* pair with Adrian," Isabella said. "He and I are comfortable together and know each other well."

"But?" the ancient prompted.

"But this traveler who has come. Elder Rhys, when…"

Isabella felt she could not continue her conversation. She had done what she should not have in kissing Trent without having been paired with him first.

"When you and he join lips," the ancient said, stunning Isabella and making her look at him.

Suddenly he laughed, surprising her further.

"I have seen the visions the two of you are having in the nights, Isabella," Elder Rhys said. "Do not worry so. What I have seen these past nights is nothing I have not seen in many night visions before. I have lived for 600 years, do not forget."

"I…" Isabella stammered. "I know I should not have…"

"You had been seeing him in visions of the night even before he came here, and he had been seeing you in his visions of the night also."

"Yes, but how can that be?" Isabella asked. "And what does that mean?"

As they neared the garden, the ancient stopped walking and turned to her.

"I think you know, Isabella," he said. "I think *he* is who you are meant to pair with. It is what has always been intended for you."

"But that cannot be so, Elder Rhys," said Isabella. "He is not from our time. How could we have always been meant to pair?"

"Nature has its ways. What is meant to be, will always be, one way or another," the ancient said. He paused as he looked closely at her. "You must decide what you wish for, and then he must do the same. If you both wish for it, it can be done."

Before she had a chance to question him any more, he began walking away from her, back along the path they had just walked along together.

"Miss Isabella, what can we help you with today?" she heard one of the gardeners call out to her. As the conversation with Elder Rhys had ended, Isabella resolved to think nothing more about his talk of pairing.

"Master Martin, I have been instructed by Cook Joan to come and fill this basket to the brim with carrots," Isabella called back to the gardener.

"To the brim, you say? Very good, lass. Come with me, and I shall find you the best that are ready for you to take back to the kitchen. We can't have Cook Joan without her required ingredients when she has a masterpiece to prepare," he said with very apparent amusement on his face.

The look reminded Isabella that it was quite alright for her to relax in her day and enjoy the simplicity of humor and laughter.

CHAPTER 22

Adrian was mindless to his job for the whole day. His thoughts continued to veer back to Isabella and the stranger who had somehow arrived and yet, at the same time, *not* arrived. He was sure it must be some kind of magic or some kind of curse.

What had not escaped him was how Isabella and Trent had looked at each other. They had shared a mutual look that Adrian had hoped only he would ever receive from her. It made him despondent. He believed she loved him as a friend. He equally believed that she would never be willing to pair with him. For that, she sought - needed - another.

"Adrian, can you help me please?" he heard a voice call out to him. When he turned, he saw Kat standing close to him. "I need to move these few bags of grain just over there, but I am still finding it difficult to lift such weights."

Adrian looked at the young woman before him. She was two years younger than him, so not an established friend. In truth, he'd never noticed her at all until she, too, had begun working in the mill during the day.

Feeling a tender and bruised heart, Adrian began to look at Kat in a new light. She was attractive. She seemed friendly and eager to know him. That meant something. As Adrian studied her further, he decided she could equally be someone to fill a void, serving as a replacement for who he truly wanted to be with.

"Of course I can do that for you, Kat," he said while smiling at her and beginning to perform the duty she had asked him to.

When he had moved the few bags she'd needed help with, he came back to her. He liked seeing her smiling shyly at him. It was refreshing to see *anyone* looking at him as she was. She wasn't the person he preferred would look at him in such a way, but his preferred person would never do so. He was resigned in accepting that truth. He felt sadness in admitting it to himself. He also felt a sliver of freedom in knowing he had to give up on thinking Isabella might feel differently about him. She was his good friend. That was enough.

"Thank you, Adrian," Kat said to him, a slight blush appearing on her face.

As Adrian looked closer at her still, he further thought about moving forward in his future without expecting Isabella to be his paired mate. If he could not pair with his preferred one, did it matter who he paired with?

Kat watched his face, enjoying the view even though she could see the extent of his thinking at that moment. She'd watched him for as long as she could remember. It had never been impossible to see how close he was to Isabella. For that reason, Kat had never before approached him. Something inside of her gave her the impression that the right time had arrived to make herself known to Adrian. She didn't know what made her think that. It was something in her subconscious, but she was sure her gut feeling was correct. She wanted him to look at her and truly see her.

"Can I walk you to the dining area at dinner time, Kat?" Adrian finally asked.

Kat smiled demurely at him, a flutter occurring in her chest. The timing of his question fitted perfectly with her chain of thought. Almost too perfectly, if she'd truly thought about it.

"Yes."

CHAPTER 23

"Oh, there you are!" Isabella heard Cook Joan call out to her as she returned to the kitchen, her basket heavily laden. "Thank you, Miss Isabella. Just in time, too, as any later and I would not have been able to cook those carrots as slowly as I like to. Oh, it shall be a grand dinner this evening! Yes, it will indeed!"

Isabella felt the basket of fresh produce pulled from her hands. The cook began washing and scraping the carrots, turning her back to Isabella as she did.

Knowing she was dismissed and no longer needed, Isabella walked out into the sunlight, wondering what else she could help with for the few hours until the evening dining time.

~~~~~

When she entered the dining area for dinner, Isabella automatically looked around for Adrian. On not seeing him, she gathered her food, sat down at the table they always sat at together and waited.

Greatly surprised when she saw Adrian enter with the young woman that Isabella identified as Kat, Isabella felt a slight pang in her heart. It was the very first time she'd seen her close friend with a woman. In that instance, she realized just how much she had come to rely on his devotion to her. Suddenly presented with the consideration that he might not always be there for her - that one day he would pair with someone other than her - she felt a new emotion she had never felt before. It confused her immensely.

"Isabella, do you know Kat?" Adrian asked her, breaking her out of her reverie as he and the young woman sat at the table.

Isabella smiled as warmly as she felt she could.

"Yes, of course," she replied. "Hello, Kat. You work in the mill with Adrian, do you not?"

The young woman looked surprised but, at the same time, pleased at having been recognized by Isabella. Kat nodded her head but didn't reply, instead moving her head to look at Adrian again. It wasn't lost on Isabella just how much admiration Kat seemed to show in her gaze towards Adrian.

"How has your day been, Isabella?" Adrian asked.

He hadn't thought through the reality of sitting between his lifelong
~~~~~

friend and his new one. As he settled in for his meal, he found the situation quite different from how he'd imagined he would feel if he escorted Kat to the dining area for their meal.

Reluctant to talk openly in front of Kat, Isabella kept to herself anything about her happenings with Trent earlier in the day or her talk with Elder Rhys. Instead, she restricted her conversation to that of the garden. She spoke of the few things the gardener had told her about this and that. That seemed to satisfy Adrian's curiosity, at least for the moment. He didn't ask for information about the traveler, even though she suspected the topic might be on his mind.

When Isabella had finished her meal, she stood up. On any other evening, she would have relied upon Adrian wanting to leave with her. With Kat being at his side, Isabella found herself unsure of what Adrian would want to do. To give her time to analyze if he'd want her to wait for him or just leave him with Kat, Isabella took her time gathering a little bread and a small amount of the carrot and barley stew. Discretely she filled a small cup and grabbed a spoon.

Adrian saw her start to move but stopped himself from standing and leaving with her. Despite him wanting to do so, Kat was beside him, and she was still eating and talking. He didn't want to make things awkward for her. He also felt that he was approaching a time when he would have to extract himself from Isabella, one way or another. He supposed the ache in his heart would ease if he could do that slowly rather than all in one go.

Remaining where he was, he saw her prepare to leave. When she smiled at him, he smiled back, and then she was gone. He felt the thud inside his chest but forced himself to turn and look at the young woman beside him. Seemingly she had no idea that the man she was talking to was at that moment heart-heavy for the woman who had just walked out.

~~~~~

Isabella looked around her to make sure no-one was around when she started walking down to the area by the pool. She was pleased to see no other villager in sight. When she got there, Trent was in the pool once more, sitting peacefully with his eyes closed.

As Trent felt her presence, he opened his eyes to find her standing at the poolside, watching him. He inhaled sharply, once again confronted with not only her beauty but the reality that the woman with the red hair, who had invaded his dreams so intensely, was standing right in front of him, smiling at him.

Pulled from his thoughts, he smiled back at her.

"Have you been in there all day?" Isabella asked him as she laughed softly.

Trent slowly made his way from the far side of the pool to the side
~~~~~

closest to her, grinning broadly.

"Most of it. It feels too wonderful to waste," he said as he started to climb out.

Immediately Isabella turned away from him but heard him laugh at her.

"It is alright, Isabella," he teased her. "I am covered on my lower half. You do not need to turn away."

Turning to face him, Isabella was confronted by him being directly in front of her. Although covered on his bottom half, his upper half was completely bare. She drank in how his chest, arms and belly looked. While acknowledging he had a long way to go to build up muscle tone again, she liked what she saw.

Trent could see the look on her face.

"I like you looking at me," he said.

After looking around once more to make sure nobody was nearby, Isabella moved forward and kissed him. As she did, she remembered one of her dreams.

"I touched you … there … in my vision of the night," she said, pointing to the center of his chest.

"Yes!" exclaimed Trent as the vision entered his memory. "Something happened … something passed between us."

Isabella nodded, remembering.

"I do not think I should touch you like that until we know what it means," she said, surprised that her visions of the night had remained in her mind for so long.

Trent nodded, absorbing the smell of food that came from a cup in her hand while he slipped on a t-shirt.

"Yes, you are right," he said. "Tell me how you have filled in the hours from when I saw you earlier, till now."

When Isabella sat down, Trent sat cross-legged in front of her, their knees almost touching as she prepared to feed him.

"I had to gather many carrots for the cook so she could make her carrot and barley stew," Isabella said. "I have brought some with me for you to try, and some bread also."

After looking around to make sure no-one was approaching, she nodded to him to indicate it was safe for him to place his hands on the ground and let himself transport into her time.

Trent felt the energy surge through him. It was confounding to him why placing both hands on the ground provided such an experience. It seemed like doing so closed some kind of circuit of time. It made no sense to him, but he had conceded long before that little that had happened to him *had* made any sense. In the life that he'd traveled from, he would have done something to try and figure out what was happening.

A screen would have been turned on, and the Internet used to begin investigating. That had been his automatic response to anything he'd wanted to learn before he'd embarked on his journey to walk away from it all.

As his mind turned to the world of computers and mobile phones, he fought to push the memories aside. That was the world he'd felt the need to escape. Yes, he had people there that he'd loved. He'd also experienced an intense amount of stress, not to mention his increasing hate of anything with a screen. It had all been far too easy to forget the simple joy of being in nature without anything electrical at all.

Refocusing on the moment he was in, Trent welcomed Isabella leaning toward him and using a spoon to transfer a small amount of the cup contents into his mouth. As his mouth burst with flavor, Trent wondered why anyone in the modern world could have let such wholesome goodness in food be replaced so easily with versions of food that sometimes tasted like cardboard. The food Isabella brought to him was nothing like he'd ever tasted before.

"Elder Rhys spoke to me again today," Isabella said as she let him take another spoonful of the stew into his mouth. "He said some things that I need to think about, but I think you need to consider too."

After he had swallowed, Trent questioned her, asking what she'd meant. He listened as she continued to speak while transferring another spoonful of flavor to him.

"He..." she started to say. Trent saw her face transform into a deep blush before she seemed to find the courage to continue. "He suggested that perhaps you and I had been meant to find one another. That we are meant to be ... *paired*."

Trent sat silent, not sure if she needed him to speak or not. He watched her as she continued to feed him from the cup, then saw her put the cup and spoon down and rip off some bread. Once she'd placed it at his mouth, he watched her focus on his lips as he pulled the bread in and began to chew. Trent suspected that if a woman had watched him so intently back in his normal world, he might have found it a bit odd. Seeing Isabella focus on him like she was, he didn't mind it at all.

While they continued to sit in silence until the food was gone, Trent looked around the area while the color was there for him to see. He then pulled his hands up and let the world go grey and brown around him once more.

Isabella saw his arms reach out to her as he knelt. She reveled in him pulling her close to him and holding her tight before releasing her again.

"Tell me more about what Elder Rhys said," Trent said as he relaxed back and focused on her face.

"He said that he believed you and I have shared dreams because we are linked somehow. He thinks that nature intended for us to be paired together," Isabella said, thoughtful. "But that could not be, could it? We are not even of the same time..."

Trent kissed her. It was his way of reassuring both of them that he was real, and so was she. Even though everything seemed to be out of a science fiction novel rather than real life, it *was* happening. There seemed no point in denying it.

"Perhaps," he replied. "But this feels real, does it not? When I look at you, I desire you, Isabella. I felt like that before I had even seen you in person. You came into my dreams, and you say I came into yours..." he continued and saw her nod in response. "Who is to say we are not destined to be together?"

Isabella was quiet for a long while. She didn't know why or how such a strange thing had come to happen to her. She was just a normal girl. As yet, she didn't even have any clear direction in her life.

"What exactly does it mean, this pairing?" Trent asked. They'd touched on the subject briefly when he'd first met her. The continual mentioning of it made him think that it meant something important to the people of the ancient township.

Isabella blushed heavily. It was a topic she didn't feel comfortable talking about, but she knew she had to answer.

"It is what happens so our population can continue," she said as she felt her face grow warmer. "There is a ceremony where the man and woman being paired are united. After the ceremony, they go to the pairing chamber together, where they remain for that night. It is expected in there that they will ... love ... so that a child will be made. After that night, they will begin to share their life together as mother and father."

Trent could see that in her culture, the pairing they talked of was similar to marriage, although the focus appeared far more on procreation than on the love that could occur between a man and woman.

"And when paired, the mother and father remain together ... for the rest of their lives?" he asked for clarification.

"Yes, until one is called forth to leave this world and go on their journey to pass to the next," replied Isabella as she nodded.

Trent nodded, taking this to be their explanation for death.

"I see," he said quietly. He'd come from a time and place where people married all the time, but also divorced. He knew he would need to view the pairing process in the village as different from modern-day marriage. Even if there were similarities, the *intention* was very different.

After a long time of silence, Isabella found the courage to speak further and ask what she wished to know.

"Have you given more thought to what Elder Rhys said to you about moving into our time permanently?" she asked. When Trent didn't immediately answer, she continued. "Do you think that ... you ... might *like* to pair with me?"

Trent didn't have to take more than a few seconds to consider the question. He guessed her asking it should have felt as imposing as when his ex-lover had implied they were going to get married. Even though the questions were similar, they didn't evoke the same feeling in him. He'd been with his last lover for a long time, but he'd never developed feelings for her deep enough to want to marry her. They'd been good together sexually, but it had never had any further depth than that.

For a moment, he considered that maybe the reason he felt so strongly about Isabella was that he hadn't bedded her yet. He wasn't oblivious to the attraction of the chase. Many times, he'd experienced a desire for someone, and that urgent need to know them had disappeared almost immediately after fulfilling the sexual urge.

As he looked at Isabella, he didn't think it was the same. There was something far greater at play than just mere chemistry between a man's body and a woman's. Although he couldn't deny her physical beauty, he knew himself. It wasn't what she looked like that had captured him. There was something uniquely powerful about her. That, combined with her not appearing to *know* the level of power she emanated, was incredible to him.

After his silent contemplation, he stood up and held out his hands, encouraging her to do the same. Confidently, he pulled her to him and held her tight against his chest.

"Oh, Isabella, do you even have to ask?" he asked before he pulled back from her just enough to allow them to look into each other's eyes. "I do not know why I was led to you or why I feel so drawn to you, but I have no desire whatsoever to disregard these feelings that I have toward you."

"You do not wish to return to your home?" Isabella asked, uncertainty in her voice.

"I left behind a life that was not fulfilling," he replied. "My world is not peaceful like this one. My world does not have the simplicity of what you have..."

Isabella hung her head low, not feeling good about his last comment.

"We are not advanced enough for you," she said quietly.

"No!" Trent exclaimed, horrified that she'd misinterpreted his meaning. "You misread my point. What I meant is that I have been living in a world where nothing is simple anymore. Everything is about money and things. I have not seen all of your village, so I cannot judge how you live your life, but I feel like I know you. I feel like I have always been meant to come here to find you."

Isabella looked up again. She didn't know what he was talking about.

In her community, there was no such thing as money. Usually, she would have asked more questions to find out about the world outside the walls of the village. Instead, she moved in to kiss him deeply. The move took Trent by surprise and made him groan at the depth of the kiss.

"If we pair, we will have children. It will be our duty," Isabella said when she pulled away from him. "It is an important part of our people."

Trent smiled at her, already sensing the shift that had taken place in him about sex and it being a method of procreation and not for pleasure. Not *just* for pleasure.

He was aware of how different he felt, standing in the arms of a beautiful woman who had been kissing him passionately. The part of him that would usually be alert and awake instantaneously in such a situation was at peace and not alert. He felt no alarm. To him, it seemed like he'd moved into a different physical form, not needing such frivolous use of his body as he previously had before he'd left the city.

"I would be honored to raise children with you, Isabella," he said and kissed her once again.

On hearing voices moving closer, Isabella quickly pulled away from him.

"People are coming," she whispered. "I must go now."

Isabella saw him nod in recognition before she turned and began to walk away as if she were leaving the pool area after bathing.

Trent watched as she greeted whoever was approaching. He then saw her turn and wave to him with a smile that to him looked incredibly sad. The sight made him instinctively want to run to her and put his arms around her again. Instead, he remained still. She had things she needed to do.

He sighed to himself. Although he suspected other people were in the area with him, in their own time, he only felt alone. It was an odd feeling after he'd trekked so far and for so long over and around the mountain range to reach the village. He *had* been alone throughout all of that time.

The difference was that when he'd been walking, he hadn't felt as alone as he did each time Isabella walked away from him.

CHAPTER 24

Before it got too dark, Trent packed up his things and once again moved up to the wide-open area he had slept in the night before. The little pup tent was up, and his sleeping bag was laid out inside. He felt refreshed after so much outer cleansing, and satisfied with the food he had received from Isabella earlier.

Lying in his sleeping bag, he thought about the option open to him. In the present moment, he was in his own time, in a place that to him looked barren and like a war zone. The waterfall and the pond were intact. He could still use them even as he currently was, but there was no growth. Since arriving inside the village walls, he'd not seen one living plant. When whatever happened had happened, it not only had destroyed the structures that someone had taken time to build. It also seemed to have destroyed the possibility of life.

He considered that he was there, and as far as he could tell, he was alive. There was a possibility that he could work hard to bring the land back to life. He could try and revive the plants with enough watering and care.

The idea wasn't a good one. Even if Trent did that, he knew he'd still be alone. Isabella could see him, but she would not be around forever. She would also be expected to move on and pair with someone. That was her duty to contribute to the maintenance of their population. If he stayed as he was, he might see her day to day, but was that any way to live?

The other option was to build up his body once again over the coming weeks and prepare himself for a return journey back to overpopulated civilization. Back to noise. Back to plastic-tasting food. Back to a life of promiscuity and sexual freedom. Even in the last point, he couldn't find any real desire or interest, even though he'd always been a relatively free and easy lover. He'd had relationships but they never lasted long. If he was honest with himself, he had come to be - and to be regarded as - an easy sexual friend to whoever wanted it.

So far, he had only seen a small part of the world that Isabella saw, but it wasn't a frightening thing to him. Perhaps they were people who lived simply. As yet, he didn't know exactly how they lived. Even if they *were* living simply, would that really be such a bad thing?

He moved lower in his sleeping bag, his head full of questions and possibilities. He knew he wouldn't decide quickly, but he also knew that he couldn't keep her hanging. She had a friend who was eager to pair with her. It would only be fair that Trent let that happen if he really couldn't find any desire to be in her world.

CHAPTER 25

Isabella lay in her bed, awake and thoughtful. There were so many things to think about. Surprisingly what most made her uncertain about what to do if certain possibilities were presented to her was the thought of Adrian.

She did not want to hurt him. She would *never* want to hurt him. Isabella considered that perhaps with him having now befriended the young woman she'd seen him with earlier, he was in a place to move on and not wish to have anything more than friendship with Isabella.

She tried to imagine seeing Adrian and Kat paired. Briefly, she wondered how she would feel about that. She focused on the possibility, but the thought did not cause any stress inside of her. It only made her think of how happy he could be if things went that way.

No, she knew that Adrian did not have to be an influencing factor in any decision she made regarding the stranger from the future. In reality, everything lay in the hands of Trent. He was the one who would have to give up his existing life in order to join hers.

If the situation were reversed - if the only way they could be together was for *her* to go into *his* time, where she would see her home very differently as she saw it now - would she want to do that, even for him? She suspected she wouldn't. The thought of leaving everyone around her was something she could not … would not … even consider.

CHAPTER 26

The next morning, Isabella rose early once more and went to see Trent in his little home. Neither of them felt uncomfortable at her entering the tent and lying down beside him. Once settled and comfortable, she kissed him without any hesitation. She knew she shouldn't indulge in it with them not having paired, but the idea of not spending the time with him was unbearable.

Feeling her lips caressing his own, Trent was confident in his decision to change over to her time. He didn't think his enthusiasm was driven by an unfulfilled sexual desire. Remarkably, as much as he loved kissing her, his body seemed to have accepted there was nothing more to come from that. Not yet, at least. The hunger he felt to be close to her was a different kind of hunger to what he'd previously felt. It wasn't just sex that he wanted. It was a much deeper level of knowing her.

They didn't speak at all for a long time. When Isabella heard voices in the distance, she pulled away.

"I must leave now," she said before kissing him lightly one more time.

"I know," Trent replied in a whisper.

As she climbed out of his tent, Trent found himself aware of how much he'd come to love being close to her. He also began to realize how empty he felt every time she had to leave.

CHAPTER 27

At breakfast, Isabella found Adrian alone and sat down peacefully beside him.

"You are always early now," she tried to tease him, given that traditionally he had always been late in the mornings before their world had begun to change due to the arrival of a stranger.

"I know it is time for me to act more responsibly," Adrian replied, smiling. "I have been neglectful of my duties for too long."

Isabella suspected he was referring to things other than breakfast but didn't question his precise meaning. Whatever was happening between him and Kat, Isabella felt she needed to leave him to that and not interfere or ask about it.

"Adrian," she said, lightly touching his hand. "I wish to talk to you."

"I am right here, Isabella," Adrian replied. "What is on your mind?" he asked before noticing Isabella look around her and begin to speak in a softer tone.

"I wish us to speak about what you asked me earlier - about you and me pairing," Isabella said in almost a whisper.

Adrian looked surprised for a moment before a look of resolve came over his face.

"Isabella, I know you do not feel about me in the way that you wish to with the person you will pair with," he said. "I accept this. You are my friend, and I am yours … always. Do not think any more about my question to you. I am at peace with not being your choice for pairing."

The speech was given with passion and devotion. As Isabella heard it, she felt tears come to her eyes. She would not speak against what he had said. She felt no need to contradict the words he had spoken, but there still remained a great deal of sadness about the statement and its finality.

~~~~~

After breakfast, she walked to the open area and saw that Trent and his gear had disappeared once more. She laughed inwardly at the fact that he'd dismantled his little house and taken it with him, even though he knew no-one else could see it.

Not seeing him nearby, she made her way down to the area near the pool. As she approached, she could see that Trent was sitting down and talking face to face with Elder Rhys.
~~~~~

She stopped walking and remained where she was, currently out of view of both of them but still within listening distance. Her interest piqued as she heard their voices talking.

"Only you can decide if you wish to change over, Trent," Elder Rhys said. "What is it that you desire?"

"I desire to be with Isabella," Trent replied. "She has told me of the pairing your people have. I would like that with her."

"Pairing is for life in our village," replied the ancient. "We do not pair with one and then pair with another when we tire of the situation we have chosen."

"I understand," said Trent as he nodded. "I have no wish to be with anyone else…"

"Perhaps not here, but what of your home?" asked Elder Rhys. "Is there any part of you that wishes to return to where you came from? Once you cross over, you will not have the opportunity to cross back again if you wish to see your own home again. Everything and everyone you have ever known will be gone."

There was silence for a while before Isabella again heard Trent speak.

"I know that I am supposed to be with her. It is important to me that I am, if you and your people are willing to accept me into your village." He paused before continuing. "I will work hard, I will love her, and I will bring children into your village that will come from different bloodstock. That must make a difference to such a small population, I am sure."

The ancient nodded in agreement.

"It is true that we should have wider breeding ideally, but we are populated enough to keep from there being problems there. We are not a small population, Trent," Elder Rhys said. "Perhaps you will think so compared to the city you come from, but you might find yourself surprised by the number of people who are here, once you can see and hear them all."

"I am prepared for that," replied Trent. "Please. Please consider allowing me to come into your world, and to pair with Isabella if she wishes to have me."

There was silence again as the ancient considered the words presented to him from the traveler who had so recently appeared.

"I will consider your wishes about coming into our world, and I shall talk to Isabella regarding the possibility of her pairing with you. Thank you for talking to me. I shall leave you now."

As the ancient walked away, he saw Isabella come into view a short distance away. He walked up to her, took her hand, and smiled at her.

"You must come and see me this afternoon, before our evening meal," he said. "We have much to discuss."

Isabella nodded. "Yes, of course, Elder Rhys."

CHAPTER 28

Walking the last leg of the pathway to the pool, Isabella looked closely at the sight of Trent sitting down on the ground. He looked peaceful and full of thoughts, so much so that he didn't hear her approach immediately.

"You are deep in thought," she said and saw him look at her, not startled at all. The ease of it made her think he'd sensed her there.

Trent watched as she sat down in front of him. When she was settled he took no time leaning in to kiss her gently before sitting back and smiling at her.

"I have been talking to Elder Rhys about the option of me coming into your world," he said and saw her nod in response.

"And?" Isabella asked. She felt nervous. It wasn't a new feeling, but it was one that she'd felt so few times that it seemed intense to her.

"And I told him that I wish to cross over so I can be with you, Isabella," Trent said. "I want to do this so that we can pair if that is what you want." He paused to let her consider an answer and speak again. When she didn't, he continued. "*Is* that what you want?"

"Yes," she breathed out heavily, her head filled with visions of how their lives could be if together in the same time. "Yes, Trent. I want to pair with you. I want to live with you and see you every day - openly. I want to have your children." They were quiet for a few minutes before she spoke again. "I want to kiss you every day - every morning and every night. I want to bathe with you."

Her blatant desire fuelled Trent. He kissed her hungrily, resolved that he had to have her not just sexually but in entirety. He'd taken time to reflect on all the options open to him. The one that kept calling to him the loudest was that of making her the greater part of the rest of his life.

"I want that too," he finally said without any doubt.

He watched as Isabella sat back. She seemed visibly shy all of a sudden. It only made her more endearing to him. He saw her pull out the food she'd brought from breakfast and start to help him eat.

"I shall miss this, though - helping you in this way," she said.

Seeing the amusement on her face, he laughed with her.

"We will find other things to share pleasure in," he told her. He didn't mind at all the intense blush he saw in response.

CHAPTER 29

"What are your thoughts?" the ancient asked Isabella as she sat inside the temple with him. He didn't expand on the question because he knew he didn't need to.

"Elder Rhys, I would like Trent to come through to our time, and for the two of us to pair," Isabella replied and then paused. "But it is not up to me, is it? He must make the decision about both of those things, and they are not one decision. They are two."

The ancient nodded.

"It is true, but he is resolved to come through and pair with you, and I believe his sincerity," he replied. "Do you have doubts?"

As Isabella remained quiet, Elder Rhys could sense something was passing over her mind, so questioned her.

"What is it?" he asked.

"I … I just wonder if he will still want me when he is around many women again," Isabella replied, her face growing red. "I am the only woman he sees, but how can he be sure he wishes to be only with me if he does not yet know who else he is going to see when he comes through to our time?"

Isabella felt the ancient's hands reach out and touch hers.

"Isabella, the two of you are entwined," he said. "Fate has secured that, and I believe it to be real. He did not have visions of the night about anyone else. He cannot see anyone else apart from you and me. You are his connection. You are his intended. And he is yours."

Isabella nodded but remained quiet. It was all very well what she wanted, but ultimately she could not force someone from another time to leave their life and their world to come into hers. Even if the reverse were possible, she was sure she would not want to leave her family or her friends. Not even for love.

"The right choice will be made," Elder Rhys said, smiling at her as he pulled his hands back. "Do not worry so. If you are not meant to be together, you shall not be. For now, you have met someone new, and I have long sensed that you wished for that."

Isabella looked at him, curious.

"How could you know that?" she asked.

Elder Rhys continued to grin.

"I see everything, Isabella," he replied. "I sense the joy that is always around us. I sense other feelings as well. In our community, we are blessed to have so many people who are so content, but it has not always been so. Now and then, there are people who feel differently and see things differently."

For a moment, Isabella thought about Adrian. He'd expressed discontent for a very long time, even though she didn't expect him to act and do anything in response to those feelings.

Looking at the ancient in front of her, she hoped he couldn't read her mind. All she saw was him smiling at her. It was reassuring.

"Thank you, Elder Rhys," she said as she stood up. "I am certain that I wish for Trent to come through to our time, and for us to be paired."

Elder Rhys stood and nodded at her.

"Then it shall be done," he said. "Before the village awakes tomorrow, we shall try to do just that."

Isabella nodded in response, smiled sadly in her nervousness, and walked out. She hoped her desires were right for her life. She'd rarely experienced doubt. It was foreign and new, but she chose to simply ignore it.

CHAPTER 30

"It is time," Elder Rhys said to Trent as the three of them sat quietly near the pool in the very early morning of the following day. "Are you certain of what you are asking me to do for you, Trent? I cannot reverse this once it is done. You will not be able to return to your own time. You will leave behind everything and everyone you ever knew."

Trent smiled at Isabella and then turned to the ancient.

"I already left my world behind, Elder Rhys," he said. "It is a world that I no longer wish to be a part of. Please accept me into yours."

The ancient nodded, stood, and walked toward the waterfall. Behind him stood Isabella and Trent, watching in anticipation of whatever was to come. Neither knew what they would see or what would happen. Both were astounded as they watched the ancient walk not into the water, but *on* the water. Over the pool he walked, stopping in the middle and turning back to face them.

"Follow," he said simply.

Together they stepped out. They each expected to fall into the water but following his footsteps, they found themselves on what felt like a hard surface even though they could not see it.

After they reached Elder Rhys, he moved further forward. Trent and Isabella remained close behind him until all three of them were directly in front of the waterfall. Raising his hands, the ancient forced the water flowing to separate into a right and a left side, leaving a dry entry point directly in the center of the flow.

Isabella thought she must be seeing things. In all her years, she had never seen anything like what was presently on display before her. Although the ancients were all regarded as sacred people of a great age, there had never been any word of any such thing being possible.

She felt Trent squeeze her hand as he started to walk forward through the space that had been provided for them in the waterfall. Once through to the other side, they found themselves in a cave.

Confronted by the sight in front of her, Isabella felt like she might faint. For as high as her eyes could see, all she saw was yellow. The high rock face looked golden with a sheen on it that made it look new and untouched.

Looking at Trent, Isabella suspected that he recognized it as well. It was the same color of whatever she had handed to him in their mutual dream.

The ancient moved to stand between the glowing rock and the two of them as if protective of it.

"This is our life source," he said. "It is what provides our village with the heat required to sustain our existence in this location. Without it, we would perish. That is why it is kept secret. Neither of you must tell anyone about it." The ancient paused and turned to face Trent. "You have seen what our village has become," he said and saw the traveler nod. "That was the result of someone speaking of this, and people coming to our village filled with greed and desperation to take this. It destroyed our home and our people then, and it would destroy us again if we speak of this. The two of you have the ability to prevent what happened to this village from happening in the future. Do you both understand?"

Isabella looked at Trent and saw him nod. She did the same. She supposed that now she would know for certain if he wished to be with her or not. Before them was something of great value. He could return home and tell his people about it if such a thing were more important to him than her and her people.

Focusing on his face and his eyes, Isabella saw no greed. She saw no malice or discontentment. All she saw looking back at her was passion and desire. His face appeared to mirror the same eagerness to be with her, as she felt to be with him.

Elder Rhys looked intently at both of their faces. He knew Isabella, but he didn't fully know Trent. He wanted to ascertain if both of them could truly be trusted. He was pleased with what he saw as he looked into their souls. The traveler had been lost, seeking to find some escape from a life of extreme chaos. Now he was calm. Not only that. It was also quite evident that he was very much in love.

"Trent, this will be your final chance to say if you do not wish to come to us. If you wish to come to us, you will step forward and touch the stone," he said. He immediately saw Trent take a step forward. "Stop. Do not rush. This cannot be undone once you touch it. Be sure."

Trent turned away, walked right up to Isabella, put his arms around her, and kissed her softly.

"Is this definitely what you want?" he asked. "To be with me all the time? Not just each morning and each evening? Not just in our own time and place? You will pair with me, and we will start a family ... together?"

Isabella felt tears come to her eyes as she nodded and kissed him passionately. At that moment, she was oblivious to the ancient in their presence.

Trent pulled away and then turned back to Elder Rhys, nodding.

"I am ready," he said, his heart pounding heavily.

"Very well," said the ancient. "Step forward, Trent, and place your hands here."

Trent stepped up to the large golden rock before him and raised his hands. He stopped short of touching the rock for a moment before he firmly placed both of his palms against it.

Isabella watched as light emanated from the rock and Trent's body all at once. It looked to her like he was joined to it - as one with it. His head moved back. To her, he looked … no, she did not know what that look was. It was indefinable.

As Trent touched the rock, he felt its immense power flow through him. It was the same feeling he'd experienced when he'd touched the ground with both of his hands. It had seemed to him then as if the touch of both hands worked to make a complete circuit of power.

That had been nothing compared to the intensity that came from the golden rock face. The touch of it made him feel complete in a way that he had never felt before. It scared him. He was conscious enough to know that after that moment, he would never want to feel such a level of power ever again. Many men would. They would thrive on power like that and do anything to have access to it. For him, he knew it was too much. There was nothing attractive about it at all.

For the moment, he could not turn away. He was attached to the rock as if a part of it. He felt as if at that moment, he and the giant golden stone were one. He wanted to get away from it, but at the same time, he couldn't.

Elder Rhys watched the exchange. He had seen it once before. He knew it would be several minutes before it had worked *if* it worked. It had worked the previous time, but he did not know if it worked *every* time.

All three of them stood as if frozen in time until finally, the glow of the rock eased off. As if in slow motion, Trent's hands appeared to fall back from the rock wall. He then slumped to the ground.

Isabella ran forward, her natural instincts to care for him strong.

"Be careful!" Elder Rhys called out to her, cautioning her not to touch Trent straight away. "Wait."

Isabella watched the man on the ground before her. He seemed lifeless. She wanted to do something for him, but she trusted the words of the ancient.

After a few minutes, even Elder Rhys was concerned.

They turned Trent over. There was no life in him, but Isabella knew what to do. Without consulting the ancient at all, she reached forward and placed her hand over the center of Trent's chest. As she did, a sudden and intense golden glow came from him. His back arched as he took a deep breath of air, life once again revived in him.

Elder Rhys looked at Isabella in surprise.

"The touch, Isabella! You have the touch!" he whispered to her.

Isabella heard his words but could not think about anything he was saying. All she could focus on was Trent. It had only been instinct that had told her to do such a thing. She hoped she had done the right thing.

Trent felt like he was waking from a dream. He had been touching the wall and felt its power, and then … nothing. As his consciousness further heightened, he sat up slowly.

He felt warmth flowing through his entire body. When he looked down at his chest, he could see it glowing yellow. He touched it and felt the heat coming from it. Slowly it faded away. Overall, it had left him feeling highly invigorated and very alive.

"Isabella," he whispered as his eyes locked with hers.

"I am here, Trent," she replied as she felt tears begin in her eyes. "You are alright now."

Trent began to stand up but quickly stopped himself as dizziness flowed over him.

"Wait a few minutes, traveler," Elder Rhys said. "Your body has undergone a change. You must give it time to adjust."

"Has it worked? How do we know?" Trent asked.

The ancient nodded and smiled.

"I believe it has worked, but you will know as soon as we leave the cave and step outside," he said.

As Isabella moved closer to Trent, he accepted her arms around him. When he felt stronger, he tried to move again, ready to stand.

When all three were upright on their feet, Trent pulled Isabella into his arms and kissed her. As he did, a large aura of bright golden light instantly emanated from both of them.

Elder Rhys stepped back in surprise. Because he'd never seen such a thing before, he was alarmed. Through the light, he could see them holding each other. While he would normally not consider it polite to watch two in such an embrace, the glow emanating from them was intriguing to him. He found it difficult to look away.

When Trent and Isabella broke apart, they smiled broadly at each other. Both had felt the increased power of their desire at that moment. As they turned to face the ancient, they noticed the shock on his face.

"What is it, Elder Rhys?" Isabella asked in concern.

Elder Rhys smiled softly but didn't explain what he'd witnessed.

"Come. Now we return to our village, and our time - all of us," he said. "Before we leave, I will stress to you both once again how important it is that no-one knows about this place. No-one at all - not even Adrian, Isabella. Not even your parents. Do you understand the importance of this?"

Isabella nodded.

"Yes."

Elder Rhys led them through the parted waterfall once again, and over the pool. When they looked behind them, everything was as it should be. Water flowed freely over its usual run line. The pool was as it always had been.

Trent looked around him. The difference was so stark that he wondered if he might faint. Everything was green. He'd previously seen the area in that state for short periods of time. He appreciated that time was no longer a restriction. It was possible for him to now stand and look at it for as long as he liked.

The area was lush. Greenery was intense across the trees, the bushes, and the flowers. Roses crept all over the high, grey exterior walls. Further over, he could see more trees. Further still stood buildings. In the distance, he could hear the light chatter of people. It sounded like only a few but more than Trent had previously heard.

"The village is awakening. Let us go to the temple before we are seen. I wish to talk to both of you alone before we are around people," Elder Rhys said.

Isabella and Trent nodded in response, eager to follow him and learn whatever they could about what had just happened.

Trent found himself in awe as he walked through the village. Buildings, grass, trees, houses, a water fountain - all of it had been destroyed in his time. He was determined to do whatever he could to make sure that the other future timeline did not happen.

He recognized the markings on the front of the temple. Even in its broken state, the markings had been visible to him. As he entered the structure in its entirety, he was amazed at the sheer size of it. Once within the initial interior, he stopped and looked up to see the most amazing painted ceiling with graphical images.

"These were done by our ancestors. They tell stories of our heritage. It is important these are kept intact," the ancient said. He looked pointedly at Trent.

Trent understood fully. He had seen what one action of the village letting a stranger into their midst had done to destroy all that he was presently looking at. He nodded at the ancient, assuring him of his dedication to not let that happen.

Isabella and Trent were led through another large wooden door to a depth of the temple Isabella had never seen before.

"This is the meditation room of the ancients," Elder Rhys said. "You will not come here again until it is your time to serve as an ancient, Isabella."

She looked at him sharply, not knowing what he was talking about.

"I do not understand, Elder Rhys," she said. "What do you mean?"

"You are a chosen one," the ancient said. "That is why you could see the traveler when others could not. But more than that, you have the gift of life. That is how you brought Trent back to life in the cave."

Trent looked at Isabella in surprise. He hadn't been aware that he'd stopped breathing in the cave. The thought simultaneously scared him and intrigued him. Subconsciously, his hand moved to his chest.

"We will talk about this at a later time, but you have been chosen, Isabella," Elder Rhys continued. "It is a gift that will bring great responsibility in time but not for many years. For now, you will have a great many years for the two of you to pair and begin your family, to do your part in securing the ongoing population of our village."

Trent and Isabella looked at each other. On each other's face, they could see a complex array of feelings, including surprise, disbelief, uncertainty, and desire.

The three walked further until they came to an area with mats on the floor. The ancient signaled for them to sit with him. On doing so, they saw him look closely at each of their faces, one at a time.

"It is no simple thing that has been done today," he said. "It is not something that you should take lightly or talk about. We shall not tell people how Trent has come to be here or where he has come from. It is especially important to not say *when* he has come from."

Isabella felt shock flow through her system and Elder Rhys saw it.

"Do not worry about Adrian, Isabella," he said. "Your friend has already forgotten that he ever saw Trent. When he next sees him, it will be as if he is seeing him for the first time."

"How…?" Isabella began to ask.

The ancient raised his hands to stop her from asking the question.

"It is done, and all is well. You must not talk of this to Adrian. Trent will be a traveler who is lost, and we are welcoming to our community," Elder Rhys continued and then looked pointedly at Trent. "He will have lost his memory as far as how he came to be inside the walls."

Trent completely understood that he was to tell this story if ever asked.

"Of course," he said, confirming he understood.

"He has arrived today, and you have found him and brought him to me, Isabella," Elder Rhys said and saw her nod in acknowledgment. "I am therefore asking you to now take him and show him around the village, as you would any new person."

Isabella and Trent both inhaled deeply, understanding then that they would have to pretend as if they had never met before.

"I ask that you will wait for at least two weeks until you let people see you together as potential pairings," he said.

Isabella unintentionally let out a small groan at the thought of still not being able to be near Trent as closely as she wanted.

"Do not worry, Isabella," the ancient said. "I can see how much you wish to be together. I will not stop you. There is a small room behind the temple that is discrete. Trent can sleep in it and make it his own for now. When he is known among our people, we can work toward announcing your pairing."

The words were said as a statement, not a question. They did not require an answer from either Trent or Isabella.

"Now, come with me. I will show you to the room that will be Trent's until we find more suitable accommodation for him," Elder Rhys said as he stood and led them out of the room.

As they walked behind the ancient, Trent looked at Isabella. He felt nervous. It was something he hadn't felt around any woman since he'd been a teenager. If there was one aspect of life that he never had a lack of confidence in, it was with women. Feeling his heart as full and pounding like it was, he knew he'd made the right choice.

CHAPTER 31

Once in the small room that housed only a bed, the ancient nodded to Trent and Isabella and removed himself, quietly closing the door behind him.

Instantly Trent walked to Isabella and wrapped his arms around her, drawing her to him and holding her close. Feeling his emotions close to overloading, he thought about all that he'd seen and been through.

When they looked at one another, Isabella could see tears in his eyes.

"Are you sad? Do you wish that you had not come into our time?" Isabella asked, concerned.

Trent looked closely at her, kissed her lips softly, took her hand, and led her to sit with him on the edge of the bed.

"No, not at all," he said quietly. "I am overwhelmed with so many things going through my mind. There are many things to think about in this new life, but the one thing that I am certain of is that I have done the right thing."

"You have not seen the village properly yet, or the people…" Isabella replied.

"No, and I will not today if you do not mind," Trent responded. "Today I need to adjust to … this," he said, waving his hand around to indicate the building he was in. "A short time ago, all I could see here was rubble. Now I am sitting in it. To me, it is as if it has been suddenly resurrected. I know that is not the case, but I do need to adjust to one thing at a time."

Isabella nodded at him, feeling an intensity in her emotion. In the back of her mind was a fear that once Trent was comfortable around people, she would not be the one he chose to pair with at all. He had not seen any other women for so long. Would she still be his choice when she was not his *only* choice?

Trent saw her face grow morose as she seemed to shut down and go silent. He raised her chin so that he could look directly into her eyes. He wanted to ask her what was on her mind. Before he could, she reached up and kissed him, passion deep in the kiss.

Regardless of his hunger for her, Trent maintained his composure. Elder Rhys had indicated it would only be a few weeks before they could be paired. She was worth waiting for. For the moment, he indulged in the feelings that she brought out in him. Instinctively he moved backward along the length of the small bed, taking her with him.

Neither was sure of how much time had passed when they broke apart. What Trent did know was that he was well and truly under her spell. If he was in his time and he'd met her in his city, he would have already attempted to bed her without any thought whatsoever. He would have acted on his natural impulses and not given any consideration to that being a rash and unfeeling thing to do.

In the time he now found himself in, although he had yet to see the people of the village, or the village itself in its lively state, he felt a sense of disrespect over the ease with which he'd bedded women in the past. They had each meant something to him in the moment, but Isabella meant something *more* to him. He wanted her to be the one final woman he made love to. He wanted her to be the one he had children with and would grow old with. He didn't know about her growing internal fear that once he saw other women, she might not be his chosen one at all. If he had, he would have reassured her, however he had to, that he had no desire to be with any other woman ever again.

"I must not stay, I do not think. There are … feelings … inside of me that I am new to," Isabella said with a slight blush and a very demure look on her face.

Trent could not argue with her. "I have them too, Isabella," he said softly. He saw her look at him sharply as if surprised. "You are not the only one feeling that way."

He lifted his hand and stroked her cheek lightly, deep in thought about so many things but trying desperately to not think about making love to her.

"You are … experienced … in…" she started to say, looking down as if in deep embarrassment. "Loving a woman?"

"Yes," he replied instantly, not wanting to lie. Not to her.

"Many women?" she asked.

"Yes," Trent continued in full honesty.

He watched her facial expressions as she let the acknowledgment flow through her mind. Eventually, she seemed to deflate, right before his eyes. At that moment, he wished he hadn't treated sex as casually as he always had, but that was his past. There was no changing it.

"Isabella, I come from a world where many people do not regard … such … pleasure … as anything more than an activity that they partake in," he explained.

"It is not for making children, in your time?" asked Isabella, confused.

"Yes, but many people who do not want children still choose to enjoy it," Trent said.

Isabella shook her head.

"I do not understand. I do not *need* to understand..."

Trent kissed her softly.

"I cannot undo having been with women before you. I can assure you, however, that I never felt anything for them," he said. "Not like I feel for you. Perhaps that makes the idea of ... pairing ... seem not important to me, but the opposite is true. I truly believe that you and I are meant to be together, now and for the rest of our lives. Nothing from my life before is as important as how I feel being here right now ... with you."

Isabella felt confused but would be patient and accept whatever would happen with them. At that moment, it was a relief to be able to lie beside him and not worry about people from her time seeing her outside, doing things such as kissing an invisible person.

The thought suddenly made her laugh.

Trent was so happy to see her smiling again that he found himself laughing in response.

"What are you laughing at?" he asked her, curious at her change in mood.

"I was thinking about how it might have looked to someone from my time ... this time ... before, if they saw me holding my arms around you and kissing you," she said, grinning. "I am sure it would have seemed like a strange thing to see."

Trent smiled at her and kissed her more, for the moment not caring how it would look to anyone else. He held her in his arms and found himself quite at peace. He also couldn't help but appreciate how it felt to be on an actual bed after so long sleeping on the ground in his sleeping bag...

All of a sudden, he sat up, making Isabella jump.

"What is it?" she asked.

"I just realized that my gear will all be ... in the future," Trent said, trying to get his head around the realization.

"Yes, it will be lost to you now," replied Isabella. "Was there something that you needed?"

Trent relaxed back and smiled.

"No, nothing. It is just very odd to think that it is here, but it isn't here *now*. I may never quite understand how that can be."

~~~~~

After lying together quietly for some time, Isabella heard his stomach rumble. She smiled at him.

"I will take you to the dining area if you wish," she said.

Trent found himself salivating at the possible flavors soon to be made available to him.

"But did Elder Rhys not say we have to pretend like I am new here?" he asked. "How will we do that?"
~~~~~

"Hmm, yes," responded Isabella as she nodded. "Let us go and see him to ask him how he wants this day to go. I am sure he will have already considered such things."

When they stood up, Isabella moved toward the door. Before she opened it, she felt Trent take her hand once more, pull her close and kiss her deeply. As he did, Isabella found herself wishing they could quickly move to the pairing part.

~~~~~

Walking through the temple, they found Elder Rhys sitting in meditation. Isabella looked at Trent, not sure whether to disturb the ancient. As always, Elder Rhys was already aware of their presence.

"Do not be concerned. I am finished," he said, standing up and greeting them. "You have a question for me."

"Yes," Isabella said. "Shall I take Trent to the dining area for sustenance, or bring some here for him?"

"I think it is time, Isabella," Elder Rhys replied, glancing from her to Trent. "We can introduce him to the people and announce his arrival to all if you are both ready."

Trent felt nervous. He had left the city to get away from crowds of people. Suddenly he wondered if he was about to feel claustrophobic once more.
~~~~~

CHAPTER 32

As Trent and Isabella followed the ancient out of the temple, once again Trent felt himself in awe of how the village looked compared to how it had looked to him before his change. Although the area was small compared to the world he'd known before, it was vibrant, alive, and lush. It was beyond logic that things could grow so easily as high up above sea level as he knew they were. Considering that, he had to wonder if the villagers even knew they were on top of an icy mountain. The grey exterior walls were so high, even from the inside of them, that there was no real way to see how much land and depth of valleys there were outside of the walls. It felt warm and pleasant in the village. He considered it quite possible - maybe even *likely* - that the residents had no comprehension of where exactly they were on the planet. He found himself wondering if perhaps they did not even comprehend that there was any life at all beyond where they were.

~~~~~

As they walked behind Elder Rhys, Trent started to see more and more people, but he remained relaxed. He could see the village and knew that the possible population of it could in no way be anywhere near what he had grown up in and had grown to hate.

Wherever they walked, people stopped and stared but then came up and greeted Isabella and the ancient. They would then move forward to smile at Trent and nod their heads. They did not speak directly to him, seeming very shy about him. He was glad of that as he did not know if he could speak at that moment either. He was relaxed, but he was also overwhelmed.

~~~~~

They seemed to walk a long distance, past what Trent assumed were homes. He saw a fountain, from which someone was filling a jug of water. After that, he could see what he thought might be a blacksmith, working with metal, shaping what appeared to be small knives.

Finally, they entered a large enclosed area with a great many tables installed into it. Everything he saw helped Trent to gain an understanding of how many people lived in the village. It wasn't just a few, but it equally wasn't anything like the crowds he'd grown tired of in his own city.

"Hush, everyone," Elder Rhys said, speaking at a volume that neither Trent nor Isabella had heard him speak at before. When there was silence, he continued, addressing the sea of people looking directly at him, Isabella and the stranger beside her. "Please. We have a visitor in our midst. This is Trent. He has come to us this day from outside the walls. I am sure you will have questions for him about where he has traveled from, but for now, he has no recollection of anything before today. He needs, most of all, to receive sustenance to help his body regain strength. I have assessed this young man. He is to be trusted, but he is also to have peace. Please give him the space he will need. He is currently quite confused and needs to be able to find his way in our community."

Trent was overwhelmed by the power the ancient exuded at that moment. After a nudge from Isabella, he moved forward one step, raised a hand slightly, and smiled at everyone, making the crowd clap. Even in that, they were quiet. Trent smiled at the realization that in the village, he might never again experience great noise like his life had been full of before he embarked on his journey to find peace. Until that moment, he'd wondered if he might regret not having the option to return to the modern world. The crowd before him, being calm and at peace, helped to reassure him that he'd made the right decision. He didn't need noise anymore.

"Come with me. Let me show you the food," Isabella said, smiling at him and making him yearn for her.

Even though it was not their first meeting or first day together, seeing her among the people, and seeing her as a contrast to them, Trent felt like he was seeing her for the first time all over again. Although she was stunning to look at it, what was even more evident to Trent was seeing just how much people truly liked her. It increased his pride at the possibility of being the one to be paired with her.

"Cook Joan, this is a new friend for us, Trent," he saw her say to an older woman in a stained apron. "He is eager to try your special food, but I think he should not eat too much too soon."

"Oh, Miss Isabella!" the cook replied. "Yes, of course. Today I have this bread here, and with that is a very special tomato rice dish. Take a little of each, and you will be fine with that, Mr Trent," the cook continued as she smiled broadly.

After Isabella showed Trent where the plates and foods were laid out each day, they sat down in her usual seating area.

Trent looked at the food before him and felt his hunger and his appetite. Uncertain of eating traditions and not wanting to insult or offend, he looked to her for guidance.

"Eat, Trent. It is good," Isabella said, spreading some of the tomato rice on her piece of bread and taking a large bite.

It was the first time Trent had seen her eat. He couldn't help but be enraptured as he watched her indulge in the food.

Isabella laughed at him.

"Eat!" she commanded him and immediately saw him laugh at her.

Trent tentatively picked up a piece of bread and spread the tomato rice on it. On tasting it, he openly showed his appreciation for the flavor.

"Hmm. This is so delicious," he mumbled through food-filled cheeks, making her laugh even more at him.

Suddenly Isabella sensed someone on the other side of her. When she turned, she saw Adrian sitting down.

"Isabella, who is this?" she heard him ask as if he'd never seen Trent before.

Isabella felt relieved. Just as Elder Rhys had said he would, Adrian had forgotten already having met Trent previously. She looked closely at Adrian, finding it difficult to comprehend that some part of his memory seemed to have been taken from him. It saddened her, but at the same time, she could see why it had been necessary to keep Trent's real situation a secret from everyone in the village.

"Adrian, please meet Trent. He was lost, so will be staying with us now," Isabella said and watched Adrian tentatively reach out his hand toward Trent.

"Hello, Adrian. It is good to meet you," she saw Trent say while shaking Adrian's hand.

Trent felt amazed that Adrian did not remember the day he had met him. Although the ancient had said that would be the case, it was still difficult to believe it could be a reality.

Adrian started to discuss everyday things. Isabella found herself wondering how much of his memory had been removed from him. She couldn't know for sure if he remembered the discussion they'd shared about pairing together. She suspected that might be the case when he suggested she walk partway with him to the mill.

It was a conversation she didn't want to have again. If they spoke of it again, she knew he might be hurt once more. She didn't want that. If she kept away, he would hopefully keep spending time with Kat.

"I will not today, Adrian," she replied. "Elder Rhys has asked me to show Trent around the village and introduce him to our ways. But I shall see you at dinner?" she asked and saw him nod in response.

When they had eaten and washed up, Isabella invited Trent to walk with her to meet the people she interacted with daily.

"Cook Joan, is there anything that you wish me to fetch for you from the garden?" she asked as they walked past the food preparation area.

"Oh yes, Miss Isabella, if you please," the cook replied. "I require four green apples and some sweet basil - just a handful of that. That would be wonderful, thank you."

Isabella smiled at the cook and veered Trent away to walk outside. As they walked, she watched his face. She enjoyed seeing his curiosity as he looked at everything and everyone.

Eventually, they reached the fork in the path, near where Trent had slept in his tent. Although everything looked different, he was able to find his bearings and understand where they were.

"This is where I slept?" he asked and saw her nod and smile in reply. "And where you came into my tent?"

Isabella knew he was trying to tease her and make her blush but she didn't mind at all. She laughed at him while nodding again. "Come. This is the way to the garden and the orchard."

~~~~~

Once in the large garden area, Trent was able to get a better view of it than what he had been able to see on that first day. The level of self-sufficiency of the people overwhelmed him. He had already gained an understanding that there were no animals in the village apart from chickens. They, as a community, didn't appear to eat meat at all. For a moment, he wondered if that had anything to do with everyone looking healthy and youthful.

"Miss Isabella, what has the cook asked you to seek today for their creations?" one of the gardeners asked.

"Just sweet basil today, if that is possible," Isabella replied. "I can pick the apples I need to find if you are able to gather me one handful of the basil?"

"Of course. It is right over here..." the gardener said and wandered off to retrieve the right amount for her.

Trent marveled at what he saw. There was no form of tender. People seemed to have specific jobs and got on with them for the benefit of all people in the community.

"How do people get chosen to do each different job, Isabella?" he asked her, his mind full of curiosity.

At first, Isabella did not understand the question. After consideration, she guessed things must be different where he had come from.

"People do not get chosen for a job, Trent," she said. "People do the things that they enjoy. These gardeners are here because they love to be in the land, growing food. The cooks are in the kitchen because they love to create masterpieces of food that they can share with everyone else."

"And your job?" he asked her, not yet sure where she fitted into the jigsaw of society within the large grey walls.

Isabella felt sheepish as she smiled at him.

"I am still seeking to discover what I am meant to do but I think..."
~~~~~

she said before her voice drifted off to silence.

"You think … what?" Trent asked.

Before Isabella replied, she gave him a demure look that sent his pulse racing.

"I think I shall be happy to have and raise many children," she said. "I shall like to be a mother and a contributor to our population."

Trent had to quickly dismiss thoughts going through his mind. Thinking about making babies was the last thing he wanted to dwell on as he got to know the community as a whole. He was relieved when the gardener came back with the herb.

"Here you go," the gardener said. "The best apples are on that tree over there. Can you reach?"

"Yes, thank you," Isabella replied and watched the gardener walk off to carry on with his tasks.

Trent followed her as she walked to the apple tree and picked a few apples off the tree. He said nothing more to her as they made their way back to the kitchen to deliver the spoils, but his mind was racing ahead to whenever the day of pairing would be.

As if sensing his feelings, once they had made the delivery, he heard Isabella whisper to him, "May I walk you back to your room?"

~~~~~

Once inside, with the door closed behind them, she approached him with a passionate hunger that was evident in the way that she kissed him and pulled him to her. Trent groaned heavily with the degree of desire he felt. He wondered if he really could wait another few weeks.

"Oh, Isabella, I feel a desperation to be closer to you, and I apologize for that," Trent said as he pulled away from her.

"Why would you apologize?" Isabella asked. "Do you think I do not feel the same?"

He looked at her and could openly see the arousal on her face, even if she didn't fully comprehend the new feelings inside of her. He quickly took his mind backward and pushed the arousal away from its forefront.

"Come and sit with me on the bed," he said as he refocused his thoughts. "I would like to hear about your life. Are your parents alive? Do you have any siblings?"

"Siblings?" Isabella asked.

"Other children of your mother and father," Trent replied.

"Oh, no, my mother and father bore only me. They are good people, and they are as much as I could ever have wished for," she said and paused. "Would you like to meet them?"

Trent was taken aback by the request, but found himself nodding slowly.

"I would," he said. "Not today, but perhaps tomorrow? If you feel
~~~~~

comfortable to introduce me, that is."

"They would have to meet you before … the pairing. You must ask them if they approve of it," Isabella said quietly.

The thought did not scare Trent. He'd carefully avoided meeting the parents of any of the women who'd passed through his life. He'd not wanted to give any impression he wanted to have those women in his life for an extended period of time. It was refreshing to find that the thought of meeting Isabella's mother and father wasn't in any way something to worry about.

He raised her hand to his mouth and kissed it gently.

"Happily," he said, excited at the prospect.

"We must get you some clothes!" Isabella exclaimed unexpectedly. "You have nothing with you now!"

Trent laughed at her. He'd forgotten that what he was wearing was all that he had from his entire former life.

"We shall go and see the tailors immediately," Isabella continued. "They may have something of the right size already."

Trent watched her as she jumped up and held out her hand to him.

~~~~~

Once fitted with three new shirts and two changes of pants, Trent found himself warming greatly to the people of the village. No-one seemed to have bad feelings or any need to be greedy. Everyone just wanted to help one another and work together to provide an environment that was conducive to peace. It was exactly what he'd so desperately desired when he'd left the city and his other life behind.

As he lay in bed that night - the first real bed he'd been in for so long - he pondered all that had happened. There was a magical wonder in how he had come to traverse the life he had lived before to the life he was presently in. It could not in any way have been expected, but he wasn't afraid of it. In contrast, he found himself highly eager to simply embrace it.
~~~~~

CHAPTER 33

Two weeks passed before Trent and Isabella were summoned to the temple again. During that time, Trent allowed himself to slowly meet and get to know people while observing how things were done in the ancient village. There were so many contrasts to the modern world he'd left behind, but nothing negatively so.

"Both of you have previously spoken of becoming paired to one another, to remain paired for the remainder of your days," Elder Rhys said as Trent and Isabella sat in front of him. "Now that you, Trent, have been among our people and come to know those who are here, do you still wish to pair with Isabella?" the ancient asked and watched Trent's face as he looked at Isabella intently.

"Yes!" Trent replied without any hesitation. "With all my heart."

"And Isabella, do you still feel the same? Do you wish for this?"

"Yes, Elder Rhys," Isabella said before she smiled at Trent. "I very much do."

"Very well," said the ancient, nodding. "I approve of the two of you being a match but we must get the approval of your parents and the other ancients, Isabella. I will speak to my equals this evening in the privacy of the temple, but shall we go and see your mother and father now? Do you agree to this?"

"Yes, Elder Rhys," replied Isabella. She wasn't nervous about what her parents would say. Overshadowing that possible emotion was a strong eagerness to go through the pairing with Trent. New feelings had begun to emerge in her body. She wanted to stop running away from them and face them head-on.

The three of them walked to the small home where Isabella had grown up. Isabella's father and mother welcomed the trio into their home with open looks of curiosity on their faces.

"Tomas. Crisiana. I have come here with Isabella and our new friend, Trent, to speak to you of their wish to become paired," the ancient said. Immediately, all heard a gasp from Isabella's mother. "It may come as a shock since Trent has only been with us a short time, but I have witnessed them together. I give my blessing to the pairing. I believe they are meant to be together - that they were always driven to find one another."

Isabella saw her mother and father look at each other, sharing language with looks that only they could decipher.

"If you believe that then we give our blessing also, Elder Rhys, if it is truly what our daughter desires," said Isabella's mother, Crisiana. "Daughter, is this what you wish for?"

"Yes, Mother," replied Isabella. "I very much do."

"Very well then," said the ancient, standing to leave once more. "I shall take my leave now, and I shall consult with the ancients this evening. Trent, Isabella, come and see me after you have eaten tomorrow morning. I shall let you know then what has been decided."

"Thank you, Elder Rhys," four voices said as he made his way toward the door.

"I will walk with you," Trent said, beginning to fall in step behind the ancient. Before walking out of the small home, he moved back toward Isabella to give her a hug and a kiss on the cheek. "I will see you in the morning?"

Isabella nodded at him before he left, walking out into the night.

"Isabella, are you sure about this?" Crisiana asked her daughter, one major subject of concern present in her mind. "I had always thought you would pair with Adrian."

"Yes, Mother," Isabella said. "Adrian did mention it to me once before, but I do not feel the same way about him as I do about Trent. I wish for Adrian to always be my friend. I cannot think of him in the way that I feel I should think of the person I pair with."

Both parents walked up to her and held her in an embrace.

"Then you have our blessing, Daughter," her father said. "It is long past time that you did so and started your own family."

CHAPTER 34

When Isabella went to breakfast the next morning, she was pleased to see Adrian already there. As she sat down next to him, she received a brilliant smile in response to seeing her.

"Are you well, Isabella?" he asked. "It seems like I hardly ever see you at the present time."

"Yes, Adrian, I am well. I wish to speak to you though," she said. She knew him well. Her words had successfully commanded his full attention. "I … I have asked the ancients to consider … to consider allowing Trent and I to pair."

Adrian was stunned, not sure he'd heard correctly. Until that moment, he'd thought he would never be surprised by anything his closest friend could say. The effect her words instantly had on him contradicted that belief.

Isabella knew that his silence alone was an indication of how shocked he was. It was the exact reaction she'd hoped to avoid. While she knew it had been best for Elder Rhys to help Adrian forget having met Trent previously, it didn't make it any easier to think that she might be about to hurt her lifelong friend again.

"I do not understand, Isabella," Adrian said. "You have just met him. How can you wish to pair with him so soon, when you and I have known each other all our lives? I thought…"

Adrian fell silent. The two of them looked at each other, sadness mirroring in their eyes.

"You do not esteem me as much as I esteem you," he said all of a sudden.

Isabella felt her emotions react strongly to his words. She couldn't think of anything to say to him. Moments later, he stood up and walked away from her, no more said.

Before Isabella stood up herself, she was confronted by Kat sitting down beside her.

"You have hurt him, Isabella, but I cannot be angry or sad about that," the young woman said. "I have wished for him to not want to pair with you, so he might notice me. Perhaps now, he shall."

Isabella looked at the young woman beside her and felt intense sadness for her to have said such a thing.

"Kat, I believe Adrian esteemed you greatly long before now," Isabella said. "If he has not shown you affection yet, do not think it is due to me. It is possible that he is simply unaware of how you feel. Go to him and tell him. Make sure that he listens. Sometimes he needs to be told something several times before he truly hears it. Tell him and make him listen, and he will come to you happily, I am sure."

Kat looked at the beautiful woman beside her, with her mane of flowing red hair. It was no wonder that she had not one but two men wishing to pair with her. Kat wasn't happy. Words formed in her head. 'How it must be to have anyone want to pair with you, let alone two men', she murmured to herself inside the peacefulness of her mind.

Isabella had no more words to say to the young woman. She stood up, washed her dish, and immediately walked to the temple. Stopping outside Trent's door, she knocked quietly but heard no answer. After a few minutes, she knocked again, slightly more loudly. Eventually, she heard movement on the other side of the door. When it opened, she saw Trent looking very sheepish and tousled.

"Is it morning already? I am still finding that I am so tired in the mornings," he said as he quietly padded back to his bed and climbed under the covers.

Isabella closed the door and moved to sit on his bed, looking down at him. Covered as he was, she thought he looked more like a young child than the mature man that he was. She leaned down to kiss him.

Trent eagerly accepted her kiss. The taste of her lips intensely fulfilled him when they kissed. It was yet another thing that had him convinced that they were destined to be together as partners.

"Trent, are you sure you wish for this? For us to be paired?" Isabella asked as she pulled away. "If you have doubt, we do not have to…"

"Isabella, I wish for nothing more than to pair with you and start our life together," Trent reassured her.

That someone so beautiful could have any such doubts still surprised him, until he considered that the people of the village didn't seem to have any comprehension about 'beauty' as it was perceived in the modern world he'd left behind. He'd always believed that skin deep was less important than the depth of someone's heart. In the world he'd left behind, that belief hadn't stopped him from seeking out women that others deemed to be the most striking to look at. He hated to admit it, but it was true.

As if to convince himself that he wasn't just attracted to Isabella by her extreme beauty, he pulled her close to him and kissed her again. He shouldn't have even questioned his feelings, but for that moment, he had. As his lips moved against hers, he knew it wasn't her outer beauty that held him. There was something much deeper between them. It was something he'd never felt with anyone, no matter how 'hot' they'd seemed.

Isabella found herself being kissed once more and was soon lying on top of him. She rested along the length of Trent as he held her tightly.

The friction that came from her moving as she kissed him, produced the familiar feeling of sexual arousal in Trent. He quickly nudged her off him to stop the effect. He didn't want arousal to play any part in him devoting the rest of his life to her. Quickly, he began speaking as a diversion.

"I am eager to pair with you," he said to her as he moved a subtle distance away. "To do that, we must go and talk to Elder Rhys this morning, to see what the ancients have decided, must we not?" he asked as he saw Isabella climb off him, smiling at his enthusiasm.

"Yes," she replied as she looked at him lying still under the blanket. "Let us do that now."

Aware that his body was not in a relaxed state, Trent fondly smiled at her and waited for her to move further away.

"Yes, but please turn around, Isabella. You do not get to see all of my body until we are paired," he quietly said as he laughed softly at her.

He heard her giggle as she presented her back to him. As he slowly climbed out and dressed, he was glad to feel his body's evident arousal disappear. He didn't know what Isabella knew about sex, but he would go forwards in that assuming it was something they as a people did not talk about. He would maintain his expectation that they only found their way in that on the evening of the pairing.

The thought should have been enough to settle his body. It seemed to only fuel him again.

Taking a deep breath, he thought about his most recent ex. That was all it took to finally dispel any shred of arousal.

"Let us go," he said before seeing Isabella turn around, smile at him, and then walk toward the door.

CHAPTER 35

As Isabella and Trent sat before the ancient, they were greeted by a smile. It made both of them hopeful about the news to come.

"The council of ancients was unanimous," Elder Rhys said. "If the two of you still wish to, we will grant you permission to pair. What say you?"

"Yes, thank you," Isabella and Trent both replied, making them laugh together.

"We have established a home for you to live in, and we can have the pairing ceremony as soon as you wish," the ancient went on to say. "When shall it be? We do not need to prepare as it is an evening of speaking as a community."

"As soon as possible, Elder Rhys, please," Trent said as he reached over and took Isabella's hand in his. "If Isabella agrees?"

"Yes! Oh, yes, please, Elder Rhys. Tonight?" she asked.

Elder Rhys burst out laughing but maintained a look of friendliness and humor on his face.

"Of course," he said, nodding and grinning. "I understand you have had to wait much longer than others know you have, and I can see the fire in each of you for one another. Come with me now and see your new home. After the ceremony and your night in the pairing chamber, it shall be yours."

Trent and Isabella walked hand in hand through the village as they followed the ancient. All homes were similar. There was no need to inspect, but they did so out of respect. After walking through the modest structure, they each gave their thanks in appreciation before preparing to leave once more.

"Isabella, go and speak to your mother and father and tell them to be ready tonight to give you away," Elder Rhys instructed. "Trent, I would like you to come back to the temple with me so we can talk."

The two young lovers hugged before parting, both eager to get on with the evening.

~~~~~

"Tonight? Why such a rush, Daughter?" Isabella's mother, Crisiana, asked her. She couldn't hide the hint of panic in her voice.

"Mother, do you not wish for me to pair with Trent?" Isabella asked.
~~~~~

"Is there something you wish to tell me?"

"No … no, Isabella, you have just taken me by surprise," Crisiana said. "We do not know this man, but your father and I do trust in the judgment of you and the ancients. We will be ready tonight. Of course we will."

Isabella threw her arms around her mother and held her.

"Thank you!" Isabella exclaimed. "I will make you proud, helping to build the population of the village."

"That is very good of you, Daughter, but make sure also that you are *happy* with him," said Crisiana. "It is for the rest of your life. You must be certain."

"I am, Mother," replied Isabella as she grinned. "I am."

CHAPTER 36

"Please sit with me, young traveler," Elder Rhys said as he and Trent entered a small chamber in the temple. "I wish to talk to you about pairing in our village."

Trent briefly felt like he was a teenager again, about to get 'the sex talk' from his father. After a moment, he conceded that what he was about to be told wasn't the same thing at all.

"Our village has stood here for more than 5,000 years," the ancient began to say. "As you know, the land survives by a golden source that runs through veins under this entire area. But this village is also kept alive by doing what we can to maintain peace and harmony. Part of that is ensuring that men and women are paired correctly. When we pair, we pair for life. Therefore I firstly want to make sure that you have noticed other women in this village, and you still see Isabella as the one - the *only* one - that you wish to be with."

Trent was surprised but respected the question. He'd had enough women on his arm purely because of what they looked like. He wasn't proud of it, but it was the truth. He had no right to be offended by being asked such a thing, even in an ancient culture.

"Yes," he replied, knowing fully in his heart that it was the truth. "Isabella is the only woman I wish to love and have as my partner for the rest of my life."

"Good," replied Elder Rhys as he nodded and smiled. "Now tonight the ceremony will comprise much talking on my part. After you are paired, you will be led to the pairing chamber. There, you will stay for the whole night. It is during that time that you are expected to join in the hope that a child will begin to grow in Isabella's belly."

Trent nodded. "Of course."

"Go now then, Trent," the ancient said. "Rest and prepare yourself. I shall send Isabella to come and get you when the time is right."

As Trent removed himself and walked to the pool, he found his mind full of contemplation. The idea of settling down with someone for the rest of his life had never appealed. He'd surprised himself that he was so eager for it. He realized then that it hadn't been the idea of being with *someone* long term that had always kept him off that path. It had been *who* he'd been with.

Entering the pool area and seeing no-one around, he was pulled from his thoughts by the warmth of the sun. After removing his shoes, socks, and shirt, he waded into the pool in his pants.

In the water, he lay on his back and floated, looking up at the sky. The blend of the warmth of the water, the sound of the waterfall nearby, the freshness of the air that he breathed, and the beauty of the sky above him, all contributed to his contentment. He couldn't help but appreciate that he had just wanted to get some peace and solitude when he'd left the city. What he'd found instead was pure paradise.

He'd closed his eyes and fully relaxed, continuing to float and feel like he was meditating, when he heard her voice.

"I see you are being more modest now that other people can see you," Isabella teased as she watched him and saw him give her a brilliant smile.

"I have no wish to shock anyone," he said, teasing her back. "Will you come in?" he dared to ask. Her response was to remove her shoes and wade in, wearing the simple green slip dress that she had on.

As Isabella waded toward him, Trent put his feet down and stood on the pool floor. He was entranced as she confidently walked into his arms. It continued to amaze him that they had known each other for such a short time. Despite his usual self-confidence, when he looked at her and found himself immersed in her beauty, he still could not get over the fact that she wanted him. She could have chosen anyone to pair with.

Moving back toward the far-away wall of the pool, he guided her to float on her back before him. As he used one arm to steady her, he used the other to gently wash her hair in the warm water, letting his fingers run through the long red mane and loving how it felt to do so. As he began to caress her scalp in the warm water, he heard her groan in happiness. The sound made him smile.

"I wish for tonight to come sooner," she said.

Trent found himself aroused instantly. He was also glad that he'd decided to bathe with his trousers on. That she could affect him so completely without even seeming to have any idea about purposely-delivered seduction continued to surprise him.

Isabella put her feet down and turned to lean into him, putting her arms around his neck and kissing him deeply.

"We should not do this in public, should we?" he asked her, desperate to not cause any offense to anyone within the large grey walls.

"Yes," Isabella replied with reluctance as she pulled back. "You are right, Trent."

He watched as he saw her dive under the water briefly before coming up again. As she stood, Trent could see the full outline of her body in the wet dress. He forced himself to look away, desperate to not dwell on her physical appearance. It was too late. She had seen and smiled at him.

"It is acceptable to me for you to look at me, Trent," she said.

Her voice appearing to express the new sensation of passion simmering inside of her, Trent knew that the night ahead could not come soon enough.

"It is enough for me to be able to be with you tonight, Isabella," he said, not attempting to hide the pleading in his voice. "Help me to be patient … please."

His comment was met with her giggling once more, but she said nothing.

After the two of them climbed out of the pool, they sat beside one another on the large rocks nearby to dry out. As they lay on the rock formations, Trent considered the design of them. They seemed to be shaped like they were meant to provide flat platforms for an extended human body to lie along. Perhaps their very existence was for people to lie in that spot and dry out with the sun heating from above and the heating of the rocks from underneath. For a brief moment, he wondered who really was the more technically advanced. People in the modern world who needed all sorts of gadgets to do anything at all? Or people like those of the village who had mastered how to survive and be happy with so little?

CHAPTER 37

"Village members," Elder Rhys called out to the crowd that had gathered around the large water fountain near the temple. "Tonight is the night that our beloved Isabella pairs with her chosen mate, Trent. The other ancients and I have looked into each of these young people and looked forward. We, the ancient collective, approve of this match. Is there anyone here who does not approve of it? Please speak now if there is."

Isabella was surprised at the question in his speech. It was the first pairing she'd attended herself. She hadn't known it was open for anyone to object if they felt the need to.

Instinctively she looked around the sea of faces until she found the one that was most important to her. For a moment, she wondered if Adrian would stand up and speak. Instead, she saw him smile at her and nod. Although it was a small gesture, it was enough to tell her that all would be well in their friendship.

"Very well. Isabella and Trent, please step toward me," Elder Rhys said and waited as the two did as he'd instructed. "You are both honorable and good. You have asked to be paired, and it is granted. You shall now take your place among our people as one. You will do your duty to help our society continue to survive through procreation and the delivery of children. Is this a responsibility that you accept as part of your pairing?"

"Yes," they both responded, looking intently at each other.

"Then it is so," the ancient said, nodding at each of them. "Isabella and Trent, please retire to the pairing chamber for this night."

Trent watched the ancient and then looked around the people who had amassed for the simple ceremony. It was a far different type than the grandiose weddings he'd attended in his previous world. For a moment, he couldn't help but think about the woman he'd last walked away from. She'd wanted the biggest wedding of all. She'd been one of those people who'd desired not the marriage, but instead the perception of glamour and money that came from having a showy wedding.

He pushed the thought from his mind. He felt relieved to not only have escaped that situation but to have left the entire 'high society' behind. Although he'd always appreciated and made use of money, it had never been what was important in his heart. His heart. That was now taken forever. He knew that for certain as he turned and looked at Isabella. She was his present and his future. There was nothing scary about that.

The two of them seemed to be simply dismissed as the ancient and all of the village people slowly dispersed and went their own ways to their own homes.

As Isabella led the way to the pairing chamber, she held Trent's hand tightly. She felt no different, knowing she would sleep with her body next to his. She wanted that. She knew nothing about what was to come, but it did not scare her.

Walking in, the two of them could see that the room had been prepared with candles that smelled like the lavender-colored roses that climbed the tall outer walls of the village. There were cups and a large vase of water, from which Trent poured them each a drink.

Despite all of the sexual experience he'd gained throughout his adult life, Trent was nervous. His night with Isabella would be different. Not only did he believe she was a virgin, but he also suspected that she didn't know anything about sexual pleasure. In his world and time, sex was talked about all the time. He suspected it was never spoken of in the ancient village. The thought that she knew nothing both fuelled him and made him determined to take his time and make sure that things were slow for her.

After sipping her water, Isabella moved forward toward the bed that sat in the middle of the room. There, she lay down. She looked at him in anticipation as he slowly walked over and lay down beside her.

They faced one another, both reaching out and caressing the other's cheek before leaning in and kissing softly. There was no need to hold back. They were where everyone knew they were. They were to do what everyone knew they were to do. Despite their growing desire to be closer since the moment they'd met, neither felt any need to rush.

Isabella savored the kisses. She did not know how it all worked, but she knew that she wanted to keep kissing him. She couldn't get enough of that. Already it felt like she had waited an eternity for the right time when she could keep kissing him without having any real reason to stop.

As their kissing deepened, Trent felt his hunger increase. He groaned in the realization that she, too, was kissing with a slight sliver of aggression. It was something natural inside of her - something glorious, waiting to be set free.

Isabella felt a need to be free of the barriers between them. She pulled away from him and stood up to remove her shoes. As she did so, she saw him do the same.

Both standing, Trent pulled her tight against him and kissed her deeply. The sensation made her moan in the depth of her throat. It was a sound that further heated him.

She ran her hands over his arms and chest, through the fabric of his shirt, before she removed it from him, revealing his chest to her. It wasn't the first time she'd seen him like that, but something about the two of them being alone made it seem different to her. She wanted to see more of him.

Trent kissed her neck as she wrapped her arms around him again, her hands naturally beginning to caress his back. Trent could feel her body wanting to give in and follow her natural sense of desire and passion. He remained as he was for a long time. He held her and kissed a soft part of her neckline that she appeared to enjoy having kissed.

Suddenly, he saw her stand back from him. He watched as she lifted her shift dress and removed it completely, leaving her naked in front of him. He breathed out a deep breath at the sight. She was utter perfection. The life that her people lived comprised of no stress, no preservatives, no meat, no fat, and no salt. The combination of so many aspects of modern life not existing for her people had resulted in them being of a natural human form. She was exquisite. Her shapely but toned body, combined with her long red hair flowing down her back, made Trent reach another level of hunger.

He quickly shed his clothing and immediately saw her look at him from head to toe, stopping for a long while at where he couldn't hide his arousal. She looked alarmed at first but then seemed to relax once more as she climbed onto the bed and lay down on her back. Although she appeared to be waiting for him to join with her, Trent had a long way to go before that would happen - a *very* long way.

~~~~~

Isabella watched him move over her and braced herself. She didn't know what he would do to her, but she had to be ready, so told herself that she was. Instead of advancing on her in such a way, she felt him hover over her, kissing her lips gently and moving between them and her neck. The feeling being blissful to her, she reached out with her hands and stroked him wherever she could reach - his hair, his neck, his back, his shoulders, his arms. Touching him felt as heavenly as how it felt when he kissed her.

Isabella felt him move slightly as he kissed down over her breasts, using his tongue to lick the tips of them. A jolt flowed through her body that was new to her. Although it surprised her, she liked it very much. He remained there for a long time before moving further still.

Gently he nudged her legs apart and kissed her thighs while his hands caressed up and down her legs. Isabella next felt something of a magnitude she had never known could be done with two bodies. She looked down and saw that what was causing such a feeling was him
~~~~~

kissing her where he was. It was exquisite. She didn't try and stop him from doing what he wanted to do to her. She had no desire whatsoever to *ever* stop him from doing what he was presently doing to her.

Trent was entranced. Her body was so natural, even down to the fact that she had natural hair around her groin. That was something that every woman he'd ever been with had worked hard to eliminate and never have when he was with them. He found that not only did he not mind her having hair there, but he loved it. It was natural and untouched. Something about that only fuelled him on further.

She was far more relaxed than Trent had thought she might be for her first time, but he could feel and see her body writhing so much that it appeared to be a natural thing for her to do. She was instinctively sexual as a woman. That thought amazed him. He had left behind so many fake people - people who worked so hard to not be who they naturally were. The simple honesty of Isabella was a beautiful thing to him.

He lapped at her, determined to remain patient until he could see her experience orgasm. That, he realized, would be different for her. It would be *completely* different because she possibly had no awareness of there even being such a thing as an orgasm.

"Oh, Trent, what is happening?" she asked.

The words made him smile. He knew women. He knew she was starting to venture toward climax. He pulled away long enough to talk to her and soothe her.

"It is alright, Isabella," he said quietly. "Relax and let it flow over you. It is nothing to fear."

Isabella took his word for it and let her head rest back once more as she felt him resume his attentions to her. She felt her body tensing again. This time she remained still and let it happen. Soon she felt her body reach an entirely new place that she had never known existed. She felt different parts of her body lightly dancing as if she were alive with new feelings all over her.

When she relaxed, Trent moved forward and kissed her on the lips once more. He loved how she instinctively put her hands on his hips and pulled him to her. He nestled between her legs for a long while as they kissed deeply. He then looked at her, maintaining her eye contact as he nudged forward only the slightest amount. Once there, at the very outer edge of her, he lay still again and kissed her more. He enjoyed delivering light kisses to her lips and her neck while feeling her hands moving over his back.

"Isabella..." he breathed out, close to not being able to hold back for much longer. "I must ... move into you," he said quietly, almost as a whisper.

"I am ready," she said, running her hand through his hair and pulling him to kiss her again as he edged in a little more.

He would not rush her, even though he was almost at a breaking point. As if reading his desperation, Isabella naturally lifted her hips toward him. As a result, Trent found himself deeper inside of her.

It was a completely new feeling for Isabella, but not one she disliked. She felt like it was what her body had been wanting even since before she had come face to face with Trent. It had known there was something needed. Finally, she felt like she'd found it.

With his own climax dangerously close, Trent pushed the final journey into her until he was buried as deeply as he could be. He moved outward and inward one more time before he released, determined to orgasm deep within her to ensure the best chance of her conceiving. It was pleasure, but it was also something the community expected to happen to produce a child.

Isabella felt and heard him reach the same point she had. Afterward, he seemed to slump on her, quiet and thoughtful for a moment before he kissed her again. He didn't rush to move. She was glad. It was the most special moment of her life to date. She didn't want him to pull away too soon. She wanted to lie still, joined with him for as long as possible.

"Are you alright? Did I hurt you?" Trent asked her with tenderness in his voice as his hand lightly caressed her hair and cheek. His questions were greeted by a smile on her face.

"I am alright. You did not hurt me," she replied, looking into his eyes. "This is new for me, but I like being this close to you."

Trent watched her face as she said the words. He wondered at his decision to have taken sex so lightly in his life before. He couldn't remember that he'd ever before been with a woman for her first time. The fact that he couldn't remember distressed him. It was a further reminder of how little he'd regarded people in the past.

He prepared to move off her, suddenly aware that his weight was on her, but she only held him closer.

"Please do not go yet," Isabella said. "Can we stay like this for longer? It feels nice." Seeing an intense blush on her face made Trent's heart flutter. "Having you … inside of me … being joined like this feels nice."

He kissed her with the intense longing and emotion that he felt inside of him. How he had come to be in such a place with such a woman, he had no idea, but it felt like he had always been moving towards her. It almost seemed as if he'd been nudged along by life and fate, with every intention of ensuring the two of them became one, entwined together as they presently were.

As their kissing deepened, he felt himself growing once more. He heard her moan at the sensation, as if she did not realize what was happening. He took his time, moving only a small amount and with great care in the speed of his movements. Pulling away from their kiss, he looked into her eyes to make sure she wasn't in any discomfort but only saw arousal at the movements he was creating in her.

Isabella had not known that pairing with someone could feel like it already did. She had thought they would have to join once, and then she would be with child. She had not anticipated the feelings that were occurring in her from them being joined as they were. She had not known that it would not be only once that they did it. The revelation made her smile. If they would keep doing such an act to create children, it was something she would relish for the rest of her life.

Having climaxed so soon before, Trent maintained a steady rhythm inside of her over a longer time. He could see on her face and hear in her sounds that she was enjoying the sensations she was experiencing. It drove him on to make it last even longer and to let her become familiar with everything that was happening between them.

When Isabella started to naturally move her hips underneath him, meeting his movements with hers, she heard him groan. It drove her on to keep doing it.

With the intensity of her moving in such a way, Trent could not hold back anymore.

Isabella heard and felt him climax again.

"Oh, Isabella," he breathed out heavily as his body convulsed.

He relaxed on top of her for a moment and then lifted himself out of her. Remaining as close to her as he could, he maneuvered them so they could both move under the covers they had been lying on top of. Once settled, he pulled her into his arms, her head rested on his chest, and he kissed her forehead softly. Such a part of being entwined with her - the lovemaking - he had not thought would be as overwhelming to him, given how many women he'd previously been with. The opposite was true. Lying with her in his arms, he felt like he had finally found home.

Isabella lay quietly and felt herself falling asleep. Her body finally grew relaxed in the knowledge that it had undergone something new and exciting. She wondered if a child had already been formed. The thought made her smile against his chest. Hearing Trent's breathing deepen to indicate sleep, she let herself also drift off, the smile secure on her face.

CHAPTER 38

Trent woke the next morning to find Isabella lying beside him, watching him. Pulling her close and kissing her softly, he intended it as a light good morning kiss. Instead, it caught with her, like a match to a flint. With no hesitation, she moved her body against his and turned the soft kiss into a passionate one.

"Please," he heard her say quietly, seeming to him to want him to move inside her.

Trent lowered his finger down while he kissed her and encouraged her body to relax as he caressed her at her core. At the same time, he felt her hand move down and touch him. It wasn't long before he felt her convulsing against his hand.

It was the first time Isabella had touched a man in such a way. She found the sensation of holding him to be strange, but it woke her up even more as she heard him moan quietly at her touching him.

Lying side by side, Trent moved so that he was at the right height to pull her uppermost leg over his hip. There he slowly nudged into her. He saw Isabella's eyes go wide at the different position. Once adjusted, she seemed to naturally find her way and started to move with him once more. It didn't take long at all before Trent found himself lost in the sea of pleasure again.

Finally, both satisfied, he kissed her softly again before he saw her smile at him.

"I like this," she said shyly.

Trent laughed softly at her. "So do I."

"We must leave here this morning, and then we shall live in our own home," she said.

Trent nodded before laying soft kisses over her lips, forehead, and cheeks.

"I must find an occupation," he said and saw her look at him curiously. "If I am living here, I must contribute. Who would I speak to about what I should do?"

"We all find our own place - everyone except me," Isabella said. "I am still trying to find my place, but what did you do where you came from?"

Trent found himself wondering how to even answer that question, given that he'd been a software designer.

"I did not do anything like what the people here do," he said. "I would like to try some different things and see if I have any skills in anything that can be of use to the village."

Isabella nodded at him. She understood perfectly the uncertainty of not knowing which aspects of village life one was meant to help others with.

"Let us go to the morning meal. Then I shall introduce you to some people in different parts of the village," she said. "You can talk to them and see who needs help. Perhaps that will help you decide."

Trent kissed her, taking one more moment to look at her as she was. Her natural state of being relaxed and sated continued to intrigue him. He knew he could lie and look at her all day. Determined to be better than that, he started to pull away and dress.

"Yes, let us go and eat," he said to her. "I shall not get anything done today if I keep lying here and looking at your beautiful face and lovely body."

Isabella heard the compliment and blushed heavily, but smiled at him and moved to dress also.

Once ready, and having tidied the room, they left together, stepping out into the sunshine on their first morning as a paired couple.

CHAPTER 39

"Isabella," Adrian addressed her as she sat down beside him with Trent settling on the other side of her. "Are you well?" he asked her quietly.

"I am well, Adrian," she replied, smiling.

"Good morning, Adrian," Trent said quietly, and after a moment found the greeting returned.

"Adrian, how is work at the mill? Is there need of another hand down there?" Isabella asked her lifelong friend and saw him nod in acknowledgment.

"It has been slow with the water flow slower than usual, but it has been increasing once more in recent days. Do you wish to work in the mill, Trent?" Adrian asked the traveler.

Trent looked uncertain before he answered.

"I do not know yet what I can do," he said. "I thought I might spend some time in different areas as I am needed until it becomes clear where I should be."

Adrian nodded.

"I can take you down to the mill after we finish eating if you wish," he said. "The mill has many aspects to it. There will be many things you can try to see if you wish to keep working there."

"Thank you," he heard Trent say.

Adrian wanted to not like the traveler, being the one who had secured Isabella's heart, and so quickly. There was nothing he could sense about Trent that would warrant such a harsh judgment, so conceded he had to let go of any difficulty in his feelings. Looking closely at Isabella and studying her face, Adrian could only see great happiness. He had to appreciate the traveler for that.

~~~~~

After finishing their food, all three washed and put away their dishes. Once out in the sunshine, Isabella turned to Trent.

"I will go and do some chores now," she said and pulled him close to her. "I will see you at the evening meal?"

Trent nodded at her, drinking in her beauty before pulling her even closer and kissing her. When they parted, he saw her smile at Adrian before she then walked back into the kitchen.

"I believe that you do very much love her, Trent," he heard Adrian
~~~~~

say, and redirected his view to the man beside him.

"I do," Trent replied as they started to walk. "I love her very much."

"It is good to see my friend so happy," Adrian said, nodding.

Trent considered the words. He had thought Adrian wished to pair with Isabella himself, and yet there was no hint of malice in his voice at all.

"I will always work to make her happy, Adrian," Trent said. "You have my word on that."

The two of them walked the rest of the way in silence, each in their own thoughts.

~~~~~

On return to the kitchen, Isabella sought out Cook Mary.

"Ahh, Miss Isabella. How are you today?" she asked with a gleam in her eye that made Isabella laugh.

"I am well, Cook Mary," Isabella said, grinning. "How can I help you this morning?"

"Yes, please collect the eggs that are waiting, and then perhaps some spinach. Take this basket with you. After getting the eggs, fill the basket to the top with as much spinach as you can fit in there, and that will be lovely for a nice spinach and egg pie for our evening meal."

Isabella nodded and smiled.

"Of course," she said before walking out into the sunshine once more. For a moment, she stood still, feeling its warmth on her face.

"Daughter," she heard her mother's voice say from beside her. "Are you well?"

Isabella smiled at her mother, Crisiana, before feeling bold enough to lean in and put her arms around her. It was a move that was rare and seemed to surprise her mother.

"Yes, I am very well, Mother," Isabella replied.

Crisiana looked at her daughter and could see on her face that the evening had been a success and would hopefully result in a child soon. She said nothing more to Isabella, instead smiling at her and then walking along as always, as part of her day.

Isabella watched her mother walk away. They had always been close but had seemed shyer of one another in recent years. Isabella found herself wanting to be close to her again if there was a chance she was already with child.

Dispelling the thought, she moved on with her chores. After gathering eggs from the chickens and going to the garden to get the spinach, she took all back to the kitchen.

"Can I help you with anything else, Cook Mary?" she asked.

For a moment, Isabella felt a distinct feeling of loneliness. It was an odd thing to have experienced, but she accepted it. She'd felt it before. It
~~~~~

came now and then. It would pass.

"Oh, no," replied the cook. "Thank you, Miss Isabella. This is all that I needed."

Isabella once again stepped outside, feeling an emptiness inside of her. She walked to where the tailors worked and looked at them longingly.

"Miss Isabella, do you require new clothing? Or perhaps something mended?"

"No," she replied, unintentionally sighing at the same time. She saw the elderly woman move closer to where she stood.

"You sound as if you need an occupation, young one," the woman said.

"Yes, I think you may be right," replied Isabella. "I know that I help people when I am needed, but I do not have an established thing that I do each day. I feel as if I should."

Her words were greeted with a smile from the woman before her.

"You have just had your pairing, have you not?" she asked and saw Isabella nod with a touch of blush on her face. "Then I think your place will soon be centered around raising a youngling, Isabella. Being a mother is the most demanding role of all. Do not underestimate how taxing it can be, or how incredibly rewarding it can be. Be patient and a child will come. Then you may find yourself wishing you had *more* time."

Isabella nodded, smiled, and then bid the older woman farewell. Not sure where to go or what to do, she walked down to the pool. Seeing no-one there, she waded in, wearing her shift dress as she always did. She blissfully relaxed into the warm water. After a long while, she moved to sit against the far side of the pool and closed her eyes. In the background, she listened to the waterfall while she remembered the night before.

She was in awe of how the night had panned out. So many things about it she had been unprepared for - not just the act of child making itself, but also how wonderful it would feel. It was something no-one had ever talked to her about. She had embarked on it completely blind. Despite her inexperience, she believed that she and Trent had fitted well together and both had equally enjoyed their time together. The way he had made her feel when he'd touched and kissed her, and the way he'd felt when inside her, was a beautiful thing. She could not wait to do with him again and again.

As if she had sent the thought directly to him, she heard his voice break through her memories.

"You are thinking about pleasurable things, I think," Trent called out to her.

Isabella was briefly startled. When she opened her eyes and saw him at the edge of the pool, the feeling was replaced by happiness and eagerness to see him.

Trent had watched her for several minutes, looking at her face and the serenity of it, combined with a slight blush that he thought might mean she was thinking about their time together.

As she smiled at him, he felt the need to be closer to her. He removed his shoes and shirt before walking into the pool and directly over to her. As he stood in front of her, he kissed her. In turn, she moved both of them so that he was sitting on the submerged ledge and she was in front of him. As if it were the most natural thing in the world for her to do, she straddled him and put her arms around him to kiss him deeply. The combined confidence of her, and the physical feelings evoked, made Trent moan even though he wanted to be silent, being outdoors.

They broke apart. Both looked around before Isabella felt his fingers find their way under the water, reaching up under the hem of her dress and start to stroke her as he had done that morning. She didn't try and stop him. With the passion she felt, she kissed him again while she was taken to that place once more. She felt herself rise and then give way to incredible release.

Trent watched her face as she sat slightly apart from him. It wasn't long before he felt her hand reach down under the water and begin caressing him through his pants.

"Can we?" she asked as if reading his exact thoughts of that moment.

Subtly, he reached down and slid down the top of his trousers, just enough to set himself free. Pulling Isabella to him, he saw her eyes change in her level of desire as she realized they could join even under the water.

It took some minor movements and adjustments for both of them, but then she began moving down on him. Her movements were subtle enough that if anyone appeared in the area, it wouldn't be too obvious what they were doing.

Trent alternated between kissing her lips, kissing her neck, and watching her face. Her expressions were astounding to watch. That, combined with the exquisite feeling of her body moving up and down on him, and the warmth of the water around him, resulted in him reaching his final point, forgetting for the moment to be quiet.

Suddenly, he heard her giggle. When he opened his eyes, he saw her looking around, checking that no-one else was around.

"You must not be so loud," she whispered into his ear with extreme amusement evident in her voice.

Trent held her tight as he laughed softly.

"Yes. You just looked so beautiful," he said before she kissed him.

After a long time of kissing, Isabella edged off him so he could resurrect his clothing under the water. When he had, she straddled him once again.

"You went to the mill with Adrian?" Isabella asked.

"Yes, I visited and watched different people doing different jobs, but they do not need me there now," replied Trent. "I shall return tomorrow after breakfast and help then."

"We have the rest of today to spend together?" Isabella asked.

For a moment, as he looked at her face, Trent wondered how much his body could take in one day. Prior to their night of pairing, it had been so long since he'd subjected his body to physical pleasure.

Isabella saw him laugh at her, and the sight made her laugh with him.

"What did you have in mind?" he asked, resolved that it didn't matter how his body felt. He wanted her just as much as she seemed to want him. There was no point in fighting that.

"We have not yet been in our home," Isabella said.

Trent took a moment to think about that. He had never owned a home. It had always been out of his reach financially, with the high-living life he had chosen for himself. To think that the people in the village simply lived in homes for the duration of their lives and then they were handed to someone else once empty, without any consideration for anything financial, was astounding to him. It wouldn't work in the modern world. In the village, it obviously did.

"Then I think we should go and see our home," he said. "Shall we sit in the sun for a while to dry out and then go and make ourselves at home?"

CHAPTER 40

Isabella approached the door tentatively as if it did not feel right to be entering the home. She had known the previous occupants. They had been an elderly couple who had always been there since she'd been born. They'd left the world more than a year earlier, but the small home had remained empty since then, still seeming to be theirs.

She felt Trent come up behind her and reach around, placing his hand over hers to show his support, but waiting until she felt ready. Finally, Isabella found strength and opened the door.

Walking inside, Trent again appreciated how simply the people of the village lived. Not needing to eat in their homes, the structure seemed primarily made to house a small table, a few chairs, and two tiny rooms, each with a bed in it. They did not seem to need or wish for anything more. He found himself in awe that people could live with so little, and yet so much of the population of the world he had come from constantly needed more.

Isabella closed the door after them and looked at his face to try and interpret how he was feeling. Knowing nothing of the world he had come from, she had no idea how he would find their home. She needn't have worried.

Once alone again, Trent pulled her into his arms and kissed her, not intending it to be a precursor to lovemaking but simply out of the strength of emotion he was feeling.

"Isabella, this is perfect for you, me, and our children," he said to her, truly believing the words in his overwhelming emotion. "Nothing could be more perfect."

Isabella molded her body against his. A smile formed on her face before she reached up and placed her lips on his again.

Trent groaned in wonder of her eagerness. He was excited, especially considering she was someone who, 24 hours earlier, had never known the pleasures of sex and physical intimacy.

"It may take some time before a child is within me," she said demurely.

The words and the tone made Trent's heart ache at the sight and sound of her. He felt her take his hand in hers as she started to lead him toward the bed.

"We must keep practicing, must we not?" she asked.

Trent found himself smiling shyly at her as he listened to her speak. He could not put his finger on what it was about her. It was like she knew how to affect him directly at his core, even without any outside influence that the world he'd come from provided. The way she moved, the way she looked at him, and the way she kissed him all seemed to come from instinct.

He walked with her as she stepped backward toward the edge of the bed. As he stood with her, he put his arms around her and nudged her so that she moved back. When she lay on the bed, Isabella instinctively wrapped her legs around his hips and held him firmly in her arms. He hadn't intended to grow so aroused so soon after their time in the pool. There was no helping it. His body was screaming at him that it still hadn't had enough of her. He felt his pants become taut once more.

Isabella enjoyed the weight of him on top of her and his body starting to rock back and forth as they kissed deeply. She felt in her a deep and growing hunger to be closer to him. Thoughts of the outside world were once again completely discarded as her mind closed. All she could sense, feel, and think about were the feelings he was invoking in her.

Trent indulged in the feelings that passed between them. Once more, he was confused by how he - someone who had so much sexual experience - could never have felt when he'd been with other women like he did when he was with her.

He let himself settle, wrapped around her, while he absorbed a sense of urgency falling over him. Unable to hold back, he stood up and removed his clothing quickly before returning to her. He pushed her slip dress up and over her head, leaving her naked. Again he took in the sight before him, wondering at how beautiful the natural state of her body was compared to others he'd been with who had worked so hard to be anything but natural.

Isabella pushed him gently onto his back beside her and knelt beside him, looking down and along the length of his body. She studied him, looking from his head to his toes and back again.

Trent trailed her eyes. He felt incredibly vulnerable and open to her. Seeing her looking at him - *really* looking at him, without any diversion to anything else - made him feel drawn into her. Seeing the expressions on her face was something new and never before seen by him. He couldn't remember having ever seen anyone really look at him like that.

As he kept looking at her, he saw and felt her embark on a new journey. She brought up her hands and ran them over his arms, shoulders, and chest. He lay still, as if in a spell, watching her eyes as they moved along with her hands, touching him and caressing him as they explored.

Isabella looked into his eyes to make sure her desire to explore his body was acceptable. When she looked at him, she saw only acceptance and a peaceful calm over him. Moving closer, she bent her head to kiss his lips softly before sitting up again and resuming her exploration. She moved her hands down over his chest and enjoyed the feeling of his belly. It was currently slightly sunken due to his extreme recent weight loss, but she looked forward to seeing him build and fill out as his appetite increased. From there, she moved over and past his most intimate area and down to his feet. Touching each one lightly, she made him jolt away from her fingertips, making her giggle softly.

Trent lay back and felt her hands start to stroke his legs - shins, knees, and up to his thighs. He made no move to hide his arousal. There was no need. She didn't seem embarrassed about him being in that state at all.

"Turn over," she whispered.

Trent negotiated how he could comfortably do that, being as aroused as he was. Finally, he found a half-turned position that presented his back to her. Straight away, he felt her hands moving over his calves, thighs, up over his buttocks, and then over his back and shoulders. The next thing he felt was her kissing the back of his neck softly, just below his hairline. He couldn't help but moan at the sensation.

Under him he was hard, desiring her but not wanting to interrupt her journey of exploration. Hearing her tell him to turn over once more was welcome to him, as was feeling her move over him and lie down along the entire length of him to indulge in kissing him.

Trent wrapped his arms around her and secured her head down with one hand to keep their lips together as he devoured her tongue with his. The sound of her groaning was followed by her moving her body as she took him inside of her. He instantly felt like he would never find anything so perfect in his life. He didn't know where her instinct for it came from, but he couldn't doubt that in every way, it felt like they were made to fit together. He lay still and let her move as she felt she needed to.

Finding her way to let the pleasure increase from the way she was moving, Isabella discovered a new way to reach the same point that Trent had previously taken her to. An intense wave of emotion flowed over her as her body tensed.

Trent felt and heard her climax as she was rubbing against him while he was deep inside her. The sensation of her self-induced pleasure was exquisite and immediately resulted in the same reaction in him. He pumped up into her as her muscles clenched around him.

They lay together with her on top of him, neither moving for some time. Both felt blissfully sated.

Trent kissed her passionately before he heard Isabella laugh softly.

"I think we can do this all day and all night," she said.

Trent laughed in response to her enthusiasm.

"People might miss you if you hide away with me all day and all night," he said.

Isabella gave him the most brilliant smile.

"Yes, you are right," she said with a look of amusement on her face. "Only nights then."

Trent moaned at the thought - both for the consideration of how he had been eager to rest his body and let it recuperate from the long journey to the foreign but magical place, and for the desire he felt for the idea, liking it very much.

Isabella pulled off him and cuddled into him, letting out a sigh of contentment.

The sound inspired Trent to turn and look at her. As he did so, he became aware that he could see a glow appearing on her lower belly. He pulled away from her, thinking that he must be seeing things. When he turned toward her once more and looked more closely, the golden glow was still visible. Not only that, but it was growing stronger and brighter.

"What is it, Trent?" Isabella asked him, seeing the concentration on his face. "You look worried."

Trent looked at her face. Whatever was happening inside of her, she didn't seem to feel it.

"Isabella. Your belly," he said quietly, pointing to the glowing.

Isabella looked downwards and finally saw the small light shining through her skin as if it was translucent. Automatically, she put her hand over it. Through her hand, she felt a warmth of comfort that made her feel extremely protective.

Trent watched her face change as she touched the glow. He then saw her reach her hand out and take his, moving it to her belly. As he touched her skin, he instantly felt the warmth and the pull of it. It was a different kind of feeling. Not being like anything he'd felt before, he found it difficult to determine what it was.

It was impossible to pinpoint, but it felt almost like an extremely strong need to do whatever it would take to protect Isabella. Somehow it inspired in him a determination to be the best man he could be, from that moment in time and on for the rest of his life. As odd as it was, it suddenly seemed as if everything - his future, her future, and the future of everyone - depended upon it.

"How are you glowing like that?" he asked her quietly and saw her shake her head.

"I do not know, but it feels nice. It feels like it is meant to be," she said and saw him nod in agreement.

"Yes," Trent replied simply.

Whatever it was, it made them each feel the pull to look after one another and ensure they both remained calm and happy.

"Is it..." he started to ask. He dismissed the idea, thinking it could not be possible, but the same thought had already blended into Isabella's mind.

"A child? Have we just made a child?" she asked him.

Trent was as surprised as she was to hear the question come from her lips. He touched her belly once more and enjoyed the feeling of the heat before he pulled his hand away. As he did so, the glow began to fade, leaving him wondering if it had indeed happened.

"I must speak to my mother about this," Isabella said. "Perhaps it is normal for this to happen to women?" she asked.

Trent nodded but kept his doubts to himself. He knew of no such thing happening in his time and place. He expected that since the villagers were still human, child-rearing shouldn't be any different, but he had to concede that things *were* different from modern society. He could be no judge of what was normal or not.

"Shall I come with you?" he asked her.

Isabella kissed him again, gently and softly, taking longer to enjoy her lips against his, before she started to move.

"No, I should like to speak to my mother alone, if you do not mind, Trent," she said as she stood up and put on her dress. "She may not feel comfortable with you there when I ask her about such things."

Isabella looked at him, lying naked on the bed. The sight made her smile before she leaned over and kissed him again.

"I very much like the way you look, lying like that," she said with a distinctively suggestive tone in her voice.

Trent found himself blushing once again as if he were the one who had never had sex before. He stood up and pulled her close.

"And you are very beautiful, Isabella," he said. "I am very lucky to be in this place, with you ... paired with you."

They kissed softly before she pulled away.

"I must go. I shall see you perhaps at dinner?" she asked and saw him nod in response.

Isabella ran out the door, eager to find her mother and talk to her. When she finally located Crisiana, she pulled her aside.

"Mother, can I please talk to you about something private?" she asked and immediately saw alarm on the face before her. "It is not about anything bad ... I do not think."

"Of course, Isabella," her mother replied. "Do you wish to talk in our home or elsewhere?"

"Yes, I think inside your home is best," Isabella said, feeling a slight longing for the home she'd grown up in and previously also considered hers. Now she would regard it as only being that of her parents.

The two of them walked to the house. Once inside, her mother invited her to sit and talk.

"Is all well with you and Trent? Is there a problem?" Crisiana asked her daughter, feeling extreme concern. Isabella was normally carefree and happy.

Isabella smiled shyly at her mother.

"All is well, Mother. Trent and I are … happy," she said and felt her face go deep red. The look on her face resulted in a knowing glance from her mother even though Crisiana did not say anything with words. "But I must ask you, when you became with child - when I was in your belly … did you … glow? Here?" she asked, moving her hand to her lower belly to show the location the golden glow had emanated from.

"Glow? No. Glow how?" her mother asked.

"It was like a golden light, coming from my skin," replied Isabella. "When I touched it, I felt warmth from it. Trent could see and feel it also."

"No, Isabella. I do not know what that means. I cannot help you with this. I do not think that happened when you were in my belly," Crisiana said, taking her daughter's hands in her own while a look of concern crossed her face. "Oh my daughter, are you alright? Should we be worried about this?"

"I shall go to the temple to see the elders. They may know what it was…"

"It is not still happening?" asked Crisiana.

Isabella shook her head.

"No, it happened for only a short time this morning," she said and stood up. "I shall go to the temple now. Thank you."

Crisiana hugged her daughter tightly to her before letting her go and watching her walk out of the door.

CHAPTER 41

As Isabella walked into the temple, she once again felt an overwhelming sense of being home. Whenever she entered the large structure, she felt she was where she was meant to be. That was normal. What wasn't normal was her belly growing warm and reacting to it also. She placed her hand over the area and again felt the comfort of heat emanating from it.

She was standing like that when she heard a voice call out to her. For a moment, it startled her.

"Isabella!" she heard Elder Rhys exclaim with more surprise in his voice than she'd heard before.

Isabella saw him move toward her and glance at where her hand rested. When she looked down, she could see the golden glow visible through her dress.

"Elder Rhys. What is it?" she asked, raising her eyes to meet his. "I do not know what is happening."

They both looked down at her belly area. As the ancient moved closer to her, the glowing intensified, growing even more visible through her dress.

Isabella could feel the power growing inside of her. It wasn't a feeling she enjoyed at all.

"Stop!" she called out to the man before her. "Please. As you draw nearer to me, it is growing stronger. I do not think … I do not know … what it is yet."

Although he was an ancient and hundreds of years older than her, Elder Rhys bowed down to her request. He was intrigued by the situation.

"Of course, Isabella," he said quietly, backing away from her. As he did so, both of them could see the strength of the golden light ease off.

"What is it?" she asked him. She naturally expected an ancient to have the answers. Instead, she only saw him look at her, perplexed as he shook his head.

"I have heard of some women who were destined to be ancients going through this, Isabella, but it has not happened in my lifetime, so I cannot say for sure," Elder Rhys said. "Your time is not yet. I do not know how or if this could be related."

Isabella took a moment to decipher what he'd just said. He'd mentioned the possibility before, but she'd dismissed it.

"You truly think that I am destined to be … an ancient?" she finally asked.

"Oh yes, I have no doubt about that," he replied. "You are a chosen one, Isabella. You are destined to live a very long life. Over your lifetime, you will learn many secrets, and you will develop your powers fully."

Isabella looked at him, surprised.

"My *powers?*" she asked.

"You know already that you have the power to heal through touch. You brought Trent back to life," Elder Rhys said. He paused a long while before asking his next question. He knew it was a personal one but felt that the answer was incredibly important, not only to him but also to their people. "As for what we have just seen … what you have just *felt* … you and Trent have … joined in love?"

Isabella felt her face darken in unease at the personal nature of the question but nodded.

"Yes."

"I have never seen such a thing, but I do believe that it must be your child, Isabella," he said. "You and Trent saw each other long before he came here, and now he has been able to successfully establish himself among us, in our time. The two of you, I believe, were always meant to be. That means both of you have been chosen, Isabella, perhaps for a higher calling … a greater purpose … but perhaps for the creation of the youngling now growing in you. I think that he - or she - is where your path has been leading you toward all of your life. The child will be chosen also."

"But I do not know if there *is* a child yet," Isabella said, confused about what was happening within her.

She saw Elder Rhys look at her with a look of calm, acceptance, and kindness.

"I think you do know, Isabella," he said. "You feel it. You can feel its strength within you - the combined strength of you and Trent. Focus on it and let the feelings engulf you. I think it is fair to say that you *are* with child now."

Isabella remained quiet, allowing herself to feel the plethora of emotions flowing through her. There was excitement that it could be true, and she might be carrying Trent's child. There was fear about what the combined strength of them meant. He had crossed distance and time to be with her. The result was something new that no-one had seen. Nobody knew what would follow on from that. She felt happy that she'd been so lucky to find such love finally, after thinking that she would never find it. She also felt sadness that if she already were with child, her private time with Trent may have to end, at least for the moment.

CHAPTER 42

Back in their home, Trent sat quietly for a short time after Isabella had left. His thoughts focused on the mystery surrounding the golden glow he had seen coming from her belly. When he'd touched her there, he had felt energy similar to what he'd felt when he had touched the ground upon his arrival at the village. It also resembled the power he'd felt when he'd touched the golden rock that had enabled him to change over. It was a power that he already knew could be all-consuming. That kind of power made him fearful.

The possibility that his child, only really hours or even minutes old in its first stages of formation yet, could emanate that kind of power, made him wary. He was reluctant to yet believe that could be the situation.

He lay down, using the moment alone to let his thoughts go free about all that had happened so far. Eventually, he felt his body relax once more. His mind finally found peace. He did not know what he could do for, with, or about Isabella. He put trust in her mother or the ancients for being able to provide her with guidance. If she were pregnant, there would be a child to raise, and she will have finally found her place in their village. She will have found a place that she seemed to have been seeking for a long time, wondering where she was supposed to be and what she was supposed to be doing.

In contrast, Trent still had to find a place to fit in and a way to contribute. He sensed that everyone in the village just got on and did the tasks that they naturally veered toward. So far, he didn't know what that meant for him. In one way, he was regretful that in his former life, he had chosen to get caught up in working with computers. That had been something that didn't even prepare him for being able to survive should something major happen, such as a grand scale electricity outage. Really, in his thirty years of life so far, he hadn't at all learned how to simply survive. He did not know how to grow food. The food that he knew how to cook, came from other food that was processed. It was never entirely fresh.

With that thought, he quickly jumped up and got dressed. He was determined to learn, at the very least, what he could about the land. Growing things. He had never done that in his life but at the very core of humanity was the basic need to be able to eat to survive. It was as good a place as any to begin living a different life. He would still go to the mill the next day as he had told Adrian he would, but for the remainder of the day, he would go to the garden and find someone to start teaching him the basics of growing food for survival.

CHAPTER 43

Isabella left the temple no less confused about what was happening in her body than she had been before her visit. She walked out into the sunshine, absorbing the simple joy it provided. In that, there was never anything of concern.

After visiting her home and seeing Trent was not there, she went to the kitchen to ask the cooks if they needed any assistance.

"Oh, yes, please, Miss Isabella," the cook said, grinning at her. "Your timing is perfect. Can you go down to the garden and fill this basket with tomatoes, please? The reddest ones that are there so I can slow cook them overnight for a tomato and mushroom pie for tomorrow."

Isabella smiled at the cook and took the basket, glad to have an occupation to take her mind off things. Upon arrival at the vast growing area, she was surprised to see Trent kneeling on the ground beside one of the gardeners, listening intently to what he was saying.

As she approached, both looked up at her. Instantly Trent jumped up to go to her, kissing her softly before she turned to the gardener.

"Master Martin, Cook Mary has asked me to fill this basket with the ripest tomatoes. Shall I get them?" she asked before seeing the man stand and walk to her.

"Oh no, Miss Isabella! I shall get those for you. Master Trent here has come here today to ask to learn about gardening so he can come with me … if you wish," the gardener said, redirecting his sentence to Trent.

"Yes, of course," Trent replied, reluctantly moving away from Isabella.

Standing back, Isabella watched with amusement as he trotted off on an adventure to learn something new.

When they came back, Isabella took the basket and found Trent eager to walk with her.

"Did you go to the temple?" he asked her, having spent time trying unsuccessfully to not worry about her.

Isabella nodded at him as she smiled softly.

"I did. Elder Rhys is not certain, but he thinks that we do now have a child growing inside of me," she said while subconsciously moving her hand to cover her belly. "He is not certain what the golden glow means, but he thinks that you are a chosen one also, Trent. That is why we dreamed of each other, and why we could see each other in both times."

Trent stopped walking suddenly and looked at her.

"*I* am a chosen one?" he asked. "But that cannot be. I am not even of your people..."

"I know, but it is what he believes," Isabella replied, putting down the basket long enough to move closer to him and put her arms around him, something he eagerly received as he looked down into her eyes. "I do not want us to just focus on this, Trent. I have only just found you. We have only just ... begun..." she said, feeling herself begin to blush. "I would like us to move forward as normal and see what happens but not stop our journey of getting to know one another."

Trent kissed her lips and nodded at her.

"Yes," he said. "I surely do not know enough about you yet to already stop learning. Are you walking to the kitchen with this?" he asked and picked up the basket when Isabella nodded at him. "I shall walk you there."

"How did you like the gardening?" she asked him, eager to change the subject.

Trent smiled broadly at her.

"I liked it very much," he replied. "I think that is what I wish to learn and do, but I shall go to the mill soon and talk to Adrian to see if they will need me down there."

When they approached the kitchen, Isabella turned to him.

"I shall walk with you to the mill if you will wait for me. I should like to see Adrian, also," she said.

Trent nodded and watched her walk into the kitchen area.

"Here you go, Cook Mary," Isabella called out. She was immediately greeted with excitement.

"Oh, Miss Isabella!" the cook exclaimed. "They are the reddest tomatoes we have had for a long while. Thank you so much."

Isabella laughed at the cook's enthusiasm before waving and turning back to Trent. When he held out his hand to welcome hers into it, she gladly accepted the gesture.

They walked in silence, each in their own thoughts until they reached the mill. As they entered, Adrian immediately saw them from where he was moving bags of grain.

"What are you doing here?" he asked both of them with a smile on his face.

"Trent wishes to talk to you about work, and I just wanted to see you," Isabella said.

As she spoke, Trent saw an intensive look of admiration appear on Adrian's face as he looked at her. Although Trent didn't want to feel it, for a moment, he felt a little jealous. It was an absurd thing to feel. If the two of them had been meant to be together, they would have paired before he'd arrived. He shook the thought quickly from his mind.

Hearing and watching Isabella speak, Adrian found himself captivated for a moment. As he'd done many times before, he shook his head and forced himself to wake up and come back to the present moment. She was his lifelong friend. Any chance of that ever changing had now been extinguished forever.

"Of course," he said, refocusing on Trent. "How can I be of assistance to you?"

"When I was here this morning, I assisted, but I feel like I am pulled in another direction, Adrian. I wish to work in the garden, but I did say I would come back here tomorrow…"

Adrian watched Trent speak and sensed a concern that might flow over to Isabella. To prevent that, he called one of the elders over and asked Trent to speak to him.

"Oh no, that is understandable, Trent," the elder before them said. "We all have to find our own way and our own place. If it is the garden that is calling you, that is where you should go."

"Thank you," Trent replied.

He continued to be astonished that such decisions were not so easy at all in the world that he'd recently left behind. So many things were different in the older society but only for the good. He'd even become aware of how his language was changing, the more he spoke to people of the village. No slang. No swearing. No anger. He found himself continuing to question whether the world, in moving forward into modern society, really had changed for the better.

Broken from his brief thoughts, Trent watched the elder nod, smile, and quietly walk away.

"Will you go to the evening meal now?" Adrian asked and saw Isabella nod. "I shall walk with you then."

CHAPTER 44

During their meal, Adrian leaned in close to her to whisper in her ear.

"Isabella, can I still talk to you?" he asked and saw her nod in reply. "In private?"

Isabella looked at him and nodded again. He was usually a confident and merry person. As he voiced his questions, he looked less so.

"Yes, of course you can, Adrian," she said. "Do you *need* to talk to me in private?"

Adrian smiled sadly at her.

"If I can…" he said, sounding doubtful.

"Why would you not?" Isabella asked, confused.

"Trent…"

Trent heard his name mentioned and looked around from his side of Isabella.

"Are you talking to me, Adrian? I am sorry. Did I miss something?" he asked and immediately saw Adrian go a shade of red.

"No," Isabella said. "Adrian would like to talk to me alone. After dinner I shall spend some time with him, Trent, if you have no objection."

"Oh! Oh no, of course not," Trent said. "Adrian, you do not have to feel awkward about asking such a thing. You and Isabella have been friends for your whole lives…"

"Yes, but now she is paired with you…" Adrian replied, his face showing a slight discomfort.

"Yes … but that should not - and *will* not - change her friendship with you," Trent assured Adrian, surprised even at himself for not feeling jealousy over their friendship. As he finished his meal, he stood up, then leaned down to kiss Isabella before moving away. "I will go home and see you when you return."

Isabella nodded at him and watched him walk away, wondrous again at where he came from and what the two of them meeting actually meant.

"I am sorry, Isabella," said Adrian. "I did not intend for him to leave."

"Adrian, he had finished eating," Isabella replied. "There is nothing to worry about. Now it is just the two of us. Talk to me. What has you so serious today?"

She saw Adrian look around him as if scared someone would hear.

Finally, his eyes rested on hers, and he spoke.

"I think it is time for me to pair also, Isabella. I wish to ask Kat," he said and immediately saw Isabella burst out laughing. "What is so funny?" he asked. Her reaction had instantly left him feeling surprisingly vulnerable.

"Oh, Adrian!" Isabella exclaimed. "Of course you should do that! She has been yearning after you for so long."

"What are you talking about, Isabella? You do talk nonsense sometimes," he replied. The mock look of surprise and disbelief on his face made her laugh harder.

"No, I do not!" she said.

Adrian couldn't help but begin to laugh with her. They'd not shared any true fun in a long time. It felt good to feel relaxed in her presence once more.

"I take it from your response that you have no objection then?" he asked after a long time, his tone changing again.

"Why would I object to you finding someone to pair with?" she asked and took his hand in hers. "Be happy. I am."

Adrian felt some loss and sadness flow over him. He hid it, squeezing her hand and smiling at her.

"Thank you," he said quietly.

"You are my dearest friend," Isabella reassured him.

"Maybe I *was* your dearest friend…"

"Why do you say such a thing?" she asked in surprise. "Why do you think we are not still friends?"

"No, I just meant that now Trent is…"

"Adrian, no matter how much it appears that he and I should be together, to share our lives, I barely know Trent. The person I know best of all is *you!*" Isabella said. "I will never turn my back on that. I will never turn my back on *you*. I believe that you will feel the same way when you are paired…"

As if sensing she were the object of conversation, Kat appeared beside them, sitting down near Adrian.

"Hello Kat," Isabella said before starting to rise. "I shall leave you two alone." She put her hand on Adrian's shoulder and squeezed it before exchanging a smile with him.

As she walked away from them, she felt a moment of sadness. The words she had said - that she knew Adrian intensely and hardly knew Trent at all - had been true. Despite that, it *did* seem that she and Trent were meant to be together. Something higher than all of them had made it so, and who were they to deny it.

CHAPTER 45

On her way home, Isabella found herself drawn to the temple. She stopped in front of it. Anyone seeing her might have thought she was looking at the front façade of it. As she stood and faced it front on, she felt a warmth in her belly that. For that moment, she wanted to stand still and focus on it.

"Isabella," she heard in her mind. It was a woman's voice that was calling to her. "Step into the temple, child. Do not stand outside."

Isabella opened her eyes, wondering if what she'd just heard was real. She looked around her but saw no-one who could have spoken to her. At first, uncertain of whether to return to her home or do as the voice had requested, she found her curiosity heightened to a point where she knew she could not just walk away.

Stepping forward, she entered through the large doorway and slowly made her way through the chambers.

"Isabella, are you alright?" she heard a man's voice ask. When she turned around, she saw Elder Rhys looking at her. Concern was evident on his face.

"I..." she stammered, keeping her distance from him as she remembered the earlier feelings she'd experienced when she'd stood close to him. "I heard a voice. It told me to come in here."

She watched the face of the ancient before her. He looked surprised and then startled.

"My voice?" Elder Rhys asked.

Isabella shook her head in response.

"No, it was a woman's voice," she replied.

"What did the voice say?"

"She said my name, and then she told me to come into the temple," Isabella informed him.

Elder Rhys looked at her with confusion in his thoughts.

"There is no woman here, Isabella."

"Perhaps it was another ancient..." she started to reply but saw him shake his head.

"No," he said. "There are no women ancients at present. You will be the next one, I suspect, but for now, there are no other women here."

"Perhaps just one of the elders..." she said, trying to figure it out, like a deep puzzle that was testing her.

Elder Rhys was thoughtful but doubtful. Although he didn't agree with her theory, he smiled softly at her and reassured her.

"Yes, perhaps," he said in almost a whisper.

Isabella continued to study his face as he spoke. She appreciated his assurance, but she equally suspected his words had only been said to make her feel better. Understanding there was no answer for her to find, she said her goodbye and walked out of the temple. When she reached the temple exterior, she stopped momentarily to listen in case the voice spoke again. It was of no use. There was nothing more to be heard.

She turned away and made her way home. There she found Trent waiting at the small table, looking thoughtful. When he saw her enter, he smiled at her as he stood up, moved to her, and kissed her.

"Is all well?" Trent asked her. When he saw the confused look on her face, he continued. "With Adrian? He wanted to talk to you alone."

"Oh! Yes, Adrian is well," replied Isabella, nodding and smiling. "He is considering asking Kat about going through the pairing with him."

Trent moved with her until they were both sitting at the table.

"And how do you feel about that?" he asked.

Isabella looked at him with the same surprise she had shown Adrian at the question.

"I think he needs to be with someone, and Kat seems to wish strongly to be with him," she said. "It will be a good match, do you not think?"

"I know neither of them, but you know them both," said Trent.

"I do not know Kat very well. She has fewer years than Adrian and I, but I trust Adrian in his choice. It is nice…" she started to say and then wondered if she should.

"It is nice … what?" Trent asked her, realizing it was the first time he had seen her uncertain of what to say about anything.

"It is nice to know that … that is, I was worried that when you and I paired, he might not … be happy. It is good to see that he is," she said quietly.

Trent watched her, thinking once again about the life he'd left behind. His previous world had seemed to be a world of greed and jealousy. The people of the village did not appear to have such feelings. He was sure that if the situation of Isabella going off to be with a different man, happened in Trent's world and time, the man who had previously declared his love for her would not want to still be her friend. Adrian had watched Isabella choose Trent, and he still seemed intent on being in her life - in *their* life - as if it did not occur to him to feel hurt, jealousy or anger.

In many ways, the people of the village seemed less advanced but Trent could not help feeling that observation was entirely untrue and it was actually the opposite that was real. In their dealings with each other and with their humanity, they were far more advanced than anyone he had ever met in the modern world he'd grown up in.

"What are you thinking about? Your mind looks active," he heard her ask with a smile of amusement on her face.

"I was thinking…" Trent said, standing up and reaching out to her to pull her into his arms. "I was thinking that you are looking even more beautiful this evening."

He then pulled her into his arms, delivering her a kiss that took them to an even more loving place for hours to come.

CHAPTER 46

The next morning Isabella awoke with a vision of the night fresh in her mind. She'd not experienced any more night visions since she and Trent had grown close then paired.

"You cannot win against me, Isabella," the woman had said to her from a distance. It had sounded like the voice of an older woman, but in the vision, Isabella could not see her face. "You shall not become an ancient, gaining the knowledge of the generations who came before. *I* will be the next ancient, and I will bring much prosperity and a new way of living to our people ... to *my* people."

Upon waking, Isabella felt deep unease. She experienced new emotions that she was unfamiliar with. Her heart was beating quickly. She could also feel that her belly was warm. She sat up, reached down to look, and saw that it was glowing slightly.

"What is it?" she heard Trent ask quietly. When she turned, she saw him lying beside her with a worried look on his face. "Isabella, what is wrong?"

She could hear the concern in his voice, but she felt like she was momentarily stunned. She lay back down again and pulled his hand over so that it settled on her belly. When she looked at him, she saw a relaxed smile had come appeared his face.

"I like this heat," he said. "I do not understand it, but I like it."

Isabella turned onto her side and saw him do the same so that they were facing each other. She pushed the night vision out of her mind. She did not understand where the voice kept coming from or who the woman was. She believed she needed to keep herself calm and relaxed to inspire calm in the child growing within her, if that *was* what was inside of her, causing the warmth and glow in her belly.

"I am so happy that you found me, Trent," Isabella said and watched as he studied her face. "I am happy that you are here with me."

Trent brought up one hand and pushed her hair aside before caressing her cheek softly.

"You are speaking of happiness, but Isabella, you do not seem happy. What is bothering you?" he asked. He waited for a reply, but she gave none. "Please tell me," he encouraged her again.

There was silence for a long while as the two of them looked at each other. Finally, Isabella spoke.

"I have been hearing a voice - a woman's voice," Isabella said. "The same woman was in my vision of the night last night. I know it is only a night vision..."

"Isabella, you and I both know that there can be much, much more to dreams, so let us not instantly expect it to be nothing," Trent said. "What happens in the dream?"

"I have only had the one. In it, she talked as if we - her and I - were in some kind of competition to become ancients," Isabella said. "She said she would not let me become one, and that she would lead our people - *her* people, she said."

Trent looked at her, feeling a depth of concern. Before he'd met her - before he had actually set eyes on her - he would never have paid much attention to dreams. Isabella having appeared before him after he'd dreamed about her, had changed his thoughts on dreams entirely. He knew that for as long as he lived, he'd never again dismiss one as being unimportant.

"How are you feeling about it? Is it worrying you?" he asked her.

"I am not sure," Isabella replied. "When I heard her voice last evening, I followed her instruction and went into the temple, but only Elder Rhys was there. He said there was no woman there who could be talking to me. Now that she has appeared in my vision of the night, I am not sure if she is real or not."

As Isabella looked at Trent, she saw the protectiveness in his eyes. Seeing it made her move as close to him as she could and push her body up against his.

Trent welcomed the move, pulling her closer still and tightening his arms around her. He had left behind a world of women who wanted to be independent and never lean on any man. He'd never given it much thought previously but found himself loving how open and vulnerable Isabella was. He loved being a man who she would move close to for support and protection. It was just another thing that made him wonder at the life he had lived before fate had guided him to her.

"I think for now we can only watch what happens next. Very few visions of the night go on to mean anything," Isabella said. "I will remain aware of what is happening, but I will not let it consume me, Trent," she continued and saw him nod at her in agreement. "Are you going back to the garden today to continue your learning there?"

Trent smiled at her, accepting her effort to change the subject.

"I will," he said. "I am quite excited to be learning something new, to be honest. I have never learned about such things in my lifetime, so it is good for me." He was silent for a moment before continuing. "Shall we get up and go have some breakfast? Although I do like the thought of lying here with you all day…"

Isabella laughed at him and tenderly pushed him away.

"Gardening awaits for you!" she teased him as she stood. "I am sure the cook will wish for me to fetch ingredients for them, so let us go and have our morning meal, and then I will walk with you."

CHAPTER 47

As they sat down in the dining area, Adrian appeared and sat down beside Isabella. Sensing his presence, she turned to him and smiled. She knew he'd intended to talk to Kat the night before about the two of them pairing. She was eager to hear the outcome of the conversation.

"Adrian! Is all well?" she asked him.

She wasn't specific in the question she was asking, but Adrian knew her well enough to decipher the meaning. He laughed in response.

"Yes, Isabella, everything is well," he said. "I will tell you all about..." he started to say before another voice appeared and spoke over him.

"You will tell her all about what?"

The voice startled Isabella. It sounded similar to the voice she'd heard the night before when she'd been outside the temple. It was also similar to the voice that had spoken in her last vision of the night.

The sharpness of Kat's tone startled Adrian and Trent, but Adrian smiled at her before he spoke.

"I tell Isabella all sorts of things, Kat. She is my confidant. She knows far too many secrets for me to let her slip away from me," Adrian said with a light-hearted teasing in his voice.

Isabella watched the interaction between Kat and Adrian. She sensed that not only was Kat not happy with that explanation, but also extremely *unhappy*.

"Well, that will change soon. You will not need Isabella anymore once we are paired," Kat went on to say.

The words surprised everyone within listening distance. It was so unlike the people of the village. There was something in her tone that Trent in particular noticed. It was a tone that would have fitted perfectly in his previous world of jealousy and greed.

Adrian found himself extremely uneasy, sitting between his closest friend of many years and the woman he'd only the night before talked about pairing with. Kat had always been easy going and nice. What he'd just heard from her lips had not been nice at all.

Isabella, being the straightforward person that she was, immediately determined to bring any issue out into the open.

"Kat, why do you say such a thing?" she asked.

The question had been on the minds of Adrian and Trent even though both were too polite to have voiced it.

"He will be mine then, Isabella," Kat replied. "You will not be needed anymore. You have Trent. You no longer need to talk to Adrian. When he needs to talk, he shall talk to me."

Isabella was about to say something more when she felt Trent's hand move over hers and squeeze it. The movement brought her attention back to him instead. She saw the look he gave her. She deciphered it as a look that told her not to say whatever she was about to. She knew it was only a suggestion but conceded that perhaps it was not the way to go. The person who would most suffer from any such action would be Adrian.

She kept her focus on Trent as Adrian begun a new conversation with him, keeping his attention from Kat.

"How was the garden yesterday, Trent? Do you think you will keep learning about food growth?" Adrian asked to cover up an unidentifiable feeling in his gut.

Trent instantly reacted in the way he suspected Adrian wanted him to.

"I very much enjoyed what little I learned yesterday. I am eager to get back there today to start learning and doing more," said Trent. He moved his eyes from Adrian back to Isabella and saw that she had eaten all that had been on her plate. "Speaking of which, I shall go there now. Are you finished, Isabella?" he asked her and saw her nod in reply. "I will wait while you talk to the cook. If you do need something from the garden, we can walk down there together."

Isabella nodded and turned back to Adrian. She saw a different look on his face. It was one she'd never seen before, even though they had been friends for a great many years. She put her hand on his shoulder and squeezed it as she stood up.

"Have a good day, Adrian," she said to him, smiling. She then moved her vision over to the woman sitting next to him. "Kat," she said, giving her a slight nod before turning and moving away with Trent.

As Trent and Isabella washed, dried, and put away their dishes, they both remained silent, each in their own thoughts.

"Cook Mary, do you wish for me to gather anything for you?" Isabella called out to the cheerful woman in the kitchen area. In the back of her mind was a deepening concern for her friend. She fought to dispel it.

"Yes, please, Isabella!" the cook called back as she moved forward. "Mushrooms today, please. Oh, and some thyme, if you please. It is time to make some more lovely mushroom spread, I think," she said.

The mention of the mushroom spread caused Isabella to turn and look at Trent. Both of them remembered the way she'd had to feed it to him. It seemed like much more time had passed since then than actually had.

"Mushrooms and thyme," Isabella said as she returned her gaze to the cook. "Yes, I shall go and get that for you now. Do you have a basket I can use?"

After the cook handed Isabella a basket, she and Trent began walking out of the kitchen, heading for the garden. Partway down the path, Trent stopped, turned to her, moved forward, and wrapped his arms around her.

"I hope you are not distressed by Kat's words, Isabella," he said.

Isabella put the basket down on the ground and pulled him close to her before kissing him.

"I was surprised by them, but I shall move on with my day as if I did not hear them," Isabella said. "But..."

"But what?"

"Her voice ... her voice was so similar to the one I heard," Isabella said quietly. "I know it cannot be so. Kat does not have any powers, I do not think. If she were the one I heard in my vision of the night, she would have shown it. I do not think that she looked like she had shared the night vision."

Trent looked at her and considered what she was saying.

"Perhaps it would be best to stay away from her for the moment," he said. "Until we are sure she is no threat to you, will you stay away?"

Isabella looked at him, not even knowing what the word meant.

"Threat? What is that?" she asked.

Trent leaned in and kissed her, remembering that her people did not know much of the language that he was used to. They didn't know the words because they didn't have many of the *feelings* that his population of humanity had experienced and expressed so freely.

"Just do not think about her words," he said. "You have far more happy things to think about."

"Oh? And what happy things would they be?" Isabella asked, teasing him with a suggestive smile.

Trent laughed at her and kissed her again before pulling away from her and resuming their walk.

"You know exactly what I mean," he said quietly and saw her blush softly. The sight made his heart melt and his mind forget Kat and Adrian entirely.

CHAPTER 48

Isabella sat quietly on the grass as Trent went away with Master Martin to the area where the mushrooms were grown so he could learn how to harvest them. Having reassured the gardener that she was in no hurry at all and the two men could take as long as they wished to, Isabella took a moment to close her eyes, breathe in the air, and enjoy the sunshine on her face.

"I am coming for you, Isabella. You will not win," the woman's voice said in her head all of a sudden. Isabella felt her body tense. In her belly, she felt distress. She placed a protective hand over it and felt the warmth emanating from the glow that was once again present.

In her head, she ignored the voice and spoke through her thoughts to her unborn child.

'All is well. You are safe. Your father and I will not let anyone harm you,' she soothed in her thoughts. As she let the mantra repeat in her mind, she felt the warmth lessen. The feeling of distress was reduced. Her body was at peace once more.

She'd hoped the voice had stopped. It hadn't.

"Your child will not be born," it taunted. "No child will ever be born from your body. I will not allow it."

Isabella felt her protective instinct come alive with a forceful strength. She contemplated whether to try talking to the voice in response. Hearing the men returning, she opted to not try it. Pushing her thoughts and memory of the words from her mind, she stood up and smiled at them. As she saw the smile on Trent's face, she vowed to herself to not mention her latest hearing - not yet anyway.

"Here you go, Miss Isabella," the gardener said to her as he handed her the basket of thyme and mushrooms.

Isabella smiled her thanks before the gardener walked away, leaving her and Trent together.

"Mushrooms! Have you seen where they grow and *how* they grow?! I had no idea," Trent said, feeling incredulous. In response to his enthusiasm, he saw her laugh at him. It was something that always made him happy. "Do you want me to walk you back?" he asked and saw her shake her head in response as she continued to grin at him.

"No. You enjoy the garden. I am going to take these back to Cook

Mary, and then I might go into the pool to bathe," Isabella said.

Trent's attention was immediately captured. In his memory, he could see images of her in the pool previously. He couldn't hide how that affected him.

"Garden!" Isabella said, seeing his facial expression.

Trent refocused with a sheepish smile on his face before kissing her and turning away from her.

CHAPTER 49

After walking into the kitchen to deliver the produce, Isabella went to the temple again. Feeling her belly grow warm as she entered, she found herself approached by Elder Scott.

"Isabella, what brings you here?" he asked her, startling her as she had not seen him for many years.

"I… I do not know," she stammered, suddenly shy.

She warily watched as he moved closer to her. She was relieved to note there was no reaction to him. It felt nothing like the times Elder Rhys had moved closer to her since the night she'd become paired with Trent. .

Elder Scott walked right up to her, curious about the young woman before him. He had watched her grow up, as he had done with all of the children and young people of the village.

"What is bothering you?" he asked. "You seem very thoughtful."

"I have been hearing a voice. I do not know where it is coming from," Isabella replied. "I thought it was only one time, but today I have heard it again."

"Come and sit down," the elder said to her, his curiosity growing. "What does the voice say?"

"It … *she* … keeps saying that she will make sure that I will not give birth to my child - that I will not give birth to *any* child," Isabella said. "She says that she will make sure of it."

Isabella saw a look of alarm cross the elder's face. For a moment, she wondered if she should be talking to him. He was an elder, but she did not believe he was an ancient. His title had been given to him because of the number of years he had lived, not because he had any power of foresight or anything else.

"Elder Scott, do you know of any women ancients?" she asked, wondering if Elder Rhys had been incorrect when he'd answered the same question.

Elder Scott shook his head.

"I do not, but you do know, Isabella, that I am not an ancient," he said. "They are a people who maintain privacy. Even living here, I cannot be certain who all of the ancients are. Generally, they keep themselves from everyone else, even those of us elders residing here in the temple structure."

Isabella nodded at him, feeling a sense of helplessness all of a sudden.

"What about women *elders?"* she asked.

"There are several elders here who are women," Elder Scott replied, nodding. "I do not think any of them would have the ability or the power to talk to you through your mind. I believe that would only be something that an ancient could do."

Feeling a little dismayed and distraught, Isabella stood up.

"Thank you, Elder Scott," she said, eager to be away from the temple. "I do not think there are any answers for me to find here today, so I shall leave you. Thank you for your time."

The elder watched as she stood and began to walk away. He felt a slight frustration that he wasn't an ancient, and couldn't offer her any insight into something that was so obviously upsetting to her.

CHAPTER 50

Isabella waded into the pool, lowered her head under the water, and took some time to massage her scalp and hair. After rising once again, she sat on the ledge of the outer side of the pool. She fondly remembered the two times she had been in the pool with Trent and the way it had felt when he'd massaged her hair.

She'd never truly considered what it would be like to be paired with someone. She had always known it would be expected of her, just as it was of everyone in the village.

As her mind drifted to Trent, she couldn't help but feel happy and contented. As if that very thought had flowed through her body, she closed her eyes and felt her belly grow warm. When she looked down, she saw the now-familiar glow start to appear.

"Enjoy the happiness while you can, Isabella, because it will not last," the foreign voice said in her mind. "Keep away from him. He is not yours. He is mine."

Isabella opened her eyes sharply at the discovery that the new words appeared to have a far more personal aspect to them than those spoken previously. She didn't know who 'he' was. Trent? She didn't think so. He knew very few people in the village. It was difficult to believe that another woman would have made herself known enough to him to believe that she was meant to be with him. No, not Trent, Isabella thought to herself as her mind cast back to that morning in the dining area. Not Trent. Adrian!

She slowly moved out of the pool and onto one of the large flat rocks nearby to let her body, hair, and clothing dry. As she lay still, allowing the warmth of the sun and the rocks to do their magic, she waited in expectation of the voice to return. It didn't. Regardless, her mind was busy. The recurring voice in her head had something to do with Kat, she was sure. But how?

Once she felt completely dry, she walked down to the mill. As soon as she entered the large building, Adrian saw her and walked over to her, a large smile on his face.

"Isabella! Who have you come to see?" he asked, his heart full of happiness to see his lifelong friend.

"I wanted to see you and make sure you are alright," Isabella said simply. Her words were greeted with what she recognized as a look of confusion on Adrian's face.

"Me?" he asked. "Yes, I am well. Why would you think I might not be?"

Adrian looked at her. He knew her expressions well. There was no hiding that she did appear seriously worried about him.

"I am not sure," Isabella replied. "I just had a feeling…"

At that moment, almost as if she'd approached with the stealth of a stalker, Kat appeared. Her voice seemed loud when it called out from behind Adrian.

"Hello, Isabella," she said. "What can we help you with?"

Isabella watched and saw the same expression on Adrian's face that she'd noticed earlier that morning.

"I have come to talk to Adrian," Isabella replied before redirecting her attention back to her close friend. "Can you come with me?"

As soon as she'd asked the question, Isabella believed that she shouldn't have. Discomfort visibly fell over Adrian.

"We are too busy today," Kat said. "He will not be able to leave until the evening meal."

Isabella watched the individual expressions on the two faces in front of her. Listening to Kat's voice and manner of speaking, she considered it was Kat who had been speaking to her, but not *this* Kat, she thought to herself. There was a different tone to it, or perhaps a maturity. It was as if the voice that had been plaguing Isabella was an *older* version of Kat. If that were the case, the version of Kat facing Isabella might not even realize that her older self had been doing what she had to Isabella.

Deep in her thoughts, she watched both of their faces and found herself wondering at Adrian. He was older than Kat, so senior to her in the mill. Despite that, he was letting Kat say what would and would not be happening. Isabella wondered if Kat had some kind of power over Adrian.

"I see. Then I shall not keep you, Adrian," Isabella said, keeping her concerns to herself. "I will talk to you at the evening meal." She added and saw Adrian look at her with regret and sadness, but say nothing.

Isabella turned and quietly walked away. Part of her wanted to run back to him, pull him into her arms, and remind him of who he was. She wanted to make sure he remembered that he was her good friend and a good person who would give anyone the time they needed from him. Another part of her worried that he was getting into a situation that was not good and might get worse as time passed. She also suspected that any input she tried to have into that situation would only result in his pain.

She walked away. For now, that was all she could do.

CHAPTER 51

After spending the day in the garden, Trent returned to their home and found Isabella lying on their bed. She looked extremely contemplative.

"I am going to go and bathe, so have come home to ask if you would like to join me," he said as she finally seemed to focus on him.

Trent watched her stand and move to him before putting her arms around him tightly. She said nothing for a moment. He held her close, remaining quiet while waiting for her to speak.

"I did bathe earlier, so will not go in the pool again, but I will walk with you and watch you if you have no objection," she said to him, smiling up at him and kissing him lightly.

Trent suspected something was worrying her but didn't raise the subject. He could only hope that she would tell him in time when she was ready and needed to talk.

"I would like that greatly," he said. "Come. If we go now, it will still be early enough to go to dinner when I am done."

As they made their way through the paths and down to the pool, Isabella pulled him into easy conversation about his learning in the garden. She keenly listened as he eagerly shared information about what he'd been told during the day.

"The food they grow here is incredible, Isabella!" he exclaimed, honestly excited. "The colors, the flavors … I have never seen produce like this ever."

"Do you not have such foods where you come from?" Isabella asked him, her curiosity piqued.

"Yes, but nothing is as it is here," he replied. "And that is exciting for me."

After watching him discard his shoes and shirt, she saw him wade into the pool and dive under. She laughed as he came up. Always, he was a joy to watch.

"Do you think you shall want to stay in the garden? At least for now?" she asked him.

"I do," Trent said as he used his fingertips to massage his scalp in an effort to remove the dirt he could feel. "I think that I shall like to keep learning and doing what I can in the garden. I never felt it before, in my old life, but I think it is where I am meant to be. It is what I am meant to do."

Isabella continued to watch him. She loved the sight of his face, his eyes, his chest, and arms …

Trent saw her face change and grinned at her.

"I can see your thoughts, Isabella," he teased her as he saw her blush and smile sheepishly at him.

Moving out of the water, he took her hand and led her to the drying stones. There he lay down as close to her as he could without getting her wet.

"Tell me what has happened today," he said. "I feel like there is something you need to talk about."

"Yes, I have heard the voice again today," Isabella replied. "I think I may know who it is but…"

"But what?"

"I am not sure it is possible," she continued. "I believe I must be mistaken."

Trent waited patiently while watching her face. She looked like her mind was working hard. He didn't speak, hoping she would enlighten him to her thoughts. Finally, she looked at him deeply, her eyes looking directly into his.

"I think … I think the voice is Kat's. But it sounds like an older voice, as if…"

"As if Kat … of the future?" Trent asked and immediately saw her face change to disbelief.

"Yes, that is what I thought, but it could not be," Isabella said. "That is not possible."

"Isabella, I think you and I both know that it certainly *is* possible for people to communicate over different times," Trent replied. "What did the voice say?"

"It warned me to keep away from him, and I thought at first that she might be warning me to stay away from you, but…"

"Adrian?" Trent asked and saw Isabella nod at him. "Yes, she was not happy this morning."

"Yes," Isabella agreed. "I went to see Adrian at the mill earlier. When I spoke to him, Kat put herself beside him and said that he could not speak to me. Trent, it was like she had him in some kind of … I do not know. He did not seem to have full control of himself."

Trent watched and listened, becoming more alarmed all the time.

"But Isabella, your people are peaceful. It seems to me, as an outsider, that you have no malice or hatred here. Where would she have learned such feelings of jealousy from?"

"Jealousy?" she asked him. It was another new word for her.

"Yes," he replied. "Jealousy is when you do not like the thought of someone being with someone else - well, no, sorry, not necessarily a person. Sometimes you might want something - anything - that someone else has. The feeling can be very strong. It is a desire to have that thing or person for yourself."

"Yes, you describe that as how I thought Kat was this morning," Isabella agreed. "I do not think she wanted anything I have, but I did feel that she did not want me to talk to Adrian. It seemed that she would like Adrian and me to be apart from one another and not be friends anymore."

"Yes, that is what I thought when she spoke this morning also," said Trent, nodding.

They lay quietly until Trent felt he was dry. Making their way to their evening meal, both wondered what would happen if they saw Adrian and Kat there.

~~~~~

When they arrived, Kat and Adrian were already seated and seemed to be enjoying conversation together. As Isabella and Trent approached, both saw the look that came from Kat. Trent didn't know Kat but he'd seen a similar facial expression many times. He had no doubt it was intended to intimidate and make Isabella not want to sit beside Adrian. Despite Kat's effort, Trent saw Isabella completely ignore the look and sit beside her friend regardless.

"How has the rest of your day been, Adrian?" she asked.

Adrian turned to face her and smiled.

"It has been busy at the mill, but you know I enjoy that more than when it is too quiet," he replied.

Trent watched the interaction, but more so, he watched the face beside Adrian. The emotions that showed left Trent wondering if anyone in the village would rightly understand them. Seeing the seat beside Kat was empty, he stood up and moved to the other side of her. There he sat in an attempt to draw her attention away from Adrian and Isabella.

"How has your work been, Kat?" he asked her. Her facial expression made him suspect that he'd stunned her for a moment. Her body language indicated she might be torn between the need to keep watching Adrian and Isabella, listening to every word they said, but also wanting to talk to Trent.

"My … my work has been very good, thank you, Trent. It is busy, but I enjoy working in the mill," he heard her say, her eyes flicking back to the other two as she said every few words.

He engaged her as best he could, an action that was noticed by Isabella. He saw her give him a discrete look of appreciation as she leaned in closer to Adrian.

"Will you come to our home for a visit, Adrian?" Isabella asked her friend. "I would like … I require your assistance in something personal."
~~~~~

"Yes, of course, Isabella," Adrian replied. "I can come with you after we finish our meal if you like."

"I shall come too," Kat's voice said out loud from the other side of Adrian.

Isabella saw his face change again. He didn't turn and face Kat, instead maintaining focus on Isabella.

"No, not this evening, Kat," Isabella called back. "I have something personal that I wish to discuss with Adrian. It does not concern you."

"Then he will not wish to go with you," Isabella heard Kat say. Isabella couldn't help but suddenly feel sorry for Adrian.

To her surprise, she saw Adrian turn to face Kat and speak quietly but with incredible power and strength.

"Kat, I shall go with Isabella and Trent after we eat," he said. "Isabella is a friend, as you well know. She needs me, I will be here for her. This does not concern you, and you do not need to be so concerned about her and I spending time together without you nearby. We have always done it, and we shall continue to do it."

Kat looked at him, first with a look of surprise and then an expression completely new to Isabella and Adrian. Trent, in contrast, knew it and could easily see it. On Kat's face was an undeniable look of utter contempt.

Kat stood up and left, leaving the remaining three to look at each other, not sure of what to say.

"I will come with you, Isabella," Adrian said quietly, his eyes intently focusing on hers as he saw Isabella nod in reply.

CHAPTER 52

As they entered their home, Trent turned to the two of them.

"Shall I stay? I am happy to leave you alone," he asked and immediately heard Isabella and Adrian both reply at the same time, telling him to stay.

"But thank you, Trent," Adrian said as the three of them sat at the small table in the room. "I do not know why Kat cannot be as gracious as you are about my friendship with Isabella. Sometimes I feel like she has some kind of power over me - like she can bend me to her will, removing all of mine."

"You and Isabella do have a close friendship," Trent said. "It would not be an easy thing to watch when paired with one of you."

"You do not feel any sadness or concern over it, do you?" Adrian asked Trent, who shook his head in return. "You have not seemed to have any objection to us talking still."

"Yes, but not everyone is the same, Adrian," Trent replied.

"Have you … asked her about pairing?" Isabella asked, feeling extreme protectiveness over him all of a sudden. She had previously attempted to ask the question but had so far not received any real answer. When she saw him nod, she felt another depth of concern for him.

"I did. At that time, she said she wanted that, but since then, she has seemed … different," Adrian said. "Before she seemed nice. Now, it is as if something is different about her," he continued. He was quiet for some time before he spoke again, looking directly at Isabella. "I do not know what to do."

"What do you mean?" Isabella asked him, alarmed.

"Should I still go through with the pairing?"

Trent saw the surprise on Isabella's face. He quickly stepped in to take over the conversation.

"Do you have doubts?" he asked the young man before him. In his world, it was nothing to get engaged and then not get married for whatever reason. He already understood that such actions did not happen in the village.

Adrian looked at Trent, for the first time appreciating him being in their lives. Having grown up so closely entwined with Isabella as his closest friend, he didn't have other men to talk to about things.

"I should not say so, I know, but yes, I do have doubts," he replied. "When the two of you paired, I thought I could just pair with anybody since I could not with Isabella. I see now that this is not enough. I did like Kat, but she is not as nice as she seemed to be. I feel she made me see one version of her, but now I am seeing another." He paused and considered his words. "I need to pair. I know it is expected of me, but I want at least to *like* the person I pair with. I am not sure Kat and I have even that."

Trent was surprised at the raw honesty of Adrian as he spoke. He'd had no hesitation saying how he'd felt about Trent and Isabella pairing even though he had wanted to pair with her himself. Trent had observed that in telling them that, Adrian had shown no level of malice or anger about it. He'd said it in a completely matter-of-fact manner.

"You did not ask me here to talk about something personal with you, did you?" Adrian asked Isabella and saw her shake her head. "You knew that I needed to talk about Kat and that the only way that I might be able to talk to you without her nearby would be by asking me here under such a guise."

Isabella nodded at him. "Yes."

"Thank you," Adrian said. "It seems a difficult place for me to be. I want to talk to you, but Kat does not want me to talk to you. It confuses me, not knowing where my loyalty *should* lie, even though I know my loyalty does lie with you."

Isabella watched the face of her friend. He had always been a happy person, excited about life and possibilities. Now all she saw was someone unhappy. To think that he could change so much in such a short period of time made her intensely worried about how much of an effect Kat would have on him over the long period ahead that would be the rest of their lives.

"Adrian, if you do not still wish to pair with her…"

"I must continue with it now, Isabella," Adrian said. "To not do so would go against how things work with our people, as you well know."

"You could speak to one of the ancients and get their advice," Isabella replied. "It could not hurt, could it?"

"What if they are offended by me saying such things? I *could* cause hurt…"

"They are not like that, Adrian," said Isabella. "Elder Rhys is wonderful to talk to. I can go with you if you like."

Adrian looked at her face and considered what she was saying. He did not like going against the ways of their people. He never wanted to upset anyone. He equally couldn't help the ongoing feeling that something was not quite right with the situation with Kat. After considering what Isabella had said, he conceded that it might be better to ask questions at the present time than live to regret a decision later.

"I think you may be right. I will go if you will come with me," Adrian said and saw Isabella stand. "Oh, you mean now?"

"Yes, immediately," said Isabella. "Trent, will you come with us?"

Trent looked from one face to the other.

"I can if you both wish me to, but I do not need to. What do you prefer, Adrian?" he asked.

As Adrian suddenly realized he'd come to appreciate the older man who had paired with Isabella, he nodded.

"I think I would like you both there," he said. "I would feel better."

The three of them made their way to the door, but not before Isabella pulled Adrian into her arms and held him tightly. As he wrapped his arms around her in return, he caught sight of Trent over her shoulder, but only saw him smile sadly. He wondered if Kat would ever be so accepting of the special bond he and Isabella had shared all of their lives.

CHAPTER 53

As they approached the temple, the three of them slowed their walk. Isabella felt the warmth in her belly again. Her hands naturally came up and over it protectively, in the manner they had so recently discovered. Out of the corner of his eye, Trent saw the action.

"You still can feel it when you move closer to the temple?" he asked and saw her nod in response.

He placed his hand on her belly and felt the warmth. As he did so, the glow eased off as if soothed by knowing both of its creators were there to keep it safe.

Adrian saw the actions and words exchanged by Isabella and Trent but did not question what they were talking about. It was not the right time. At that moment, he had to determine what to do about his own future. He couldn't be distracted by someone else's.

When they had walked into the inner areas, they were greeted by Elder Rhys.

"I sensed you coming to talk to me. Come," he said simply, instructing the three to follow him.

Once inside a small room, they all sat.

"Adrian, you are worried about something," Elder Rhys said.

Adrian instantly felt overwhelmed, not having had the level of contact with ancients that Isabella had recently become familiar with.

"Yes. I am … uncertain … about my chosen pairing…" he said slowly and quietly, uncertain about what he could say that would not cause offense.

"Kat," the ancient said.

Adrian nodded, assuming Elder Rhys was asking a question. Upon looking at the ancient's face, he saw the older man was in contemplation and not entirely present with them at all.

Trent, Isabella and Adrian watched as Elder Rhys grew rigid and began to stare at nothing. After a long while, he came back to them in presence.

"She is here, in the temple," he said and stood up to walk out the door.

Adrian looked at Isabella and Trent with a look of confusion on his face. He was sure that Kat would be angry at him for being in the temple, talking to everyone about her. Despite his fear, he stood up and followed the ancient from the room. Trent and Isabella followed behind.

Elder Rhys walked to where she was. In his mind, he could see what she was seeing. He knew exactly which room she was in. As she came into view, he saw Kat turn around and look at him. When she did, the ancient was instantly overwhelmed.

From behind him, Isabella saw the look on Kat's face and the way she was looking at Elder Rhys. Isabella was surprised when she saw the ancient grip his belly firmly and slowly lower to the ground, onto his knees.

Without thinking, she began to rush forward before she felt her belly warn her not to get close to him.

Trent, seeing her frustration, ran to the ancient himself. Kneeling down, Trent provided Elder Rhys with as much support as he could.

"Elder Rhys! What is it?" Trent asked. In response, he saw the ancient grip his belly and moan loudly.

Trent looked back at Isabella and Adrian. They were both focused on Kat.

"Why are you here, Kat?" Adrian found the strength to ask. Almost immediately, he wished he hadn't. As soon as the words had left his mouth, he experienced a deep ache in his belly that forced him to the ground in pain.

Isabella watched in disbelief.

"Stop!" she exclaimed. "What are you doing, Kat? You are hurting them!"

Kat turned her attention to Isabella, her face contorted into something that only Trent could recognize as deep hatred. She seemed to focus on Isabella but then looked surprised.

"You will bow before me," she said, a different voice coming out of her.

Isabella recognized the voice. It was the same one that had entered her head on numerous occasions.

"No, I will not," Isabella said, moving forward. She monitored the feeling in her belly. She would not do anything that would hurt it, but it only gave her courage, not concern.

As she moved forward, Isabella saw something begin in the belly of the woman she faced - a glowing. It wasn't like the golden glow she had noticed in her own belly. Before her, a blue glow was beginning to form.

At the same time that Isabella saw the blue, so did Trent. Having remained on the floor with the ancient, he'd temporarily escaped Kat's attention. When he saw what he saw, he did not stay quiet.

"Isabella, look!" he called out.

As soon as his voice was heard, Kat's eyes fell on him. Her look was immediately followed by Trent experiencing extreme pain inside of his body.

Isabella saw the pain Kat had caused in Trent. It drove her on to do whatever she must to stop the pain from continuing.

"You have been talking to me in my head for days now, Kat. Why?" she asked boldly.

In response, Kat only looked confused.

"What? I do not know what you…" she started to say.

To all others in the room, Kat appeared to suddenly feel pain herself. As her face revealed agony, the blue glow on her belly intensified. Her clothing hid nothing of the blue light as it grew brighter and stronger.

Isabella continued to walk forward, feeding off the feeling that was coming from her own belly. As she did so, Kat seemed to suffer from it.

"Stop! You are hurting me," Isabella heard Kat saying.

Despite the younger woman's pleas, Isabella didn't stop moving toward her. She felt empowered. More than that, she felt a new emotion - anger.

"Stop hurting them, and I will stop hurting you," Isabella said, the power in her voice evident to every person in the room.

Instantly Kat changed her focus and seemed to lift whatever force she had pushed onto the other three people in the room. The sounds of Trent, Adrian and Elder Rhys being relieved of their temporary suffering was highly audible.

"Now tell me what you want from me," Isabella said. "You must have had some reason to talk to me as you have been, contacting me through my mind instead of simply talking to me."

"Isabella, I do not know what…" Kat started to say before again feeling another stab of deep pain inside of her.

"Isabella," Trent said and saw Isabella turn to look at him. "Isabella, I do not think she knows what has been happening."

When Elder Rhys looked at the two women, he groaned heavily.

"You! You are in disguise, but I remember you," he said forcefully, directing his words at Kat.

"What…?" Kat continued to ask, seeming to not know anything about anything the people around her were saying.

"That blue glow. I have seen it before," the ancient said. "In the future, when you were here before. You came here, and you destroyed us."

Kat's eyes grew large as she tried to comprehend what the ancient was saying.

"No! I would never hurt anyone!" she exclaimed. "I do not know what you are talking…"

Once more, the pain flowed through her, making Kat fall to the ground in agony as Isabella moved even closer.

"Be careful, Isabella," Trent pleaded with her.

He had no idea what was going on. Why or how Kat was causing physical pain in other people was beyond his comprehension, but he couldn't deny that he'd felt it. Watching on, he felt useless.

Seeing Isabella get so close to Kat, Trent couldn't stop himself from standing and taking a step toward them. As soon as he did, Kat's face changed again. When she stared at him, the pain in his body became unbearable once more.

"Walk back, Trent," Isabella said, watching him suffer. "Only I can be this close to Kat now."

Trent hated having to remain back and only watch her walk into whatever was about to happen. Regardless, he nodded, retreated, and felt the pain subside.

Settled in the spot he was resolved to stay in, he watched the two women. He suspected he didn't need to worry so much. Isabella was strong. He just hoped she did have the strength in her to not be harmed by the dangerous woman in front of them all.

"My child. Oh! Do not hurt my child," Kat called out as she held up a hand to try and stop Isabella from moving any closer.

Trent saw Adrian's face react as if he were only beginning to wake up. The words had been a surprise to everyone in the room, but mostly Adrian.

"Child?!" he asked quietly.

"It is no child, Isabella," Elder Rhys called out. "I have seen it before. That glow - it is not a child!"

Isabella stopped moving and remained still for a moment. Inwardly she checked her body but knew in her heart that it was right for her to keep moving forward.

As she stepped closer, she saw Kat start to back away, moving along the ground away from Isabella. When she reached a wall, she could not move any further.

Kat watched as Isabella neared. The blue cold in her belly was intensifying to a level where she thought her body would freeze in its entirety.

All of a sudden, when they were only a meter apart, Isabella brought her hands together as if making them into a cup shape. It wasn't something she'd thought about ahead of that moment. It was her gut instinct that had made her move in such a way. Her eyes were mesmerized as she unexpectedly created magic.

Before all of their eyes, a golden glow emerged in Isabella's hands, as if coming from the golden stone that had been seen by her, Trent, and the ancient. She stood still as the glow grew in its power. It formed itself into a ball, taking on the appearance of an orb of golden flame.

Kat stood once more and braced herself as she saw and felt Isabella take the final step toward her. Kat willed herself to put out her hands and push Isabella away but found that she could not move any part of her body. The majority of her body felt frozen. She could only watch as the hand holding the golden glow moved closer and finally made contact with her own belly.

The three men watched as the contact was made. Isabella's golden flame being pushed hard up against the blue glow in Kat's belly resulted in a brilliant light filling the room. Trent, Adrian, and Elder Rhys each closed their eyes and turned from it, momentarily blinded by the light. Not able to see what was happening, they each heard a scream come from one of the women. Which one had made the horrifying sound, they couldn't tell.

Isabella felt the power surge through her like it was flowing from her and into Kat, consuming the younger woman in front of her. She heard the scream that came from Kat. Even through the blinding light, Isabella could see a blue light rise from Kat's belly and hover right in front of her face. Although she didn't know what it was, instinct told her that she had to eliminate it.

Isabella quickly brought her other hand up. She watched as a second golden flame grew. When it had formed, she knew she had to use it to directly strike the glowing blue ball that had escaped from Kat.

Bringing her other hand up from Kat's belly, the younger woman slumped down before her. Isabella could not do anything at that moment for her. Instead, she concentrated her power on her hands coming together while enclosing the blue light within them and trapping it with her own golden light. Eventually, she felt the heat reach an intensity she had never felt before. Smoke began to emanate from her closed hands, before the feeling of power disseminated into the air around her. Whatever it had been, she knew it had gone.

It was over with incredibly quickly. To others, it must have looked like nothing at all. Isabella knew at that moment that she would never forget the degree of power she'd felt flow through her. She didn't know what had happened, but she hoped that the blue entity, whatever it had been, was destroyed.

She looked down. Seeing Kat lying still, Isabella quickly moved to her. She could see that Kat was in the same state Trent had been the day that he'd touched the golden rock in the cave.

From where they remained, the three men watched as the bright light that had filled the room finally disappeared. They saw Isabella kneeling in front of Kat. When Isabella raised her hand and placed it on Kat's heart, the golden glow showed once more.

Trent watched in wonder, knowing in the depth of his soul that he was seeing what Isabella had done to him that day in the cave. He watched as he saw Isabella do just as she'd done when she'd brought him back to life.

All of a sudden, a loud gasp of air being inhaled came from Kat. Her body convulsed. Isabella closely studied the young woman. She immediately sensed a different person before her. Hearing someone begin to move up behind her, Isabella held her other hand back to indicate them to stop.

"Wait," she called out. "It may not yet be safe."

Kat opened her eyes and looked around her. In contrast to the powerful being that she'd been minutes earlier, she just looked intensely frightened.

"What? Where am I?" she asked Isabella with fear in her voice.

"You are in the temple, Kat," Isabella quietly said to her.

"The temple? No. No, I was at the mill," Kat replied, her confusion evident. "Adrian and I were about to leave to go to the evening meal."

Kat felt warmth in her chest and looked down to see what was causing it. Surprised to see a golden light glowing through her clothing, she put her hand over it.

"What happened to me?" she asked, looking around at everyone in the room.

Isabella stood up and held out her hands to assist the younger woman.

"Come, Kat. Stand now," Isabella said. "You have not been yourself, but now all will be well," she continued even though she felt no certainty that her words were true.

Kat stood and looked around her again. Adrian, Trent, and an older man were looking at her as they slowly moved forward to where she and Isabella stood.

"Adrian? What are you doing here? And who is that man?" she asked. Her confusion was evident to everyone, and everyone found it to be real.

The ancient walked forward until he stood directly before Kat. Before everyone, he closed his eyes and focused solely on her. In her soul, he searched for any trace of whatever it was that had consumed her. He found none. After a long while, he smiled at her and held out his hands to take hers in his.

"Kat, I am Elder Rhys, and I am an ancient," he said. "You are feeling confused now, but rest assured, all is as it should be."

Kat let the old man hold her hands. Feeling a level of trust emanate from him, she relaxed.

"Kat will be well," Elder Rhys said as he turned to face Isabella, Trent, and Adrian, then walked away from all of them, confident there was nothing more to fear.

Trent approached Isabella and put his arms around her protectively.

Isabella welcomed the feeling of safety that came from the action. Remaining where she was, she watched as Adrian slowly moved forward.

Uncertain what had happened or where he stood with Kat, Adrian was tentative about approaching her. So many things didn't make sense. He'd witnessed the strange little interactions between golden and blue glowing. What was at the forefront of his mind, however, was Kat having referred to the blue glowing as a child. Had she meant that? If she was with child, that would mean she would have to already be paired with someone. He knew that was not the case. The whole village would know if she'd gone through the pairing ritual.

He was pulled from his thoughts by her voice.

"Adrian, I do not feel like myself at all, and I do not think I am ready to go through the pairing yet. I am sorry…" Kat started to say.

Isabella watched Adrian's confusion transform into relief. It appeared that Kat might not remember all that had happened in the build-up to that moment in time.

Despite his confusion, Adrian smiled at Kat fondly and moved to put his arms around her.

"Do not speak of that now, Kat," he said. "I shall walk you home. Once there, you must rest." He spoke confidently but could see the intense confusion continue on Kat's face.

As if understanding the same need to test that Kat was back to her normal self, Adrian and Isabella walked toward each other and put their arms around each other. They held each other tightly before looking at Kat to see if there was any reaction to it. All they saw was her smile sadly at them. Adrian placed his hand on her arm.

"Come now," he said to Kat before leading her out of the temple.

Trent turned Isabella around and held her firmly against his chest.

Feeling exhausted, Isabella happily leaned against him. Aware that something was missing, she placed her hand on her belly. There she felt nothing.

"It is gone, Trent," she said sadly and immediately felt his hand touch her also.

"It was not our child, Isabella," Trent said. "It was something else - something wonderful inside of you that was needed for you to save us."

"Yes. But what of our child?" she asked, feeling a great sadness that registered as a sense of loss.

Trent smiled brilliantly at her in an effort to reduce her sadness.

"We shall just have to keep on trying," he said with a very suggestive grin on his face.

Isabella laughed at him and kissed him.

"Take me home," she whispered.
Trent leaned into her ear. "Gladly."

THE GOLDEN SUPREMACY

~~ Golden Desires Series: Book 2 ~~

CHAPTER 1

A battle was over. By the standards of the world as we know it, it had hardly been a battle at all. By the standards of what Trent had been taught of the wars of the world throughout recorded history, he knew it had been a battle that would hardly have been reported on in the time and place he'd come from.

Trent also knew that to Isabella and the few other villagers who were aware of what had taken place in the temple that night, it had *seemed* to be a battle - and a great one. It had been a fight between good and bad; a clash between hot and cold; and a challenge between the heat of a flame and the cold of ice.

The surprising force of an unknown entity that had existed within Kat had that night been extinguished by the power that had resided deep within Isabella. Kat appeared to have forgotten what she'd taken part in. To everyone around her, it seemed as though her body had been used without her knowledge or consent for the purpose.

Isabella's memory hadn't been so kind. She could remember every little thing with extreme clarity.

In the days that had followed, Trent had recognized despondency on the fair and beautiful face of Isabella - the woman he'd paired with so recently. Having been drawn together over great distance and time, he still sometimes looked at her and wondered if she had any idea of her level of beauty. He wondered if she had any idea how much he longed to be close to her over the few hours each day when they were apart. He also wondered if she knew how much he truly loved her, even though he'd previously thought he was a man who could not love.

Isabella had believed she'd been with child. She and Trent had both thought that was what the golden glow that had been visible on her belly had represented. It had been a light that emanated warmth from it, providing a feeling of comfort and safety.

The battle had taken that from her. It had been her strength in fighting the cold blue that had emanated from Kat. The warm, soothing feeling inside of Isabella's belly had never been a child at all. Regardless, Trent could see that she missed it as if it *had* been a baby growing inside of her. He didn't know if she was aware that she did it, but now and then he would notice her hands move to her belly. Those movements were just as they had been when she'd believed she was with child.

She'd said nothing more about the golden glow after that night. There seemed no point. It hadn't been what they'd thought it had. They had been mistaken.

Three weeks had passed since that night. Over that time, Trent felt as if something had changed inside of Isabella. She was still beautiful. She still smiled. She was still friendly. She still appeared happy.

But he knew she was not.

He and everyone close to her could see that her distinct and usual level of pleasant cheerfulness had seemed to have simply left her. It had disappeared, almost as if a once brilliant flame had just gone out.

CHAPTER 2

Lying beside her early in the morning, Trent slowly and quietly turned his body so that he could look at her. Always when he woke up, he felt like he had to see her again. He knew each morning that she was right there, lying next to him, but he had to *see* her. She had a natural beauty about her. It was a rawness that came from not being a part of a world where people worked hard to be something they weren't. That was the world Trent had come from. He'd happily left behind a busy society that never stood still. It had been a society that was hectic and stressful. It had been a society that was forever trying to have and do more.

That world he'd walked away from - literally. He had packed up only what he'd needed to survive a long trek. Then he'd walked, and walked, and walked. Once he had reached a certain point in his journey, he'd found he didn't have any great desire to go back.

After trekking across mountains that had separated their worlds, he'd found Isabella. After that, he hadn't wanted to return to where he'd come from. Time had passed with him in her village, originally in his time and then in hers. Over that period, he had come to fully understand that contentment was far easier to find in the villagers' simple way of life than it had been in his previous life. He no longer felt that he had to be so concerned with seeking more. He'd found everything he needed. He already had everything that he desired.

As they lay together in their bed, Isabella's long red hair flowed out in all directions from her. The vision made Trent think of a flame, as if she were the very heart of it. A random clump of red strands lay across her cheek. He could see a strand or two moving up and down near her nose in the ebb and flow of her breath.

His focus fell on the strands. He didn't want to move from where he was. Looking at her in such a way each morning, with her face so much at peace, he would do anything to not disturb her quiet slumber. She hadn't been her normal self since the night in the temple. It worried Trent, but he was patient. He'd seen grief. He knew it was only time that might heal Isabella.

So focused was he on the hair lying across her cheek that he hadn't noticed her eyes opening.

CHAPTER 3

Isabella lay still, watching his eyes as they focused on her. She knew that even though they were together every morning and every night, he missed her. Although she knew it hadn't been a baby inside of her, the loss of it had still affected her. Since that night, she hadn't longed to be passionate with Trent. The desire had not been there, and he'd accepted that. He hadn't tried to pressure her in any way. Every night and every morning he held her close, and that was enough.

With each morning that had passed since then, Isabella had woken with the feeling that a little more of her usual self was returning. Another small slice of the whole was present that hadn't been there the day before.

Although she had moved forward with each day as if it were like any other, her thoughts had continued to plague her. She could not pinpoint precisely what concerned her. The way everything had played out in the temple that night still seemed to her to have been far too easy. It had appeared as if she'd extinguished whatever it was that had been assaulting Kat's body and mind previously. Even though conflict was something that she had never seen or experienced in her village, her elimination of the cold blue had seemed just too easy. Perhaps she was wrong. She hoped she *was* wrong. She wasn't yet convinced that she was.

As she continued to watch Trent's face, she felt like she was almost completely back to her usual self. The thoughts would continue. The fears would continue. Despite knowing that, she could feel her heart and her body returning to their former state. She also knew that she didn't want distance from Trent anymore.

Trent reached his hand out slowly and quietly, to move the few rogue strands of hair he'd been watching. As he peacefully and carefully lifted and moved the hairs aside, his eyes met hers. At that moment, he realized she wasn't still asleep at all. Looking into her eyes, he saw something he hadn't seen for weeks. His surprise was further heightened as he watched her move closer to him and place her lips over his. He indulged in the feeling her kiss evoked in him. His body was awake, and it was hungry. When she pulled away briefly to look into his eyes and moved her body over his, he felt recognition.

She'd needed time to recover from her loss.

Now she was healed.

CHAPTER 4

In another part of the village, Adrian awoke with the alertness of his usual self. Since that night three weeks earlier, he'd simply decided that the event should be *very* forgettable. Each morning he saw his closest friend, Isabella, and believed she had moved on from it. In his view, if Isabella was fine then everything in *his* life was fine. For Adrian, it was that simple, or, at least, he thought it *should* have been that simple.

Over the days following that night, he had spent some time with Kat. As far as he could tell, she had no awareness of whatever had been inside of her. She seemed to have no memory of whatever had been done to her or by her without her consent or knowledge.

Adrian was still uncertain as to what degree her memory was absent. Before that evening, they had talked about pairing together. Since that evening, it had seemed that she did not feel the two of them pairing was a good idea after all. Adrian had fears about who or what had made Kat seem so eager to pair before that night. Had it been her, due to how she felt about him? Or had it been whatever entity had been inside of her, manipulating her like she was a puppet on a string?

In more recent days, he hadn't spent time with Kat. They both worked in the village mill but rarely had to talk to one another. He was confused. He didn't know what was real with her and what was driven by someone else - some*thing* else. In his confusion, he'd concluded that the best solution was simply to avoid her as much as possible.

He didn't want to think about the seriousness of what he'd seen that night. The power that had then come from Kat had easily caused physical pain in him, in Trent, and in the ancient, Elder Rhys. Afterward, the physical pain seemed not to exist, but the residual memory of how much it had hurt still remained in his mind. He'd never before that night experienced such pain. He equally didn't want to ever again.

Pushing those memories from his mind, as he seemed to have to almost every morning, he rose and prepared himself for the day ahead. He would go to breakfast. There he would see Isabella.

After that, the day would be good.

CHAPTER 5

Trent held Isabella in his arms. Her passion and desire had returned. He tried hard not to smile too broadly as they lay together. He was in recovery mode after she'd shown him just how full of desire she had been when she'd woken up.

Isabella moved her body, turning onto her front so that she was beside him but facing him, her chest subtly huddled against his shoulder. She looked closely at him and smiled. Her face revealed not the side of her that was a sexual goddess, but instead the side that made her appear shy and timid. It was the side that resulted in her face having a slight blush to it.

Trent loved that she could so easily and honestly demonstrate her feelings. He knew she had attempted in recent times to look happier than she'd felt. He preferred her as she was in the present moment, relaxed and not trying to hide the way she felt at all. She knew when she was feeling bashful, but she never tried to hide that underneath any kind of strong exterior. In many ways, she was the most raw woman he'd ever met in his life. He had come from a world where too many women tried to be someone else. From the moment he'd met Isabella, it had seemed as if it would not even occur to her to change anything natural about herself. She was who she was, she was *what* she was, and that was simply okay.

Isabella saw Trent's eyes sparkling and bright. She had missed being so close to him. She was uncertain why she hadn't wanted to be as close to him since the night things had changed, but she was glad to be so intimate with him again.

Trent leaned close to her and kissed her once more. As he did so, his hand reached up, and his fingers wound into her hair. He held it in a gentle hold to pull her even closer. As they eased apart again, she gave him a wide grin. His heart ached at the sight of her. Always he could look at her and just think that she was the most breathtaking woman he had ever laid eyes on.

"I have missed this," Isabella said. When Trent said nothing in reply, she continued. "I am sorry, Trent..." she began.

Her words were cut off mid-sentence, extinguished by his lips coming down on hers. For a long while, he kissed her with the passion she'd missed.

"Isabella, you do not need to say sorry for anything," he finally said before kissing softly her yet again.

"But you have not had … we have not…" Isabella started to say.

Trent watched her face as she began to get flustered. Isabella, in turn, saw his eyebrow rise as his eyes showed his amusement. Finally, Trent laughed softly and kissed her forehead as he wrapped his arms around her in a tighter hold.

"The only thing I need is to know that you are alright. Your mind is too full of thoughts, Isabella," he said. "You need to let go of some of your concerns or talk about them. You know you can talk to me, or Adrian, or Elder Rhys. Even your mother or father might be good to talk to."

"I do know this," she said. "Thank you, but I do feel better today. Shall I show you again?"

Trent laughed out loud as she moved onto her back and pulled him to guide him over and into her. There was no more laughter or serious conversation as he sunk deep inside her, relishing every single second of his joining with the beautiful woman lying beneath him.

CHAPTER 6

"Good morning, Adrian," Isabella greeted her lifelong friend as she sat down beside him at the long wooden table in the dining area. The area was vast, with row after row of the same style of wooden table. The air was alight with a diverse range of glorious culinary scents.

As she was confronted with the smell and sight of the food dishes of the mealtime, Isabella realized how famished she was after such an active morning. The thought inspired a blush on her face. It was a blush that wasn't missed by Trent. The look of amusement evident on his face as he looked at her told her he knew what she'd just been thinking about. She smiled shyly at him before turning back toward Adrian.

As she faced her friend once again, Isabella was greeted by the smiling face she knew even better than she knew her own. Lifelong friends, they'd grown up together and were close.

"Good morning, Isabella," Adrian said with his usual easy-going and happy tone. "Good morning, Trent."

Trent returned the sentiment and sat next to Isabella, eager to enjoy whatever flavors he was about to be subjected to. There had been many things he'd discovered and come to love about moving backward in time to become a member of the ancient village. The freshness and flavor of the food was one of them.

Isabella and Adrian were chatting in their usual light-hearted manner as Kat came into view. Trent had just started to enjoy a simple, small but flavor-concentrated breakfast of thick mushroom spread on fresh bread when he noticed Kat approaching. He watched her. He knew it was a general belief that she had no real understanding of what had happened in the temple that night. He understood that everyone believed she had played no real part in it. Regardless, he was wary of her.

Since the day he'd met Kat, she had shown a different nature to the other residents in the village. Although he could concede that the entity that had invaded her could be fully responsible, Trent wasn't sure if that was the truth. He wasn't sure how many of the different aspects of her actions and words had been part of her being controlled by someone else - some*thing* else - and what percentage came from her true nature.

As Adrian and Isabella ate and talked, Trent saw Kat move closer to their small group. She looked at Adrian and Isabella tentatively. When she saw Trent looking at her, she gave him a shy, sad smile. He nodded at her, not wishing her to see the doubts he had. Although he'd tried to convince Isabella that she worried too much about what had happened, and what could happen in the future, he also had concerns. He suspected that for a long time yet, he would continue to worry about what was real with Kat.

"May I sit here, Adrian?" Kat asked.

Adrian turned his head from Isabella as he finally noticed her. He still wasn't sure how he felt about her. He didn't know if she was to be trusted, or if she was honest in her dealings with him.

Kat felt uncomfortable as Adrian faltered in his response, leaving her standing as she was. She didn't want to sit if she was unwelcome. She equally didn't want to walk away if he wanted her to sit down.

Even from where Trent sat, he could see that Kat felt unsure what to do. Although he didn't particularly like her, he felt sorry for her as she stood waiting.

Isabella saw the extended look of uncertainty on Adrian's face before he seemed to remember to put his well recognized friendly smile back on.

"Of course, Kat," he said quietly but with a friendly tone. "I welcome it."

Isabella turned away from Adrian to give him some privacy with Kat. As she did so, she noticed the look that was on Trent's face.

He saw her give him a look full of questioning. He refrained from answering her unspoken question. Instead, he took her hand in his and squeezed it, as a silent promise that they would talk about his concerns later.

Adrian saw Isabella turn away from him and found himself somewhat dismayed. He knew she'd turned away to allow him to talk to Kat without it seeming like Isabella was listening. His dismay came from knowing that by Isabella doing so, she'd taken away his choice about whether he really wished to speak to Kat or not.

Resigned to being polite and doing what he should, Adrian swiveled his body slightly so he could give his full attention to Kat.

"How are you this fine day?" he asked. For a moment, he thought she was going to say something serious to him. She then seemed to regard that option before she smiled and began equally polite, unimportant conversation with him.

CHAPTER 7

"What had you so worried when we were sitting down, Trent?" Isabella asked as the two of them walked away from the dining area and toward the kitchen.

They stopped to wash, dry, and quietly put away their dishes before he turned to her.

"I am not completely certain, Isabella," he began. "I just still wonder…"

As he started to speak, Cook Joan called out. Her voice boomed throughout the area, not able to be missed.

"Oh! Isabella!" she said loudly. "If you please, can you gather the eggs soon? I shall also be needing some sweet basil and mushrooms. Oh, our meal this evening is going to be a right treat, it surely is! Here, take this basket with you and do not forget - sweet basil and mushrooms!"

The daily gathering of items for the kitchen had become Isabella's place in the village. Around her, everyone else appeared to have found their set place in the village, doing work where they just knew they belonged. There they worked all day, every day. For some it was in the mill; for some it was in the kitchen; while others had taken on roles such as village tailor.

Even Trent had given gardening a go, despite having been in the village for so short a time and never having done it in his previous life. Working there day in and day out, he'd found that he enjoyed it. The garden was where he'd stay, learning from the older and more knowledgeable gardeners. Slowly he was gaining the skills needed to cultivate food for the entire village.

In his previous life, he'd been a software designer. He'd spent years studying and working hard with computers. It had seemed important at the time. It was only when he'd arrived in the ancient village that he realized that for all the studying he'd done in the modern world, he didn't know how to do even the most simple and vital thing in life - grow food. His career had seemed highly important then. Now it meant absolutely nothing. Day to day, he didn't give it a thought. In the village garden, he'd found something infinitely more rewarding and enjoyable.

Isabella was still searching for the one place that she would belong. She wanted to find the one place that she would be able to lay claim to as her own. There was one place that would inspire her and create in her a passion to keep doing whatever it was that she was meant to do. She just needed to ascertain what that one place was.

Broken out of her thoughts, she smiled fondly at the woman who'd called out to her and nodded as she accepted the basket. "Of course, Cook Joan," she said. "I shall return with your gifts shortly."

Trent led Isabella away from the kitchen, his hand fondly resting on and caressing her lower back as they stepped outside. From there, they embarked on their usual walk to the gardens where Trent worked during the daylight hours.

"Yes? What were you saying, Trent? What do you still wonder?" Isabella encouraged him to continue. Her curiosity was piqued about what he had been going to say earlier.

Three weeks on from the strange event in the temple, Isabella did not completely know how she felt about Kat. Because of that, whenever someone else wished to speak about her, Isabella found herself absorbed in the wonder of their thoughts.

Trent looked at her, not sure if he should speak or not. He hated that she'd already worried so much. The last thing he wanted to do was compound that concern into fear. He equally was resolved to never lie to her.

"Kat still makes me nervous, Isabella," he said in truth. "I do not know why exactly that is, but there is something about her that I do not trust. I know that thing that was inside of her is now gone, but I am just not … quite … sure."

Isabella observed him as he stopped walking and turned to face her. Reading his face, she could see that he had suddenly found himself overflowing with concern. She released the basket that he reached to take from her, and watched as he placed it on the ground. Immediately afterward, she felt him move closer and pull her tightly against him. She gently rested her head on his shoulder. She gladly embraced the moment to enjoy the simple feel and smell of his body against hers. After a long pause of breathing his scent while trying to maintain calm within herself, she pulled back from him so she could look into his eyes.

"I know there is still a threat, Trent," she said quietly. "I can and do feel it. It might be Kat, or it might be someone or something else. There is no way for us to know what will happen, if anything. I have been thinking about this on many occasions. I do not think we can be prepared for it if something does happen. We must try and not be ruled by fear. I do not want it to consume us. It has consumed me enough. Please do not let it consume you too."

Trent watched her face as she spoke. He wouldn't talk about it anymore in that present moment. His fears might turn out to be nothing.

Kat might be a nice person with just a few personality issues. Greed, spite, and unpleasantness weren't things that appeared to be common among the villagers, but he guessed that didn't mean that such things never happened. They were human, after all. He equally supposed that just because she'd been unknowingly consumed by an entity before, didn't necessarily mean that she would be again.

Isabella leaned against his body and kissed him, enticing him to turn off his previous thoughts. She wanted him to focus on something far more enjoyable. They quietly stood in a warm embrace, holding each other close while enjoying the simplicity of their lips caressing. It didn't seem like a long time at all before Isabella could feel just how much she was affecting him. The speed and strength of him growing hard against her always enchanted her. It was something she'd had no previous knowledge of with sex being entirely unspoken about among the village residents. To her, it was all new, and it was magical.

She pulled away and saw him look bashful in the realization that she knew what she'd just done to him and how his body had reacted. Isabella smiled at him and laughed softly before kissing him once more. It was an incredibly soft kiss of short duration, intended only to let him know how much she simply loved being with him.

CHAPTER 8

Adrian listened to Kat talk about whatever things she wished to share with him. Even though he could show in his facial expression that he wanted to listen to her, he didn't feel that his heart was any longer in it. He no longer looked at her and thought she would be an acceptable substitute for the real love of his life.

While it was true that Isabella was now happily paired with Trent, Adrian knew that although he did need to think about pairing with someone, Kat wasn't the right person for him.

She never had been.

Polite in nature, he'd never been in any way uncaring or unkind toward anyone. Although he was not sure where he and Kat would or even could go, he would continue to treat her as a friend. He'd never known conflict, but his instinct told him that he needed to be careful where Kat was concerned. He suspected that if he weren't, she might act in a way that would make things uncomfortable - not just for him, but for a great many.

Although he generally was able to put a smile on his face, even when he was unhappy, spending time with Kat did challenge Adrian's ability to hide his feelings. Sometimes when she was talking to him, he could vividly remember how things had panned out in the temple that night. When the strange entities had battled, Adrian had worried about both Kat and Isabella, but he couldn't deny that his primary concern had been far more for the latter and far less for the former.

CHAPTER 9

"Trent," Isabella said, immediately capturing his attention utterly and securely with the tone of desire attached to that one word. She watched his face as it changed, and he looked at her intently as if waiting for her to continue. "I would like to go and bathe. Will you come with me?" she asked.

Trent gulped but then beamed at her. They had just returned to their modest but perfectly formed little home in the village after dining for their evening meal. Trent could still taste the vibrancy of the tomato baked rice they'd enjoyed. Since he'd arrived in the village, his taste buds had been treated to what he thought were the most incredible meals.

Everything that was made in the village kitchen by the cooks was created from the fresh vegetables, fruit, and grains that the villagers grew. They ate no meat. The only animals in the village were the chickens, which were used only for eggs. As far as Trent could tell, the concept of eating a chicken was not something anyone had ever considered. Before he'd discovered the village, he'd been a big meat eater, but there hadn't been one day since his arrival that he'd craved it. Learning how many ways things grown in the ground could be used to create delectable flavors was something he took great joy in at every single mealtime he attended.

When he'd arrived, worn and weary from the long trek he'd endured on foot, he hadn't been healthy. Over an extended period of time, he had walked off far more energy than he'd been able to consume. As a result, by the time he'd arrived, he had lost a lot of his muscle tone. Since he'd started to be able to eat once more, after discovering Isabella and the village, his body had slowly returned to its former self. There was no such thing as a mirror in the village but Trent sometimes considered that his body wasn't its former self, but rather a *better* version of its former self. He felt healthier than he ever had in his life. He believed that was due to the combination of better eating of more wholesome food and having far less stress in his life.

For all the people of his world - *our* world - had worked to create technology to make life 'easier', since becoming a part of the village, Trent had come to believe that the world had actually gone backward in the future. Where he'd come from, people had been far more stressed in their lives in their desperation for more. Now he knew better. The people he now lived amongst within the peaceful confines of the tall structure walls lived a far better life. They knew nothing of technology or 'advancement', but they certainly knew how to live, and love, and simply enjoy.

His thoughts flowed over him quickly. He let them until he realized Isabella was waiting for his response. It seemed as if it had been a long time since they had bathed at the same time in the warm pool of the village. As he looked at her face, he could see she was alight with passion bubbling inside of her. The thought had an instant effect on him. He blushed as he felt his body harshly react to the silkiness and suggestion in her voice.

"I will but give me a moment, Isabella," he said quietly and saw her laugh in understanding.

His body's reaction to her was still something that Isabella was in awe of. Nothing had ever been said to her about the pairing process that wasn't considered essential for the maintenance of the population. No such thing was ever talked about, so when she'd paired with Trent, she'd had no previous knowledge of lovemaking. For her, it had been a journey of discovery but one that she still found extremely enjoyable and exciting.

She knew Trent sometimes seemed embarrassed by the way his body reacted when she was close to him. She regarded it as nothing for him to worry about. She could be completely open about it and even admit that she very much liked that he responded to her in such a way.

After giving him a moment of peace, she approached him and hugged him to help his body calm down. The opposite effect happened.

Trent grinned and nudged her away from him.

"That is not helping!" he said, teasing her.

Isabella laughed louder, holding out her hand to him.

"Come, Trent," she said. "I am certain that no-one else will know how you are. Only me."

Trent shyly and reluctantly gave in and moved alongside her as they made their way to the pool. Walking beside her, enjoying the simplicity of holding her hand, he felt a fullness that he'd never felt in his previous life. In the life he'd grown up in, he'd never quite found that special something that would truly make him feel complete and content.

He'd been with many women as a partner and as a lover, but he'd never quite found that special someone. Always it had seemed like he'd thought he knew what he wanted. When he'd thought he'd found it, he still hadn't been satisfied. It had felt like an itch that never went away, no matter how much effort he put into scratching it. It had always seemed just out of his reach or even unachievable. In his previous world, he could never have imagined that he would be where he'd ended up, living a life of such blissful peace and tranquility.

The distance he'd traveled. The people he'd met. The experiences of simple things like wholesome food that was pure from nature. All had helped him to finally gain a sense of contentment, a sense of having a true home, and a sense of at last being where he was meant to be.

The two of them did not talk as they walked from their small home, along the path to the pool of natural flowing warm water. During their short journey, each was content simply being in each other's company. They needed nothing more.

As the pool area came into view, both were pleased to see no other villagers using it at that time. The area was lush with trees and bushes that complemented the inner surfaces of the structure's exterior walls. Lavender colored roses climbed in all directions over the walls with the steady year-round climate helping the rose plants to bloom every day. The strong scent that consistently drifted from them was heavenly.

Between the pathway and the pool, large flat stones lay lined up beside each other. Trent didn't know if they were natural and in the place they'd always been. They were perfectly shaped and sized for people to lie on to dry quickly by the sun from above and the natural heat rising from underneath. Sometimes when Trent looked at them, he believed that nothing in the modern world could have been so perfectly planned and designed as those large flat stones, even though they seemed to be a gift from nature itself.

The sound of the waterfall engulfed each of them, with the ongoing crash of the water hitting the far left of the pond surface. It was a therapeutic sound that Trent believed he would never take for granted. It was just one small part of his recently found paradise.

On reaching the edge of the pool, he removed his shirt and they both removed their modest shoes. In all other clothing, the two of them entered the warm water. No matter how many times he bathed in it, Trent was still in wonder of the village and its creators for so well harnessing nature in the ways that they had. He and Isabella knew the secret of the heat that kept the village warm, including the water that flowed through the pool.

In the location of the village high up on top of a vast mountain range, it should never have been warm, but it consistently was. Golden veins flowed underneath the ground, heating it. Trent and Isabella did not know what the golden formation was. They did not know how it worked. They just knew that it did. Because of those golden veins, the entire population of the village continued to thrive, as it had done for hundreds - perhaps even thousands - of years.

In the warmth of the pool, Trent instantly lost his chain of thought as he watched Isabella dive under the water. She was still wearing her standard shift dress that all women wore in the village. In silence, he breathed out deeply as he saw her surface again and stand up. The sight of her like that was one more thing that never ceased to capture and hold his attention. The villagers were not people to dress for vanity. They wore what was simple and comfortable, enabling them to get through their days without any stress or annoyances. Although the dresses that Isabella wore day in and day out were plain, when Trent saw her like that - rising out of the water with the shape of fabric clinging to her - his breath caught … every single time.

He watched her as she ran both of her hands through her hair. The movement of her hands resulted in her figure heightening and stretching further. He would never get tired of looking at her. Of that, he was very, very sure. It just couldn't be possible. Ever.

As he looked at her at that moment, his eyes traveled down her body and up again. Standing like she was, with the fabric of her dress hugging her figure so well, Trent's eyes returned after their second view to her belly. He hadn't noticed it before. It must have been something that couldn't be so easily seen when she was lying down. Peering closer, he didn't doubt that he could see a bump. He wasn't experienced in being a parent, and he'd never seen any friends in the early stages of pregnancy. What he did believe he accurately knew, however, was Isabella's body.

He considered the option to not say anything just yet. Isabella had only just gotten over feeling like she'd lost a child. Even though that was not what the golden glow in her belly had been, part of Trent thought it best not to suggest anything to her in case he was wrong. Not sure, for a moment he considered asking her about it. He willed himself to take at least a few minutes to consider before speaking of it. He determined not to plunge forward without thinking.

Isabella watched his face. In full honesty, she liked that she could stand like she was, and he would look at her in such a way. The way his eyes moved over her, from her head down to her feet and back up again, affected her in return. His eyes were dark. She knew he was full of desire at that moment. She walked toward him and encouraged him to move backward until he sat on the ledge of the pool that was naturally formed against the far stone wall. When he sat like that, his body was submerged from the waist down.

She straddled him, knowing he was hard for her. She leaned down and kissed him, before moving to make him available to her. It wasn't their first time enjoying such pleasure in the pool. She enjoyed the look on his face as she encouraged him to let her move her body down onto him.

Trent watched her face as she began to move up and down. She was skilled in doing it subtly. If anyone saw, they might not know what was happening. *Might* not.

Despite her slow and subtle movements, it didn't take long before he convulsed inside of her.

Isabella felt his body tense. She watched peacefully as his face moved from the state of climax to a more relaxed calm. As she continued to kiss him, she indulged in her feelings of desire as he used his finger to touch her under the water.

After both had enjoyed the moment through orgasm, Trent covered up and made himself presentable again.

As Isabella continued to straddle him, she felt his hands move over her stomach. They were silent for a long while before Trent found the courage to speak.

"Isabella, do you think you could be with child?" he asked. The question made him nervous. He didn't want to bring up any memory of unhappy times. It was too late. He'd blurted the question out. There was no choice but to face whatever reaction it might evoke in Isabella.

He watched her face change from the previous happiness and peace he'd seen on it to a blend of confusion and dismay.

"Why would you ask that, Trent?" she asked.

"I do not wish to upset you, but you are getting bigger here," he said as he caressed her belly. "I could see it just before. When did you last have your period?"

After he asked that question, she looked even more confused. He hadn't even considered that she wouldn't have heard that particular word used before.

"What is a period?" she asked.

For a moment, Trent had to think about how to explain and ask, not using the terminology he was used to.

"Do you ... do you bleed each month?" he asked and saw her blush deeply as she nodded.

"Yes, of course," Isabella replied. "You know that I do."

"Have you bled over the past three weeks, while we have not been intimate?" Trent enquired.

As Isabella shook her head, Trent could see the idea was finally starting to make sense to her.

"No! Trent, it has been much longer than that!" Isabella exclaimed. "Oh! Do you think I am with child?"

Trent briefly laughed in relief as his Isabella revealed her excitement at the possibility - before her face changed.

"Oh, but we have thought this before, have we not?" she went on to ask as her face changed. "It was not a child at all."

"No, the golden glow that we saw on your belly was not a child, but that does not mean that you have not been with child all this time, Isabella," Trent said, reassuring her. "One thing does not necessarily have to have anything to do with the other."

Isabella moved even closer to him while still straddling him. She wrapped her arms around him tightly.

Trent enclosed her firmly in his own and sat quietly. He indulged in the feel of her body against his, and the clean, pure scent of her.

"I do not want to hope too much," Isabella said quietly, mumbling against his neck. "Can we not speak of this to anyone until we have waited longer?" she asked, pulling away from him slightly.

"Yes, of course," replied Trent. "I will not say anything to anyone."

They sat like that for a long while, neither in any hurry to move. Trent believed he was right, but he understood her fear. He would wait with her and see if their thoughts were correct before he would say anything to anyone about her possibly being pregnant.

Pregnant. Period. Just two words that he needed to try and avoid as he kept working to blend in with the people of the ancient village. He didn't want anything from his time - their future - to be brought into their time and place. He was the one person who could introduce changes to their language and knowledge if he weren't careful. The longer he was among them, the more he was determined to not help them move forward as the world had before it had reached his own time. They were happy frozen in their own little world and ways. Most people he had known in the future didn't know or experience that same level of happiness and contentment.

Language might have seemed like a small thing for him to always consider. Perhaps it was something that would make no difference to how they lived as a village, even if they did learn new ways of speaking. Regardless, from the moment he'd stepped back in time, it had been important to Trent to learn their way of speaking, and never let them learn his.

Peaceful in their individual thoughts, Isabella and Trent moved out of the water and lay down on the large flat stones. As he lay on his back, he closed his eyes against the sun and indulged in taking slow, deep breaths. Day to day, he took for granted how fresh the air was in the village, given its location high on the mountain range. On the odd occasion, he forced himself to remember the pollution, the noise, and the smell of the large city he'd left behind. There was just no comparison between the two situations. If he had any control over it, he would be happy for the village to continue its ways and never move forward in the direction of the modern world. Village life was perfection. Life in the large modern city had never been.

"What do you think so deeply about?" he heard the sweet voice of Isabella ask from her place beside him.

He opened his eyes and looked at her. She was lying on her side, not touching him but staring intently at him. He could not help but smile at the sight.

"I was thinking that every day that I am here with you brings me great pleasure," he replied in full honesty.

Isabella said nothing in return. Instead, she leaned over and kissed him deeply.

Once again, Trent felt his body stir.

"Hmm … no!" Trent said, pretending to scold her. He was rewarded by the glorious sound of her laughing loudly. It was a sound he couldn't get enough of. It was wonderful. It was fulfilling. It was, quite simply, the glorious sound of happiness.

CHAPTER 10

Later that night, Kat lay in bed, her mind in turmoil. She felt alone and lonely. Adrian had been polite to her and had engaged her in conversation, but she knew - she *knew* - that he hadn't been interested in talking to her. Nor had he fully listened to what she'd wanted to say.

Why could he not see that whatever she'd done or said during that time was out of her control? She couldn't even remember the things he'd said she'd done. Why did he keep punishing her for something that he knew she had no knowledge or recollection of?

Knowing there was nothing about the situation in her control, she turned over and tried to relax. After a long time of fitful thoughts and frustration, her body won out over her mind. Finally, she fell into a deep sleep.

~~~~~

'Kat, do not put up with that from him' a voice said. 'He does not know your value. He does not see you like you should be seen. Walk away from him, Kat. There is someone else who wants you. Someone *better*.'

Kat woke suddenly and sat up sharply, so surprised that it had jolted her out of the odd night vision she'd been having. She couldn't remember anything visual from her vision of the night, but the voice was vivid in her memory. It had spoken directly to her. Whose voice had that been? She was sure she'd never heard it before. It made no sense that it could be real.

Looking around, she saw daylight start to creep into the room. With her mind contemplating the day ahead, the night vision was dismissed and the voice forgotten.
~~~~~

CHAPTER 11

"Oh, my dear daughter!" Crisiana exclaimed as Isabella talked to her and told her of her thoughts. "You are going to be a mother!"

"I am?" Isabella asked. "How do I know for sure, Mother? I think I was mistaken before."

Isabella felt her mother's arms wrap around her. She also felt the comfort of a broad smile against her cheek.

"No, Isabella. I think you have been with child all this time," Crisiana said, putting her hand on her daughter's belly. "Look! Feel! You are showing. I believe you have been with child much longer than you think. You might have even conceived on the night of your pairing. Have you bled since that first night?"

Isabella blushed, uncomfortable talking about such intimate things even with her mother.

"I have - once," she replied. "Since I paired with Trent, I have bled once. That was in the few days that followed after our night of pairing."

She saw her mother smile broadly at her.

"Be happy, Isabella," Crisiana said. "Be happy and remain relaxed. There is no reason why you would not be with child. You and Trent will have many children, my daughter. All will be well. We should announce this to the village…"

"No!" Isabella said sharply. She instantly saw the surprise on her mother's face. "No, Mother. Please. I would not like to share this yet."

Isabella saw her mother look at her kindly before pulling her into a warm hug.

"Of course, Isabella," Crisiana said. "I shall not say anything. You must feel right about when is the best time for you. I can see that you are afraid, as is normal. Being with child is something that is exciting but also frightening. It is something new that is happening within your body. It is something unknown but rest assured, it is natural, and it is wonderful. It is a process that has happened since the beginning of time. There is nothing for you to worry about. You know that your father and I are both here if you need to ask or talk about anything," she continued before feeling Isabella nod against her shoulder.

As they moved apart, Isabella smiled shyly in response to the happy smile on her mother's face.

"Does Trent know there is a possibility his child is within you?" asked Crisiana.

"Yes, he was the one who suggested it might be the case," Isabella replied nodding as her hands moved over her belly. "He was the one who noticed…"

Suddenly she found herself in a hold against her mother again. She laughed.

"I hope that if this is a child, I can prove to be a good mother, like you," she said.

"Oh, my daughter," Crisiana replied as she pulled away from the hug and looked into Isabella's eyes. "Your father and I were not blessed with any other children, but even if we had been, you still would have always been so very special to us. You have within you a special light that I have always known is there. You do not seem to see it, but you have greatness inside you and about you. Others have always been drawn to you. Being your mother has always been a joy to me. You will be a wonderful mother, and Trent will be a wonderful father. Of that, I have no doubt."

Isabella felt tears begin to appear in her eyes. She laughed softly as she was instantly pulled back into her mother's arms once more.

CHAPTER 12

In the dark of the night, Kat lay sleeping. As always, the village was silent at that time. It would be hours before even the cooks would wake from their slumber. Not having gone through the pairing process, Kat lived in the same house as her parents, as was normal in the village.

In a small part of her heart, she still hoped that Adrian would once again show an interest in pairing with her. She suspected he wouldn't. Regardless, when she'd gone to sleep, she'd done so thinking about him.

'I know what you are thinking - that he is the one for you,' a voice said to her in her slumber. 'You are worth so much more than that. Do not let him treat you that way. I will treat you better. I will treat you like the supreme woman that you are. You deserve so much more, Kat. If you do not believe what I say to you now, go ahead and ask him once again about pairing with you. You will see that I am right. He will tell you that he does not want to be with you. He does not deserve you. You are meant for greatness. They are stifling you. They are trying to stop you from being the powerful person you are destined to be. They are doing that because they do not want your greatness to be revealed. Once that is shown, they will not be seen in the great light that they are. They see your supremacy and know that they must try and prevent it from being noticed by others.'

In her sleep, Kat heard the long dialogue. She heard the words. She understood what they meant. She agreed with what had been said.

Even in her sleep, she smiled.

CHAPTER 13

Isabella was sleeping soundly when all of a sudden, through the haze of her slumber, she heard a voice. It was a man's voice - deep, mature, and rugged. She did not recognize it. Although still asleep, she was able to turn her attention to it. If she had true knowledge of the world Trent had come from, and the multitudes of gadgets that had been invented in his time, she would have likened what was happening to her to tuning into a radio station.

She listened to the words as they were spoken. It wasn't like it had been when she'd heard Kat's voice speaking to her before the night of the battle. Instead, it seemed like she was hearing words as if she were a bystander. It made her feel like she was standing in the village and softly overhearing a conversation two people were having a short distance away from her.

When she heard Kat's name, her body convulsed and shook her awake. Immediately afterward, she felt a deep shudder of extreme dread pass through her.

Alarmed, she sat up and looked around. The sudden wakefulness startled her. She listened carefully, almost expecting people to be in the room with her. Seeing it was still dark, she turned her head and looked down at Trent. With the smallest amount of moonlight entering the room, she could see he was lying on his front with his right arm relaxed above his head. His left arm was under the cover while his face was turned to the left toward her. She could make out his profile as she listened to his very light sound of sleep. He didn't stir even though she'd sat up abruptly. Quietly she lay back down and positioned herself so she could just look at him.

The voice in her head had disturbed her, in more ways than one. Regardless, she would not wake the man lying beside her and talk to him about it. It could wait till morning. When they were both awake, she would tell him what she'd heard and share with him her concerns.

She closed her eyes and willed herself to go back to sleep.

Subsequently, she forgot all about it.

CHAPTER 14

In the weeks that followed, Isabella finally grew certain that she was indeed with child. It appeared to her that her belly was growing at an alarming rate. She had no knowledge of how such things generally went, so she listened closely to her own body. There was nothing that she could identify that seemed or felt wrong.

Trent watched her and lovingly held her close to him whenever he could. Each night before they fell asleep, he would move behind her back and hold her from behind as his hand caressed the moderately sized but growing bump.

Sometimes he felt and heard her moving in her sleep. To him, it sounded as if she were having a conversation with someone. He never asked her about it. If she ever remembered what had happened in her dreams, she knew she could talk to him. He suspected she might not be remembering them when she woke each morning. He was happy to let that be the case. That option seemed far more attractive than her worrying about something that was happening during her sleeping hours.

They had still not announced she was with child. Regardless, it was Trent's belief that Isabella wasn't keeping it hidden from anyone who looked at her.

"Do you think we should announce that we are going to have a child?" she asked him one morning. She was surprised when her question was met with him laughing out loud.

"You are already quite visible, Isabella," Trent replied. "I am not sure you have kept it a secret."

Isabella smiled at him.

"My mother has told me we should formally announce it because that is the way such things are done in the village," she said. "I shall go to the temple today and talk to the elders to see what is needed for such an announcement to happen."

"Would you like me to come with you?" Trent asked as she moved closer against him in their warm bed. In response - or perhaps *not* in response - he saw and felt her press her lips against his and indulge him in a deep kiss that made him forget the conversation entirely.

CHAPTER 15

"Isabella! Trent!" they heard a voice call out to them after they'd finally left their home and entered the depths of the temple.

When they saw him, they were greeted by the large smile on the face of Elder Scott. It had taken Trent a long while to gain an understanding of the structure of people in the village. He now understood that when people survived to a certain age, they moved into the temple and took on the title of Elder. Of those, the ones who had proven to be 'chosen ones' - villagers with powers - were assigned the additional title of being an ancient. All ancients were elders. Not all elders were ancients.

From the previous battle and earlier indicators of her powers, it had been ascertained that Isabella would become an ancient when she was of age. That would not be for a great many years yet. Her powers were only beginning to emerge. It was expected that they would increase in capability and strength over time, slowly at first before they'd start to gain momentum. It was always the way as ancients grew into their role in the village.

"Elder Scott," Trent heard Isabella say out loud beside him. He broke out of his reverie to smile and greet the elder also.

"What brings you to the temple this fine morning?" Elder Scott asked. "Is there someone, in particular, you need to see?"

"Oh no," Isabella continued. "Oh, I am not sure. I … we … have an announcement to make. I am uncertain what needs to be done in such a situation."

Trent watched Isabella's face as she became flustered. He smiled at her with clear amusement in his eyes. When he turned to face the elder once more, he saw the older man's eyes fall to Isabella's belly.

"Do you wish to declare you are with child?" Elder Scott asked softly, continuing to smile.

"Yes," the elder heard Isabella quietly reply. He knew she had a strong personal aura about her. He equally knew that sometimes, such as at that moment, she was well known to also emit a sense of shyness. It was one of the things that made her so well-liked among their people. Strength with modesty. Power with a blend of open friendliness.

"Of course," Elder Scott said. "Do not look so concerned, Isabella. It is anticipated by all that the villagers are made aware of expected children. We describe it as an informal ceremony, however, in truth, it is simply an announcement that is made to everyone. You will not be uncomfortable. We shall hold the announcement at the evening meal in the dining area. All it will involve is one of the ancients speaking for you and making the news known to everyone. It is nothing at all to worry about."

The elder looked at Isabella and saw her visibly relax.

"Thank you," she said quietly.

Looking at her, Elder Scott wistfully wished he were much younger in years so that he could once more experience the freshness of joy in meeting someone so vibrant and alive. For a fleeting moment, his mind cast back to his Kathleena. She had been beautiful. He could still remember how easily she'd made his blood heated with the way that she'd smiled at him. She was no longer in his world. She had passed, and she was well on her journey now. A small part of him looked forward to his own passing so that he could find her once again and venture on her journey with her. They had thought they'd be together forever. Forever had not eventuated. Instead, their time together had ended far too soon.

"It is no problem at all," he said as he pushed his memories from the forefront of his mind. "You and Trent can go now and move forward with your day as usual. I will arrange things with the ancients. Please relax and worry not."

Trent remained silent as he and Isabella quietly walked out of the temple. Once outside, Isabella turned to him and nestled herself against him, encouraging him to wrap his arms around her.

"Are you alright, Isabella?" he asked, slightly startled at her action. Immediately he felt her nod against his shoulder. "What is it?"

Isabella pulled away only far enough so she could look into his eyes.

"We are having a child," she said, making Trent laugh out loud.

"Yes, I believe we are, but I think you might have already known that," he said softly. He brought one hand up and stroked her cheek before pushing a stray hair aside. "Why are you so full of emotion?"

Isabella looked incredibly young and innocent at that moment as she blushed.

"It is only starting to feel real now, having told someone other than my mother," she replied.

Trent pulled her close to him and pressed her head to his chest.

"Yes, I do understand what you are saying," he said. "It is real. You are going to be a mother, I am going to be a father, and we shall love our child … together."

~~~~~

As the two of them walked into the dining area that evening, Isabella felt a new nervousness flow through her. It was as if it were only at that
~~~~~

moment, as she saw Elder Rhys call everyone's attention to make the announcement, that she really did understand and believe that she was going to have a child. She was going to be a mother. It was no longer just a matter of duty to help with population maintenance within the tall stone walls around the village. It was no longer just a thought that perhaps she and Trent would create a child together.

It was real. A tiny being was already inside of her, growing.

Although she didn't know it, it was also already gaining power.

CHAPTER 16

"Friends and family," Elder Rhys called out to everyone at the evening meal. "I am very pleased and proud to announce to you on behalf of Trent and Isabella that we will soon have a new addition to our population. Let us all take this moment to remember how blessed we are, and send them wishes of good hope in the upcoming delivery of our new little one. He or she will be loved by all, as has always been the way of our people. He or she will contribute to our land and our way of life. He or she will be most welcome," the ancient continued as he looked back and forth from Trent and Isabella to the crowd assembled before them. "He or she will be loved."

Trent was surprised by the content of the announcement. He was even more surprised when he heard the crowd speak. After Elder Rhys spoke his last words, they were echoed back from a mass of voices.

"He or she will be loved."

The stark difference of the volume of the words coming from so many people, after there had been mostly silence as the ancient had spoken, almost stunned Trent. He looked at Isabella and saw her turn and smile at him. The combination of the reception of the people as a collective, and the look on her face, resulted in him feeling his eyes water with intense emotion.

Isabella saw tears beginning in Trent's eyes. She laughed softly at him as she squeezed his hand tightly.

It was only natural that at that moment, Trent should move closer to her, slide one hand around her back, and let his other hand rest on her belly. In response to the movement, Isabella leaned her head on his shoulder and looked out over the crowd in front of her.

"I give you my blessing, Trent and Isabella," Elder Rhys said. As soon as the words were spoken, he walked away, leaving Trent to assume the ceremony was over.

Isabella watched as most people resumed their dining. Her mother and father, Crisiana and Tomas, came to her and pulled her into a hug, before turning to Trent and doing the same.

"You have my blessing," Tomas said and heard Crisiana repeat the words.

The formality of the situation left Trent speechless. He didn't know all of the ways of the village yet. Ceremonies, in particular, made him wary of saying or doing something that he shouldn't. As Isabella's parents moved away, he experienced another set of arms wound tightly around him and Isabella.

"I am excited for you both," the familiar voice said, full of animation.

"Thank you, Adrian," replied Isabella as she returned the hug. "Shall we sit?" she asked, guiding the two men to a large dining table.

Trent's senses filled as he looked excitedly at the food before him. Fresh bread with a creamy apple and mushroom spread was soon in his hand and not moving fast enough toward his mouth, as far as he was concerned. Every meal, constructed with love from the produce of the people, was a miracle to him. Eating it, he knew he'd never want to return to the diet of fast food and preservatives he'd grown up on.

Adrian watched as Trent began his assault on the food in front of him. Trent was oblivious to everything and everyone around him for a moment before he realized Adrian was laughing softly.

Isabella turned to Adrian.

"He loves the food, Adrian," she said to her friend, her face full of love and happiness. "You and I must let him enjoy it."

Trent smiled at both of them without stopping his chewing. They could tease him all they liked. He understood that they did not know just how special the food of the village was. After years of living on food that sometimes had made him think he might as well be eating cardboard or plastic, he would never tire of the tastes that were so abundant in the magical paradise.

"I am happy for you, Isabella. Are you pleased?" Adrian asked. In response, he received the broad grin that revealed Isabella's happiness.

"I am happy, Adrian," she said. "I do wish to be a mother. I am ready. I know I am." Seeing Adrian give her a sad smile, she took his hand in hers.

"You will be a good mother, Isabella," he said. "Of that, I have no doubt. I am very happy for you both."

"But what can I do to make you happier?" Isabella asked. "I wish for you to find what I have found with Trent. It is time, do you not think?"

She saw Adrian sigh.

"I know it is, Isabella," he said. "I do believe that I am ready for it. I do not know who I am to pair *with*. I want to be sure, and I do not feel sure about anything to do with Kat. I feel that I *should* be sure with the right person. Do you think so?"

Isabella nodded.

"I can only speak for myself," she said. "It was very easy for me to want to be paired with Trent but is it always the way? I do not know. Have you spoken to your mother and father about it?"

"No. They have enough to keep them busy while my sisters are still so young. I do not wish to bother them," Adrian said and paused before he continued. "I shall find my happiness, Isabella. I do not think I am meant to be alone. I shall like to be paired and become a father."

"And you will be," she reassured him. "Do not doubt that, please."

CHAPTER 17

Since his heart to heart discussion with his lifelong friend, Adrian had been considering options for pairing. He knew he was a man who others regarded as always being open and friendly. Although in the village there were women his age who possibly would agree to pair with him, in his heart, he wanted to find someone who truly wanted to be with him.

As he'd moved through the approach into adulthood, he knew he'd always yearned strongly for one person. That one person, he could not have. It had saddened him on many an occasion when he had considered the fact, but he did not resent it. He'd accepted that as the way things were, and he did honestly feel happy for Isabella in her choice. There was nothing about Trent that had caused Adrian any concern. It was very clear to anyone who saw them together that the two of them were both equally happy to have been paired together.

As thoughts flowed through his mind, Adrian sat in the dining area. It was early in the morning - *very* early for him since he was so often running late in the mornings. He'd wanted to get there earlier to take some time to simply look around. Perhaps if he turned his head this way and that, his eyes would find someone who was looking at him, wishing they could get his attention. Perhaps someone was thinking of him and hoping they could pair with him.

Once he'd looked around, he knew it had been a futile effort. It had been a childish thought of imagination. It was a small village. Everyone knew each other. Sometimes he wondered if they knew each other too well. There was never any intrigue or mystery about anyone, except Trent, of course. He had come from somewhere else. After his arrival, he had very quickly secured Isabella's heart.

Adrian didn't know any details about where Trent had come from. He'd tried to ask several times. Trent would only say that he did not want to talk about it. He'd said that he had a new life, and that was where he wanted his focus to be. He didn't see the point in talking about the world he came from. It wasn't as peaceful and enjoyable as this world was.

Even Trent's terminology confused Adrian when he thought about it. What did Trent mean when he referred to the village as 'this world'? He must have come from the same world. He'd only walked into the village. How far could the 'world' he'd come from be?

Abruptly, Adrian turned his mind from that thinking. He respected Trent and understood his desire to keep that aspect of his life secret. Adrian would push no more about that. He needed to find his own place in the village. He needed to find his own someone to pair with and start contributing to the population of his people. That was his responsibility, as it was everyone's. He did not know what would happen if he didn't choose someone. Would the elders of the village choose someone for him? As he pondered that possibility, he smiled to himself. Perhaps he didn't need to do the work and find someone after all. Maybe if he waited long enough, someone else would find that someone for him!

"You are here early today, Adrian," he heard the familiar voice say.

He turned to smile at Kat. Her timing in breaking into his thoughts about pairing right at that moment made him briefly wonder at the coincidence of it. As always, he quickly questioned silently what was real with Kat and what was just his imagination. It was a passing concern that he quickly dispelled.

"Good morning, Kat," he replied. "I woke early today and found myself quite hungry! You must try this apple and mint pie. I am not sure which cook came up with this creation. I have not tasted this dish before, but I have to say that I am enjoying it immensely!"

Adrian tried to sound enthusiastic and friendly. When he looked at her closely and studied her face, he saw the look she gave him. It made him feel like she could see right into his soul. It also made him wonder if she knew he was not being completely truthful in how he felt about her.

When Kat next spoke, it appeared that she'd completely dismissed whatever she had been thinking about. It was also clear that she certainly did not seem to want to talk about food.

"Adrian, I wish to talk to you about you and I pairing," she said bluntly.

The words made Adrian splutter the water he'd been drinking.

"Kat! Why are you bringing this up?" he asked. "You said you did not still wish to pair with me..."

"Yes, I did say that, but I was not feeling quite myself. I believe I was too hasty," Kat said. "I now wish to discuss it again. You and I both need to pair sometime soon, and we get on well enough. There is no-one else I wish to be with."

Adrian looked into her eyes, searching for something. It was a move that Kat saw and accurately understood.

"It is only me, Adrian," she said. "I see you looking at me like I have another person inside of me. I do not. I am asking you about the possibility of our pairing."

They sat silent for a long while, studying one another. It was exactly the kind of situation Adrian had been trying to avoid. How could he be sure it was only Kat mentioning such a thing? Did he want to risk becoming paired with her and then having her as a life partner? Did he want to risk being paired with something else?

"Please talk to me. Tell me what you are thinking," Kat said, breaking him out of his thoughts.

Adrian found it difficult to find any words to adequately express his concerns. Knowing she was waiting for a response, he complied and forced an answer out to not upset her.

"I … I am not sure, Kat. Perhaps you could tell me why you wish to pair with me now when previously you did not want to," he said, wondering what was driving such a change of heart in her.

"Why do I need a reason?" she asked. "As I have said, you need to be paired, as do I. We are comfortable around each other. Could that not be reason enough?"

Watching his face, Kat saw his confusion. Realizing he wasn't instantly agreeing to the pairing, her mind thought back to her vision of the night. The voice had said that Adrian would not pair with her. She'd asked Adrian about it because the voice had told her to. She didn't know whose voice it was, but she'd still felt compelled to do as it had instructed her to. Not only that, but it looked to her like she was about to get the answer from Adrian that the voice had said she would. He was going to turn down her request to pair with him. He was going to prove the mystery voice right in its prophecy.

Adrian considered the thoughts that had been running through his head minutes earlier. He had been wondering who he could pair with. He'd been trying to figure out who would want to pair with him. Now someone was asking him but was that reason enough? Did he want to consider the opportunity again with Kat? He'd agreed to it the first time, believing the two of them could be happy enough together. That had been before she'd told him firmly that she did not want it to happen. Now she was again saying that she did. What was driving her to change her mind so much?

Curious to see how far she would go in the conversation, he decided to challenge her.

"Alright," he said and watched her face closely as it changed before him. Very evident on her face in response to that one word was her distinct look of surprise.

"Alright?" she stuttered as if it were the last thing she'd expected to hear come from his mouth. "What do you mean, 'alright'?"

"I mean, yes," he said. "If you wish to pair with me, then let it be so. When would you like to arrange the pairing ceremony for?"

As he continued to watch her face, he saw her become deeply flustered. It seemed she'd wanted to confront him and ask him to pair with her. It equally appeared that she hadn't wanted or expected him to agree to go through the pairing process with her.

"I … I must go," she said suddenly and stood quickly, picking up her cutlery, cup, and plate, and simply walking away.

Adrian watched her as she moved to the clearing area. She looked normal but tense as she washed, dried, and put everything away. Before she left the area entirely, he saw her turn and look at him. He could not fathom the look on her face in that instant. It made him wonder if it were actually Kat or if it was the face of someone else.

CHAPTER 18

Kat rushed out of the dining area. As the fresh air hit her face, she stopped and closed her eyes. She was confused. She knew she had just asked Adrian about pairing with her, but it felt to her like the idea hadn't even been hers. The words seemed to have tumbled from her mouth without her consent, but she was conscious of it. It wasn't like the other times when Adrian and Isabella had told her of things she'd done - things that she couldn't *remember* having done. She had been fully aware she was asking Adrian about pairing. She just didn't quite believe that the idea or the desire to do it had actually come from her.

She shook her head, trying to shake away the thoughts and concerns inside of her. She found herself wishing desperately that the previous few minutes had not happened.

"Kat? Are you alright?" she heard Isabella's voice ask. Kat categorically did not want to talk to her, but she inhaled deeply, opened her eyes, and smiled as best she could.

"Good morning, Isabella. Good morning, Trent," Kat said. "Yes, I was simply enjoying the fresh air. Thank you. I … I must go to the mill now," she continued before swiftly walking away from them.

Trent looked at her as she left.

"That was not a true smile," he said softly. The words had been spoken mostly to himself, but Isabella heard.

"No, it was not," she agreed.

CHAPTER 19

"Adrian, is Kat well?" Isabella asked her friend as she sat down beside him in the dining area. "We saw her leave. Something did not seem right."

She saw a look of concern cross Adrian's face briefly before he seemed to remember he should always be happy. A large grin replaced the seriousness.

"Isabella! Good morning!" he replied with a noticeable overindulgence of enthusiasm. "Good morning, Trent!"

As Adrian said the words, he could tell by a raised eyebrow that Trent wasn't believing his feigned high level of happiness at that moment. It was a facial expression Adrian had never seen before Trent had arrived in the village, but he'd gotten used to it. Now he understood its meaning. It was Trent's funny way of silently expressing he did not quite believe what he'd just seen or heard.

Isabella reached out and took her friend's hand in her own.

"Adrian, you do not need to pretend with me," she said. "Did something just happen between you and Kat?"

She saw Adrian's face relax. He smiled sadly at her as he took a moment to think before he spoke.

"She asked me about pairing with her," he said quietly, feeling confused once more. "Again!"

"Is that a good thing or not a good thing?" Isabella asked.

Adrian watched as she let go of his hand and turned to begin eating. He saw her look back at him as she took a bite of the large slice of apple and mint pie before her.

"I do not know," he replied. "How can I know? I do not even know for sure that it *is* Kat who was speaking to me." He looked around so that Isabella and Trent were both in his view. "Do either of you think there is a possibility that whatever was inside of her before is not gone? That she still is not truly Kat at all?"

Adrian looked at their faces and could tell from their somber expressions that they had also questioned that very possibility.

"You have doubts also? Both of you?" he asked and saw his two friends nod in response.

"It is on my mind, Adrian," Trent replied. "Of course, it is. She seemed well that night after Isabella extinguished whatever that thing was that came out of her, but something about her does make me nervous. I am sorry to say it..."

"No!" exclaimed Adrian. "Please do not apologize. I am also uncertain of what is real. It is confusing since it was she who wanted to pair at first, and then she said she did not. Now she has decided she *does* want to..."

Isabella reached out and squeezed his hand again.

"Adrian, do not do anything you are uncertain of," she said to him.

Adrian nodded at her, for a moment appreciating the beauty of the friend before him. When he realized that witnessing the happiness of Isabella and Trent was not helping with his confusion, he rose from his seat.

"I must get to the mill," he said as he put one hand on Isabella's shoulder. He smiled sadly at both friends before walking away.

Isabella turned to Trent. They continued to look toward each other, but neither focused on the other. It had all happened weeks earlier. The cold blue entity that had been inside of Kat had been extinguished by the warm gold of Isabella. The blue was gone. It was dead. Why did it keep feeling like the battle wasn't over at all?

CHAPTER 20

Kat moved through her day without speaking to anyone. She worked in the mill, not far from Adrian, but she did not speak to him. Her mind was alert and full - *too* full! For days, she had started to feel like she was muddled and didn't know what was happening to her. She had asked Adrian about pairing, but she wasn't sure that it was what she wanted at all. Why had she asked him if she wasn't sure? What had driven her to do such a thing?

At the end of the workday, she walked out of the mill. Breathing in the warm air as she stood still and absorbed the sunshine hitting her face, she intended to walk alone to the evening meal. She was surprised to hear Adrian call out to her.

"Wait," his voice carried to her, making her turn. "Kat, please, we must talk about…"

"There is nothing to talk about, Adrian," Kat responded, flustered. "Please forget I said anything this morning."

"But … but this morning, you said that you wanted…" Adrian began to say in his confusion.

"I was being silly. Please disregard what I said," Kat replied.

Adrian found himself stunned at her change again. He stopped walking and watched as she turned and resumed her movements up the path to the dining area. Partway up the long path, she stopped and turned to him again.

"Are you coming to dine?" she asked as if their previous moment hadn't happened.

Adrian found himself immersed in confusion but began walking again. Although they strode alongside one another, the two journeyed to the dining area in silence.

~~~~~

"I do not understand what you wish for, Kat," Adrian said as they sat with their meals. "If you wish to pair with me, then let us arrange to do that. Why have you changed your mind again? What possibly could have happened since this morning that could make you not want to pair with me now?"

Kat felt her head become fuzzy with not knowing … *anything*. She felt frustrated because it seemed to her that even she couldn't accurately
~~~~~

ascertain what she wanted.

"I think that I do want to pair with you, but I keep feeling uncertainty," Adrian heard her say quietly. In response, he took her hand in his.

"If you wish to be paired with me, I will agree to that … happily," he said. Her facial expression appeared intense. He wanted to help her stop looking so worried.

"Yes?" she asked timidly, a complete opposite to the person she'd appeared to be in the temple weeks earlier. "You will pair with me?"

Adrian gulped but nodded softly. He didn't know who he was supposed to pair with, but she was there, and she wanted to be with him. *Sometimes* she said that was what she wanted. In reality, he knew he could never be paired with the person he truly always had wanted to be with. Did it really matter who he did pair with then?

CHAPTER 21

"Kat! He does not deserve you. I keep telling you," the voice started to say in her head while she slept.

This time she found the strength to speak back. "No!" she exclaimed inside the confines of her vision of the night. "You said he did not want me, but you are wrong. I asked him, just as you said to, and he said yes. He wants to pair with me."

"No! That cannot be!" the phantom voice said forcefully. "If he said yes, he is only saying it to appease you, Kat. Can you not see that? He does not want you. He wants another that he cannot have. You are just a replacement. You are not the person he truly wants. Do you want that for the rest of your life? To be with someone who does not even want to be with you? To be someone's replacement for the person they really want to be with? Kat! You know you are worth so much more than that. You are a woman who needs to be recognized for your supremacy over all others."

Kat forced herself awake. She did not want to hear any more.

The words remained clear in her head as she sat up and took a deep breath. She didn't understand where the voice kept coming from, but she didn't want to hear it.

She lay back down and resolved to not fall back asleep for the rest of the night.

CHAPTER 22

At breakfast the following morning, Kat sat with Adrian and chatted to him in as friendly a manner as she could muster. It was difficult, with the extreme tiredness she was experiencing due to her lack of sleep.

They talked about unimportant things that were easy to talk about. They each avoided conversation about pairing. It was confusing for both of them, so they were equally happy to simply avoid the topic altogether.

That night, Kat felt dread as she prepared for bed. She hadn't let herself go back to sleep the previous night. Throughout the entire day, she'd felt the exhaustion that had flowed on from that decision.

Finally, she succumbed to the extreme need to sleep and fell into her slumber. It wasn't long before the deep voice began working its way into her visions of the night once more.

"Please do not pair with him, Kat. I want you more than he does," the voice taunted her. "You are worth so much more. You will be valued by me. You will be *loved* by me."

"You do not even know me," Kat replied in her consciousness of slumber. "Why do you keep talking to me? Why do you keep trying to sway me toward you and away from him? What do you want?"

"I want you," the voice said. "You will see. You and I are meant to be together."

"If that is so, then show yourself to me," Kat challenged it. "Show yourself to me in person. Stop speaking to me like this, hiding your true self. Talk to me so I can see who you are. You say you want to be with me and that I should not pair with Adrian, but he talks to me every day, as a real person. That is more than I get from you."

~~~~~

The night visions continued for many weeks more, forcing Kat to initially dread sleep every night. With it happening so regularly, however, she began to notice she was finding a new level of strength. In her visions of the night, she began taking enough control to visualize the voice away. Once she'd mastered that, it became easier to at least return to a peaceful slumber each night, even if she did still have to listen to the initial unwelcome onslaught of words.
~~~~~

CHAPTER 23

Over the same few weeks, Adrian found himself beginning to panic. Kat seemed friendly enough toward him, but every day she looked like she was changing a little bit more.

In physical appearance, she seemed to be changing into someone else completely. He could see darkness under her eyes. When he questioned her, she would simply say that she had not slept well the night before. It was an acceptable reason, but something felt different in the way she was acting toward him also.

"Kat," he said to her one morning in the dining area as he sat beside her. "When shall we see the elders about setting a date for our pairing?"

He saw her express a look of being startled before she mumbled a reply.

"Oh … Adrian. There is no hurry, is there?" she asked. "It is just that I have not been feeling very well lately. Could we talk about it later?"

Adrian nodded and said nothing more. He wondered why he ever let himself get pulled into the same conversation, over and over. He'd learned that Kat said one thing, and then she said the opposite. He'd also accepted that whatever would or would not happen between the two of them, she was the one in full control of the outcome. He was just a passenger along for the ride.

CHAPTER 24

As the weeks passed, the voice in Kat's head in the evenings seemed to become progressively more intense and increasingly louder. She tried to fight it with all of her willpower in an attempt to keep it at a distance. She desperately wanted to find a way to go to sleep and keep a wall up around her mind so that it could not invade her at all. Somehow it kept breaking through, demanding she give it her attention when it seemed to know that she was trying not to.

After much trial and error, she had begun to master turning the voice off after a period of time of having to listen to it. Her strength in being able to fight it had grown with each subsequent night that it had invaded her. It wasn't an ideal solution. In truth, she felt desperate to be rid of it altogether. It was a constant source of confusion. The voice was insistent that it wanted her and that she should not pair with Adrian. Although it persisted in its messages, the owner of the voice did not appear before her. She didn't know who it was. She didn't even know if she could be certain that it was *real*.

CHAPTER 25

Deep inside of him, Adrian started to feel even more panic. He was unsure about what was happening with Kat. Whatever it was, it made him more and more nervous. Her reactions to him flowed back and forth in an erratic movement. One morning she'd be enthusiastic about talking to him. The next, she would sit elsewhere in a very obvious attempt to completely avoid him. Then she would return to his side, happy and chatty. Afterward, she would be somber and morose.

In the silence of his mind, Adrian questioned whether he might be dealing with two different people.

That thought scared him deeply.

~~~~~

One evening, as he sat with Trent and Isabella in their home and he looked at his closest friend, Adrian was surprised by how quickly her belly was growing larger. Nobody could have any doubt that she was with child.

He felt a new level of protectiveness flow over him as he looked at her. They had been close friends all of their lives. Normally he would do anything for her. With her being in her current state, he wasn't quite sure what he could do to help her with anything.

"How are you feeling, Isabella? Truly?" he asked quietly, realizing how in awe of her he was. He always had been to an extent. Visually seeing her belly growing and knowing that a small person was inside of her pushed his admiration to a new level.

"I am well, Adrian," Isabella replied, happiness evident on her face. "I feel myself getting larger. Some days when I first wake up, it feels like I've woken up much larger than I was when I went to bed! I do not, however, feel as if anything is wrong. I am happy."

Adrian smiled at her in response to her words.

"I am ashamed to say that I am quite envious of you, Isabella," he said. Not only have you found someone to pair with, but now you are also going to become a mother. It has all seemed so easy for you."

When Isabella looked closely at him, she saw his eyes beginning to water. She reached out her hand to his.

"You must be patient, Adrian," she said. "The right person that you are meant to pair with will come along. Put it from your mind. Let it just
~~~~~

happen as it is meant to."

Adrian remained quiet. He had no wish to argue with her about her theory. It seemed too good to possibly be true, but he had no desire to upset her with his view on the subject.

"What is happening with Kat now, Adrian?" he heard Trent ask from his place at the table beside Isabella. "Has anything been resolved?"

"No. I feel like I live in a constant state of uncertainty where Kat is concerned," Adrian replied. "Some days she wants to pair. Some days she does not. In truth, I do not mind which it is to be. I simply wish that she could be constant in her thoughts. It is this ongoing changing of her mind that causes me more vexation than whatever the final answer is to be."

Trent looked at him and said nothing more. His fears about Kat being taken over by an entity again continued to increase. He'd kept those thoughts to himself. He would do anything to avoid upsetting Isabella as their small child grew inside of her.

"I must return home. Thank you for making the time to talk and listen," Adrian said before standing, hugging each, and quietly leaving their small home.

Once they were alone again, Isabella turned to Trent.

"I wish so much for Adrian to find someone to pair with, Trent," she said. "He is a good man. He deserves to be loved. He deserves to have what I have with you."

Trent felt overwhelmed in his love for her. He stood up to guide her out of her seat and into his arms.

"Yes," he said. "I would wish everyone to find what I have with you too."

Sensing the depth of his emotion, Isabella leaned against him and reached up to kiss him softly. It was intended as a simple expression of her love for him. As soon as her lips touched his, she realized she was more than a little bit hungry for him.

As they moved from lip caresses to deep indulgence with their tongues tasting one another, Isabella felt her body awaken as if it were absolutely starving. She could tell by the positioning and movement of Trent's hands that he was holding back and thinking far too much. It wasn't a time that she wanted him to think. It was a moment in which she wanted him to act.

Trent tasted her mouth and wanted more - *needed* more. He always felt like he could never get enough of her. She'd been a virgin and completely unknowing about anything sexual before the night they had paired. Regardless, Isabella had shown him right from that first night that she had natural sexuality about her. Embedded within her was a sexual and sensual instinct. She'd affected him right from their first moments together as if she had always known how to use her body to please someone.

Trent indulged in the feel of her lips and the additional friction that was occurring in his body from the feeling of her tongue caressing his. It made him moan deeply and try to pull her even closer. As he did so, he was reminded by the swell of her belly that another person was present. A tiny person was living and growing inside of her womb. The thought was a startling and sobering one. He reluctantly pulled his lips away from hers and looked into her eyes.

"What is it?" Isabella asked him, concerned that something was seriously worrying him. She was alarmed to consider that perhaps something serious had happened. She hoped it wasn't something he'd not told her about.

Trent looked at her and pulled right away. Having come from a modern world, he felt he should know when it stopped being safe for a pregnant woman to have sex. It made no sense that he *would* know that. He hadn't been in the medical profession, nor had he had anything to do with any woman when she was pregnant. The unknowing caused a slight concern in him.

Isabella remained quiet in the belief that she could read his emotion by what his face revealed. She hoped there was nothing to truly be concerned about, but patiently waited for him to speak.

Trent took her hand, quietly led her to the bed, and prompted her to lie down beside him. There they lay, on their sides, facing one another.

Isabella continued to wait for him to speak. During his silence, she seized the moment to just look at him. She saw him every day and every night, but sometimes she forgot to really *look* at him. Pushing aside the glorious way he made her feel when he touched and kissed her, she conceded that she'd also always loved the way he looked. She loved the waviness of his brown hair. She loved the way that he kept his facial hair short but visible. It was different from the many men in the village who preferred to grow long beards. Since Trent had arrived, Isabella had noticed other men had started to do as he did, shortening their facial hair. She didn't think he'd intended to make any changes to the village or the people in it, but little things had begun to change regardless.

Since Trent had made the decision to move from his time in the future to her time, and he'd been able to eat well and regularly, his body had changed. He had been bony when they'd met, due to the long journey of walking he'd been on before he found her. His body had not been in good shape then.

As Isabella let her eyes travel over his arms and chest, visible through the simple shirt he wore, she was reminded of how well-formed his body was. When they stood together, and when they lay together, they fitted each other perfectly. When she thought about them fitting together perfectly, her mind wandered into the realm of how it felt when he was moving inside of her. Since Trent was, at that moment, lying quietly with no urgency for them to talk, Isabella let herself dwell on exactly that thought.

As she lay still, deep in her observations and thoughts, letting her mind wander to aspects of their lovemaking, Trent watched her face. He could tell she was thinking, so he did not speak for a long while. He believed he would never get tired of watching her face. It was always easy for him to see when she was deep in thought. Sometimes her face blatantly revealed her thoughts as they turned to the subject of pleasure. As much as he'd wanted to be serious in his concern about harming her or the baby while she was pregnant, he couldn't help but smile at her when he understood where her thoughts had taken her.

Although facing one another, Trent could tell by her face that she was somewhere else entirely. He waited patiently, letting her indulge in whatever thoughts of pleasure she was enjoying at that moment. The expression on her face was far too enjoyable to watch for him to even consider saying anything and breaking the moment.

When Isabella had long focused on the thought of how Trent always felt inside of her, she let out a sigh. At that moment, she suddenly became aware that he was watching her. She quietly laughed as she felt her face begin to blush heavily. She knew he could always read her face, but she did not mind. It was refreshing to know he often understood what she was thinking about, without her having to try and talk about it.

"Where were your thoughts just then, Isabella?" Trent asked. The grin on his face was wide enough to make her laugh even more. "Yes, I can see it all over your face. Whatever you were thinking about, you were very much enjoying it!" he further teased her.

Isabella moved closer to him and brought up her hand to stroke his cheek lightly with her fingers before leaning in and kissing him softly.

Trent lifted his hand and caught her wrist so he could kiss her palm.

"I was thinking of you. I was remembering how it feels when you are inside of me," she said boldly but quietly, almost in a whisper.

Isabella instantly heard him let out a deep breath. She saw him move so that he was no longer looking into her eyes. She waited for him to compose himself and formulate the words he seemed to want to say. Finally, he spoke.

"I do not know when we must stop doing that," he said quietly, feeling remarkably shy in contrast to his usually confident nature. He raised his eyes again and once more looked into hers. "I do not want to hurt you or our child."

Isabella smiled at him as she ran her hand through his thick hair.

"Trent, this is what you are worried about?" she asked and saw him nod.

"I am apprehensive about it, yes," he said. "I cannot bear the thought of anything happening to you. If I were to harm you in any way…"

"I am well," Isabella replied. "I do not know if there is any possibility of harming our child or not when we join, but I cannot bear you pulling away from me. If we do not join, can we not still be close?"

As she said the words and asked the question, Trent felt her hand glide across his body as it moved down. Feeling her touch his chest, belly, and down to his thigh made him yearn for her touch. It equally made him desperate to touch her.

Isabella saw his eyes change and darken before he leaned forward and kissed her lips. Softly at first and then with increasing pressure, his tongue made its way to meet with hers. Wrapping their arms tightly around each other, neither ventured toward anything more for the moment. The taste of each other and the way their tongues danced together in perfect harmony was not something to be rushed away from.

She moved her hand onto him through his clothing. Both groaned at the touch. Trent loved the natural feeling of pleasure that came from being touched by her.

Isabella loved the glorious understanding that his hardness was the result of how he felt about being with her. It told her clearly how much he loved her touch. At that moment, she needed to be much closer to him.

Trent felt her begin to pull his clothing off. The movement had such eagerness and almost desperation about it that he laughed softly as he helped her. When he'd removed all of his clothes, he lay naked beside her.

He saw Isabella study all of him, from his eyes, down over his torso, and down his legs. He felt her hand move down to his ankle and slowly move up his upper leg. All the time that she was touching him, he watched her face. The way that she looked at him, and the degree to which she seemed to study his body, he adored. He wanted her to always look at him like that.

Inside of him, he felt desperate to touch and pleasure her. He held back. On her face, he could see that it was more important to her to let her hands enjoy their journey. She avoided touching him directly on his erection. Instead, she moved her hands skillfully around him so that she could explore his torso further. Finally, her hands and her eyes returned to his eye level. As her hands cupped his face, she placed her lips on his.

They kissed for a long time, neither wanting to rush. Isabella eventually felt one of his hands move, and his fingers lightly caress the tip of one of her breasts. Through the fabric of her slip dress, she knew he'd artfully found her nipple and was touching it lightly. It was enough to send her nerves to a higher degree of desire.

Trent heard her moan softly. He kept his fingers in the one place, teasing her for a long while.

Not wishing to take things slowly anymore, Isabella sat up and removed her dress before lying back down again. As she did, she found herself nudged so that she was lying on her back.

Trent moved over her and straddled her outer thighs to not put his weight onto her. Concentrating on her belly being visibly swollen helped to sober and keep his body calm as he focused solely on her.

Isabella felt him kiss her deeply. She desired to feel him move into her. That was what her body seemed to need. She forced herself to focus on his lips instead.

As his mouth moved from her lips and down to her neck, Trent heard her moan deeply. He had reached one of her pleasure points and chose to stay there for a very long while. The sound of her in such pleasure was not something he could ever move away from quickly. He felt her hands on his shoulders, trying to move him from the spot. The discovery made him laugh softly at her. He kissed her before moving his lips down her body, stopping to give each of her slightly swollen breasts the attention he always felt they deserved.

Finally, Isabella felt his kisses approaching where she needed them to be. Opening her legs wide, her head moved backward as she felt his tongue begin its journey of pleasure. The feeling of him kissing her there never ceased to amaze and fulfill her. As her belly had increased in size with the child inside of her growing, so had the depth of her feeling of pleasure. It wasn't long before she felt the blissful and highly intense waves flow over her.

Trent moved over her and kissed her again, surprised at how quickly she'd climaxed. He opened his mouth to speak and tease her about it. Before any words escaped his mouth, he found himself physically pushed off her and onto his back. The movement was so forceful that he chuckled at Isabella's heightened sensuality that seemed to have come from her pregnancy.

Without any hesitation or movement toward kissing him on his lips, Isabella seemed to dive straight in. As soon as Trent's back was flat on the bed, she wrapped her lips around him.

From the first contact of her mouth on him, Trent could think no more. She had perfected her movements with her lips and tongue when she caressed him like that. He was happy to lie still and focus on the feelings she evoked in him. He could feel his orgasm building. His body was desperate for release. When his climax hit, he couldn't even think about keeping quiet as muscles throughout his entire body clenched and then started pulsating. After a long while, he felt her remove her mouth, reposition herself, and then kiss him directly on his lips, full of passion.

Neither spoke for a long time. There was no need for words. Trent had been concerned he could hurt her. They both knew that. They wouldn't join again until after the birth of their child, but they equally would not give up their sexual pleasure.

CHAPTER 26

Trent woke to the sound of Isabella screaming. The intensely sharp and horrifying sound cut through his dreams and struck directly at his heart. He knelt on the bed and looked at her, fearful that a new battle was about to begin. He was relieved to see that in the moonlight, despite the agony that her screams had indicated, she was smiling.

"I think it is time, Trent," Isabella said with a look on her face that momentarily stunned him. "I can feel the baby moving downwards inside of me."

Trent took a moment to consider the words. They weren't words he'd ever heard anyone say, but he hadn't known any close friends who had yet had children. Perhaps he'd always misconceived that labor took a great many hours.

"Oh, I think it is almost here," he heard her further say as she moaned deeply. Trent was speechless. He would never claim to know anything about childbirth but didn't think it usually happened so quickly. He expected she was more likely embarking on a long night.

He watched calm appear over Isabella's face as she pushed back the covers. Directly in Trent's sight was the view of a baby being born. He remained still, kneeling in the same spot, as onto the bed, a tiny person slid down and out of its mother.

Trent couldn't move. In front of him was a little being, moving and opening its mouth to cry.

Isabella looked at Trent and laughed. Childbirth was unknown to her. She'd never seen it happen or even heard anything about it. Anything that personal was never discussed among their people. All she knew was that it *did* happen, over and over again, and it was required to keep the population of the village steady.

The small amount of pain she'd experienced quickly disappeared. It was replaced by a warmth spreading over her belly.

Seeing her look down, Trent followed her view and saw it too. His eyes moved to the golden glow that had begun to appear. He leaned over with his hand and touched it. He knew it was as it had been before. The glow was back. Looking at Isabella's face, he guessed that she had come to the same startling conclusion.

Suddenly a small cry alerted both of them that there were more pressing matters than just a golden light emanating from its mother's belly.

Trent, broken from his thoughts, looked around for a cloth to wrap the child in. Gently he secured the fabric and pulled the small infant into his arms. In the moonlight, the tiny body looked like it had a faint golden haze around it. Trent immediately dismissed it as not being real. He then put it down to a trick of the light and filed what he'd seen away in his mind to be forgotten.

"He's perfect, Isabella," he said.

When she looked closely at Trent, Isabella saw his eyes watering as he smiled at the child.

Suddenly aware of how open and uncomfortable Isabella must be feeling, lying on the bed in the way that she was, Trent passed the small package to her to hold.

"You hold him. I shall bring some water to clean you," he said.

Isabella smiled at him. Cleanliness was the last thing on her mind. She looked down into the small face and laughed.

"You are real," she said with a wondrous sound in her voice. "You are here, and you are real!"

Trent took his time, cleaning Isabella and fussing over her to make sure she was alright.

"Trent!" she laughed out loud to him, making him smile bashfully. "Come and sit down here with our son," she said as she reached out with one hand, inviting him to sit with her.

Trent settled on the bed so they were both sitting up. The baby nestled in his mother's arms and easily took his first taste of Isabella's milk.

"What shall we call him?" Trent whispered as they watched the small mouth drink in hunger.

Isabella opened her mouth to say something. As she did, a faint voice inside of her head seemed to call out to her. She heard what it said and immediately repeated it. She didn't want to think about where the voice came from. All she knew was that the voice and the name at that moment were right.

"Cesare," she said.

"Cesare?" Trent asked softly, curious.

"Do you object? Is there another name you would prefer?" she asked.

Trent smiled at her and kissed her.

"No," he replied. "Cesare, he shall be."

CHAPTER 27

The new family relaxed together until the sunshine finally broke through, replacing the moonlight in the room.

"We shall need to find him some clothing, Isabella. Why did we not think of that before?" Trent asked and heard Isabella laugh softly in response.

"It is alright, Trent," she replied. "We only need to visit the tailor. They will have clothing that is suitable. We can stop there on the way to the morning meal. I would also like to see my mother and father."

Trent smiled at her and happily received the bundle back once again. He hadn't told Isabella as much, but in his previous life, he'd never wanted to have children. They were something that hadn't been part of his life plan - whatever plan that had been. As he held the small infant in his arms and looked at the beautiful woman beside him, he began to consider that perhaps he'd always been meant to be a father. He vowed silently to himself that he would be a good one.

They walked toward the door to introduce their little one to the world, and the world to their little one. Before they stepped outside, Isabella moved close to Trent and kissed him deeply.

"I do not know if we shall have privacy for a while, Trent. I think Cesare will sleep with us until he is older," she said.

As the words came out of her mouth, Trent saw an extremely seductive glow on her face, along with a look that Trent, being from our world, would only describe as a smirk.

"Isabella," he said, laughing. "Your body just gave birth. I do not think we will be having any of that for a while yet!"

He saw her blush as she laughed softly in response. The sound of her chuckle made his heart sing. She was happy. Nothing could be more important to him than that.

"Come, Trent," Isabella said. "I shall not tease you more. Let us go and find this little one some clothing, and then begin our day."

Trent looked at her in surprise. Being bedridden for days, as he had always thought any woman would be after giving birth, simply did not seem to be any kind of thought to her.

~~~~~

As soon as they stepped outside of their modest home, people on their
~~~~~

way to their work or the morning meal threw up their arms in surprise and joy.

Isabella laughed as one person after another stopped them on their journey to the village tailor to collect clothing for the infant.

Finally, they reached their destination. The tailor was enraptured.

"Oh! Isabella! Oh, how wonderful. Here now. Give him to me to hold while you look through this pile of infant clothing. He is a good-sized little one. Any of these will fit."

Isabella grabbed a handful of items, including one to put her son into immediately. While the tailor helped her to dress him, Trent looked on in wonder that before him was his son.

After gathering the baby and his clothing up, they turned to leave and once again began a slow journey as they were greeted by different people of the village.

"Daughter!" Isabella heard her mother call out to her. When Isabella turned with Trent toward the direction the voice had come from, they saw Crisiana running toward them. "Isabella! Trent! The little one has arrived? Oh, let me see."

Isabella handed Cesare over and watched tears appear on her mother's face.

Crisiana looked at Trent. She leaned in to hug him before taking Isabella's hand in hers and squeezing it tightly.

"We must have a celebration. It is tradition. Have you been to the temple yet?" she asked.

Isabella shook her head.

"Not yet, Mother," she replied. "I shall go there after we dine."

"Yes, of course," said Crisiana. "You must look after yourself. The two of you should go now and eat in the dining area. I shall look after this little one for you," she continued as she gushed over the small bundle in her arms.

Trent looked at Isabella and found her looking right back at him with one eyebrow raised. He didn't know if she was aware that she'd picked it up from him. Whenever he saw her do it, he laughed silently on the inside and loved her even more.

CHAPTER 28

Inside the dining area, Isabella immediately went to find Adrian. As he saw her approach and sit in the seat beside him, she saw a look of surprise on his face as his eyes moved to her belly.

"Isabella, I am sure you were bigger than that yesterday," he said with an honest look of confusion on his face.

The words of her good friend made Isabella laugh.

"That is because the little one who was living in there yesterday has now moved out," she replied and quietly waited for him to comprehend what she was saying.

Suddenly, she saw him jump up.

"You are a mother?" Adrian asked, full of excitement. In response, he saw Trent and Isabella both laugh. "Oh, Isabella!" he said, pulling her close and hugging her tightly. "Where is the little one? Is all well? Are *you* well?"

As Trent and Isabella sat down and began eating, Isabella smiled at Adrian.

"I am well, Adrian, and so is our son," she replied.

"You have a son?" he asked with a wistful sound to his voice.

"Yes," Isabella replied. "Cesare. Our little Cesare has arrived and is currently being held by my mother."

"But you, Isabella?" Adrian asked. "How can you be so well so soon after giving birth? You look like you did nothing out of the ordinary last night at all!"

Trent had been silently asking the same question since the birth of their son but had not voiced his curiosity over it. Perhaps it was just the way it was with the people of the village. Perhaps it was another cultural thing or a by-product of no stress or unhealthy living. He'd decided that the reason didn't matter. Isabella was fine, and they had a son. A son!

~~~~~

After they'd finished their meal and washed, dried, and put away their dishes, Trent and Isabella left the dining area. Looking around outside, they saw Crisiana standing right where she had been, chatting to people as they walked past.

When the couple reached her, she smiled broadly.

"He is beautiful but he does not have hair like yours, Isabella,"
~~~~~

Crisiana said. "Nor yours, Trent. I think this one will have a different color again," she said as she handed the bundle to Trent. "Oh, my daughter, I am happy for you."

"Thank you, Mother," Isabella replied as she received a hug from her mother. "I will go to the temple now and talk to the elders."

~~~~~

As they approached the temple, Isabella started to feel slight warmth and familiar discomfort in her belly. She reached down, placed her hand over it, and recognized it. The feeling made her stop walking. She remembered having seen it briefly straight after she'd given birth. At that time, she had pushed it from her mind and subsequently forgotten it.

Trent noticed Isabella had stopped walking. He turned to her as he held Cesare, asleep in his arms. Looking at her face, he saw alarm.

"What is it?" he asked, instantly concerned.

When he saw her look down at her hands and then move them, Trent saw the glow. As Isabella tentatively took a step toward the temple, the glow shone brighter, just as it had done months before.

"I may not be able to talk to the elders, Trent. Can we go in there slowly? You may need to carry Cesare to introduce him," she said.

Trent nodded and held out his hand to her.

"Of course," he replied. "You need to tell me when you feel discomfort or pain that is at a level too uncomfortable to bear."

As they slowly walked into the temple, Isabella monitored the feelings inside of her. When they were in the middle chamber, she started to feel the slight level of pain she'd felt the last time she'd experienced it. As the pain increased, she stopped walking once more and saw Trent turn to look at her.

"Elder Rhys is coming," Trent heard her whisper. He was about to question how she could know that since there was silence. Before he voiced the question, the ancient appeared.

"Isabella. Trent," Elder Rhys said, moving forward. When he saw the look on Isabella's face, he halted in his steps.

Trent saw the ancient's eyes drop to her belly automatically as if he'd already suspected what was happening.

"You have the glow again, Isabella?" Elder Rhys asked, horrified at the possibility. He saw Isabella nod, confirming his fears. "What does it mean? I thought it was over. Is there another among us? Another like Kat?"

Isabella looked lost in her inability to give him any answers.

"I do not know, but I feel the discomfort once more, so please keep your distance from me, Elder Rhys," Isabella said and saw him nod in response.

On the previous occasion when Isabella had exhibited a golden glow
~~~~~

in her belly - the same golden glow she'd used to fight Kat's cold blue that night in the temple - it had been realized that Isabella could not be close to Elder Rhys without feeling great pain. The closer she moved toward him, the greater the pain became. Neither knew why it happened, but both were very aware that it did.

"Of course," Elder Rhys said, moving a step backward. When he turned to look at Trent, he finally saw the bundle in his arms.

"Oh! It has happened!" he said as he moved closer to Trent and Cesare.

When he peered inside the cloth wrapped around the child, he saw the small eyes open and look directly at him. As he raised his hand to run a finger lightly over the baby's cheek, small fingers grabbed and held it. Elder Rhys smiled at the movement. Such a move from any newborn child always made him smile, but something was different with the infant he looked at. As soon as the small hand wrapped around his finger, he felt a warmth flow over him, like he was suddenly engulfed in a warm breeze.

"It is good to see you, old friend," he heard inside of his head. The words were as clear as if someone was standing right beside him, whispering in his ear.

Trent and Isabella both saw the ancient's face change for just an instant. For just the slightest moment, he seemed to be startled before he appeared to then regain his composure and move away from Trent and the baby.

"Elder Rhys? What is it?" Isabella asked from her safe distance.

The ancient turned and looked directly at her.

"He is a most charming youngling," the ancient replied. "I congratulate you both. Now tell me, what name does this young one go by?"

"Cesare," Isabella said and instantly saw the ancient look faint. "Trent, please bring Cesare back to me so you can help Elder Rhys."

Trent quickly crossed the distance to transfer the baby into Isabella's arms. He then moved back to the ancient, put out his arms to steady him, and walked him to the nearest chair to help him sit down.

"Are you unwell, Elder Rhys?" Trent asked but saw the ancient shake his head in reply.

"No. Thank you, Trent, but I am well," Elder Rhys said. "I felt a little uneasy for a moment. It has now passed. I am fine."

Elder Rhys felt confused. He knew the voice he had heard. He recognized it but knew it could not be. No, it could *not* be.

"Who could it not be?" he suddenly heard Isabella ask. He looked up at her in surprise.

For a moment, Elder Rhys thought he must have spoken his thoughts out loud instead of quietly in his head. Trent's reaction proved otherwise.

"Who could who not be?" Trent asked Isabella and saw her look of confusion.

"Elder Rhys just said it could not be," she said quietly, uncertain herself if she had truly heard it.

"No," she heard both Elder Rhys and Trent respond at the same time.

"He did not say anything, Isabella," said Trent.

The ancient looked at Isabella again.

"No, but I thought it," he said quietly.

Inside his head, he looked at her and let a question pass through is mind. 'Can you hear me?'

"Yes," Isabella said. At that moment, both of them knew something had changed. "Yes, I can hear your thoughts. How can that be? That has never happened before. I have never heard your thoughts before, Elder Rhys!"

"I do not know, Isabella. It is indeed a mystery, as is the timing of your golden glow returning," the ancient said and lowered his head to think.

"Shall we leave you?" Trent asked him and saw the elderly man nod wearily.

"Yes, please," Elder Rhys said. "I must meditate and assess, but we shall hold a celebration for the birth of little Cesare. Yes, perhaps tomorrow during the evening meal?"

"Yes, of course, Elder Rhys," Isabella said, growing increasingly concerned about him.

Quietly, the young couple left the temple, saying nothing as both focused on their own thoughts. As soon as they were out of the temple, Isabella felt relief in her belly. Unintentionally, she'd been clenching her abdominal muscles tightly while inside the temple. Finally, she felt able to let them relax and go free once again.

"Could we go back to our home now, Trent? I feel a little tired," Isabella asked shyly and saw him grin at her.

"Of course," he replied. "I would not expect anything else. I take it you do remember you gave birth to a child just a few hours ago?" he asked, teasing her.

Placing his arm around her shoulders, he held her as they walked.

Already, Isabella found comfort in holding little Cesare as he lay sound asleep in her arms. She'd spent no time with infants. She'd never known the comfort that could come from someone so tiny.

Back inside the house, Trent sat with Isabella while she fed the baby. When Cesare seemed to have his fill and had fallen asleep, Trent encouraged Isabella to lie down on the bed under the covers.

"Sleep for as long as you need to sleep, Isabella. I will be right here," he soothed her and watched as she did as he'd suggested.

Trent looked on. Within only a minute or two, sounds came from Isabella proved to him she was fast asleep. As he watched her in her slumber, he found himself even further amazed at the people of the village. Isabella had given birth to the baby in his arms only hours earlier. Since then, she'd been walking around the village. If anyone had said anything about that, Trent might have assumed it was just Isabella's strength that enabled her to do that. Nobody in the village having asked if she shouldn't be recovering in bed, suggested to Trent that what she'd done was simply what mothers did when they gave birth in the magical place. They had a baby, and then they got up and got on with their day as if childbirth were the easiest thing in the world.

He thought back to the world he'd left behind. Not having been a father himself, he had no practical experience or first-hand knowledge of such things. Regardless, he was fairly sure that, in general, women remained bed-bound for quite a lot longer than a few hours after they'd delivered a child.

The small bundle in his arms moved slightly, bringing his attention back to his newborn son. His son! He wondered if he would ever tire of thinking of those two words.

At the same time that the baby moved and repositioned himself, Trent saw Isabella do exactly the same. He was not surprised. He was no longer sure anything would ever surprise him again.

CHAPTER 29

"Trent," he heard Isabella call out to him softly from the bed, a long while after he'd seen her drift off in slumber.

Hearing her voice, he turned to look at her. He'd been deep in thought while watching his son sleep. When his eyes focused on Isabella again, he saw her smiling at him and holding out her arms in a silent request.

He moved slowly to the bed, taking care not to wake the sleeping infant. For a moment, he lay the child down in front of Isabella. Trent then moved so that he was behind her and able to put his arm over her and hold her close.

"Have I been asleep long?" she asked and felt Trent kiss the back of her neck.

"Quite a while, but it is to be expected," he said. "Your body has gone through an amazing thing. It needs rest to recover."

Isabella turned slowly and steadily until she was facing him. Looking into his eyes, she pulled him down to kiss her. Indulging in the moment, they were soon reminded of the third person in the room as Cesare cried out. Isabella turned back, scooped him up, and helped him to calm and feed.

"This is my place, Trent," she said. "I have been wondering where my place is in the village. This is it - with you and Cesare."

As she watched their son suckle, Trent saw Isabella beaming. It was the first time since he'd arrived that he considered how nice it would have been to have one thing from his past life - a camera.

CHAPTER 30

Elder Rhys was unsettled. Things he'd never heard of happening were starting to occur with increasing frequency. He knew that Isabella was central to much of what was happening, but he equally believed that she wasn't the cause of it. Although she was somehow at its core, none of what was happening was her intention.

Of most alarm to him, was her recently discovered ability to read his thoughts. He didn't know if she could read all of his thoughts, or if she had to be within a short distance. As if testing her, he sent a thought out, just in case. 'Can you hear me, Isabella?'

Hearing only silence, he laughed to himself. It appeared Isabella had only heard his thoughts when she'd been in the same room as he was. There had been nothing about her manner that had suggested she'd known any of his thoughts before that moment.

"But I do, old friend," another voice said in his mind. "Oh, Rhys! You know me! Do you remember that time, when we were boys, when we ate too many apples in one sitting..."

Suddenly, Elder Rhys started laughing as the memory came to him. Then he became serious once more.

"Who are you?" he asked.

"You know," the voice replied. "You knew when you heard my name because it is the same name I used before."

"Cesare?" Elder Rhys asked, confused.

"Yes," came back the reply.

"But you are gone from this world," said the ancient. "You left more than one hundred cycles ago."

"It does not feel that long to me," the voice said. "It feels like I was with all of you just moments ago."

Elder Rhys sat still, trying to calm his mind and control his thoughts. He found he couldn't. When he heard a laugh in his thoughts, he knew it very well. It made him smile.

"I do not understand this," he thought.

"Nor I, but please listen to me, old friend," the voice replied. "There is someone in the village of ill intent. They are here to cause great harm to everyone. I can sense them. At different times I can hear some of their thoughts. I think that is why I have been brought back. I believe I am here to help you all."

"You are … no … not possible…" Elder Rhys said.

"Yes, Rhys!" the voice continued. "My soul is able to communicate through the child. I am returned, but I cannot do anything in that state of body. Instead, I need to guide and inform you so that you can do whatever is necessary to keep the evil away."

"You are not … the child itself?" asked Elder Rhys.

"No. I do not know where I am," replied the voice. "I am not always in the child's mind. I think I am flowing in and out. The child is special. He will grow with great power, but he will not realize that for many years. For now, he is a mere infant. He is unaware of my using him for communicating with you. I can reside in him, but not always be at the forefront of him. He must grow as all children do. He will never be aware that I am inside of him."

"And what of the time when this deed is done, and the evil is stopped?" Elder Rhys asked. "What will become of you?"

"I do not know," the voice replied. "It does not matter. I am already gone, as you know. This is only a short visit, I believe. We will not be sure until what needs to be done, is done."

Elder Rhys sat in peace for a moment, wondering what to do.

"He is already here, and he is communicating with someone," the voice continued. "I do not know what his intention is, but I do know that it is not good. I sense that he means to deliver great harm."

"Very well, old friend," the ancient said. "You must let me rest and think without you in my mind. It is enough that Isabella has lately been…"

"Isabella?" asked the voice.

"Yes. She is a young woman…" Elder Rhys began to explain.

"She is the child's mother?"

"Yes," he clarified.

"She is a chosen one, Rhys," the voice said. "She must be protected at all costs. It is vital to the survival of our people."

"Of course," Elder Rhys replied, beginning to feel extremely tired.

"Yes, I can tell you are weary," said the voice. "I shall leave you now, old friend. I will wait to hear from you. I believe if you think as if calling out to me, I shall hear and be able to respond. I shall not enter your thoughts unless I feel something is very urgent that you should know."

"Thank you," Elder Rhys said.

Although there was no audible indication that his old friend had left his mind, Elder Rhys immediately sensed he'd been left alone. He was glad. It had been good to speak to a close friend from his past, but it was equally confusing. In many ways, it made no sense. In other ways, it helped in the ancient's understanding of all that had been happening.

Weary, he began to walk to his bedroom. There he lay down to rest his body and rest his mind. Whatever was coming, he suspected his strength might be needed.

CHAPTER 31

"He is a joy, Isabella, is he not?" Isabella heard her father, Tomas, ask. They were sitting in the home of Isabella's mother and father in the evening. As Tomas held Cesare in the crook of one arm, he watched and smiled as the infant squeezed one tiny hand around one of his fingers. "When shall the announcement be made?"

"Tomorrow during the evening meal, Father," Isabella replied.

She watched as the smile on her father's face broadened in happiness, and he nodded.

"Very good," Tomas replied. "I am sure everyone will wish to meet you, little one."

Trent looked at Isabella and saw her smiling. She'd been beautiful since the day he'd met her, and even before that day, in his dreams. Since giving birth, her beauty had moved to another level. It had deepened, perhaps due to the added responsibility of motherhood.

After spending so long wondering where she should be and what she should be doing, Isabella believed she was meant to be a mother. That was her place in the village. That was her intended role. For so long, she'd been searching for where she belonged. Now she knew.

As Isabella sensed Trent looking at her, she turned her head to face him. Since the birth of Cesare, her emotions had been different from usual. She could feel them returning, growing stronger every day.

When she looked at him, Trent saw on her face a look he knew too well. He shook his head slightly at her. It was a silent reprimand, meant kindly. He knew she'd accurately understand his silent message to not look at him like that in front of other people - especially her parents. He saw her smile shyly at him before turning back to her father and her son.

Something changed at that moment. One minute, Tomas was smiling proudly and holding the baby. The next moment, he seemed to seize up. Isabella saw it happening and reached forward to grab Cesare before he could fall from her father's arms.

Right before their eyes, Tomas appeared to turn a shade of blue, with a slight haze of green present around his mouth. He appeared to be choking and unable to breathe as if the air had been sucked out of him. All watched as he fell to the floor.

Trent rushed forward in the hope of exerting the limited first aid and

CPR he'd learned prior to finding the village. He tried to do what he could remember. He couldn't remember much. Should he lie Thomas flat? Raise his chin? Press on the chest? Was it five compressions to two breaths? Two compressions to five breaths? He was frustrated with himself as he remembered that he hadn't taken enough notice during the workplace first aid training he'd been forced to do. Regardless, he was still determined to try.

It wasn't enough. Crisiana fell to the ground and pulled Tomas into her arms. Trent stood and put his arms around Isabella as she stood frozen in shock.

"Isabella?" he asked gently. He wondered if she had the power within her that she'd been able to harness to bring him back from death in the cave when he'd changed times. "Isabella!" he repeated with more force.

When Isabella finally looked at him, Trent spoke quietly to her, close to her ear.

"Isabella, do you have the power to do something?" he asked and finally saw her face clear.

Isabella looked at her hands, uncertain if she did have anything inside of her that could help her father. Knowing she should at least try, she passed Cesare to Trent and then moved forward.

"Mother, please let me get closer to Father for a moment," she said, gently but firmly trying to nudge her mother away. "Mother, please."

Crisiana heard the words and let her daughter move forward. She watched as Isabella placed her hands onto her father's chest.

Isabella knew she had done exactly that when Trent's life had faded in the cave on the day that he'd been transferred from his time to hers. Even though it had worked, and he'd been saved, she didn't know *specifically* what she'd done to make it happen. She equally didn't know how to summon the power again.

She held her hands over her father's chest, silently calling for the power of healing to come to her. Slowly she saw a small golden light appear. It gave all in the room some hope before, as quickly as it had started to brighten, it dimmed once more. Isabella tried again and again but without success. After a long while, she heard her mother speak.

"Isabella," Crisiana said as she moved to her daughter and put her arms around her. "It is good of you to try, but he is gone. Let him rest in peace. We must go to the temple and summon one of the ancients."

Trent looked at Crisiana, his surprise rising to yet another level. He could see she was upset, but once more, the level of commitment to just get on with what needed to be done astounded him.

"I will go and find Elder Rhys," he said and began to walk out with the baby cradled in his arms. At the door, he looked back and saw Isabella and her mother holding each other tightly.

One life arrives, and almost immediately afterward, another ends, he thought to himself.

What were the chances of that happening?

CHAPTER 32

"Elder Rhys," Trent called out as he entered the inner sanctum of the temple. Whenever he'd entered the large structure with Isabella, she'd always seemed to have an instinct about where the elders were, without any need to look around or call out. Not having the same foresight, Trent realized how naturally she'd always led them to where they needed to be in the expansive building.

He walked further until he found himself in the meditation room. In there, he saw the ancient, Elder Rhys, on the floor, deep in meditation. Not wanting to interrupt, Trent stood quietly. It seemed like a situation that demanded urgency, and yet, with Isabella's father having passed already, somehow there didn't seem so much urgency after all.

"Trent," the ancient said before he opened his eyes and focused on the man and child before him. "Something has happened."

Trent nodded and moved forward quietly.

"Yes. Isabella's father has passed," Trent informed the elderly man. He saw no surprise whatsoever on his face. "Crisiana asked me to come and find someone here to bring back to their home."

He saw Elder Rhys stand up and move forward toward him.

"I can come with you now," the ancient replied. "Let us go."

Trent was so surprised again that he ventured to find the courage to ask a direct question.

"Elder Rhys, why do you not even seem surprised that Tomas has died?" he asked. "Even Crisiana did not seem as surprised as I would have expected."

The ancient stopped walking and turned to face Trent directly.

"Trent, things are different here," Elder Rhys said. "Life begins, and life ends. We must all do our part while we are here. When someone leaves us, we must farewell them and bid them a safe journey."

"A journey … to where?" asked Trent, intrigued.

Elder Rhys smiled at him as he resumed walking again.

"You will see," was all the response he provided. "Come."

"It was not an accident, old friend. Nor was it natural," the voice of his old friend Cesare said in his head. "Be careful! The person who did this is in the village. He hides in plain sight."

Trent looked at the ancient with concern when they had stopped walking.

"Elder Rhys, are you alright?" Trent asked. "You look ... scared. What has happened to make you look so worried?"

He watched as the ancient appeared to try to brush off whatever thought had passed over his mind. Instead of words, the response Trent received was a soft smile.

"All is well, Trent," Elder Rhys said. "Come. We must go now and see that Isabella and Crisiana are well."

~~~~~

"Elder Rhys!" Isabella called out as the two men entered the doorway.

She moved as if she were thoughtlessly going to hug him. As she did, she was reminded sharply of how her body reacted when she was in close vicinity to him. As soon as she felt the golden glow and discomfort in her belly, she retreated. As she moved backward, she almost doubled over from the pain that had begun to grow when she'd stepped too close.

"Yes, stay back from me, Isabella. It is best for the moment," Elder Rhys said as he moved to sit beside Tomas's body.

Crisiana watched as the ancient looked down the length of her husband, head to toe, and then back again. After a visual inspection, she saw Elder Rhys raise his eyes to rest upon her face.

"Are you at peace, Crisiana?" he asked her and saw her nod while her eyes began to fill with tears. "Do you feel that our dear Tomas lived a good and fulfilling life?"

Trent watched the conversation with a feeling of disbelief. That people could so easily accept death was something he knew could be the most difficult thing for him to understand in the new world he'd fallen into.

After Elder Rhys saw Crisiana nod once more, he placed a hand upon her shoulder.

"He was a very good man. We shall prepare him for his farewell tonight," he said and saw Crisiana nod silently again. "I shall return to the temple now and speak with all of the elders. Tonight we shall say farewell to Tomas."

Isabella watched the ancient stand. She hadn't before experienced the departure of someone so close to her. She had attended farewell ceremonies before, but only of people who were fellow villagers and not family.

"Trent, may I ask you to help me also?" Elder Rhys asked, looking closely at Trent. "You have not before attended a farewell ceremony. I wish to talk to you about what will happen tonight."

"Yes, of course," Trent replied as he passed the infant back to Isabella.

The two men walked out of the small home. Once outside, Trent saw
~~~~~

Elder Rhys turn to him, expressing concern on his face.

"Trent, I feel there is more to this than a natural death," the ancient said. "We must not talk within close distance of anyone else, but I wish you to come into the temple with me so that we can be sure no-one can overhear."

The ancient saw a look of alarm cross Trent's face but said no more. The two of them walked silently through the village and entered the large temple structure. They passed through the rooms until they reached the small bedroom that Trent had first used when he'd arrived. Once inside, with the door securely closed, Elder Rhys expressed what was on his mind.

"I do not think the death of Isabella's father was a natural one," he said. "Did you notice the green tinge to the skin around his lips? That is an indication that he has died before his time, Trent."

"What do you mean, Elder Rhys?" Trent asked. "What does the coloring indicate?"

The ancient looked morbid as he sat down on the small bed in the room. Trent knew that Elder Rhys was already 600 years old. He found himself wondering how that related to the lifespan of ancients who passed through the village. Was Elder Rhys young at 600 years old? Was he nearing the expected age for an ancient to leave their world? He was pulled out of his reverie as the ancient's voice spoke once more.

"I fear Tomas was poisoned," Elder Rhys said in almost a whisper. "It is not something that is common here, as you may guess. People here live in peace. Our world is not like the one you have come from. There is no need for greed as everyone lives as they wish to live. They eat what they wish to eat. Everyone is equal here. There is no need to harm each other."

"But?" Trent asked, foreseeing there could be more to the situation than what was being presented to him.

"I have seen this kind of death before. It must be at least 300 years ago, mind you. There has been nothing like this for a very long time. I am very dismayed and shocked by this."

"Are you certain about this, Elder Rhys?" asked Trent. "Could you be mistaken?"

The ancient shook his head slowly. He didn't try to hide his feelings of sadness and extreme weariness that he suspected showed on his face.

"I do not believe that I am," he replied. "A natural death does not produce such coloring on the face."

Trent absorbed the words and thought briefly of the world he'd left behind. It had been a world in which technology had been designed for exactly such a situation. Even though not a scientist, he did know that with technology, it was easier to determine what had happened to someone to result in their death. He quickly dismissed the thought. For all the advancements of modern technology, Trent still didn't believe that it had ever really brought populations of people any great sense of contentment and fulfillment. The more people had owned, the more still they had wanted. It was a world he was glad to have left behind.

"What can we do?" he asked.

"The death must be treated as a natural death. If it is not, I fear we could cause panic among the village. We must keep quiet about this, but I shall consult with the other ancients as we prepare for the farewell," the ancient said and paused in silence for a moment. "Tonight, Trent, we will follow the normal farewell proceedings as we have always done here. I do not know how you say farewell to the dead in your world, but here, we will hold a celebration of his life. One of the elders will speak, and then I shall begin the procedure to say farewell to Tomas. After that, the village members will join together in their thoughts and help to send him on his next journey."

Trent looked at the elderly man. He had no idea what journey he might be referring to but assumed it must be similar to how one of the many religions in his world said goodbye to the dead. He wouldn't ask about it. Instead, he would wait and see what happened. Briefly, he remembered back to when he had arrived in the village. At that moment, he had been in a different time, having arrived at least 300 years in the future. Even having passed through the time as he had, he still found it difficult to believe that such things could happen.

Regardless of his curiosity and inability to understand the how, they *had* happened. He remembered that when he'd arrived, seeing the village in ruin, one of his first thoughts had been wondering where the people had gone. Not living people, but *bodies*. If an entire race had been wiped out, why had there not been any skeletons visible among the ruins?

Once more, he dismissed his thoughts of curiosity. No good could come from such questioning. He believed that what he knew about the future, he had to always keep to himself. If he questioned too much about how things were done in the village's present time, he expected questions would flow back to him about the time and world he'd left behind. He didn't want that. The people of the village lived in harmony. Their systems and way of living worked. The death of Isabella's father was one thing, but it was quite another to consider that it was the first unnatural death in more than 300 years.

"You are thinking of your world," the ancient's voice said out loud, startling Trent from his thoughts.

"Yes, I was for a moment," Trent replied. "But that is gone now. Please tell me what I can do to help Isabella and Crisiana, or help you."

Elder Rhys nodded in acknowledgment.

"Come now," he said. "I shall gather up some other elders, who will take responsibility for removing Tomas from his home and bringing him here. They will cleanse him and prepare him for his upcoming journey. If you wish to help bring him here, you are welcome to. If you feel it more important to stay with Isabella and Crisiana, please do so. They will both appreciate you being there to lean on, I am sure."

The two men left the small room. Trent was introduced to five elders he'd not previously met, who returned with them to the home of Crisiana and Tomas.

On entering the small home, Trent saw Crisiana and Isabella holding each other, with little Cesare receiving equal attention from both women. The two women looked up as the door opened. Trent immediately moved forward to provide further comfort to them.

Isabella watched as Elder Rhys provided instruction to the elders. She noticed that he stayed well back, close to the door. When she caught his eye, he nodded. They each understood that they must not be in very close vicinity. They both silently acknowledged that it had something to do with the golden glow that was beginning to emerge in Isabella's belly once more. Isabella didn't know why it was beginning again, nor did it make any sense that when it was present, she couldn't be in close vicinity to Elder Rhys. How the two things were connected, neither knew.

Through his communication with the soul of an old friend he'd always trusted and believed in, Elder Rhys at least understood one thing. He knew there was a danger in the village. He also suspected that the golden glow was preparing Isabella to fight another battle.

CHAPTER 33

In the evening, after the time of dining, the village assembled in the vast open area in front of the temple. The introduction to Cesare was postponed. It was more important that Tomas was sent on his journey via the farewell ceremony. Many villagers had already met Cesare that morning. His introduction to the village in its entirety could wait.

When Trent and Isabella had gone through the pairing process, it had been the first time Trent had seen any large assembly of the villagers. The number of people had surprised him then. Although the village within the great walls on top of the mountain was substantial in physical size, day to day, it seemed to Trent that few people lived in it. Until that moment, he had thought he'd seen everyone in one place on the night of pairing. He now realized he certainly hadn't.

As he looked around him, he could see substantially more people than there had been at his pairing to Isabella. He held Isabella's hand tightly with one hand while Cesare securely remained sleeping and settled in the crook of Trent's other arm. Looking down at the small bundle he was holding, Trent already felt like he'd been a father for an immense amount of time. It was hard to believe that just one day earlier, the little person lying in his arms hadn't been out in the world, but rather, nestling soundly inside his mother's belly.

Trent saw Isabella look at him as she squeezed his hand tightly. On the other side of her was Crisiana, whose hand was also being squeezed by Isabella. Trent looked at both women, once more amazed at how calm they were. Looking around the crowd, it continued to surprise him just how calm *everyone* was.

~~~~~

"Friends!" Elder Scott called out to the crowd as he stood upon the raised stone platform in front of the temple. "This night, we say farewell to a much-loved friend and father - Tomas. He was well known to you all as a fair, honest, and generous man. His love was known in all its fullness by Crisiana, who paired with Tomas a great many years ago. Together they gave life to their beautiful daughter, Isabella.

"Although this time of life saddens us, it is also a time to celebrate a great life lived by a great man," the elder continued. "Would the deliverers please bring Tomas to us so we may say our final farewell?"
~~~~~

Trent watched as six men carried Isabella's father and placed him on the stone platform in front of the elder. The body was wrapped in green cloth, bound tightly in a way that reminded Trent of the Egyptian mummies he remembered seeing at a museum in his previous life. The difference was that Tomas's face had been left clear for everyone to easily see.

Looking around, Trent was curious to find out what they were going to do with the body. He'd not wanted to ask, but he was very aware that there didn't seem to be any kind of cemetery within the walls of the village. He'd also not seen one outside the expansive walls before he had fallen through the holographic portal to the village when he'd first arrived. As far as he knew, no-one from inside the walls ever ventured outside of them. He didn't even know if anyone knew they *could* go outside.

Feeling Isabella squeeze his hand, Trent's attention was once more brought back to the present. He refocused on what was happening around him.

"Elder Rhys, please step forward and prepare Tomas for his ongoing journey," Elder Scott said before the two men swapped places.

"Tomas," Elder Rhys said as he knelt over the body. His eyes were focused on the body, but his voice carried enough for everyone to hear his words. "You have lived a great life. This has been confirmed by Crisiana, your paired partner for all of these years. It is now time for you to leave us and continue on the next stage of your journey. We thank you for your commitment to working and living among us, and for the joy you have brought to us over all of these years that you have been with us. Do not be afraid. A new journey awaits you. Go now, our friend. It is time."

Elder Rhys stood up and redirected his words to the villagers amassed before him.

"It is now time," Elder Rhys called out. "Please ensure that each of you is holding hands with at least one person. The bond must be strong. There can be no broken link."

Trent turned to see people behind him, for as far as he could see, doing what they'd been instructed to do. He looked down at Cesare, wondering how he could link with anyone. The answer to his silent question came as Elder Scott approached.

"Trent, the link between you and your child is already complete. I shall take one of his hands in mine, and provide the link between you and the next person."

Isabella watched as the elder took one tiny hand in his, and then reached behind with his other hand. The person behind instantly reached forward to join hands.

"Is everyone linked in the chain?" Elder Rhys asked. Everyone listened to see if anyone was not. No-one spoke. "Very well. It is time. Please, everyone, bow your heads and give thought to the gratitude."

Trent was curious but did as he was bid. There was silence as the villagers carried out the instruction. After a few minutes, the voice of Elder Rhys could be heard once more.

"It has begun," he called out. "Please ensure you continue to hold hands, and maintain the silence, but raise your eyes and watch as we see and encourage Tomas to begin his journey beyond."

Trent looked up. He was shocked to see a golden glow begin to emanate from the body of Isabella's father. He blinked to see if it were real. Such a glow was not new to him, but it was the first appearance of it he had seen in such a situation. He intently watched as it became brighter and spread its light further. It was incredibly bright but different from the light of the sun. Trent found he could look right at it. He didn't sense it would do any damage to his eyes, as looking at the sun might.

His awe continued as the golden glow moved upwards, and Tomas's body began moving. As it lifted off the platform, it appeared to hover without anything holding it. If he were in any other place at that moment, Trent would have believed he was watching a professional magician or illusionist at play, but there was none of that.

The body hovered for a short time with the golden glow surrounding it. A comforting feeling of warmth spread from it.

All of a sudden, Trent realized that there was only a glow. There was no longer a body within it. The glow was alone, and it was hovering. He watched as it moved. Slowly but steadily, it moved away from the platform and began a slow circle of the entire assembly of villagers. It circled everyone, then Trent saw it move from the opposite side it had traveled down first. When it looked as if it would move forward to return to the platform, Trent instead saw it move toward him. For a few moments, it hovered in front of Crisiana, then Isabella. It then moved in front of Trent and right up to Cesare. The infant watched the glow with a smile on his small face.

The glow continued to hover for a few more moments, close to the child. It then moved backward and returned to its previous place on the platform, hovering but remaining still once more.

"You have leave of us, Tomas. Go forth on your new journey. You have our blessing," Elder Rhys continued.

All of a sudden, the golden glow became brighter and then reduced in size. Moments later, it was gone.

Trent looked at the platform, not believing his eyes. The glow was gone. The body of Tomas was gone. Where both had been, now there was simply nothing.

Isabella squeezed his hand. Still surprised, he turned to look at her. He could tell by her facial expression that nothing was out of the ordinary for her. She had seen the event of farewell before. She didn't appear surprised by it at all.

Trent wanted to ask questions. He didn't understand. Even with all that he'd seen and done, and the level of power he'd experienced flowing through him from the golden stone, he was still stunned by what he'd just seen. It was as if just when he'd accepted one thing as being different in the village compared to the life he had come from, another level of surprise was delivered to him.

He remained quiet and didn't ask any questions. Instead, he held Isabella's hand tightly and watched everyone for cues so he could anticipate what happened next on such a night.

Slowly the villagers began to disperse and return to their homes for the evening. Trent watched their faces and could hardly compare their reactions - or lack of them - to any funeral he'd ever attended. How did they accept death so easily without emotion?

He turned toward Isabella and saw her move forward and into his hold as she took Cesare into her arms. Beyond Isabella, Trent could see Crisiana. She was not crying. She seemed void of emotion as she turned and her eyes met Trent's.

"You are sad, Trent," she said. "I thank you for that. Tomas regarded you very highly. He was very glad of you being Isabella's choice for pairing. It was a great day today, with Tomas being able to meet Cesare. That is something that I shall treasure for the rest of my life, however long that will be."

Trent watched as she turned from them and began to walk away, seeming to head toward her home.

"What will she do now?" he asked Isabella quietly. He only saw confusion on her face.

"What will she do?" Isabella asked. "What do you mean?"

Trent looked at her, reminding himself that he shouldn't keep thinking about the past life he'd lived, and the ways of the world that he knew before.

"She is alone now," he said and saw Isabella smile sadly at him.

"My mother is not alone. She has me, she has you, and she has Cesare. She has all of these people," she replied, using her hand to signify the many villagers still nearby.

"But she will live alone," said Trent. "Will she be alright living alone?"

"It is the way of our people," Isabella said. "It is the order of things - the *right* order of things. When she is of the age deemed suitable by the ancients, my mother will be declared an elder and will move into the temple. There she will be surrounded by people of similar age to her and older. She will not be alone, Trent. I do thank you for worrying about her, but she is an incredibly strong woman. She will be well."

Trent looked at her closely, trying desperately to turn his thoughts off. He knew he shouldn't be so concerned about things that the villagers didn't seem to worry about. As he closed off his thoughtful mind, he leaned in and kissed her gently on the forehead.

"Of course," he said. "Come. Let us go home."

CHAPTER 34

Crisiana walked away from the farewell with a pit of emptiness inside of her. She had reassured Trent that all was well, and she would be fine. Although she knew there was no need for sadness, given the great life that Tomas had led, she did feel his death deeply. It was not the way of their people to grieve, but she did feel like one half of her had been removed.

She walked into her home. It had been the home that she'd shared with Tomas as they'd brought Isabella into the world and then raised her. The three of them had been happy together. Tomas had wished for more children, but they had not been blessed with any after Isabella had been born. They had not questioned that. If they had been meant to have more children, more children would have come.

Having closed the door behind her, she looked at the small table with the chairs around it. She focused on the spot where she'd seen Tomas fall to the ground before her eyes. It was the place where she'd held him as the life had flowed from him. As she looked at that spot, she didn't want to be in the room. She assumed that in the morning, it would hurt less. In the present moment, it hurt greatly.

She walked into their bedroom and settled herself under the bed covers. It would be the first night in a long life that she had not had the comfort of Tomas's body beside her.

Her tears began to flow.

CHAPTER 35

When Crisiana woke the following morning, she naturally reached out to touch Tomas. It took a few minutes for her to remember that he was not there, and he would never *again* be there. She knew she would soon have to get up and start her day as was expected of her every day. For the present moment, she let herself feel and weep. She would not rush that. She would smile when she left their home - only *her* home now - but for a brief moment, she just wanted to indulge. She wanted to be honest in admitting that already she missed him and would continue to miss him for the rest of her life.

~~~~~

"Crisiana," a man's voice said as she made her way to the dining area several days later.

She'd cried well into each night since Tomas had departed, and again for a long time on waking each morning. The intense level of loneliness she'd never felt before. Even when her mother and father had each passed, she'd not felt as she did over Tomas's passing.

As she turned toward the voice, she saw Antonio coming toward her. Having grown up together, they were the same age and had attended lessons and activities together as children. As with so many villagers, she still saw him around the village from time to time. He was always polite when he passed her. She wouldn't say the two of them were good friends, but certainly friendly acquaintances.

"Antonio," she said, giving him a warm, friendly smile. "How are you?"

Antonio took in the sight of the woman before him. He, too, regarded her as an old friend, although underneath, he had other thoughts. Those thoughts, however, he wouldn't reveal at the present moment. He wasn't sure he'd even reveal them any time soon, but in the future, he would decide if she was suited to his needs. If she were, he would make it clear to her what usefulness she could play in his plans.

Crisiana saw him return a smile, although a sad one.

"I am well," he said. "Are you well? I am so sorry about the loss of Tomas. I know he will have a safe journey ahead of him."

"Thank you," Crisiana said, holding back tears that threatened. "I do feel his absence already, but I understand that it is not a bad thing to be
~~~~~

called to the journey."

The two of them walked further in silence until they reached the dining area.

"Will you dine with me, Antonio? I do not wish to sit alone," she asked him and saw him smile at her.

To her, it was a smile of friendship.

To anyone else who might have seen - anyone else who might have been a bit more observant - they might have seen a completely different type of smile altogether.

CHAPTER 36

As Trent and Isabella entered the dining area, Isabella saw her mother washing the dishes she had used, preparing to leave. Beside her was a man that Isabella did not recognize. It surprised Isabella but did not stop her from stepping forward.

"Mother," she said softly and immediately saw Crisiana turn and face her.

Isabella saw the unknown man look briefly at her before quietly walking away without saying a word. Although it surprised Isabella somewhat, given how friendly people generally were in the village, her attention immediately moved to her mother instead.

"Isabella, are you well?" Crisiana asked and watched as Isabella passed Cesare to Trent.

"Yes, I am well, Mother," Isabella replied as she extended her arms around Crisiana. "Are you?"

Crisiana smiled sadly at her daughter.

"I shall be well," she said. "I did miss your father greatly last night, but I shall adjust to that. It makes me happy to see you so happy. And you, Trent," she continued, shifting her gaze to him. "I know you love my daughter deeply. I am thankful that she is able to experience such love."

The three of them were silent for a moment before Cesare cried out and broke the serious moment. Isabella saw her mother's face change as she smiled and reached toward Trent, eager to relieve him of the bundle in his arms.

"Oh, such a lovely little one," Crisiana said. "I would like to spend more time with him, Isabella, if it would not disrupt your routine."

Trent watched the woman currently holding his son in her arms. He could not deny that however old Isabella's mother was, she was still an outstandingly beautiful woman. As he considered that, he felt sadness about each person in the village only being paired once in their lifetime. Who knew how much longer Crisiana would live. It seemed incredibly sad that she would do so alone and without any partner to love and be loved by. As that thought passed through him, he suddenly felt a tear come to his eye. It was not unnoticed.

"Trent, please do not be sad," Crisiana said to him as she softly bounced Cesare in her arms. "To know the love that I shared with Tomas is a wonderful thing. I shall miss him for a long time - perhaps every day and every moment for the rest of my life. I am blessed to have been loved by him and to have shared that time with him. Through him, I have gained my beautiful daughter, who now shares such love with you. You are a good man to be able to feel and share your sadness. I will be well, and I have this little one to focus on now!"

Isabella began to cry even though she tried to stifle her sobs. She felt loved and secure as Trent wrapped his arms around her and held her tightly. When she felt his lips touch her forehead, she closed her eyes to indulge in the comfort that came from being in his arms.

"If the two of you are going to eat, I can watch this little one while you do so if you wish?" Crisiana asked, breaking Trent and Isabella out of their hold on one another.

It wasn't an offer that needed to be accepted, but Isabella and Trent could both see Cesare as a way for Crisiana to start to heal from the death of Tomas.

"That would be wonderful, Mother," Isabella said. "We will not be long. Where shall I find you after we dine?"

"I do not feel like rushing today," Crisiana replied. "I shall go for a walk down through the gardens. Will you come and find me there?"

Isabella nodded and watched as her mother left the area with the small bundle in her arms. Even as the distance between them widened, Isabella watched and could tell by the movement of her mother's head that she was deep in conversation with Cesare. The sight made Isabella smile.

"I think your mother might wish to spend much time with him," Trent said quietly.

Isabella turned toward him and saw the smile on his face.

"Yes, and I think it will be good for her to do so," she said and wrapped her arms around his body once more before pulling away again. "I am sure you will wish to eat," Isabella teased him.

Trent laughed but could not deny it. He very happily followed her to sit down and begin their meal.

CHAPTER 37

For each of the nine mornings that followed, Crisiana noticed Antonio situated in the same location each day. She found his company to be a comfort, but as the days passed, she started to wonder if he had another reason for being so attentive to her.

She'd decided she wouldn't ask him. Not yet. She would wait until more time had passed. She knew he had long ago paired. That made her wary about what he could want from her. She did not want to cause any discomfort between the two of them if she was wrong. He knew she'd just lost Tomas. Any good friend would not do anything that could be perceived as an attempt to replace someone's recently departed partner.

~~~~~

"Crisiana, may I sit with you this evening?" Antonio asked as he approached her at a table in the dining area one evening.

Crisiana nodded and smiled at him, but Antonio found himself wondering what she was thinking. She seemed to be friendly, but he thought that underneath her smile, there could have been the slightest amount of distrust emerging. Although it was subtle, he was sure it was there. Anybody else might not have seen it. He wasn't just anybody else.

"Yes, of course, Antonio," Crisiana replied. "Please do sit down and join me. How was your work today?"

Each of them continued the charade of small talk during the evening meal. When Crisiana moved to leave, Antonio finished his meal at the same time and followed close behind her as she washed, dried, and put away her dishes.

"Would you like me to walk you to your home?" he asked and was pleased to see her smile at him while nodding.

~~~~~

Crisiana was nervous about her old friend. There was something different about him. They'd never been very close, but there was an odd vibe emanating from him that she could not ignore. She had thought it was perhaps a desire on his part for them to be more than the slight friends they'd always been. Her heart beating faster than normal highlighted her feeling of general unease. It was something she didn't want to ignore.

"Well," she said, turning to him as they reached the door to her home.

"Thank you, Antonio. Goodnight."

She was startled when he leaned closer and kissed her on the cheek. As she pulled back from him, she saw him attempt to smile shyly. His mouth looked shy. His eyes did not.

"Crisiana, you are a beautiful woman," he said. "You should not be alone. Let me help you to remember how beautiful you are."

Crisiana stood before him with her eyes lowered as she considered the words being said to her. When she finally found her incredible depth of internal courage, she raised her eyes so that she could look at him directly before she spoke.

"I thank you for trying to make me feel better, Antonio. I am not alone," she said. "I have many people around me very often. They are all that I need," she said as she placed her hand on his arm. "I was paired with Tomas for a very long time. He and I shared something wonderful and raised our daughter together. I do feel like I have been taking your time away from Ariana. If losing Tomas has helped me to consider anything, it is that we must enjoy who we are paired with while we can. I value your friendship. You have been a great strength to me these past days since we said farewell to Tomas, but please spend less time with me and more time with Ariana."

Antonio looked deeply at her. He believed she was essential to his plan. He needed to make sure she was in the right place at the right time for his plan to come to fruition.

He was not happy with her response, but he was fast-thinking enough to do what he could to not let that show. Instead, he bowed and then smiled once more at her.

"I will not pressure you to do anything you do not wish to do," he said. "I only want to be your friend, as we always have been. You know that I am here for you … always."

Crisiana watched as he removed himself and started to walk away. She continued to watch him until he was not in view anymore. Her thoughts were erratic. Her manner was bothered. Something was not as it seemed where he was concerned. That deeply troubled her.

CHAPTER 38

Isabella and Trent both watched Crisiana from a distance. Sometimes when they saw her, she had a look about her that said all was not well. Whenever they asked her about it, she was adamant that she was fine. She was still a little sad at Tomas's passing, but that was only to be expected.

The young couple made it a new priority to invite her to spend evenings with them. Sometimes she accepted and seemed to gain great joy from spending time with the two of them and Cesare. Other evenings she seemed to want to be on her own.

They worried about her but knew they could do nothing. Both of them put her look of stress down to her grief. They didn't want to push too hard. They could only wait and see if she would talk to them in time if there was something that she felt she needed to talk about.

Crisiana welcomed the invitations to visit her daughter in the evenings. On some nights, she could not bear it and just needed to be alone. On other nights she was desperate to have an excuse about why she could not see Antonio. She had hoped he wouldn't approach her as often after her words to him. In reality, his efforts to spend time with her actually seemed to have increased. It made no sense to Crisiana.

Even though he never mentioned Ariana in their conversations, Crisiana believed he was happily paired. Regardless of its population, everyone knew when a couple paired, and Crisiana clearly remembered the pairing of her friend to Ariana many years earlier. She also remembered the announcements of each of their children's births. Why was he pursuing her and trying to spend so much time with her? What was his intention?

None of it made any sense. The only explanation that might have made sense was that he was indeed concerned for her as a friend. That explanation might have been easily accepted if it were centered around anyone else. Something about Antonio made that explanation not accurate. There was something more going on with him, and Crisiana sensed it the more they spent time together. She couldn't think what it could be, but her intuition had always been right, and she'd never had any reason to disregard it easily. It wasn't the 'if' that confused her. No. It was the 'why'.

~~~~~

One evening when they had gone out for a walk together after their evening meal, Crisiana found Antonio seemed particularly pushy. Increasingly, it seemed like he was no longer trying to be a friend to her, but instead was beginning to try and control her. It appeared he wanted to be able to make her do things that she didn't particularly want to do. He pushed and pushed, until one evening she snapped.

"No, Antonio, I do not feel the same way as you do!" Crisiana exclaimed. "Please do not ask again. My answer will not change. I think of you like an old friend and nothing more."

"I know that we are meant to be together," Antonio said, his voice pleading.

Crisiana physically moved into a stronger position so she could easily walk away from him when she had said what she was about to say.

"I do not know why you are pursuing me. I do not trust what you say when you say it is because I am beautiful. I do not trust your intentions, Antonio," Crisiana replied. "I will say this one final time. You and I shall not become anything more than friends. You are paired with someone else. Why do you act as if you are not? We are not to become paired. I shall not share my body with you if that is what you wish me to," she said and stopped a moment to watch his facial expression. "Do not worry, however. Your pursuit is not something I have spoken of to anyone else. Nor shall I. Please, let us forget all of this and move forward as the acquaintances we have always been. Whatever you wish for, Antonio, you must find with someone else. I am not open to your plans or your desires."

Antonio stared at the woman before him. He had miscalculated her as being suitable for his plans. She was not flexible or easily manipulated. No, he needed someone much more malleable for his needs.

For a moment, he considered doing to her as he had done to Tomas. He decided against it. As far as he was aware, no-one knew Tomas's death had been intentional. It would be asking for suspicion if Crisiana died just as suddenly.

He looked at her and nodded.

"I understand," he said simply, and then walked away. He was finished working her over. He did not need her.

For now.
~~~~~

CHAPTER 39

The question about Tomas's death was not discussed any further, but it had remained on Trent's mind. He hadn't told Isabella of the fears of the ancient, Elder Rhys. It was still difficult to believe that Tomas had been poisoned. It was horrible enough that Isabella had lost her father so suddenly. Trent had no desire to bring up something so horrific to her. Even though he spoke of it to no-one, now and then the thought appeared at the very forefront of his mind.

Elder Rhys had said nothing more about it but did that mean that nothing was being done to find out what had happened? Surely not. Trent didn't want to believe that even in such a peaceful village, someone being killed could be something they would just turn their back on and not deal with in some way. Perhaps to the general population who didn't live such long lives, the idea of someone being killed did not even exist in their minds. But Elder Rhys admitted he had seen it happen once before. What had they done in that situation? Had they sought out the murderer and done anything to ensure justice was served for the action?

He resolved to go to the temple the following morning and talk to Elder Rhys about it. In Trent's time and world, it would have been called a murder. He suspected there was no such word in the current time and place. Silently he wondered about the progression from people living as they did in the village, to living as they did in the world he'd left behind. The villagers were peaceful and content. They exhibited no desire for more. They showed no symptoms of greed or malice. How had the world arrived at the place he'd left behind, with thousands of murders every single day across the globe? Somewhere, somehow, between the century he was in and the one he'd left behind, something had gone very, very wrong.

Before he'd changed and moved from his real time to that of Isabella, Trent had seen the state of the village. All he'd seen then was rubble everywhere. There had been no living person except for Isabella, who wasn't really in his time at all. The village had been in ruins and appeared to have not been seen or heard of for centuries. It had become a forgotten city. Elder Rhys had told Trent that was due to the greed of someone who had visited the village when it was healthy and alive. That person had gone away and then returned, bringing more people to try and take the golden stones that resided in and under the land. No-one had won in that. One group's greed had killed both groups. All had perished, along with the village itself, never to be heard of again.

Trent had been told by Elder Rhys that the destruction had occurred in their current future, but he didn't know when. It was sometime between the time he stood in now, and the time that he'd left behind. But when? He'd been told he would have the power to stop it from happening a second time. How could he know that if he didn't know when or how it happened? What could be his role in preventing it from happening again? He had no powers like Isabella did. Even *her* powers seemed limited.

They had both been told that her powers would grow as she grew older. She was expected to become an ancient, but what did those things really mean? She had exhibited the power to bring him back to life moments after he'd changed times and his heart had stopped beating. In contrast, she hadn't been able to do anything when her father had died in front of them. To what extent were powers if they didn't work reliably, every time they were needed?

"Trent!" he heard Isabella's voice call out to him. They were lying in bed. He'd thought she was sleeping while he'd been allowing such thoughts flow through his mind. When he turned to her, he saw her looking at him sleepily.

"Stop thinking!" she said and saw him smile at her acute perception.

"Sorry," he replied as he cuddled into her and laughed softly. "I did not mean to wake you with my noisy thoughts."

He heard a soft chuckle escape her lips and felt her smile as she kissed him lightly.

"I can tell you are deep in thought when your body tenses so much," Isabella said. "Please relax and stop thinking!"

Trent kissed her forehead and relaxed against her. At that moment, questions would not be answered. They may *never* be answered if he were completely honest with himself. They could wait. Remaining in the present was far more important. He was paired with the most beautiful, caring, and loving woman he'd ever met. He was a new father to a young son. He had finally found a type of good hard work that he enjoyed and was gaining a huge amount of knowledge in - knowledge that would serve as something vital to life.

No, he didn't need answers to all of his questions.

He had all that he needed.

And that was enough.

CHAPTER 40

Although he looked calm on the outside, Antonio was infuriated as he made his way to his home after his discussion with Crisiana. It wasn't a major setback, but it was annoying all the same. He had something he had to do. Crisiana being so difficult was upsetting to him, but he wouldn't show it.

As he entered his home, he saw Ariana - the woman he'd paired with 30 years earlier. She had been all that he had desired. He had no reason not to be content with her and the offspring they had together produced. If she were hurt in any crossfire from what he was working toward, he would be devastated about that.

Now he had to put his second plan into place. He had been positioning Kat for a long while through his newly acquired ability to enter her night visions. She was young. She would be very pliable. His nightly efforts toward her had continued, even during the time he'd been focusing so heavily on Crisiana. He knew he'd already gotten to Kat in a small way. At different times he'd walked past her and read thoughts in her head that were about him. Not him, as in his physical self, of course, but his voice and his words. She heard them during the night and kept thinking about them during the daylight hours that followed.

His uncertainty with Kat was whether she would be able to look past his age. He only had to get her to like him just enough. She had inside of her what he needed. She could be the most magnificent being to control if only he could fully win her over.

"Are you well, Antonio?" he heard Ariana ask from across the room.

He smiled at her and moved forward to put his arms around her and hold her tightly. Since the birth of their last child two years earlier, he knew she hadn't considered their joining as important. Regardless, as he looked at her, he couldn't help but kiss her fully on the lips. To his surprise, she reacted instantly and positively. Her body melded against his as her arms wrapped around him, and she kissed him back with great passion. Antonio pulled away and looked into her eyes. What he saw heated him.

"Yes, please," she said almost so quietly that Antonio was uncertain if he'd heard correctly. "It has been too long."

Antonio kissed her again, his hunger evident. He had been completely obsessed by something greater than him that had seemed to have taken over his thoughts lately. As Ariana took his hand in hers and led him to their bed, he pushed all thoughts of his plan from his mind.

CHAPTER 41

Kat was eager to get to the morning meal to see Adrian. When she thought of him, sometimes she felt eager to pair with him. Other times she didn't like the idea of pairing with him at all. Sometimes it felt good to be around him. Other times it didn't.

The voice inside of her head didn't help. It felt like whatever it was, was making her think that pairing with Adrian wasn't a good idea. She knew she'd have to pair eventually. Whatever it was that was talking to her had so far not revealed itself. She didn't even know if it was real. Perhaps it was just something not working right in her thoughts.

She walked faster as she considered Adrian. There was no reason to take any notice of the voice that had been appearing in her visions of the night. It meant nothing. It wasn't even real.

~~~~~

"Good morning Adrian," she said as she sat down beside him at the dining table.

Adrian turned to look at her. For a brief moment, panic set in as he pondered yet again what was happening with her. He didn't know where the two of them were going or not going. As quickly as he thought that, however, he pushed the thought away and replaced it with a smile.

"Kat, how are you this fine day?" he asked.

The two of them talked happily, despite both being uncertain of the situation they were in, or what should be happening between them.

When they'd finished their meals, they stood up and moved to wash, dry, and put away their items together. Just before they were to walk out, Kat heard a voice approaching.

"No, all is well, Crisiana," the voice said. "I appreciate your friendship. I am sorry if I offended in any way."

Adrian saw Kat's face go pale as she slowly lifted her head and looked forward. Following her line of sight, Adrian saw Isabella's mother entering the dining area. Looking back at Kat, he could see her eyes were focused on the man beside Crisiana.

"Kat, are you alright?" he asked but found her too focused to hear him.

Kat had heard the voice and felt a familiar feeling come over her. As the older couple before them moved in their direction, Kat saw the
~~~~~

woman make eye contact with Adrian.

"Adrian, good morning to you," Crisiana said.

As she did so, Kat looked at the man next to her. He turned and looked at her, as if seeing directly into her soul, right through her eyes.

"Good morning, Kat," he said.

At the sound of the words, Kat felt faint. She had no doubt it was the voice she'd heard in her night visions so many times in recent weeks.

Crisiana and Antonio walked past the young pair. As they did so, Adrian saw Kat's eyes follow them. When he turned to look, he only saw the backs of the older couple moving to prepare to dine. Adrian was curious about what had caught Kat's attention so much.

"Kat, what is it?" he asked her, concern growing inside of him. "You have gone very pale."

Kat forced her attention back to Adrian. She felt intense confusion inside of her but knew she had to act normal if things were to progress with him. She was confused about whether she wanted them to progress, but she still could not upset him and prevent him from wanting to pair with her.

~~~~~

That night in bed, Kat was nervous. She wanted to hear what the voice had to say. She wanted to be sure that it was the man she'd seen in the dining area earlier that day. There was little doubt in her mind that the man she'd heard was in fact who had been speaking to her in the hours of sleep for so long. Despite her certainty, she wanted confirmation that her thoughts were correct.

She willed herself into slumber, and through the night realized she was indeed being spoken to.

"You looked beautiful this morning, Kat," the voice said. "Do you now know who I am?"

In her night vision, Kat affirmed. "Yes, I saw you. I recognized your voice as you walked into the dining area this morning."

"I wish to see you, Kat. Alone. Soon," the voice continued.

Even in her sleep state, Kat could feel her heart start to beat faster.

"Yes. I wish for that also," she said in her head. "I want to speak to you, face to face, but with nobody else nearby."

The voice in her vision of the night continued to talk with the same smooth and melodic tone.

"Good. I am glad," it said. "Tomorrow evening, I shall come to you as I am now. You will meet me then, when I give you directions."

"Yes," Kat confirmed, knowing that her concerns were real regarding the irregular night visions. Something greater was happening inside of her and to her. She didn't understand what it was or what it could be, but she knew that it was indeed real.
~~~~~

CHAPTER 42

Within her peaceful slumber, Isabella heard the conversation. She visualized standing very still. She was afraid that if she moved, she might make some kind of sound. She didn't want to alert Kat and the man she was speaking to that a third person was present and hearing every word they were saying.

She heard the invitation, and she heard the acceptance. She wasn't alarmed and didn't wake herself up, but she did find the determination even within her vision of the night, to keep the knowledge at the forefront of her mind. She hadn't given more thought to the conversation she'd heard previously. That had left her conscious mind soon after it had happened. Now that it had happened again, she remembered.

In her vision of the night, Isabella imagined herself waiting until no more words were heard. Then, in her imagery, she simply walked away.

~~~~~

When Isabella woke the next morning, the voices and words echoed in her mind. She knew Kat was one of those who had been speaking, and it was the Kat they all knew. In the build-up to the previous battle, Isabella had thought that the Kat who was interacting with them was an older version of herself. She'd sounded similar but not quite the same. This time, however, it seemed to definitely be Kat of the present time.

Isabella lay still and awake, thinking. When she felt Trent's arm fall across her as he slowly awoke, she turned her head to look at him and watched as his eyes opened and focused on her. The smile he gave her immediately switched on her desire. She started to turn her body to face him. As she leaned over to kiss him, another small voice broke their silence, almost as if knowing what Isabella's intentions might have been.

Trent laughed.

"That is a sign that you are still to let your body rest, Isabella," he said with a blend of fondness and teasing in his voice.

Isabella laughed softly with him as she watched Trent leave the bed, stand, and approach their newborn child. Lying still, she saw him pick Cesare up and hold him close in his arms. Instantly the crying eased off as Trent smiled at the small bundle he was carrying back to the bed. After Isabella sat up, Trent passed Cesare to her and allowed her to hold and feed.
~~~~~

"Adrian has not met him yet," Trent said softly, trying not to disrupt Cesare's bonding time with Isabella. "Do you think we should introduce them finally?"

Mention of her friend inspired further recollection of Isabella's night vision, and Kat's part in it.

Trent saw a look of concern cross Isabella's face.

"What is it?" he asked and saw her slowly turn to face him.

"Kat," Isabella began to say. "She has been … that is, I *believe* she has been … conversing with someone through her visions of the night."

"How would you know that?" Trent asked.

"I am not sure how or why it has happened, but two times now, I have heard their conversation in my night visions," Isabella replied.

Trent cringed inwardly. There had been times when he'd thought something had been happening in Isabella's sleep. He'd chosen not to ask her about it in the hope that she would forget and remain relaxed.

"You are part of the conversation also?" he asked, once again wondering if the surprises would ever stop.

"No," Isabella said as she shook her head. "It was more like I was listening to it from a distance. I do not think they knew I was there."

"Who is the person she is talking to?" Trent asked.

Isabella looked thoughtful as she tried to remember if she'd heard the voice before, but she could not place it.

"I do not know. His voice is unfamiliar to me, but they mentioned meeting tonight, alone," she replied as she felt Cesare fall away from her breast.

When she looked down, she saw he'd fallen asleep again. She smiled in wonder at the tiny being that had been born from her body. For a moment, she was preoccupied with the small hand that she let rest around one of her fingers. She indulged in the simplicity of the moment, treasuring it. Inwardly, she wondered if she and Trent would be blessed to have another child together. When she thought about that, she felt a familiar level of desire flow through her. She turned her head to look at the man beside her.

Trent had been watching her facial expressions as she had been looking down at Cesare. As always, he was enraptured. Silently he wondered if she would ever stop getting more beautiful. When she turned to him with the look on her face that she had at that moment, he was speechless. He saw her lean her head back against the wall behind them while keeping her eyes on his. As he saw and felt her raise one of her hands and touch his cheek with it, he closed his eyes and indulged in the incredible feeling that came from her touch.

Isabella watched as he turned slightly and kissed the palm of her hand. When his eyes opened, she saw tears beginning in them.

"Why are you sad, Trent?" she asked him gently with hardly any more than a whisper.

Trent smiled at her and leaned over to kiss her on her lips and forehead before easing back to the same position once more.

"Not sad," he said. "I love you so much, and I am very happy to be here with you. Everything about you is incredible."

Isabella smiled at him, pleased with his words. The desire was intense inside of her but she dismissed it. She knew that Trent would not wish for her to rush to intimacy with her body so soon after Cesare's birth. Although she felt like fire was running through her veins in desire, she was happy to wait as long as Trent thought it necessary to.

CHAPTER 43

When Trent and Isabella entered the dining room that morning, they both noticed that Kat was already seated and talking to Adrian. As Isabella looked at Trent, he could see the concern on her face. He took her hand in his and held it tightly as they made their way to the table Adrian and Kat were sitting at.

"No, Kat. I do not understand," Isabella heard her lifelong friend saying as she approached. "You are confusing me. You say you wish to pair with me. Then you say you do not. I do not understand at all."

As Isabella and Trent sat down beside him, Adrian finally became aware that they were close by. Feeling frustrated at his conversation with Kat having taken another turn, he turned away from her and turned instead toward Isabella. In the background, many voices could be heard chattering with a happy tone to them. The unhappiness of Adrian in the seconds before was a stark contrast.

"Good morning, Isabella. Good morning, Trent," he said with a smile that both knew did not reflect how he was truly feeling.

As both of them returned the greeting, Isabella saw Kat rise and leave the table without saying anything to them.

"What has happened, Adrian?" Isabella asked and watched as her friend slowly released the smile façade and let his face relax.

"I do not know," Adrian said. "Kat tells me she wants us to pair, then she says she does not, and then she says she does. I do not know what is happening. Why does she keep changing her mind? It is the same thing, over and over. Either she wants to pair with me, or she does not. Which is how she truly feels, and which is pretend?"

Isabella reached out and put her hand on his shoulder. As she did, Adrian noticed the bundle that Trent held in his arms.

"Is that...?" Adrian started to ask, making Isabella laugh softly. "At last, I get to meet little Cesare?"

Isabella felt a little sad that she hadn't proactively introduced her friend to her son earlier. As she watched him move around her to sit beside Trent, she knew Adrian did not mind.

"Oh my, you are so tiny!" he exclaimed as he reached into the cloth encasing the infant and lightly touched Cesare's cheek. "Oh, Isabella!"

Trent watched Adrian's face and laughed softly. He'd never been truly certain how well Adrian had accepted him being paired with Isabella. In front of him, he could only see true joy. Adrian showed no anger or resentment.

"He has different colored hair, Isabella," Adrian said as he lightly touched the light waves on Cesare's head. "It is almost ... golden."

Adrian lifted his head and looked past Trent to smile at Isabella. She returned his smile briefly before turning to her food, suddenly feeling the depth of how ravenous she was. Seeing her start to eat, Adrian turned his focus back to Trent and the bundle in his arms.

"I do not know what I am to do as far as Kat is concerned, Trent," Adrian said. "She leaves me so confused."

Trent looked at the younger man before him and could almost feel the uncertainty emanating off him.

"What exactly has happened this morning that has upset you so much?" he asked.

Adrian was silent for a long while before he replied.

"Last time we spoke about pairing, she wanted it to happen. It was she who wished for me to agree to it," Adrian said. "This morning she has told me she is now uncertain again, so we must not rush and make any plans. I do not understand why she does not just say we are not going to pair ever. Would that not be a much easier thing to accept, than this saying yes and then saying no?"

Trent nodded.

"Perhaps, but Adrian, you may say that *you* do not wish to pair with *her* ever," he said and waited for Adrian to reply. No reply came. "How much do you truly wish to pair with Kat?"

Adrian looked directly into Trent's eyes. Trent knew how Adrian felt about Isabella, and Adrian knew that Trent knew how he felt. There was no need for any disguise of the fact.

"Trent," he said quietly, hoping Isabella would not hear. "I think you will understand that I do not see it likely that I will pair with someone I truly ... care about. All I can hope for is someone easy enough to get along with to start a family with."

"I can take Cesare now," both men heard Isabella say, breaking into their low-toned conversation. "Pass him to me, Trent, so that you can eat."

Adrian smiled at Trent and then stood up to move around the other side of Isabella, seeing his opportunity to finally speak to her. Before he had hardly moved, he knew Trent would already be devouring the food that he seemed to always eat with great relish and enthusiasm.

"He is wonderful, Isabella," Adrian said. "I am so happy for you. You are truly blessed, are you not, with Trent and now Cesare?"

Isabella looked into the normally happy face of her good friend. She was startled to see his eyes threatening with tears.

"Oh, Adrian. I do so wish it were all easier for you," she said. "You are such a good man and a great friend. I know there must be someone who you are meant to pair with..." Isabella started to say, without considering which words she wanted to follow.

"You do not think Kat is the one, do you?" asked Adrian.

"Only you can know that," Isabella replied. "Nobody else."

Adrian remained silent as he looked at her face.

Isabella could see him studying her - her eyes, her face shape, and even her lips. She didn't mind him looking at her in such a way. There was nothing behind it except a long friendship. Even if there had been, she knew him well enough to know that he fully understood her love for Trent.

"I must go to the mill and begin my work for the day," Adrian said, standing up suddenly. He placed one hand on Isabella's shoulder and looked down at her. "I am happy that you are so happy, Isabella. I do believe that I will find the same happiness. I just wish it did not take so long for me to find it."

Looking over at Trent, the two men nodded at each other peacefully before Adrian turned and began his journey out of the dining area.

Isabella turned and watched Trent demolishing his meal. The sight made her smile.

When he looked up at her, he saw once more his eyebrow-raise-move on her face. He smiled sheepishly at her, amused by her ever-changing facial expressions.

"The food here, I shall never tire of," he said before returning to his meal enjoyment once again. The flavors of zucchini and garlic bread filled his mouth as he moaned in appreciation, making Isabella smile.

They sat in silence as Isabella shifted her focus back to the infant in her arms. Cesare was looking up at her as if seriously considering what she was thinking. It shouldn't have, but just for a moment, the intensity of his stare alarmed her. He looked like he was actively listening to the words that were being said around him. Isabella smiled at him, expecting that wouldn't be possible for a newborn infant.

"Adrian is not happy," Trent said, breaking Isabella out of her thoughts. "Perhaps he shall like to visit us in our home this evening. What do you think?"

Isabella's face broke out into a wide grin.

"I think that is a very nice idea," she said.

CHAPTER 44

Adrian endured the day of work in the mill. He was aware that Kat was in the same structure as he was, just as she was every day. They had not directly crossed paths, but that was normal.

Less normal was his focus on her. She had been on his mind all day. He was trying to decide if he should simply say no to her about the possibility of them pairing. If he did that, where would that leave him? He had to pair with someone sometime. If only the person he had always wished to pair with…

As soon as that thought entered his head, he dismissed it. It was a pointless thing to invest time into considering. Isabella was the one person Adrian had always wanted to pair with. Isabella was also now happily paired with Trent. Adrian would not even attempt to deny that. The two of them obviously shared something deep and meaningful. They shared what Adrian wished to share with someone.

He was ready to give to someone what he saw Isabella and Trent giving each other. They leaned on one another. They made each other smile and laugh. Everything about how they looked at one another said how they felt toward each other.

Yes, he knew he was ready for pairing with someone who he could share a similar life with. He just had to find a way to find out who that someone *was*.

CHAPTER 45

Kat finished her evening meal hurriedly. She was excited about the evening to come.

She hadn't given Adrian another thought since their conversation that morning. Since then, only one man had occupied her mind. She didn't even know his name. He wasn't someone she'd ever interacted with in the village to date.

Now that she'd seen him, she found herself thinking about him more and more. His voice. His words. Everything about him intrigued her. From the little she had seen of him that morning, she knew he was much older than her. She didn't care about that. What he looked like, she hadn't given another thought to.

She was drawn to him. That was all that she knew for sure and all that she cared about. Something new was happening in her life - something new and exciting. It was something so new and exhilarating that she wanted to keep it to herself and not share it with anyone else.

Throughout the entire day, she was distracted by a slow-growing obsession inside her head. There was only one thing she wanted to do.

She could not wait to go back to the home she shared with her parents, go to sleep, and hear his words once more.

CHAPTER 46

Adrian sat in the small home of Trent and Isabella. There was an occasional emotional pain he felt when in their presence. It wasn't something that had grown out of spite or resentment. It was seeing them as happy as they were that caused his emotions to sometimes change. The happiness of his closest friend and the man she'd paired with seemed to accentuate the lack of happiness and level of loneliness Adrian sometimes felt.

Despite the minor uneasiness, he enjoyed his evening with them. He felt like he was pulled in towards their infant son. There was something about Cesare that seemed different. Adrian hadn't been around enough infants to know if he was identifying something real or just imagining it. There was no denying that when Cesare looked at Adrian, it seemed like he was really seeing him. It wasn't the way a child looked at an adult, but rather, the way an *adult* looked at an adult.

"Thank you, Trent. Thank you, Isabella. I shall leave you now and return to my home. I will see you in the morning perhaps," Adrian said, standing up in sudden eagerness to be away from the infant.

As he walked from their home to his own, his mind returned to Cesare. He was only an infant. Despite his age, he did seem much older in his way of looking at everyone. There was an aura about him that made Adrian think the infant already had an understanding of the village and the people in it.

Adrian shook the thoughts from his head, knowing they made no sense and were just silly and unimportant.

CHAPTER 47

"Kat," she heard the voice call out to her once she fell into her sleep that evening. "Come to me. I am waiting for you behind the temple. Come to me now."

Kat heard the voice in her head as it had been previously, in her night vision. Listening to it, she found she had the power to act on it and wake herself almost immediately. Quietly, she left the safety of the home she shared with her mother, father, and two young brothers.

Walking toward the temple, she had a moment of doubt. She couldn't help but wonder if everything was just a part of her visions of the night with no reality to them at all. As she walked around and along the long side of the large stone temple structure, she felt her chest become heavy. She stopped still, clutched her hand to her chest, closed her eyes, and breathed deeply.

After a moment, she began to walk again. As she rounded the corner at the rear of the building, she saw the silhouette of the man behind the voice. He started to move toward her but then seemed to reassess that action. Instead of approaching, he seemed to stop still.

"Kat," the same voice said to her. "I have been waiting to be able to see you like this, in person."

As he spoke, Kat noticed that he hadn't completely stopped at all. He was very slowly walking toward her. One step at a time, he gradually advanced.

Kat said nothing. Her heart felt extremely heavy in her chest. When he reached her and stood directly in front of her, she looked around. Nobody was nearby. She didn't consider she could be in danger or physically hurt, because such things never happened in the village. Because they didn't happen, the residents did not give such things a thought. They did not know fear, so never felt it in any circumstance.

"May I hold your hands?" the voice asked.

Kat nodded slowly, still too overwhelmed to speak. She watched as he stepped right up to her and slowly raised his hands upwards. As he did so, she naturally moved hers also. She was entranced as he took her hands into his.

Antonio relished the trust he had already gained in the young woman. He held her hands firmly and looked into her face. If he'd been anybody else, he might have found her attractive and a beauty, but he wasn't anybody else. He had a purpose, and she was going to help him make it follow through to fruition. He just needed to hold her attention. He just needed to get her to believe in him. Not forever. Not even for a long while. No, what he needed was for her to want to get closer to him, and stay close to him, just long enough.

"You are very beautiful," Antonio said, all the while monitoring her face to assess her naïveté and her level of ability to be manipulated.

He leaned down and kissed her hands - first one then the other. He sensed the tenseness emanating from her but did not let go of her hands. Instead, he stood up straight and looked into her eyes again.

"May I kiss your lips?" he asked.

Kat was startled but slowly nodded her head. She'd never been kissed, but she'd seen her parents do it sometimes when she'd been much younger.

Antonio leaned in and placed his lips on hers. He hadn't kissed young lips since he'd paired with Ariana. Although currently doing it for a purpose, he found that he liked it. Because he liked it, he indulged in it. For a moment, he almost forgot who he was kissing and why. When he felt her tense up, he pulled away. In doing so - in seeing her face - he understood that it was probable she'd never been kissed before. He knew he had to be careful. He didn't want to scare her. He needed her.

Kat watched as the man before her took a step back from her. He maintained his hold on her hands and looked into her eyes, but from a slight distance.

"I do not know your name," she said all of a sudden.

Her shyness showed greatly to Antonio. He resolved to be kind to her and smiled at her.

"I am Antonio," he said before kissing both of her hands once more, still watching her facial expressions.

"Antonio," Kat said dreamily as if she'd never heard the name before.

For a moment, Antonio thought she might be so easily led that she might not ask any more questions. He was wrong.

"What do you want from me, Antonio?" Kat asked. "Why have you chosen me to visit in the visions of the night? Why are you here with me now?"

Antonio studied her face. He felt a pang of annoyance flow over him but pushed it down into his soul. He was determined to not affect her as he'd affected Crisiana.

"I am sorry, Kat," he said, willing himself to appear timid at that moment. "I have been watching you for some time. I am not sure why, but you did catch my eye, and I have been thinking about you very much. I noticed and thought of you long before I contacted you. I never thought there might be a chance you would want to meet me."

"But *how* have you been contacting me in my visions of the night?" Kat went on to ask.

"I do not know," Antonio replied. "You were just there. I have taken it as a sign that I am meant to know you. I am meant to be close to you. Do you think that? Do you think that we are meant to know one another, and be close?"

He watched her face still and saw her expression soften before his eyes. Her demeanor changing gave him cause to rejoice inwardly. Yes, she was malleable. She was in her prime stage of life to be coaxed into anything with enough flattery.

Kat nodded. The words that came from him made perfect sense to her. She believed that he must be the reason she'd been so uncertain about Adrian. Adrian wasn't the man she was supposed to pair with - Antonio was! As her heart began beating faster, she became bold. Moving closer to him, she leaned her chest against his and reached up to place her lips on his. The move surprised both of them.

They kissed for a long time. Although Antonio would rather have not been, he found himself aroused by the feel of her lips on his, and her enthusiasm to keep exploring the magic of it. He didn't give any thought to Ariana. She could not be a casualty in his plan. He would make sure of it. He knew that with Kat, he had to be very careful and extremely aware of how she was feeling. He could not let himself enter a situation where she might reveal what was possibly going to happen between them. He equally could not let himself get carried away in emotion over her.

He pulled away from her and smiled.

"Oh, Kat. Your lips feel like they were made for mine," he started to say and immediately saw her blush. "I must not stay, and you must get home. Your mother and father will wonder where you are if they have discovered you are not in your bed. Go now," he said and kissed her lips quickly one more time.

"Can I see you again?" she asked.

Antonio smiled broadly, this time with true pleasure, although not for the reasons she might have suspected.

"I would like that very much," he said. "What if we meet here each evening? Shortly after the sun leaves the sky, and dark is upon us?"

He saw her nod and pull away from him.

"Till tomorrow evening then," Kat said. "Goodnight, Antonio."

As he watched her walk away from him, he remained where he was. He waited a suitable length of time to ensure he would not be seen anywhere near her as she made her way home.

Overall, he was pleased with the interaction. It had been short but very sweet. He smiled as he considered how much easier things were going to be with Kat. It had been an error to think Crisiana would be suited to the cause. She was too mature. She had a mind of her own. Kat, in contrast, was the perfect age for Antonio's needs.

He smiled further as he finally calculated enough time had passed for Kat to be safely at her family home. Walking out from behind the temple, Antonio thought about his earlier time with Ariana. It had been a surprise but an extremely welcome one.

Thinking about it again, he began to walk faster. He'd just touched young lips and rediscovered youthful enthusiasm. That meant nothing. What his lifetime with his beautiful Ariana had provided was far more important and far more fulfilling.

CHAPTER 48

Isabella and Trent lay in bed, holding one another.

"Are you worried about her?" Trent asked.

Isabella remained silent for a long time before she answered.

"A little," she said. "Part of me thinks it might have been a good idea to find them and hear what they would be talking about. A different part of me thinks it best to let them meet and plan whatever they shall plan so that we can see where things will lead."

Trent considered her words.

"It could be simply a matter of him finding her attractive," he said, even though he had never seen anything attractive or even likable about Kat.

"Perhaps," Isabella replied with doubt in her voice. "If she is being pursued by someone else, that could explain why she has been putting off pairing with Adrian. If that is the situation, should Adrian not know that someone else is trying to lure her into pairing?"

Trent said no more, not sure what was the best advice to give. Isabella's friendship with Adrian was solid and had been formed over a long period of time. He had to have faith that she would know exactly what the right thing to do was with regard to her close friend.

Instead of responding, Isabella felt him move further down under the covers and gently coax her to do the same. As his arms nestled around her, she leaned in to kiss him. The subject of Adrian, Kat, and the mysterious man Kat was meeting could wait for another day.

CHAPTER 49

The next evening Kat met Antonio again. She had been thinking about him all day long although she hadn't seen him even at the morning dining.

Her thoughts had wandered back to Adrian now and then throughout the day, but she didn't maintain focus on him for long. Neither had approached the other that morning, and she didn't miss dining with him. She was very aware that Adrian might be entirely forgettable, given the right circumstance occurring in her own life.

As she approached Antonio that second night, she instantly moved right up to him and kissed him. She took him by surprise as he was not aware of her forwardness. Once her lips were on his, he indulged in enjoying it. The previous evening, after he had seen her, he'd returned home, glad that Ariana was once again eager to be intimate with him. He had greatly welcomed that after his lips had been on Kat's.

As he stood with the young woman in his arms again, it was a surprise to him as he was very aware of the age difference between them. She was of an age where she should be considering pairing, but as yet, she had not. He knew with great confidence that he'd had some influence over her in that regard.

She also hadn't yet asked him if he was paired with anyone. It did not seem to have occurred to her that he might be. She did not seem to consider at all that at his age, it was extremely likely that he was. He expected that the question might arise.

As he kissed her deeply, he felt her arms wrap around his neck. Her body against his was alluring to him, but he was determined to maintain focus. He wouldn't let emotions overpower his plans for her.

Once again, they kissed and briefly talked before he encouraged her to return to her home. They continued this pattern for some weeks. Each evening resulted in them being a little bit closer than they had been the night before.

Their conversations in Kat's visions of the night had completely stopped, leaving Isabella unknowing of what was happening, if anything.

~~~~~

"Oh, Kat, we mustn't," Antonio said to her one evening as she held him close to her.
~~~~~

He desperately wanted her to submit to him. He equally knew it was important that he played the role of the caring man who would not harm her. He'd already spent enough time with her to know how to manipulate her. He'd already learned how to make her think something was her idea when in fact he'd led her to that decision.

"I wish to be closer to you, Antonio," Kat murmured against his lips.

She knew she should not have been seeing him as she was, but she was drawn to him. He was everything she would want in someone to pair with. He excited her. He thought and told her that she was beautiful, and he saw her value. That was something she'd never been sure of with Adrian.

She wasn't knowledgeable about physical love, but she understood that her body was desiring of *something*. When she pressed her body hard against his, she felt his body change. It felt nice to realize it was because of her.

She was learning things about her own body also. On each of the previous few nights, she'd felt Antonio's hands grow increasingly intimate and forward in their caresses. She liked it. When she'd felt him touch her breast through her slip dress, she'd experienced a jolt like no other. Even that didn't compare to the way she'd felt when his hand had moved lower. He'd touched her there several times. She wanted him to keep touching her like that.

As they kissed and touched, Antonio found she was even more eager than usual. He found it difficult to maintain his distance and not rush. He didn't want to put things off forever. Moving forward was essential with his plan. It was only fear of making her afraid that kept him moving things along slowly.

After he felt her shudder against his finger in pleasure, he took her hand and placed it over himself through his clothing. It was the first time he'd been so bold. He needed it, but he was also nervous that he might be moving things too quickly. As if she were naturally made for such actions, he felt her begin to move her hand over him.

Kat watched his face. When she saw how it was making him feel, she rubbed harder. As he groaned softly, she understood she was making him feel similar to how he'd just made her feel.

"How can I…?" she started to ask.

Antonio tentatively lowered his pants enough to let her hand encase him. She instantly started moving her hand directly over him, surprising him with her enthusiasm. Not wanting to wait any longer, he edged her back against the wall of the temple. As he kissed her deeply, he moved forward until his erection touched her lightly, right at her entry.

Kat felt him pressing against her. Having no understanding of physical pleasure, she also had no understanding of any physical pain or discomfort that could come from a woman's first time. The result was that she was relaxed as he slowly pushed inside her.

The feeling of being filled up entranced her. She had never felt anything like it as she focused fully on the feelings in her body.

Antonio looked at her face and was surprised even further. He felt like he might never finish being surprised by her. Pushing into her fully, he remained still to allow her to acclimatize to him before he slowly moved out and then in again. The sounds coming from her told him he certainly was not hurting her.

In fact, quite the contrary.

~~~~~

As their nightly rituals continued, they remained a secret. Antonio and Kat never spoke to one another on the odd day when they were both in the dining area at the same time.

Each night was magical, particularly to Kat. She had forgotten things were not quite as they were meant to be, with her being so enamored and distracted in emotion.

Seeing just how wrapped up she was in their physical connection, Antonio thought he might never have to concern himself with admitting his home truth to her.

Once again, he was wrong.

~~~~~

"I do not understand, Antonio. We have ... joined. You must pair with me. If you do not, what will happen to me?" she asked him one night.

Antonio fought to hold back his natural reaction to speak badly to her. Instead, he did as he always did with her and moved his mind into that of a kind-hearted person. He knew how to appear as a person who actually cared. Regardless, he took his time to watch her face as he spoke.

"Kat, I cannot pair with you. You must see that. I am much older than you," he started to say, hoping he could dissuade her of her hopes before he had to mention he was already paired. "You must pair with someone younger than me."

"I *had* someone younger than you, who I could have paired with," Kat replied, desperation evident in her voice. "I could have paired with Adrian. You told me I must let him go. Did you not tell me that because you wished to pair with me?"

As he watched her becoming distressed, he pulled her to him and held her head against his chest. He only had to pretend for a short while longer, to ensure that his plan had worked...

... his plan to impregnate her, with a being of supreme superiority.

CHAPTER 50

Kat lay in her bed, wide awake even though it was late into the night. The man who had encouraged her to believe she was beautiful had no intention of pairing with her. She had been fooled. She had given her body to him, and despite that being something that no-one had ever talked about, deep down she knew she shouldn't have. It was something she should never have shared with anyone other than the person she would pair with. Could she pair with anyone else now?

Antonio hadn't given a reason why he would not pair with her, and she hadn't asked. If he didn't consider her valuable enough to pair with, it didn't matter why.

She turned onto her side and brought her knees up toward her chest. What would she do now? Her mind turned to Adrian. The two of them had moved back and forth in their talks about pairing. During their last conversation, Adrian had suggested they move forward and pair. That seemed to be his current position on the subject - they *should* become paired with one another.

Despite her back and forth statements to him, she wasn't against the idea. She had wanted to pair with him long ago but had since been presented with the idea to reject him. It was the voice in her night visions that had encouraged her in that - Antonio's voice.

Suddenly she felt a coolness pass through her body and settle over her belly. As she lifted the covers, she looked down. What she saw alarmed her.

Over her belly, she could see the color blue.

And it was glowing.

CHAPTER 51

In the morning, Kat went to the morning dining as usual. The blue glow she had thought she'd seen the night before was not visible on her belly before she'd left her home. She imagined it was a trick of her eyes, perhaps due to the tiredness she had been feeling. Subsequently, she pushed it out of her mind.

Because she had no recollection of the battle in the temple earlier, she also did not remember that she'd experienced a blue glow in her belly previously. What she thought she'd seen the night before seemed new and unfamiliar.

As she entered the dining area, Kat's eyes immediately fell to Adrian. She was confused as she looked at him. Being ahead of her, he didn't know she was there as she stood contemplating her options with him. She could also see Isabella and Trent sitting next to Adrian. The sight of them made Kat's pleasant thoughts quickly turn sour.

"Yes, she is the cause of everything that has gone wrong in your life," she heard Antonio's voice say in her head. She turned around, expecting to see him. He wasn't in sight.

It was the first time she'd heard his voice during regular daylight hours, but it did not alarm her. Although she didn't want it to be true, his voice was still like a warm comfort to her. He hadn't said anything that she did not already regard as truth. Isabella was the person who had made it difficult for Adrian to want to pair with Kat when she'd first approached the idea with him. Although it seemed a very long time ago, if Isabella hadn't held Adrian so tightly back then, he would have moved forward and paired with Kat and they would now be living a happy life together. They might even be mother and father to an infant, just as Isabella and Trent were.

Yes. She agreed with the voice. It was all Isabella's doing that Kat was not yet paired, and she shouldn't be allowed to get away with that.

Her mind returned to Adrian. What was she to do there? She had already shared her body with another. She was unaware of the connection between that pleasure and the creation of new life. It did not occur to her that she might be carrying a child inside of her.

She moved forward. She needed to pair. She would not turn away from Adrian anymore.

~~~~~

"Good morning Adrian," she said as she smiled sweetly and sat next to him. "Good morning Isabella and Trent," she threw in for good measure to the two people on the other side of Adrian.

Everyone returned the greeting, but for that moment, Kat maintained her eyes on Adrian only.

Trent held Cesare in his arms but now and then raised his eyes to watch Kat's facial expressions as she coaxed Adrian into pleasant conversation. At one point, he saw Kat's eyes move briefly and meet his own. In them, Trent saw a look that alarmed him a great deal. It was a look he'd seen before, building up to and on that night. He said nothing and lowered his eyes, looking at the small bundle in his arms once more, but he had no doubt. The entity they'd thought Isabella had extinguished that night was not gone at all. It was back. It was lodged deep inside of Kat once again.

Trent then had another thought.

Perhaps it had simply never left.
~~~~~

CHAPTER 52

"The seed has been sown, old friend," Elder Rhys heard in his head. They were the first words he'd heard from Cesare in a long while - so long that he'd begun to suspect he'd only dreamed that the soul of his long-passed friend was back. "The power has begun to grow. It is within a young woman. She is not yet paired. He has seduced her. She is carrying a child that will have the soul of another - the soul of something evil."

Elder Rhys had been meditating when the voice entered his head. On hearing the words, he groaned inwardly.

"She has a child inside of her? That cannot be if she has not yet paired," the ancient said in his mind. "It is not the way of our people…"

"Listen to me, Rhys!" the voice said. "He has seduced her and played on her vulnerabilities. He has worked her and was easily able to entice her to share her body with him in joining."

"Do you know who it is? The young woman, or the man?" the ancient asked through his thoughts. There was silence for a moment before the voice spoke again.

"I do not," the voice replied. "I sense what is happening, but I do not know the people. I cannot make a judgment on who is involved. You must search for her, Rhys. You must find her and restrain her before the powers she will have, grow and intensify."

"Powers?" Elder Rhys asked.

"Yes. I sense the frustration in him," replied the voice. "He may have tried this before but failed. His previous plan did not work for him. He has delivered the strength this time in his seed, in the hope of making it more solid than the power had been last time. He has determination. That, I can feel greatly."

Elder Rhys sat for a short time longer and then moved to rise from his meditative position.

"Very well, old friend. I shall investigate," he said. "I believe I know the first place to start. Can you sense anything more that I need to know?"

"No, I can only feel that the strength is growing already. Hers will not be a regular child," the voice continued. "You must be careful. Even as it resides and grows within her, it will have considerable strength. Tread with care!"

The conversation in the ancient's head closed down as he left the room of meditation. For the most part, the village had always been at peace. Its long history was one of serenity and tranquility. The recent occurrences of things out of the ordinary happening was unsettling to him.

He had no idea how he could identify who the man or the woman were that the old soul of Cesare spoke of, but of course, there was one obvious person to begin with. He would not go directly to her. Instead, he would go to Isabella. She had been the target of Kat's aggression last time, that night in the temple. It was very possible she was going to be the target once more.

CHAPTER 53

Crisiana approached the part of the dining area where the villagers each washed, dried, and put away their items after dining. As she stood there, she heard her daughter's voice behind her.

"Mother," Isabella said, feeling like she had seen far too little of her mother since her father had passed. She saw Crisiana turn and face her. "Mother, how are you?"

As Crisiana turned, she saw Isabella standing close to her with the small bundle in her arms. Instantly, Crisiana smiled at her daughter and held out her arms to take Cesare into them.

"Oh, my daughter, how fast he is growing!" she exclaimed. "And his hair! I have never seen hair so golden. Oh, he is so lovely!"

Isabella laughed at her mother. Her joy came from seeing her mother finally starting to look honestly happy. It helped to put any fears to rest.

"You look like you are at peace, Mother," she said quietly as she watched Crisiana's face.

Crisiana looked at her daughter, smiled, and nodded.

"I am at peace, Isabella," she replied. "It was difficult at the start, adjusting to not having my Tomas beside me each night. Each day that I wake, I feel a little bit more like my usual self."

The words made Isabella think back to the weeks following the battle. She had thought she'd been with child. It had turned out that the golden glow wasn't a child at all. She had grieved for it all the same. She could only imagine how much more difficult it must be for anyone to lose their lifelong partner, knowing they would never see them again.

Her reverie was broken by the sound of her mother speaking again.

"Enjoy every moment you have with Trent," Crisiana said. "I did not consider how quickly Tomas could be taken from us. I cannot change that now, but you can make sure that you appreciate and love Trent as much as you can while he is here with us. Do not take the love you share for granted, Isabella. *Never* take him for granted."

Isabella nodded but said nothing. The conversation reminded her of the times she'd spent with her father. She could feel tears threatening in her eyes.

Crisiana saw the glistening in her daughter's eyes and smiled sadly at her as she raised one hand and cupped Isabella's cheek.

"You have sought your place in this village for a very long time, Isabella. I think that now you have found it. You are meant to be the mother to this little one, and, if it is meant to be, you and Trent will go on and have more children. Enjoy the time with this little one. He is a gift indeed," she said as she gently touched Cesare's golden hair. "I sense great things to come from him, and I look forward to seeing him grow more each and every day. I sadly hand him back to you now as I must away to go to begin my work."

Isabella received Cesare back into her arms. She watched as her mother smiled, leaned in, kissed her on the cheek, and walked away.

Trent's voice appeared behind Isabella. "She looks happy. It is good to see," he said as he wrapped his arms around her from behind.

Isabella leaned back against him, enjoying the strength she always felt when she was close to him.

"Yes, but I shall keep watching her," she replied. "I do worry about her."

Trent moved around her until he was standing in front of her with Cesare nudged between their chests. Leaning in to kiss her softly, he then pulled back and looked down to see his son looking at him and smiling. He could say no more. The look on his infant's face made him laugh softly before he turned and guided Isabella to sit down so they could dine and move forward with their day.

CHAPTER 54

"The time is fast approaching, old friend," the old soul of Cesare whispered through the thoughts of Elder Rhys. The ancient immediately stopped the activity he was doing and closed his eyes to listen carefully to what was being said. "I can sense his eagerness, but also his fear. He is afraid. He is afraid that he still might not have the strength to succeed in what he wishes to accomplish."

Elder Rhys visualized himself shaking his head.

"I still do not understand what it is that he *does* want to accomplish," he said. "What can he stand to gain by causing sorrow and destruction in our village?"

"Power, Rhys!" the voice exclaimed. "He craves power. He wants to rule and dictate…"

"You know that our village does not work like that," the ancient said in his mind. "It never has. There are no ruling powers here."

"I know you believe that, and that is how we have always perceived the village to be, but think, Rhys. Think! Who ultimately oversees everything in the village? Who utilizes the power of the golden stone to send our passed on their journey? Who welcomes the newborns into the village on their day of birth?"

"The ancients…" Elder Rhys replied.

"Yes!" said the voice. "He needs to remove the ancients, to take ultimate power of the village and its population."

"You think he wants to kill us all?"

"No, old friend," the voice continued. "He does not need to do that. Most of the ancients - even yourself - will pass and leave this world naturally in time. No, it is not the present ancients he wishes to eliminate…"

Elder Rhys groaned inwardly. He knew the target. All of a sudden, everything made sense.

"Isabella…"

The voice of Cesare's old soul toned down and became peaceful as it spoke.

"Yes," it said. "She is his greatest adversary even though she does not feel or know it. She is a chosen one. You already know that it must be within her destiny to become an ancient. She is young. She has a great many years to live, and many years to grow her powers. Yes, Rhys, he knows what she is, and he wants her gone. Before that, he wants to hurt her. He wants to take everything from her."

"You think he was the one who poisoned Tomas…" Elder Rhys considered.

"Yes, I believe that may well be the case," the voice said. "I believe he moved toward hurting Isabella more by trying to hurt her mother also."

"Crisiana? How so?" Elder Rhys asked. "I have not heard anything about this."

"It is unimportant now," the voice replied. "What we must focus on is stopping him."

The ancient remained quiet in his thoughts as he concentrated on what was being said to him.

"The greatest problem is that we don't know *who* he is," he said. "How can we find someone who is hiding in plain sight as a regular villager?"

"The mother," replied the voice. "She may not know what his intentions are, or even that he has intentions, but she might be able to indicate to you someone who has interacted with her since the death of her husband. There may be someone who has paid her particular attention."

"I will go to her, but how do we fight against him even if we identify him?" Elder Rhys asked. "Isabella is a mother now. We cannot put her in danger."

"You must, but she shall not fight alone. I will help," the old voice said, making Elder Rhys chuckle lightly even though the situation was far from amusing.

"I do not think the body you reside in will be of any benefit, Cesare," he said.

"No, I shall have to channel my power through that of another."

"Me?" the ancient asked, for a moment excited at the prospect.

Now it was Elder Rhys who heard the chuckle of another.

"Now old friend, your body is well past its time of being able to fight," the voice said. "No, there is one in the village who is stronger in body, mind and strategic ability than anyone else. He is the father of the child I am currently residing in."

"Trent? How…?"

"I shall have to prepare," replied the voice. "We must work together to see if I can channel through him. Can you make that happen, Rhys?"

"Yes, of course," the ancient said. "Now, please, go quiet and rest, old friend. I must go and speak with Crisiana and Trent. I shall call out to you when I have news."

CHAPTER 55

"Elder Rhys," Crisiana greeted the ancient after he'd knocked on the door to her small home that evening. "Please come in. Is all well?"

Elder Rhys entered the home and followed Crisiana's guidance to sit at the small table.

"All is well, but I must question you about a slightly disturbing matter," he said and immediately saw concern on her face as she joined him at the table.

"Of course," Crisiana replied. "What is it?"

"I believe that someone in the village is not as they appear, and they might be working toward hurting us," the ancient said.

Crisiana watched his face as he spoke. She had known him for as long as she could remember anything of her life. He was someone she regarded with the highest respect. She'd never had any reason to doubt his words.

"Do you know who this person is?" she asked, her voice quiet and calm.

"I do not. However," the ancient started to say before he paused to gather his words. "I believe *you* may know him, Crisiana."

Elder Rhys saw surprise pass across her usually peaceful face.

"Me?" she asked. "Why would you think this?"

"It is not an easy thing to talk about..."

He watched as Crisiana reached out, placed her hand over his, and smiled sadly at him.

"Speak, Elder Rhys," she said. "Whatever you need to say, I am prepared for."

"This man I believe wishes ultimately to hurt Isabella," Elder Rhys said. "We ... *I* ... think there may be a chance that he is going to try and hurt her by hurting you."

Elder Rhys watched Crisiana's face and saw her thoughtful before he then saw her face change slightly and take on the appearance of knowledge.

"Do you know who I mean?" he asked. "Your face shows me that you may have just thought about someone..."

Crisiana stood abruptly and walked to the other side of the room for a few minutes before she turned back to him.

"After Tomas passed, someone from my childhood did start to pay me more attention. I thought it was because he wanted to work toward pairing with me. Then, when I remembered that he is already paired, I thought that perhaps he wished to utilize my body..." she started to say as she felt her face begin to blush. "Do you think he was trying to get close to me in order to somehow hurt my daughter?"

"It is possible, but I cannot be certain," Elder Rhys replied. "There are many unknowns. Can you tell me who this person was, Crisiana? He may not be any threat at all. It may be that he did indeed seek you out for personal reasons."

The two of them were quiet as they regarded each other. Elder Rhys, having lived such a long life, could see that she was pondering something.

"What is it?" he prompted her. "You are worried about something."

"Yes," she said, casting her eyes downward. "When he first approached me after Tomas passed and left us to go forth on his next journey, I felt charmed by this man. He provided me with companionship when I was feeling alone and lonely, but the more I was around him, the more I felt something was not quite right. It seemed as though he wanted something else from me and shouldn't be trusted. It was then that I told him there was nothing he would get from me. He has not shown me the same interest since."

Elder Rhys looked closely at her. He almost did not want to ask her anything more about the man she was referring to. It felt too personal to ask for the man's name and identity, but he knew he had to.

"Who is it, Crisiana?" he asked. "*Who* is the man that you refer to?"

Crisiana took a deep breath and looked into his eyes. She was resolved that she would need to reveal the identity of her friend even though she'd rather have kept quiet about her dealings with him.

"Antonio."

The ancient was surprised. He did not in any way anticipate hearing the name that was presented to him.

"Antonio?" he questioned, making sure he'd heard correctly. After he saw Crisiana nod, he spoke again. "But he is paired with Ariana!"

Crisiana nodded again, lowering her eyes once more.

"Oh, dear," Elder Rhys said. "Let us hope he is not the person I seek. I do not wish for her to be hurt in any way, nor their children," he said before observing a tear appear on Crisiana's cheek. "Worry not, Crisiana. Whatever happened between the two of you shall remain unknown to others of the village. I have no reason to mention you know him so well, or that he pursued you, for whatever reason that he did. I am happy that you had the strength to tell him he was making you uncomfortable. You are looking happier now, and that is good to see. I shall leave you now.

Thank you for your honesty. I know it is not easy to talk about such things, and you may not have wished to disclose his name to me."

"Do you think Isabella is in danger from him, Elder Rhys?" Crisiana asked.

"I do not know for sure," he replied. "It is only a suspicion that I must investigate further. I hope I am wrong."

The ancient stood up and quietly excused himself before leaving the home of Isabella's mother, determined to gather assistance from the man Isabella had paired with.

CHAPTER 56

Antonio sat in his home that evening, enjoying hearing about Ariana's day. There was never anything overly exciting that she had to tell him, given how peaceful the village was every day. Regardless, he loved listening to her all the same. He always had. Since the two of them had re-established their nightly intimacy, his enthusiasm for her had increased even more. Even the attention he'd been giving to Kat hadn't diminished any feeling he had for the woman he'd been paired with for so long.

When Ariana had finished telling him about her day, he saw a familiar glint appear in her eyes. It was invigorating that she seemed to have found a new level of energy in their nightly passion. The pleasure was exciting enough. Ariana exuding a new level of confidence drove Antonio on even more in his excitement to be with her.

As he watched her body language, he remained still. During their long life together, he had always left the initiation of their joining to her. Out of the great respect he had for her, he had no desire to push himself on her. It was no reflection of his desire for her at that moment. He hid it well, but deep inside, he was enraptured as he watched her move toward him with her focus clear on her face.

He knew he should have been maintaining focus on other things - more important things. He couldn't help but be distracted by her. It was something he felt he could never get enough of.

CHAPTER 57

A knock on the door of the home of Trent and Isabella resulted in Isabella's awareness heightening. At the same time, the slight discomfort she felt in her belly told her who was there.

"It is Elder Rhys," Isabella said as she watched Trent walk toward the door.

Open opening it, Trent looked back at her, still surprised by her perception that seemed not only heightened but also extremely accurate.

"Trent, I wish to speak to you in the temple, if you are able to come with me," Elder Rhys said when the door had opened.

The ancient greeted and nodded at Isabella, but remained where he was without attempting to enter the home. He fully knew the degree of pain that Isabella could experience when in close vicinity to him. He still didn't understand why it happened, but he accepted and respected the odd occurrence.

"Yes, of course, Elder Rhys," Trent said, surprised but always willing to comply. He turned and moved close to Isabella to kiss her softly. "I shall return shortly."

The two men walked to the temple in silence. After making their way through to the rear of the temple, they finally sat inside a room that could be made private with the door closed.

"What is it?" Trent asked when his curiosity intensified. Although no words had been spoken, he was very aware of the level of seriousness on the face of the ancient before him.

"I fear that Isabella is in great danger," Elder Rhys said, his face grave. "There is someone among us who is ... *might be* ... working toward another strike, but this time a much stronger one."

Trent absorbed and analyzed the words he'd heard.

"You think that the last attack was directly against Isabella?" he asked. "It was not just a case of her defending the village? The entity inside of Kat wanted specifically to hurt Isabella?"

"I do think that may be a possible situation, yes," the ancient replied, nodding. "I do not know for certain, but things keep happening that are centered around her. I believe that the person in question knows that Isabella is a chosen one. He knows that she will become an ancient, and in the time from now until then, she will develop powers far greater than she has even started to grow yet."

"Do you think this person had something to do with the death of Isabella's father?" Trent asked tentatively and saw the elderly man in front of him nod.

"I do," said Elder Rhys. "I think it is his wish to make Isabella suffer before he comes back for another strike at her. Perhaps it is his hope that she will not be as strong if she is in pain from seeing those she loves suffer or leave us. If he is the man I suspect he is, I believe he has since attempted to hurt her through her mother also."

"Crisiana?" Trent asked, the tone of his voice revealing his surprise. "What has happened? I did not know…"

"No, no, worry not. It eventuated into nothing, I believe," Elder Rhys said. "I understand it was an attempt but Crisiana is too strong-willed to have given in to what he wanted from her. With regard to that, Trent, it is a very personal thing for Crisiana. I have assured her I would speak to no-one about it. I beg that you do not ask her about it or speak about it, even to Isabella."

Trent considered what was being said and nodded. His mind then moved on to a different thought.

"Do you think someone like that might have moved to another, younger mind? One that could more easily be manipulated?" he asked.

Elder Rhys looked at him intently. "Yes! Do you know of such a person?"

Trent sat down on the small bed in the room. "Yes, and so do you," he said. "Kat. Isabella has heard conversations between Kat and a man. She does not hear them often, but she did say that she had overheard the man coaxing Kat to meet him late at night, alone."

"He must need her for his plan, whatever that is ultimately," Elder Rhys replied. "There must be something special about Kat that attracts him…"

"Yes, in the same way that there is something special about Isabella," agreed Trent. "They are like complete opposites. I suppose it would only be natural for them to be absolute adversaries."

Trent sat in silence, thinking about Isabella and his young son. Even the idea of someone being intent on hurting either of them infuriated him.

"What can we do?" he asked. "How do we stop this … *thing* … without having the same strength that they have?"

"What are your fighting skills like, Trent?" the ancient asked and saw Trent's look of surprise.

"Fighting? Using my fists?" Trent asked, assuming he must be wrong in his interpretation of the ancient's question. He was surprised to see Elder Rhys nod. "I … I come from a world where fighting is fairly normal and regular. I am not a fighter, but I could hold my own against an equal or lesser opponent. Would this person not have powers though? I cannot fight against that."

Elder Rhys sat on the bed and faced Trent.

"There is something I must tell you, Trent. Your son, Cesare, is also special. He is not just a child, as you might expect," Elder Rhys said and waited a moment for his words to sink in before he continued. "Inside of young Cesare is an older soul."

Trent shook his head to show how confused he was by what the ancient had just said. "I do not understand."

"It *is* difficult to understand," Elder Rhys replied. "I did not believe it at first. It took some convincing when I first started to hear the familiar voice calling out to me. Now I have no doubts."

"Who is this older person who invades my son?" Trent asked. "You say you know him?"

"I *knew* him," Elder Rhys said. "He and I grew up together, but he left us long ago. When he passed, we sent him on his journey just as we did for Tomas recently. I had never heard of anyone coming back from their journey before, but I do believe it is him."

Trent could hardly comprehend what he was hearing.

"How do you speak to him?" he asked. "How do you *know* he is in Cesare?"

"He communicates with me through my mind," the ancient replied. "He says he is in your son, but cannot control him. It seems like he is able to use him as a means of communication more than anything."

There was silence for a long while as both men considered the situation.

"Let me assume that what you say is true and real," said Trent. "*Why* is your old friend in my son? Why is he using him to communicate with you?"

"Because he knows of the threat to the village," said Elder Rhys. "Cesare - my old friend, that is - yes, he has the same name - has said that he can feel the darkness of this man. He can feel how much this man intends to hurt us all."

"But why through my son?" Trent asked. "Could he not have contacted you directly, or entered you?"

"Trent, your son is also the son of Isabella," the ancient said. "She has only recently started to feel her powers beginning. As she matures, she will develop powers of incredible strength. Her power is already growing at a faster rate than I've ever seen in someone so young before. It is not too much to expect that any children born of her will also have powers of their own."

"You think that is something that is passed from parent to child?"

Trent asked. "If that were true, where did Isabella get them from? Crisiana and Tomas did not have any powers, did they?"

The ancient looked lost in trying to find and provide an answer to the question. As the query remained unresolved, Trent continued to speak further.

"Alright," he said. "An older man by the same name resides in my son and communicates his concerns to you. What does he suggest we do about this *thing* that is trying to cause destruction to Isabella's life?"

"Cesare believes he may be able to provide you with powers, to fight this man and end his desire for conflict."

Trent took a moment to consider that before he replied.

"You do not mean … kill him?!" he asked, horrified.

"Oh, no, not at all," the ancient replied. "Killing is not our way, but we would have to do *something*. If he is intent on bringing destruction to the village and all who reside here, something must be done. We must at least confront him and fight if we need to."

Trent stood up and walked around the room, trying to get his thoughts straight. He then turned and looked at the ancient once more.

"Where do we start?" he asked. "Do we even know who this person is?"

"I have an idea who it might be, but I have not yet investigated to find out if my suspicions are accurate," Elder Rhys replied. "I shall soon begin assessing that. For now, we must ascertain if Cesare's idea of sharing his power with you will work."

"And how do we do that?"

"This is all new, Trent. I am uncertain, but perhaps it would help to try. I can contact Cesare, I believe," the ancient said.

Trent watched as Elder Rhys closed his eyes and was silent.

"Yes," he finally heard him say, simultaneously appearing oblivious to Trent altogether.

After another long period of silence, Trent saw the ancient open his eyes and look directly at him.

"Hold out your hand, Trent," he said and saw Trent follow the instruction. "Palm up. Now focus on your palm. Will it to give you power."

The ancient saw Trent look at him with a doubtful expression on his face, but he continued to do as he was instructed.

For the long period of time that followed, Trent tried and failed to create the feeling of power he was being told he could. When he'd almost given up and was ready to leave the temple and return to his home, he took a deep breath and thought about his son. As he considered how he would feel if Cesare were put in danger and something happened to him, Trent felt a warmth flow over his palm. When he opened his eyes, he saw a golden flame hovering over it. He looked at it in amazement. It was creating warmth, but it wasn't burning him. It wasn't touching his skin, but he could feel that it was a power that belonged to him.

As he looked at it, he began to wonder what he was going to be able to do with it. He then heard Elder Rhys speak again.

"You have mastered it, Trent."

"I have this, Elder Rhys, but I am not sure how I came to make it appear," Trent replied. "I am uncertain if I can summon it whenever I wish it to. I do not think I would say that I have mastered it yet."

"It is enough for today," Elder Rhys said, nodding. "Will it away."

Trent looked at the ancient with disbelief in his eyes but again did as was asked. After several attempts to change his thoughts, imagining extinguishing the flame worked. He felt his hand cool once again.

"I must learn more if I am to use this in any way in a fight," Trent said and saw the ancient nod.

"Yes. For now, we know that you can summon it with Cesare's help," Elder Rhys said. "Trent, I feel that there is danger in Isabella having sensed the conversations of other people recently. We cannot be sure that the ability does not go both ways. Therefore I think it best that she not know you might be able to utilize this power." When Elder Rhys saw Trent open his mouth as if to protest, he continued. "I do understand you would not wish to keep anything from her, but in this instance, it could mean the difference between us taking down this person of ill intent, and not. If he has no idea that you can seize such power, he will not be expecting anything from you. This could be our advantage."

Trent didn't like the idea of keeping things from Isabella. On the other hand, as the ancient had said, doing so could mean the difference between Trent being able to help protect the people of the village or not.

He looked at the ancient and nodded.

"Of course," he said. "I will say nothing, Elder Rhys."

CHAPTER 58

As he walked back to the home he shared with Isabella and Cesare, Trent thought about what had just happened. He had no powers of his own. About that, he was certain. What he'd just witnessed had been under the control of an ancient soul that was living inside of his infant son. The enormity of all of that made Trent cringe. The more that was happening, the more he would have to keep to himself and not share with the woman that he loved. Despite it being for the best cause - to keep Isabella and Cesare safe - it felt wrong.

When he entered their home, he was saved from having to explain or lie. He smiled as he saw Isabella had laid down with Cesare on the bed and fallen asleep. Standing next to the bed for a long while, Trent took in the beauty of Isabella in her peaceful slumber.

As he turned to look at Cesare, he considered with sadness that he may never look at him the same way again. He could not shake the knowledge that someone else's soul was within him. It posed questions to Trent. As Cesare grew, would he be his own person? Or would he be guided and led by someone much older and wiser? If he were led by an old soul, would he ever really have a true childhood?

Trent shook the questions from his mind. There were no answers to be found in the immediate moment. He would have to take each day as it came and let time roll out whatever was meant to happen.

After one last glance at the bed, Trent leaned down and picked Cesare up. Slowly and quietly, he moved to the small bed set aside for the infant and lay him down in it. Cesare was sound asleep, even though only minutes earlier, the old soul within him had been actively working to help Trent. The thought gave Trent hope that perhaps the soul wasn't interacting with that of the young child after all. Perhaps his son was completely oblivious to the fact that someone else was inside of him and using him as a communication antenna.

Trent moved to the bed and lay down behind Isabella. It would be a long time before he would sleep, his mind was so active. Simply lying beside her was enough to, at least, calm and comfort him.

CHAPTER 59

The following morning, Trent woke to find Isabella awake and sitting up beside him as Cesare pressed against her chest, feeding. Before moving, Trent took a moment to absorb the sight before him. Isabella was sitting with her head resting back against the wall and her eyes closed.

Trent was glad to see her so at peace. After his talk with Elder Rhys the night before, everything he'd been told had weighed on his mind well into the night. The battle Isabella had been part of with Kat months earlier had seemed like such a huge event to all who saw it. Trent conceded at the same time that it seemed tiny compared to wars around the world. It was difficult to maintain a balance between being too worried and not being worried enough. The main thing he wanted to focus on was keeping Isabella and their son safe. Nothing else mattered as much as that did.

After a few moments of enjoying the view before him, Trent saw Isabella's eyes open, and her head turn slightly as she looked directly at him. When she saw he was awake, she smiled at him so broadly that Trent felt like he could never feel so much love or desire as he did for her at that moment. He continued to be in awe that he hadn't stopped feeling that way about her since they'd first met. He'd always been someone to attract women. He'd also always been someone who became relatively bored with them after a few months or even weeks. That he kept experiencing such strong emotions when he just looked at Isabella was a constant source of intrigue to him. He had to concede that he'd not just fallen in love with her, but he'd fallen hard. It was a love that was real, and it was deep. It was also something that he'd never before known he'd be able to have in his life.

As Isabella looked at Trent's face, watching his intense thoughtfulness, she felt Cesare's lips fall away from her. When she looked down, she saw he'd fallen asleep again. She grinned at the sight, gently stood up with him in her arms, and put him back into his own bed.

Trent watched her move away and then return. As she lay down on the bed again, she pulled the covers over her and huddled close to him. He pulled her closer still and held her tight, determined not to let the developments of the previous evening invade or even enter the closeness he enjoyed with her. He hoped she wouldn't ask about his talk with Elder

Rhys. As if knowing that he would tell her anything she did need to know, she didn't ask.

"I think it is time, Trent," Isabella whispered in an attempt to leave no doubt what she was referring to. She smiled even greater at him before she spoke again. "I am certain my body is fully recovered now."

Trent understood what she was referring to. He moaned softly at her words before he kissed her fully and let her guide him on top of her.

CHAPTER 60

On their way to their morning dining, Isabella heard her name called out by her mother, Crisiana. Trent seized the moment to move forward into the dining area to find Adrian. He wanted to discretely ask how things were with Kat, and what was happening with them. He couldn't know for sure if Kat had anything to do with the man who supposedly was intent on hurting the people of the village. He equally felt quite certain that she probably did.

The uneasy feelings Trent continued to have about Kat always worried him. He'd met plenty of dislikeable people in his lifetime. Through one experience or another, he'd learned it was always wise to trust his gut feeling when it came to such dislikes. More than once, he'd turned his back on his instinct, then paid the price for that.

"Adrian," he said to the younger man as he sat down beside him.

"Good morning, Trent. How are you this fine day?" Adrian asked, sounding as cheerful as he usually did, no matter how he truly felt inside.

"I am well," Trent replied. "How are you? Are there any developments with you and Kat yet? Any news of a possible pairing?"

He watched as Adrian's face changed and became more serious.

"No, I do not think that will happen," Adrian replied. "We have not talked in a long while. She seems very distracted these days, so I do not try to spend time with her. I am resigned to the possibility that I must look further for someone to pair with. I do not think Kat has any interest in me at all, even though at times she has said she has. To be very honest with you, Trent, I think she has been pretending with me. For what reason, I do not know. If she had ever been certain about the two of us pairing, we would be paired by now."

Trent watched Adrian's face and nodded. Looking around the dining area and noting that once again, Kat was nowhere to be seen, he wondered what Kat had been doing in the mornings. He hadn't seen her for several days.

"Be certain, Adrian," Trent said. "Ask her plainly so there cannot be any possibility of misinterpretation. You have a right to know where you stand with her, and you are right. You must not wait forever. It is your duty to assist in the maintenance of the population."

Adrian laughed softly and then spoke with a trace of affection.

"Trent, you sound more and more like a native of my village, each and every day."

The two men laughed together and spoke no more of Kat as Isabella approached. Holding Cesare in her arms, she eagerly greeted her lifelong friend before beginning her meal.

CHAPTER 61

Adrian left the morning meal feeling fresh and energized. He was ready to move forward into the next stage of his life. Every time he watched Trent and Isabella together, he knew he was ready for the same thing. He would ask Kat one more time out of courtesy. If she said no, he would be proactive in getting to know better the other young women of pairing age in the village. The thought excited him and made him hope that Kat was no longer interested.

As he began his journey down the path from the dining area to his work at the mill, he heard Kat's voice call out to him from behind.

"Adrian! Please! Wait!" she called out.

Although with a heavy heart, Adrian stopped and turned to face her. It was easy for him to put on a smile, even when he didn't particularly feel like smiling. As she approached him, he noticed the degree to which she was smiling. It was concerning.

"I am glad to see you," she said when she reached him. "I was late to dine this morning, but I wish to speak to you. Could we please go somewhere quiet for a short time before we go to the mill?"

Adrian looked at her, slightly confused by her forwardness and the strong sense of determination that was emanating from her. He experienced a deep feeling of dread coming on. As always, he covered it up with his usual friendly smile.

"Of course, Kat," he said. "Shall we walk down by the pool and talk there?" he asked and saw her nod.

They walked in silence until they found privacy. Sitting on the large flat stones near the warm water pool, he turned to her and waited for her to speak. In the background, he could hear the rumble of the small waterfall. It was a sound that helped to calm his nervousness about whatever Kat was going to say to him.

"Adrian, I asked you a long time ago if you would consider pairing with me," she said and saw him nod. "Since then, I have changed my mind several times, and I am sorry for any confusion I have caused you. I do believe that we must make a firm decision. Do you?"

Adrian nodded again but remained silent, prompting her to say whatever it was that she felt she needed to say.

"I want us to pair. You and me. Soon," Kat said.

In her mind, she was sure she had made an error in sharing her body with Antonio. That error had to be covered up and forgotten. Soon.

She waited in expectation of seeing Adrian look relieved and happy. She grew concerned when his face revealed neither feeling.

"You do not want to?" she asked him, a mild panic beginning to grow inside of her belly.

"Kat, we have had this conversation many times now," Adrian said. "I do not know what is real with you and what is not. Why do you wish to pair with me? Please tell me what your reasons are this time."

Adrian could see that Kat was surprised by his question. He could also see a level of calculation and perhaps dishonesty forming on her face.

"I ... I esteem you greatly," Kat said. "You have remained kind to me when I have not been kind to you. I believe that we could be happy paired with one another."

Adrian pondered his options. He'd considered them before and felt frustrated that he had to think about them again. A few minutes earlier, he'd been excited at the prospect of proactively seeking out someone new to approach. If he agreed to Kat's proposal, he would not be able to meet anyone else. On the other hand, if he did not agree to it, and no other woman wanted him...

"Yes, Kat, but let us do this quickly," he blurted out. "I do not wish for either of us to change our minds. We shall go to the elders and talk to them now and ask them to speak to our parents. As soon as possible, we shall have the ceremony. After that, there will be no more mind changing."

He had expected her to panic at the thought of things moving so quickly. Instead, he saw her smile with what looked like relief.

To Kat, in her situation, the idea suited her perfectly. She needed to pair with Adrian as soon as possible. Doing so would wipe all memory of Antonio from her mind and heart. She had no awareness that she might also need to pair quickly with Adrian so that it would never be revealed she may be carrying Antonio's child.

"Oh!" she said all of a sudden, jumping up. "Oh, Adrian! We shall be so happy, paired together!"

As Adrian watched her, he was surprised. He could not remember having ever seen her so happy. When she held out her hands to him, he stood and let her wrap her arms around him to hold him tightly. As he pulled away, his gaze lowered. Out of the corner of his eye, he caught the slightest glimpse of a blue glow that was emanating but slowly fading over Kat's belly.

He knew that glow. He'd seen it before, on the night of the battle in the temple. As quickly as he saw it, it seemed to fade out and was no longer there. Thinking quickly, he decided to say nothing. Whatever it was, Kat appeared oblivious to it. He filed it away as something to talk to Trent and Isabella about, and perhaps the ancient in the temple, but no-one else. It might have been a trick of the light. If it weren't, it was something far too big to talk to anyone else about.

The two of them walked to the temple and spoke to Elder Scott about their plans. In turn, he assured them he would speak to their families to gain the necessary blessings and then let Kat and Adrian know the decision about their possible pairing.

After their temple visit, Adrian and Kat wandered down to the mill to get on with their work as if it were just another regular day. Nothing more was said about their moving forward with pairing. Nothing was said at all.

In the depth of his mind, Adrian couldn't help but wonder if he had made the right decision.

CHAPTER 62

"You saw it?" Isabella and Trent both asked when Adrian told them that evening about the blue glow. The three of them were in the home of Trent and Isabella at the request by Adrian for them to speak privately.

"I could be mistaken, but I did think at the time that I saw that same blue glow over her belly," Adrian said. What he'd seen earlier that day had been on his mind ever since. As he shared the news with Isabella and Trent, he didn't miss or mistake the looks of concern on their faces.

Trent stood up, his mind active. Elder Rhys had predicted something was coming that would try and cause destruction. Isabella's golden glow had made them all further believe that theory. Adrian saying he'd seen the blue glow return on Kat was one more level of confirmation.

"The timing is similar," Trent finally said and heard Adrian ask what he meant. "Isabella has had her golden glow back for some time now. When this last happened, the two coincided in time also."

Adrian looked at his close friend.

"Why did you not share this with me?" he asked her but only saw surprise on Isabella's face.

"Adrian, I did not think anything of it. It is there sometimes, but not often. It is not harming me in any way. It is a source of strength," she said as she placed her hand on his arm to reassure him. "It is nothing to fear or worry about."

"Very well, but what shall I do?" Adrian asked. "I told Kat today that I will pair with her. I am uncertain what is the best action with regard to this … situation. I am not even sure who - or what - I could be pairing with!"

"Only you can know what is best there," Trent said, feeling quite sorry for the young man in his circumstance. "If someone is controlling her again, it might be best if you move ahead as if everything is normal. If Kat - or whatever is inside of her - suspects that you have doubts because you saw her blue glow, we do not know what will happen."

Isabella was surprised at Trent's words.

"Trent, we cannot expect Adrian to pair with someone just to keep the peace," she said. "He has the right to pair with someone for love, as we all have."

"No, Isabella, I believe Trent may be right," Adrian said quietly. "If something is beginning again in Kat, it would be best if I do all that I can to keep her distracted and happy. That will give you time to ascertain what is happening, and what threat there is to the village, if any."

The three of them sat in silence for a long while before turning the conversation to anything but the possible imminent threat to the village.

CHAPTER 63

Antonio lay in the bed he shared with Ariana. He hadn't seen Kat for a long while, knowing from his feelings and connection to her that she was already carrying his child. She had withdrawn herself very quietly - far more so than he'd expected she would. It made his plans all the easier, not having to pretend or deal with her anymore.

The seed was sown. She would bring life to his child, and that child would have extreme power. The level of power would certainly be enough to bring down the golden child of Isabella. Antonio's child would be a fair match for Cesare. The last effort to fight against Isabella had failed, but next time - through his own child - he would be infinitely stronger. Finally, the great Isabella would perish. Once she was gone, he would be one step closer to taking full control of the village and the power that ran beneath it.

That night, he visited Kat's dreams but did not speak. He just watched her. He could almost see her thoughts. From the experience, he knew that she was pursuing that boy again. She wanted to pair, but there appeared to be more to it than that. She had an instinct that she *needed* to pair. He did not sense that she understood she had a child growing in her belly, but she did sense that she had to quickly move on from her time with him.

He smiled to himself. This time he would not discourage Kat from pairing with another. He had only needed to distract her from that for the time it took to seduce and impregnate her. He didn't even think she was aware that she had a certain power inside of her - a power that made it easy for him to control and connect with her through thought. As far as he was aware, he wasn't even sure she had any understanding of how much he had controlled her before.

Yes, the timing of her pairing with someone was perfect. It would prevent any questions being asked about whose child she was carrying. As far as she and anyone else was concerned, it would be the offspring of whoever she paired with. Perfect.

All Antonio had to do was sit and wait for his child to be born. Until then, he could move on with life as if everything were normal. And because everything was lined up perfectly for him to be able to do that, there was no chance anyone would ever suspect him of anything.

CHAPTER 64

"Adrian and Kat," Elder Scott loudly said to the gathered crowd in front of the temple on the evening of the pairing. "You have chosen to pair, and it has been assessed by the ancients that your pairing will be good and sound. Is there anyone here who does not approve of it? If so, please speak now."

Everyone looked around except Kat. In her chest, she could feel her heart beating quickly. A small part of her wanted to hear Antonio call out and claim her. A greater part of her knew he would not. She'd served her purpose with him. He would not want anything more from her. It saddened her, but as she turned to look at Adrian, she was glad that she had him. She could forget her time with Antonio. Tonight she would join with Adrian. After that, Antonio would matter no more.

"Adrian and Kat, as there is no-one to object to your pairing, please step toward me," the elder said, looking at them while speaking loud enough for everyone to hear. "You are both honorable and good. You have asked to be paired, and your pairing request is granted. You shall now take your place among our people, and do your duty to help our society continue to survive, through procreation and the delivery of children. Is this a responsibility that you accept as part of your pairing?"

Both young people nodded and said in unison, "Yes."

"Then it is so," Elder Scott said. "Please retire to the pairing chamber for this night."

Adrian felt faint. He was uncertain of so many things. In all that had happened, he hadn't even considered the part of joining. As he thought about it, he was nervous. He knew nothing of how children were made. He knew nothing of procreation. As he looked at Kat, he hoped she had some knowledge and that she did not mind that he had none.

~~~~~

The two young people entered the pairing chamber and looked around. Kat could see on Adrian's face the nervousness that he felt. She felt confident in what was to come, but she also realized that she could not *show* that she was confident in it. She would have to guide him while making him think that she also knew nothing.

Adrian stood where he was, experiencing a level of fear inside of him that he'd never felt before. Despite having already gone through the
~~~~~

pairing process and secured their futures together, he still questioned his decision to pair with her. He wasn't sure they were even good friends.

As his mind wandered, he slowly became aware of her moving closer to him. He felt nervous, not only about whatever was to come, but also just about her. She'd changed her mind so many times, he was wary about her reason for having finally agreed to the pairing.

"Relax, Adrian. We shall find our way together," Kat said as she moved up to him and put her arms around him. When she felt his arms enclose her in return, she subtly moved her body against his. Instantly, she felt the reaction in his body she'd hoped for. With her head resting on his shoulder, he didn't see her smile. Nor did he see the kind of smile she exhibited at that moment.

Although the joining itself was something Kat had already experienced, she hadn't yet been naked with a man. Her times with Antonio had always occurred with the two of them still dressed, and their attire only moved aside as required. As she stood before Adrian, she found the courage to lift her shift dress off and stand still, naked before him.

Adrian felt he should look away, but he couldn't. His body reacted harshly, but he was unaware or caring about that. He followed her lead and undressed before the two of them moved together to hold one another again. Kat initiated their first deep kiss. For Adrian, it was his first kiss, but he quickly caught on. Kat was surprised when his shyness was replaced by a natural instinct of need. He kissed her with passion as he walked her back to the bed.

Lying back, Kat let the same smile grace her face as she moved and nudged him until he was inside of her. Almost instantly, she heard him reach that same place she'd heard Antonio reach many times before. Her smile changed but remained hidden. It was done. She had no need to think about Antonio anymore.

As they climbed under the bed covers, Adrian once again saw the blue glow briefly appear over Kat's belly and then fade away. He still said nothing, pretending he hadn't seen it at all. He could feel the coldness that had come from the color over her belly. It was a coldness that made him feel even more nervous about what he'd just committed himself to by pairing with the woman lying in his arms.

He lay awake well into the night, his mind full of conflicting thoughts. He had paired with Kat. After the desire expressed by her that she wished to pair with him, and all the times that she'd changed her mind and said that she didn't want to, now it was done. They were lying in bed together, and they were sealed together for life. Adrian tried to determine what emotion would describe how he felt about that. All he found was conflict.

The two of them had joined. It was the first time he'd known of such feelings in his body. He hadn't experienced any logical feelings that had made him want to join with her. His body had acted like he presumed it was supposed to, in order to create a child. It wasn't unpleasant, but he did wonder if it could be better with someone that he'd very much wanted to join with. He had no knowledge of what it should have entailed, but somehow the few minutes that they were joined together didn't quite seem enough. Perhaps that was all that it took to make a child. One joining of just a few minutes. Was that truly all it took? To create life? He'd never thought about how it happened. It felt like such a small act for such a big result. He supposed that would be it, over with now. Kat would be with child, and they would not join again until another time when she wished to be with child again.

For all the longing Adrian had experienced in wanting to find something wonderful with the right person, all he felt on his night of pairing was that it all seemed like a bit of a letdown. There was nothing that could be done about that. The decision had been made. The deed was done. He was paired with Kat.

Now he would have to live with that for the rest of his life.

CHAPTER 65

When she woke the next morning, Kat felt initially disoriented. Very slowly, clarity forced its way through her sleepy daze as she remembered that she was now paired with Adrian. Forevermore, whenever she woke in the mornings, he would be there right beside her. Was she glad about that? She didn't know the answer to that question. Her thoughts and feelings had been drifting from one extreme to the other over many weeks. In the depths of her heart, she knew something was wrong that was making her experience such extreme emotions. It no longer mattered. They were joined and would be only paired with one another.

Turning over, she saw him lying next to her, still asleep. It was the first time she'd seen him like that. He seemed at peace. She watched him for a long while, still trying to determine her feelings. For her, ultimately, it was a pairing of convenience. She had always liked him well enough but he didn't excite her as Antonio had.

Whatever she'd shared with Antonio was now over. Now she had a new man to focus on. As she continued to watch Adrian sleep, she kept looking closely at him. She considered that even though he wasn't Antonio, he was still a man. It hadn't felt bad when they'd joined the night before. There had been nothing about it that had left her not ever wanting to join with him again.

Focusing on him, her thoughts fell fully into the realm of pleasure. By the time his eyes opened, she was heavily aroused at the thought of getting to know his body better. They had joined the night before, but she wanted more.

When Adrian woke and saw her, he also felt conflict in his thoughts. They were now paired, for that day and every day in their future. When she moved closer to him, he didn't try and stop her. Instead, he held his arms open and let her move so that her chest was touching his. Under the covers, he could see her naked body in full. His body jumped to attention at the sight. The night before had seemed rushed. His instinct had told him that. He was eager to try again, taking more time to explore.

When Kat kissed him, she was driven on in her excitement as she felt Adrian's lips engulf hers. The night before, he'd mostly responded to her. As he grew more assertive, she liked it.

Through her time with Antonio, she knew where she liked to be touched. She longed to take Adrian's hand and guide him but feared that if she did, he'd wonder how she knew how those spots felt like that to her. She held back, instead letting him lead and explore.

Adrian moved his hands and lips over Kat's body, taking his time. If he was going to be with her for the rest of his life, he was going to get to know her much better than he already did. His fingers moved over her skin, touching almost every spot on her.

Nothing felt wrong. Nothing felt bad. Adrian enjoyed the feeling of her skin under his fingertips. He loved the way the tiny hairs on her arms rose to meet him in tiny little bumps as his fingers glided over the softness of her skin. He loved the feeling of the curve of her hips. He loved the way her nipples became hard and her breathing changed as he lightly touched them. Down he kept going. Her legs were toned and smooth. Between them, he vowed he was never going to rush. It was an area of unexplored territory. He'd sunk deep into there the night before, but he wanted to learn it all and gain the knowledge to affect her completely.

Kat lay still for a long time. She had expected that since she'd previously joined with Antonio, she would be the more confident one out of her and Adrian in their joining. As she focused on his touch, she realized she'd been wrong. Adrian was a nice person, a caring person, and someone who everyone liked. As the two of them lay in bed together, he showed another side of him. It was a side that was strong, forward, and determined to learn, to give, and to please. When she felt his fingers explore where Antonio had done so, Kat told Adrian how good it felt, driving him to keep touching her that way.

Under his hands, Adrian could hear and see the effect his touch was having on her. Her body was moving subtly, reaching up to meet his touch sometimes. At other times, it ground down onto the bed. Around watching how her body was responding, Adrian also watched her face. Her lips remained parted as her breathing continued to become louder and deeper.

As he kept touching her and pushing her forward to where she wanted to go, Kat reached out and took him in her hands. She stroked him idly and slowly as she felt her body moving into the final stage of preparation for climax.

Despite her hand moving over him, Adrian didn't stop his efforts. He soon saw and felt her body convulse. It might have seemed to him that she was in extreme pain. Having had his first orgasm the night before, he believed that was what she was experiencing. Her hand felt good on him, but he wanted to see her through in her pleasure before he focused on that.

Kat felt all of her muscles twitch. It wasn't her first orgasm, but it felt far more intense than what she'd experienced with Antonio. It also felt more intimate, like it meant something. When her body relaxed, she concentrated on Adrian. She would encourage him to move into her again. For the moment, she kissed him while stroking him firmly but slowly.

Adrian let the feelings flow over him. He liked the way she was touching him. When she lay back and guided him onto her, he happily slid inside of her to once again experience the feeling of magic that came from that. It took longer than it had their first time. He was glad. The knowledge of it taking longer the second time made him wonder if it got longer every time. What a thought that was.

Kat moved with him once he started to move more intensely. The feelings were unexpected but glorious. Suddenly the decision to pair with him seemed like the best decision she'd ever made if every night was going to be the same.

Hearing him moan heavily, as she felt his body tense, she knew he was there. When he seemed to recover, he lifted his head and looked intently at her.

"Can we do this often?" she asked.

Adrian grinned.

"I hope so."

CHAPTER 66

After two months had passed since her pairing with Adrian, it was visibly clear to anyone who saw her that Kat was with child. She'd managed to hide the blue glow from everyone. Now and then, she would feel the coolness spread over her belly. In those moments, she would cover herself with her hands in an attempt to hide it. She assumed, as Isabella had a long time earlier, that the glow was a baby. She had no reason to presume otherwise.

From a distance, Antonio continued to monitor her through her visions of the night. He always kept himself on the outside of the visions, like he was looking in through a sheet of one-way glass. He liked watching her, but he had no desire for her to see him. Silently he was monitoring the health of his child. He was pleased that Kat was taking such good care of herself.

At times when he felt the blue glow appear in her, the coolness flowed over him too. It was like an old comfort to him. Refreshing and calming, he hadn't felt anything like it before, but he liked it. He knew he had nothing to worry about. Even though Kat didn't understand the importance of the seed that had been planted within her, she wouldn't put his child in danger.

CHAPTER 67

One night when Antonio was observing Kat, he was alarmed to sense that he wasn't the only observer in her vision of the night. It hadn't occurred to him that anyone else in the ancient village would have the ability to enter someone else's night visions. It disturbed him to realize he wasn't a lone spectator, after all.

At the discovery, he felt strong uneasiness flow over him. That uneasiness quickly escalated to a feeling of fear. Although he was lying in bed with Ariana asleep at his side, the desire to get out of bed and go to Kat pulled at him. He desperately tried to ignore it, telling himself he must be imagining things.

After a long while of his feelings slowly intensifying, he knew he couldn't ignore them any longer. Silently, he removed himself from the warmth of the bed he shared with Ariana and prepared to leave. Something was wrong. Even though he believed Kat must still be asleep, Antonio couldn't shake the feeling that he had to act. He could not let his child be put in danger.

When he left his home, he didn't know where he was to go. He stood still and closed his eyes to try and focus on what Kat was seeing at the time. Although he'd expected she must still be asleep, he quickly realized that she'd woken in the time since he'd left his bed. He wasn't in her vision of the night at all. He was, instead, connected with her in her wakefulness.

As if in his own visual reality, what he could see made him think he was seeing through her eyes. He didn't recognize the surroundings she was seeing but knew it was not her home, nor the home of anyone else in the village. The structure she was in was too large to be a simple home of the village. The ceiling and the walls were grand and far too large. The sheer size of what he could see left him certain of where she might be. He'd never set foot in the village temple. Throughout all of his life, whenever he'd looked at it, something about it had made him feel uneasy. Even though he'd never seen the interior of the structure, he was sure of his belief that it was where Kat was in that instant.

Also, through his sight, he could see other people. Not only did that make Antonio deeply unhappy, but it also made him fearful. He had no doubt they had some kind of plan for Kat. The possibility made him increase his speed to get to her. In truth, he didn't care so much about whatever might ever happen to Kat, but the child inside of her belly had to be saved at any cost.

A vision entered his mind again. In it, he could identify who was in the temple. He wasn't at all surprised by the faces he saw. In contrast, he was greatly surprised by the level of anger he felt when he noticed one of them was his silent adversary, Isabella.

CHAPTER 68

Kat had been awakened by a calling. At first, she thought it must be Antonio. As she focused more, she realized she was unfamiliar with whatever it was that was calling her. Waking up, she wasn't even sure what it had said to her. Her mind was foggy. She couldn't focus, but she knew she was needed to do something for someone.

Confused, she sat up in the bed, her movement waking Adrian.

"Kat, are you alright?" he asked, sitting upright and placing one hand on her arm. "What is it?"

Looking at him, she briefly wondered what she was doing with him. She liked him well enough, but did she like him enough to lie beside him every night of her entire future? They were beginning to work well together. She liked sleeping with him and beside him, but for the rest of their lives? It was only a brief thought before she soon was immersed once more in the imagery of the calling.

Adrian watched her face. He had to acknowledge to himself that she didn't appear to be fully with him. Her face looked like it was in a dream state rather than a state of wakefulness. When he looked down, he saw the blue glow had not only returned but seemed to have done so with increased strength. The intense cold emanating off it was almost unbearable as it reached him.

Even in her dreamlike state, Kat could see Adrian's movements. Following his line of sight, her eyes fell to her belly. What she saw made her smile. She took his hand in hers and placed both over the area. The degree of coldness coming off it caused Adrian to shiver and want to pull his hand away. When he looked at Kat, he kept his hand still. It was obvious to him that she was gaining some kind of reassurance from it.

"Our child, Adrian," Kat said with a blissful smile on her face.

Adrian smiled back but silently wondered whose mind was controlling her thoughts and words at that moment. Was it truly Kat, or was it an entity he'd seen before?

He had to think. The glow wasn't disappearing as quickly as it had when he'd noticed it on earlier occasions. It continued to be visible, slowly but persistently growing brighter. It also continued to exhibit the level of strength that Adrian hadn't seen before. Even during the battle that had happened between Kat and Isabella previously, the blue glow he'd seen had looked weak compared to what he saw spreading over Kat's belly.

"Bring her to the temple," a voice suddenly said inside of his head. Adrian was startled, not having experienced such a thing before. "Adrian, the entity inside of Kat is growing in power. Bring her to the temple, and we shall remove it as we did last time."

Adrian looked at Kat in wonder that she did not also hear the voice, but he could tell by her facial expression that she'd heard nothing. Although he didn't recognize the voice, something in his instincts told him to trust it and believe what it said.

"Kat, we must go," he said as he studied her face to see her ability to understand him. It seemed useless. Whatever held her attention also held her captive.

Without further explanation, he rushed her to ready herself before she would ask questions.

Kat asked nothing, also feeling a pull to leave. Power was surging through her. It was a feeling she liked very much. Quietly she walked with Adrian while enjoying the coolness she felt as she moved her hands over her belly.

As soon as the two of them were inside the temple, they were met by Elder Rhys and Elder Scott.

"Come, Adrian. We believe we must eliminate…"

Kat finally heard and seemed to understand what was happening. Straight away, she started to object.

"No!" she called out to them. "You will not take my baby from me!"

Although she was screaming the words, she made no attempt to remove herself from the situation. The conflict between the words she said, and her lack of any kind of action, made Adrian further believe she must be in some kind of trance.

With no further verbal objection from Kat, they walked deeper into the temple. There, Trent and Isabella were waiting. Elder Rhys stood back with Cesare in his arms, keeping a safe distance from Isabella. They still did not know why she felt pain when in close vicinity to him while the golden glow was present in her. The reason was irrelevant. Pain was pain. It had to be avoided.

CHAPTER 69

Antonio considered again where the group must be. He'd avoided the village temple all his life because of the feelings it produced in him. He'd always felt like he didn't belong there. He wasn't welcome, but it was more than that. There was something about the large structure that produced a sliver of fear in him.

As he moved in the direction of the building, he felt his fear intensifying. He was angry at Kat for doing whatever she was doing, but he was far more fearful about the child growing in her belly. No matter how he felt, he had to do whatever it would take to protect his unborn child.

In his rare moments of clarity, Antonio didn't know how or why things had happened that he didn't understand. He seemed to experience only moments of confusion before something would take his consciousness over. When that happened, he lost himself.

For a moment, he stopped still, placed his hands on either side of his head, and closed his eyes. He wanted to scream but dared not. Something wasn't right. That was as far as his thinking got before the real Antonio was pushed aside in his mind once more and the entity took hold again.

His child might be in danger. He feared the worst. He believed they suspected Kat's child was his and that it was the spawn of great power. They would try and rid her of the child, he was sure. He could not let that happen. He started to run.

CHAPTER 70

Isabella watched Adrian lead Kat into the room. The blue glow was now extremely bright and visible not only over her belly but all over her torso. Isabella saw Kat place her hands over it in a protective movement. For a moment, watching the hands lie over the cold blue, Isabella felt sorry for Kat. She knew that movement well. She understood the need to protect a small life beginning . She also understood that the glow over Kat's belly had absolutely nothing to do with a child being inside of her.

Trent stood a distance away. As yet, he hadn't told Isabella he'd been learning how to harness the power of the old soul inside their son. He understood the reasoning behind that decision. If Isabella knew nothing, no-one could gather the knowledge from her mind. He was equally glad of the decision because he didn't want her to rely on him if there was any chance that he wouldn't be able to assist when the time came. In his mind, if she thought he would fight with her, she would be more vulnerable if it turned out that he couldn't.

Instead of making anyone in the room aware of his recent training, Trent stood off to the side. Although ready to watch and see if he could, in any way, provide her with assistance when the time was right, he remained still, quietly showing support for her to battle the entity alone.

Kat moved closer to Isabella. As she did, a confused smile appeared on her face. She was looking at Isabella's belly.

"You have a child also, Isabella?" she asked as if the two of them were firm friends exchanging pleasantries.

Isabella looked down and let her hands rest over the warm glow she could feel. In some ways, she envied Kat for not knowing that the glows weren't children. She didn't try and correct Kat's statement. She could see that the woman Adrian had recently paired with was not herself at that moment. She wasn't thinking straight. It presented a strong instance of déjà vu with the situations being so similar. Isabella found strength in knowing this time they were prepared and knew what had to be done.

Everyone braced for powers to activate in a war among themselves. When Kat's didn't, Isabella moved closer. She felt that she needed to act as if she intended to attack. Whatever it was that was residing in Kat, Isabella wanted it to think she was becoming aggressive. That was the only way she considered she might be able to encourage it to come out.

CHAPTER 71

Antonio ran into the temple structure. He was unfamiliar with it but he could sense where Kat was - or, at least, where his *child* was. He walked quietly in the hope of hearing voices, but he didn't need them to know which direction to take. The feeling of guidance that came to him was strong. He assumed it was his child providing him with it, so put faith in it.

As he came to the doorway of the room that he knew they were all in, he stopped and closed his eyes for a moment. An attempt was made by him to reach Kat through thought, to control her. The attempt failed. He tried several times to push into her mind. It was a pointless exercise. Whatever she was doing, her mind was closed off to him.

Unable to connect with her, he started to panic. Why could he not connect with her?

He positioned himself so that he could look into the room without being seen. From his viewpoint, he could see Kat and Isabella facing one another. Off to the side were two elderly men, plus the men Kat and Isabella had each paired with. The numbers were acceptable to Antonio. Kat and him against Isabella. Two against one. He disregarded the other people in the room. They weren't fighters. They were there as spectators only. They served no role whatsoever at that moment. He was finally going to be able to put an end to Isabella. The thought made him feel stronger. It wasn't part of his original plan, but he grinned as he considered that he might soon see his adversary silenced for good.

CHAPTER 72

Isabella took her time trying to assess where Kat's mind was at. She looked aware, but at the same time, it seemed like she didn't quite understand that something was out of the ordinary. She didn't quite seem to have made the connection that *everything* was out of the ordinary at that moment. Just as she'd fluctuated and changed her mind again and again about pairing with Adrian in earlier months, Kat now looked like she was fluctuating in her knowledge of what was happening. There were moments when she seemed to be fully present and confused. Those times were of short duration before her eyes would cloud over and she looked gone again.

As Isabella looked into Kat's eyes, she wondered what the younger woman could have been thinking. In her own belly, Isabella could sense extreme heat as her power seemed to understand that the cold it needed to extinguish was close by.

She moved another step closer to Kat and started to bring her hands up in the hope that if she could summon the golden light, the blue light would escape from Kat also.

Trent watched as a dim light appeared over the palms of Isabella's hands. She was subtle, not making any real move toward Kat, but Trent could see it beginning. As that happened, he tried to psych himself up to play a similar role if the situation later demanded it.

Kat saw Isabella moving closer but didn't assume any defensive position. She could see the movement but couldn't perceive any danger or threat from it. Her hands rested over her belly. The coldness was once again a reassuring comfort to her. Her baby was safe. No-one was going to harm it.

When she saw Isabella's hands come up to chest level, Kat was entranced by the golden light emanating from them. She stared at it, captured by its brilliance. It didn't occur to her to move out of the way in case Isabella meant to cause her harm. The light was just too beautiful.

CHAPTER 73

From the safety of just outside the doorway to the room, Antonio watched what was happening for as long as he could. He could see Isabella getting dangerously close to Kat. The sight made Antonio begin to fret for the life of his child.

He continued to try and connect with Kat through her thinking but it seemed like she'd built a wall around her mind. It felt like a barrier had been erected that was impenetrable to him. The discovery intensified the anger he felt growing within him. He was angry at Kat, and he was angry at all of the other people in the room. That they thought they had any right to interfere with his plans was infuriating.

For a long while, he felt like he was frozen in time. He watched all that was happening. It wouldn't have seemed much to people of the time Trent was from. To all in the room, it felt like a war.

When Antonio saw the golden light igniting in Isabella's hands, he resolved to intervene. No matter what happened to him, he had to try and save the child. He couldn't just stand still and let them destroy the power flowing through it. It hadn't even taken a breath of life yet. There were many years that it would need to grow and develop. There was no way he could risk its life being cut short before it had even begun.

Antonio took a deep breath, studied the placement of Kat and Isabella in the room, and took a step towards the fight he knew he had to contribute to.

CHAPTER 74

"He is coming, old friend. Ready yourself and ensure all are safe," Elder Rhys heard inside his head. He looked down at the infant in his arms. For a moment, he expected the infant to look like the voice speaking, but of course, the tiny Cesare that Elder Rhys held was not the same Cesare that was speaking.

The ancient moved further away to provide a greater distance between himself and the two women.

"He is coming," he said out loud, causing all except Isabella to turn and look at him.

Kat realized she wasn't party to a conversation the others in the room had already had without her. Even as she looked at Adrian, she saw no surprise on his face. To her, it indicated his deceit. He couldn't be trusted, she thought to herself. She shouldn't have paired with him.

As if sensing her exact moment of doubt and weakness in her mind, Antonio appeared. At first, Kat thought she must be seeing things. As she refocused on the others in the room, she could tell that they could see him as well.

Antonio pushed ahead quickly, moving towards Kat. He shoved Isabella back before positioning himself between the two of them.

"You will not kill her baby, Isabella," he said and saw the surprise on her face.

There was no doubt in Isabella's mind that his voice was the same as she'd heard as an onlooker in the visions of the night. She composed herself and pulled herself to full height as she faced him straight on.

Even though she was a woman, younger, and not quite as tall as he was, being so close to her, Antonio felt intimidated. He didn't like it but he could certainly acknowledge that although day to day she looked innocent and nice, she exuded an extremely commanding presence. She was a natural fighter. He considered that perhaps even she didn't quite know the extent of that yet.

They stood, looking at one another for some time before Isabella considered his words and responded.

"I am not trying to kill her baby," she said. "Why would you think that I would?"

"You think you are meant to rule but you are not," Antonio continued, his speech starting to sound like it belonged to someone else.

Before their eyes, they saw Antonio lift his hands. Above them, a blue light formed. It surprised everyone in the room. At the same time, the blue glow that had resided on Kat's belly started to move.

Trent watched, stunned, as he saw the blue glow slowly move up her body from her belly, over her chest, and then up and past her neck. Once it had moved completely out of Kat's body, it began to hover in front of her face just as it had previously. In addition to Kat's blue light, it was easy to see that Antonio had control of further cold blue with his hands.

"Two of them!" Trent whispered, loud enough for all around him to hear.

"They must both be extinguished," Elder Rhys heard in his mind. The sound of the voice that whispered it to him reflected the fear that the older soul felt.

Kat moved her hands up, making it seem like she was catching the blue glow hovering in front of her face. She held it captive in her hands. The movement scared Trent, but he maintained outer calm as he began to focus on his hands. He almost felt like he was pulled into a trance as he watched Kat begin to move the blue light from one hand to the other, over and over. It was similar to watching a child pass a ball back and forth from one hand to the other.

A safe distance away, Elder Scott and Adrian stood off to the side. Adrian watched again with horror the unbearable view of his close lifelong friend facing the woman he'd recently paired with. He had a lifelong love for Isabella. He had a lifetime commitment to Kat. They were having a child. They might go on to have many more. It was an excruciating situation to be in.

All he could hope for was some kind of resolution to end the conflict once and for all. He didn't know if he would ever be truly happy being paired to Kat, but he equally didn't want anything bad to happen to her. They were only beginning their journey together. They needed time to truly bond. Their life of being paired together couldn't end so soon. It couldn't.

CHAPTER 75

Antonio calculated moves in his head. He and Kat were the only two in the room with power, and they were up against Isabella. Although she had friends in the room, none of them had the ability to help her. It would be so easy to extinguish her at that very moment, as long as he could get Kat to work with him.

Subconsciously, he tried to communicate with Kat again. He hoped that her seeing him step up to defend her might have convinced her to drop whatever barrier she'd put up.

He was wrong. Nothing had changed. He was unable to communicate with her silently. If he wanted her to follow his lead, he would have to speak out loud, for all to hear.

"We can finish this now, Kat," he said. "You know that Isabella wants to kill your baby. That is why they have all conspired together to bring you here tonight. She knows it is a threat to her and she needs it to die. Don't let her hurt your child. Don't let her *kill* your child. I am here and I can fight with you. We can completely rid this village of her. Once we've done that, we shall all be at peace."

Kat heard the words as her head cleared slightly. She felt conflict inside of her mind. What Antonio was saying made sense to a degree. Isabella had never seemed interested in being friends with Kat, and of course she would be jealous of Kat having paired with Adrian. Even though Isabella was paired and happy with Trent, she'd liked Adrian following her around and idolizing her. She must have hated that he'd paired with Kat.

On the other hand, Kat considered that Isabella was a mother herself, and a loving one as far as Kat had seen. It was difficult to imagine that she would harm Kat's child. It was difficult to think she would harm *any* child.

Kat looked from Isabella to Adrian and then let her eyes rest on Antonio. She could see clearly that he had seduced her and made her believe things that were not real. As the haze in her thoughts cleared, she knew she didn't want to bring pain to anyone in the room with her.

As quickly as she'd had that thought, her mind switched and something else took over. With great speed, she brought her hands up. The blue glow exploded into a force of power that could be seen by all.

Trent, Isabella and Adrian realized belatedly that the force behind the blue was stronger than last time, and not only by a small amount. It was large and it was brilliant. It looked like an incredible ball of blue flame, glowing brightly, hovering, and ready to be used however its manipulator chose to use it.

Simultaneously, the same thing happened in Antonio's hands. The bystanders could only watch from their safe distances. The levels of power emanating from Antonio and Kat were intimidating. Even having known that Kat had been used by a man, they had not anticipated he'd also have such power within him. Fighting one entity had been bad enough. How would they deal with two?

Everyone watched on in horror at the sudden realization that two sources of power were now being aimed directly at Isabella, compared to the one that she had growing in her hands. Her golden flame was gaining momentum in its growth. Trent hoped it would reach at least the size of one of the blue flames before either of them was released and used for an attack.

At that moment, Trent concentrated his thought to his hands, willing the powers - *any* powers - to come to life for him to use. He looked at Elder Rhys with pleading eyes, silently asking him to speak to the old soul inside his son, and request more help.

Out of the corner of his eye, he saw Kat and Antonio both prepare to release their blue lights. Both had grown in size to resemble large balls of blue flame. Both appeared set up to fly directly toward Isabella.

Without any more time to wait, Trent did what came naturally to him at that moment. Everyone was surprised when he bolted to the center of the room. Isabella's flame seemed to scream from her hands with great force, heading directly for Kat. At the same time, Trent saw Antonio's start to do the same, heading directly for Isabella.

Trent didn't even need to think or concentrate. Just as the blue flame left Antonio's hand, aligned perfectly to assault Isabella, Trent felt a huge sense of power flow through him. Without it needing time to build in his hands, he instantly let a large ball of golden flame fly. It caught Antonio off guard and took him down to the ground. Trent immediately disregarded any reliance on 'powers' and moved to Antonio. One thing he could rely on was his knowledge of regular human strength to subdue and restrain the man who had just attempted to attack Isabella.

"You won't win, Isabella," they heard Antonio call out in one voice. It was the same voice that Kat had always heard in her visions of the night, and in person when she'd spent time with him. It was also the voice Isabella had heard when she'd found herself in the same night visions as a bystander listening to the conversation between a man and a woman.

If any of them had known Antonio from much earlier on, they would have recognized it wasn't the true voice of Antonio at all. Not the *real* Antonio.

Trent looked up in time to see Isabella's golden flame attack and engulf the blue flame that had flown at her from Kat. When the two flames came together, the room filled with a blinding light. Nothing could be seen.

For a long while, all that could be heard was a high pitched scream. It reached into the minds of all in the room, as if the sound of death itself. Something was happening between the two of them but it was external to the people in the room.

A long time later, the room returned to normal. Neither the blue flame nor the golden flame could be seen. The piercing screech had ended. Nothing more could be heard. Both were gone.

In that instant, Kat fell to the floor as if having fainted. Both she and Antonio were down. For a brief moment, Trent wondered why each of them only seemed to get one flame attack to use in their fight. Perhaps he'd seen too many movies in his previous life. In his head, he could imagine each of them having the ability to summon forth more of their attack strengths. It seemed unable to be done. It was a one-shot attempt for whatever the entity was that had a preference for Kat, and it was assumed it was the same for Antonio.

No-one rushed to approach Kat. All hoped that whatever had just happened, she was rid of what had been leading her and controlling her, as had been the case on the previous occasion. It didn't occur to anyone to wonder where the blue flame from Antonio had gone. It seemed as if it had simply disappeared when Trent had fired his own unexpected shot of power.

Trent again looked down at the man underneath him. He had been struggling and yelling but now seemed subdued and confused. Everyone then heard a different voice come from the man.

"What...?" he asked, shaking his head as if clearing it. "What is happening? Why are you on top of me?"

The voice reflected anger and confusion but what surprised everyone was that it wasn't the same voice they'd heard from him ... ever.

Trent was uncertain what to do. Was the man he was restraining really confused, like Kat had been last time they had gone through this? Or was he pretending?

He couldn't take the risk of letting the man get up immediately so continued to restrain him and ignore his words. He wouldn't make the decision alone about what to do with Antonio. He would wait until everyone in the room caught their breath and expressed their thoughts on the matter.

Adrian reluctantly moved forward and toward Kat. He saw her look at him as if he were an enemy of hers. It was as if to her it seemed like he cared nothing for her and only wanted to attack her. At that moment, he deeply regretted having given in and paired with her. He knew deep in his heart that they would never be truly happy together. Pushing the thoughts aside, he knew that he had to focus on something positive. Whatever had been inside of her seemed to be gone again. That was the right thing to maintain his thoughts on. That was far safer than thinking about his long life ahead with her as his paired partner, and all that would bring.

As he approached her, he reached down to where she was huddled on the floor with a look of extreme confusion on her face.

"Adrian? I do not know why I am here. Is this like before? Did it happen again?" she asked, sounding more and more confused and desperate with each question that came from her.

Adrian was relieved to see the look of contempt she'd appeared to give him minutes earlier, had been replaced. He reached out, took both of her hands in his, and guided her to stand. He had an awful feeling of dread inside of him. It was a dread that was confirmed when she let her hands move over her belly and asked her next question.

"Am I with child?"

She asked the question so loudly that every person in the room looked at her.

Isabella heard Trent moan heavily in the realization that Kat had not been herself, not just for the present day, but for the preceding *months*. Everyone was speechless in contemplation that in her own absence, she'd paired with Adrian and was carrying his child.

Isabella looked at her closest friend. For the first time in their lives together, she had no idea what was the right thing to do. Would he want her to comfort him and help him through what was no doubt going to be an extremely uncomfortable time, explaining things to Kat? Would he want to be left alone with Kat to talk things through? Would he simply just want to be alone?

The only person who didn't seem horrified by Kat's surprise at her own state was Antonio. Trent looked down at him once more, sensing the man's impatience to move.

"Who are you people?" he asked. "I do not know what is going on here, but I wish to go home to my wife and children. My Ariana is large with child. She is due to give birth any day now and will need me."

To most people in the room, the significance of his statement meant nothing. They hadn't known Antonio before so his words meant nothing.

To Elder Rhys, they said a great deal because Ariana *had* been with child … and had given birth to that child two years earlier.

~~~~~
~~~~~

As everyone focused on themselves and each other, the entity escaped its own demise by once again taking on the appearance of diminishing. While all eyes were on the warriors in the room, it slipped unnoticed into one in the room - someone who now would be a new puppet. One that no-one would ever suspect.

CHAPTER 76

One by one the participants and the spectators in the evening's events pulled together and let their minds begin to rest. Whatever it was that had now happened not once but twice, it was previously unheard of to any of them. There was no way of knowing if it was going to keep repeating. There was no way to know if there was any way to keep Kat and Antonio permanently free of whatever it was that had been controlling them, but if it happened again, at least they knew what to expect.

Trent pulled Isabella into his arms and held her tightly before they welcomed their infant, Cesare, into their hold.

"It isn't over, Rhys, but I can feel myself fading," the ancient heard in his head at the moment he handed the child to his parents. "It has been good to be able to speak to you again. I do not know where I am. I do not know what is happening. I feel like the distance between us is growing, like..."

Elder Rhys stopped still. On the outside, he looked calm to those around him. On the inside of his head, he called out as loudly as he could in an effort to find his old friend again. All he found was silence. That friend had passed over and left the village a long time ago. Having heard his voice again had reignited old feelings. Since he'd become an ancient, Elder Rhys had accepted that he was regarded differently from the general population. Some, such as Isabella and Trent, accepted him as the man he was. Others were afraid of him. It wasn't general knowledge who the ancients of the village were but he had never hidden that he was one of them. Someone had to be the voice for the ancients and he'd been chosen for that role a great many years earlier.

As he pondered his friend having left again, suddenly he felt weary. He was more than 600 years old. He'd lived a good life. He'd lived a *great* life. Now he was tired. He looked around the young people who were in the temple with him. He didn't know what had been happening or why. He didn't know what the ultimate cure was for whatever had started invading the people of the village. First, it had only seemed like Kat was affected. Now it seemed like Antonio had been as well. For all he knew, hundreds of people in the village might have something else inside of them. That thought made him wearier still.

"Elder Rhys, are you alright?" he heard Isabella ask. As she moved closer, he felt relieved. The golden light of her belly had gone. It had served its purpose and eliminated the blue light of Kat. Isabella could once again be in close vicinity of the ancient without feeling pain because of it.

"I am well, Isabella, but I am tired," he replied quietly. "I shall leave you all now."

"Shall I walk you?" Trent asked.

The ancient almost said no, but when he looked at the young family he reconsidered.

"Yes," he said. "I would appreciate that, Trent. Thank you."

Trent let Cesare settle in Isabella's arms and immediately began walking with Elder Rhys. Where the ancients resided, Trent had no idea, but he would follow the older man wherever he needed to go. It was the least he could do, given how much support Elder Rhys had given him since his arrival in the village from his previous life in his previous world.

CHAPTER 77

Kat stood with Adrian. She was deeply confused. In her mind, she could see images like snippets of things that she must have dreamt about. It *felt* like she had dreamed of such things. When she placed her hand on her belly, she could not deny that it couldn't have been just a dream.

As she looked at Adrian, she felt a variety of emotions flow through her. Long ago, she'd wanted to pair with him but they had never discussed it further.

"Whose child am I carrying, Adrian?" she asked quietly. She saw the expression on his face. She saw him rub his eyes. She had asked the question but she already knew the answer. "You and I?" she asked and saw him nod while looking sad and regretful. "We are paired?"

"Oh, Kat. I hardly know where to start…"

"Perhaps at the beginning. Do we have a home? Together?" she asked and saw him nod again. "Then please, take me there. I feel tired, but I wish for us to talk. I do not remember us pairing. I do not remember … this," she said, pointing at her belly. "You must be patient with me. Please."

Adrian looked at her. She was timid and almost shy of him. He remembered her being like that before the very first conversation they'd had about pairing. He was horrified to think that she could have been under the influence of something else for that entire time.

"Of course, Kat," he said, smiling. "Come with me now. Let us go to our home and I will answer any questions you have. Do not worry. We can take things slowly. We can start over…"

"But I am already with child…" Kat said.

Adrian smiled at her. "Yes," he said, wondering how things would be moving forward if she couldn't remember the two of them joining. "All will be well. Do not worry. I will take care of you."

He helped her to move. He expected things would be interesting in times to come, but he had paired with her. He would work with her to move forward and accept the place they were at. He would be patient and he would be gentle. He would do his best to support and care for her and their child. The grounding was there. They just had to start building on it.

CHAPTER 78

Antonio desired to leave the temple as soon as he was freed from Trent's hold. He felt muddled as if he was supposed to have remembered something but suddenly couldn't. He began to walk toward the door but then stopped. His head was so cloudy. Something seemed seriously wrong.

"You are confused, Antonio," he heard a voice say. When he turned around, he saw one of the older men who had been in the room. "Do not be. I can help you remember," the older man said again as he stepped right up to Antonio and placed his hand on his shoulder.

As soon as the hand touched him, Antonio felt power surge through him. He closed his eyes and focused on the feel of it. A brilliant cold flowed through the hand, through his shoulder and then through his entire body. It was like a comfort.

Slowly his mind became clearer and his memory returned. He wasn't back at the time when Ariana was due to have their last child, as he'd thought a few minutes earlier. No, much had happened since then. He had power inside of him and it fuelled him greatly.

He stood taller and once again became the person he'd been for the past two years. He then opened his eyes and looked at the elder in front of him.

"Thank you," he said as he placed his hand over that of the older man.

Elder Scott removed his hand but nodded at Antonio. "Do you understand?" he asked. If anyone else had heard the question, it wouldn't have made any sense. There was no context to it. There was no indication of what the subject was that was being asked about.

Antonio understood completely. He nodded. "I understand."

Neither said anything more. Antonio turned and left. It was time to return home to his beloved Ariana.

CHAPTER 79

Isabella watched Trent and Elder Rhys walk off into the further depths of the temple. She watched Adrian talk to Kat before gently leading her out toward the main entryway. Even Elder Scott had left, seemingly to soothe Antonio.

In the large temple room, she was alone, but she did not feel any great desire to leave in a hurry. Looking down at Cesare, she saw he'd fallen asleep. She couldn't help but smile. She closed her eyes and stood still for a moment. The temple had always been a special place for her. It had called to her for a long time before she'd finally set foot in it. Now it was a place where she felt she truly belonged.

It wasn't time for her to be there full time yet, but when the time came, she would be welcomed by the large structure and the people in it. Of that, she had no doubt. It was meant to be. It always had been.

After a few minutes, she felt Cesare move, nudging her out of her thoughts. Finally, she began to walk out. She had much to think about. Elder Rhys had been telling her over an extended period that she was gifted and she had powers that would grow strong throughout her lifetime. What were they, and *where* were they? How was she to develop them when she didn't even know what they were?

She had questions. If she was to become an ancient and have the so-called powers that Elder Rhys had indicated to her she would, she would need to get answers.

As she entered their small home and put Cesare down into his bed, she determined that she had to be more proactive. The following day, she would go to Elder Rhys and ask him to start training her. Whatever it was that she was meant to learn, she needed to at least start being taught.

Suddenly feeling exhausted, she removed her slip dress and crawled under the covers of the bed. Trent would wake her when he returned. For now, she just needed a little sleep…

~~~~~

Trent escorted Elder Rhys to a small doorway where the ancient thanked him and dismissed him. Trent nodded, smiled, and walked away, eager to return to Isabella and their son.

As Elder Rhys made his way into the small bedroom, he felt the tiredness fall to another level. He had lived long enough. It was time for
~~~~~

him to pass and go on his own journey. He readied himself and then lay on his bed. In his head, he willed a quiet passing to come.

He was ready.

~~~~~

Trent entered the small home. On seeing Isabella asleep, he quietly undressed and moved under the covers with her. He didn't know what toll the golden glow had taken on her when she had to use it as she had, but he expected she must be exhausted from the psychological aspect of it, even if not from the physical. He lay his head down and let himself drift off to sleep.
~~~~~

CHAPTER 80

"You think you eliminated me, Isabella?" the voice taunted her in her vision of the night. "Ha! You silly little fool. It is not over. It is only … just … beginning."

Isabella woke and sat upright in alarm. For a moment, she had to wonder if she'd imagined it. She knew better. When she saw or heard things in her visions of the night, they were an indication of something she needed to pay heed to.

The voice had mocked her as if wanting to ridicule her or challenge her. That was new. Previously, it hadn't given any indication of its presence or its intention. Isabella was intrigued by its boldness, making such an announcement.

In the same instant that Isabella woke and sat up, Elder Rhys did the same. Moments earlier, he'd been ready to leave the world and pass to the next. The voice he'd just heard reminded him that he couldn't leave yet. He still had too much to do. He had a young apprentice who needed to be trained. She needed to be guided. She needed to build her strength.

The voice they'd both heard was not one either had heard before. It had given no indication of when it would strike, but it had admitted it had full intention of doing so. That gave the two who heard it a new determination. There was now no doubt. It was coming, somehow, sometime. When it did, they would be ready to fight. *Really* fight.

EPILOGUE

Two years had passed since the final battle had happened. Still, whenever Trent thought about it, he conceded that once more, in the world he'd come from, it wouldn't have been regarded as any kind of battle at all.

For some time after the last battle, and the voice she and Elder Rhys had both heard, Isabella had waited for another strike to come. As yet, it hadn't. Perhaps the voice they'd heard hadn't been real. Perhaps it had simply been meant to taunt them, to create a panic that would keep them under stress and paranoia.

The effect on Isabella and Elder Rhys, however, had been significant. Immediately after that night, they had begun training. In the depths of the privacy of the vast temple, Isabella's knowledge was expanded. Her abilities to call forth the strength to summon her powers when she needed them were growing. Two years in, there was still a long way to go, but Elder Rhys had found a new purpose to remain in the land of the living. He wasn't yet ready to lie down in surrender to permanent slumber. Isabella would be the next ancient, and he was going to make sure she knew everything she had to for that role. She thought she had limited powers. He knew she was wrong. She was going to become the most powerful ancient he had ever or heard of.

~~~~~

As Trent and Isabella sat in the dining area with Cesare beside them, they looked at him with pride. Almost three years old, he still confounded them with the brilliance of his golden hair, but other than that, he appeared to be a normal child. He seemed just like any other in the village.

Next to Cesare was his closest play friend. Being the daughter of Isabella's closest friend, Esmeralda was also a child who stood out. Her hair was so black that, to some, it seemed to have a blue tinge to it. She was a year younger than Cesare, but the closeness of their parents had resulted in the two children who looked like complete opposites, being brought together as friends.

Although nothing more had happened with entities since that night, Isabella could sense her power growing by the month, or it could have been the little life growing inside of her. Cesare would have a brother or
~~~~~

a sister in the coming months, and he seemed happy with the fact. *Everyone* seemed happy … particularly someone who kept an eye on the group from afar.

Elder Scott watched with a silent glee deep within him. He was unaware of the happiness and excitement that was embedded in him because it wasn't him driving it at all. Whatever it was that was inside of him, sat patiently and waited for Cesare and Esmeralda to grow.

They would pair. He would make sure of it. So far, his efforts to eliminate the youngest chosen one had failed. He needed time to watch and see if Isabella *would* be the youngest chosen one. Yes, she would need to go. She would need to be destroyed, but the entity would not lose sight of the possibility that there was yet another chosen one to be discovered - Cesare. It would be many years before anyone would assess or see anything that indicated that he would be. If he were, eventually it may mean that he and his mother would both need to be removed from the population.

It would take time but a plan was well underway. If the power of Cesare were not used to fight the power Esmeralda had inherited from her biological father, but rather *join* with her, the combined result would be spectacular.

Yes, the entity gleefully regarded. Not one *fighting* the other. No. One *merging* with the other, to produce an offspring more powerful than even he had ever heard about.

Although excited at the prospect, he would be patient. They thought they'd eliminated him when they'd seen the blue flame disappear. Even with his having delivered his one warning to Isabella afterward, they didn't know he was inside the elder they considered their friend.

Watching.

Waiting.

It would be a long wait till the young ones were of age to pair.

But the wait would be well worth it.

THE GOLDEN UNITY

~~ Golden Desires Series: Book 3 ~~

ANN M PRATLEY

CHAPTER 1

Trent Solace sat back in his chair and pondered how his life had played out so far. Fate had proven to be a surprising thing. He'd started his life in a busy city that housed well over a million people. On the odd occasion when he took a moment to think about the hustle and bustle he'd left behind, he could still hear the intense noise of it in his memory. He hadn't thought anything of the lack of silence when he'd been growing up. Now, as he remembered, he couldn't help but wonder why the modern world had wanted to become so densely populated and busy.

Two decades on from embarking on a journey to escape the sound, the technology, and the people, he was glad fate had led him away from it all. On his initial trek to be away from everything and everyone, he'd started to dream of a young woman with vibrant red hair. The more he'd hiked, the more vivid the dreams had become.

As he glanced across their table, he still saw Isabella as the beautiful woman that she was. Although they were both older, she was no less desirable to him twenty years on than she had been when he'd first met her.

He still didn't know or understand why fate had brought them together. He suspected he could spend his entire lifetime wondering how they'd been able to dream of each other over such distance and time. That was a pointless exercise. Although it sounded like something out of a fiction novel, they *had* dreamed of each other, and they *had* later met in person.

Upon first glance at each other in reality, they hadn't been in the same time. Isabella had been in the ancient village as it had stood in the past. Trent had been in modern times. What Isabella had seen when she looked around the village was color, life, and vibrancy. What Trent had seen were only the grey remnants of destruction. It had taken time for each of them to believe that they were in the same place - just not in the same time, instead being hundreds of years apart.

Despite the time difference, something much greater than themselves had enabled him to see her, and her to see him. How it had worked, neither knew. In the end, it hadn't mattered. Trent had been presented with the option to remain in his own time or pass back into hers. Although it had meant committing to never again seeing anyone or anything from the life he'd left behind, Trent hadn't needed long to make that decision.

No matter how much time had passed since his travel back through time, Trent still considered himself the luckiest man in the world. Two decades on, he had no regrets about having made the decision to transfer from the time he'd grown up in to that of the ancient village. As soon as he'd done that, he'd been able to freely experience the lushness of the small community and the unique and hidden land the villagers inhabited.

Located atop a mountain range that people shouldn't have been able to easily survive in, golden veins under the ground provided a microclimate that was anything but cold. Since he'd arrived, Trent had never felt even *slightly* cold. The temperature was constant in the land, in the air, and in the water that flowed naturally through the pools housed within the structure walls.

As he once again considered his good fortune, he noticed that Isabella had stopped eating and was smiling at him. He knew that smile well. It was enough to relax him and wish for the two of them to have some time alone. It wasn't going to happen at that moment. To keep his mind off such pleasures, he looked further around the room at their three children.

Considered the golden child of the village, Cesare was tall for his nineteen years. He'd grown up known and much admired for his kind and happy nature and the brightness of his hair. Trent didn't know where the color came from. Given that he had dark brown hair and Isabella had vibrant red hair, Trent had originally thought it odd that Cesare had been born with hair that was almost yellow. Over time, he'd stopped thinking about it. There were magical aspects to the ancient village that were somehow related to gold. Whether that had anything to do with Cesare's hair or not, Trent had no idea, but it did make it easier to accept.

Off to the side, Trent looked at his two younger children. Marco, at seventeen, wasn't as pure as his older brother. While no children in the village seemed to get into trouble that was anything like what Trent had seen in his youth, Marco did like to push some boundaries. Trent had found a new source of amusement in his ongoing challenge to act as a strict father who was intent on guiding his younger son. Marco needed to be guided, but he was also humorous in his attempts to do anything. It had proven difficult for Trent to maintain a stern look in moments when one was needed since Marco only ever made people laugh.

The youngest of the three was Alessia. Whenever anyone saw her, there could be no doubt that she was Isabella's child. Red hair had never been common in the village, but mother and daughter shared the same colored mane. They were also similar in many other ways. Alessia had her mother's shyness. Although Trent had never seen her shun anyone, she was even more timid and curious than Isabella had been when Trent had met her. Alessia was the child that remained very close to her mother, even at her current age of fifteen.

Since they'd become parents, Isabella had more than once dared to ask Trent how life had been for children in the world he'd left behind. Each time she'd asked the question, he'd only told her that life in the village was far healthier and pleasant for children. Despite the two of them having been paired for so long, he'd still never shared too much detail with her about where he'd come from. He was continuously grateful that she didn't ask him about it very often. Trent had made sure she knew the future wasn't a happy place. She knew, as he did, that her village had previously suffered and been extinguished in the future.

No matter how long Trent was in the ancient village, the concept of time difference still challenged his mind. When he'd passed through the walls of the ancient mountaintop structure, the buildings had been in ruin. That had happened more than 300 years before the time Trent had been in then. In the time he was currently in, it hadn't happened yet. He expected and accepted that he wouldn't still be alive when that time came. That didn't matter. Even if he was long gone by then, he was determined to do whatever he could to prevent the destruction of the ancient village a second time around.

Thinking about the two instances when Isabella had used an internal power to extinguish an odd but intense entity that had emerged from another villager, Trent naturally returned his eyes to her. Eighteen years had passed since any such thing had happened. As far as the majority of the village's population knew, there had never been any conflict within the tall stone walls that contained the village. Only a few people knew about the small battles that had occurred on those nights in the great temple of the village.

Nothing more had happened like that, but Isabella and Trent continued to expect that it might happen again. Both of them had embarked on training after that day. Although their training was contained within the village temple, out of view of the general public, it was something both had taken seriously. They had a village to protect. That had been enough to inspire Trent to begin his training. That he also had three children of his own to protect made him even more determined to keep working as though he might be needed in some kind of battle in the future.

"You are very deep in thought," he saw Isabella say as she smiled at him. "What is holding your attention so completely?"

Trent returned the smile. With their offspring so close, he wouldn't tell her all of the thoughts that had been running through his mind. He equally wouldn't tell her how much he wanted to be alone with her. As he looked at her, he knew she could sense his desire for her. She'd always had a particular look that she gave him when they weren't touching or speaking but wanted the same thing. The look never ceased to fuel him.

"I was thinking about how beautiful you look tonight," he said as he leaned over the table toward her.

The look she gave him told Trent that she knew he wasn't quite being truthful. It also told him that she didn't mind that at all.

CHAPTER 2

As Isabella grinned at Trent, she felt blessed. As was the way of her people, she'd not been told anything about the pairing process before she'd gone through it. She'd known it was designed and required to maintain the village population. She'd known the expectation was to procreate and produce children. She'd not realized just how pleasurable her life would be once she'd paired.

Every day, she appreciated how fortunate she was in Trent having been summoned to the village through time. She had no idea what exactly had brought him to her, but she was glad it had happened. Prior to his arrival, she had considered she would probably pair with her closest friend, Adrian. That pairing would have made sense to anyone who knew the two of them. They'd grown up together and, for the most part, they'd always gotten on well together.

Before Trent had arrived, Adrian had declared that he wanted to pair with her. Isabella had needed more time to consider how they would be if they did. In the ancient village, when two people paired, they lived out the rest of their days together. At her then age of twenty-one, it had seemed a daunting decision to make. Then Isabella had met Trent. After that, the decision to pair hadn't been difficult at all.

As Isabella gave thought to Adrian, she felt a little sad. He'd always been a cheerful person. After Isabella had paired with Trent, Adrian had paired with Kat. Since that time, he hadn't been as happy. To some, he was a master of pretending he was, but Isabella could read him well. She could see through the smiles he gave to everyone.

In the presence of others, he and Kat both smiled and pretended, but that was all it was. They'd had one child but no more. Isabella had never asked Adrian about that. She hadn't needed to. She suspected by their body language that Kat and Adrian weren't physically intimate. That made Isabella even sadder. Thinking about the glorious feelings that she shared with Trent when they were alone, she considered that everyone should experience such joy.

Intimacy wasn't something she and Adrian talked about. Even in their extremely close friendship, that would have been uncomfortable, particularly for Adrian. That side of the pairing process was something nobody shared with anyone. There was no village equivalent of 'the sex talk' that some modern-day parents bravely attempted with their offspring. When two people paired in the ancient village, they did so blindly when it came to the act of joining.

The one blessing that had come from the union of Kat and Adrian had been their daughter, Esmeralda. Although she was one year younger than Cesare, their friendship was as strong as the one Isabella had shared with Adrian since they'd been infants. There was no surprise that the offspring of Isabella and Adrian would get on so well, given that their parents had always been so close. It was more of a surprise that the offspring of Isabella and *Kat* did.

Isabella didn't know if Esmeralda had ever known or sensed the natural dislike her mother had for Isabella. There had been many times over the years that Esmeralda had been in the company of Isabella. If Kat had tried to encourage her daughter to not trust or like Isabella, it had never been evident in the way Esmeralda acted towards Isabella.

Around the village, Esmeralda and Cesare were often seen huddled together, talking and laughing. It made Isabella happy that her son could experience such a close friendship, even if it were with Kat's child. She wasn't sure what Kat thought of her after all the years that had passed since their short but intense battles within the temple. She wasn't even sure how many of those moments Kat remembered. At the time, it had seemed like Kat had no awareness of anything that had happened. To help all move on, Isabella and Trent had never again spoken of the instances to Adrian or Kat. Many years had passed. It was hoped that all was well and peaceful and would continue to be.

Looking at Trent, Isabella could easily read his desire. She knew his moods, his body language, and his facial expressions well. He wanted her - of that, she did not doubt. Knowing that was always bittersweet since she equally longed for alone time with him. It hadn't been easy since they'd started their family, but they'd made time when they could. Thinking about it, she realized it had been more days than she could count since they'd last been intimate. Considering that made her long for him even more.

She embraced the feelings inside of her heart and her body. There was no dismissing just how much she wanted him. Even if they had to try to be utterly silent and hardly move, she was determined that she would have him once all were in bed. It was long overdue. She didn't often put her needs ahead of her family. That night she would.

CHAPTER 3

As Trent climbed into the bed he shared with Isabella, he tried to dismiss his desires. Their home was small. There was no complete disconnect from the sounds within. He'd often wondered about that particular design of homes in the village. There had been times when he'd considered suggesting a change to the home design. He never had. Anything that might be considered an improvement from the future, he desperately wanted to avoid. The world had changed between the time the village was in and the time he'd left behind. In his opinion, it had changed and not for the better.

Under the covers, he felt Isabella move close to him. It wasn't long before he felt her hand on him. Although it startled him, Trent couldn't bring himself to chastise her. Instead, he reached down with his hand and began lightly touching her. It was a pleasure and torture all at the same time, having to remain so quiet. There had never been a great deal of time when they'd halted their intimacy, but they'd certainly learned to control their desire since they'd started filling their small home with children.

"Fill me," he heard Isabella whisper close to his ear. The blatant desperation in her voice made Trent smile in the darkness.

"Not yet, my beautiful Isabella," he whispered back before finding her lips with his.

Focusing on the movements of his hand, he lowered his head and kissed one nipple just as he knew she loved. It took only a few minutes before he felt her climax against his fingers. The sound of her trying to *not* make any sound made Trent chuckle quietly.

Moving her hand to his cheek, Isabella guided his head upward so that she could return the kiss. Trent indulged in the taste of her mouth as her hand worked over him. It was a simple pleasure but a successful one. It took little time for him to feel his orgasm creep up. When it did, he pulled away from her kiss and clenched his jaw. It was all he could do to stop himself from letting out the deep groan that his body wanted to release.

Pulling her even closer to him, he focused on the feelings that flowed through his body. As he came out of the moment, he could tell by the feel of Isabella's face against his that she was grinning. Even in the dark, he could imagine how happy she looked at that moment.

"I did need that," she whispered in his ear.

Trent chuckled again. "As did I."

"I still would like you to fill me," Isabella said.

Trent couldn't stop the louder laugh that escaped him.

"That might have to happen another day," he whispered before kissing her, moving onto his back, and guiding her to nestle against his chest.

Although he'd expected they'd go to sleep, he wasn't surprised when he realized that Isabella had other plans. Feeling her move her body so that she was straddling him, he didn't mind at all when her lips came down on his. Reaching up and running his hands through her hair, he indulged in the feelings evoked from her deep, indulgent kisses.

He knew it was impossible to deny her, and, in truth, he didn't want to. Despite their long-term mutual desire for each other, they now rarely joined. While there could have been some frustration from the rarity of it, Trent didn't mind the long gaps between their intimate joining. Through those gaps, he'd learned to appreciate the power of anticipation and the power of reconnection.

When his body responded as she wanted it to, Trent waited for Isabella to do what he knew she would. Feeling her move down on him, he once again had to clench his jaw. It was something he'd learned to perfect during his time since becoming a father. There was nothing like the feeling of his Isabella moving on him. For her, he held back until he felt her clench around him. After she did, he held back no more.

CHAPTER 4

In a village house not far away, Adrian lay in the bed he shared with Kat. As was often the case, he was wide awake even though he knew he should be trying to sleep. Most nights, he slept little. One constancy in his life was his body and mind seeming determined to evade such an essential requirement for happy living.

Beside him, Kat slept. He listened to her breathing, the rhythm of it providing an odd form of comfort to him. It had been so long since they'd paired that everything felt the same, day in, day out. He'd felt that way before he'd paired with her. In some ways, he'd *always* felt that way. He could vividly remember talking to Isabella about his general desire for something exciting to happen, even before Trent had arrived in their village.

Thinking about Trent and Isabella, Adrian felt his discontent drop to an even greater level. Nobody who ever saw the two of them together could deny just how happy they were to be paired with one another. For a long while, Adrian had thought he and Kat might have been able to find the same happiness. He'd given up on that hope years earlier. There had been a brief length of time when they'd been close as friends and then as lovers. That period had ended almost as quickly as it had begun. When Kat had told him that she wanted them to continue being intimate after the birth of Esmeralda, he'd believed her. If she'd been telling him the truth in that desire, she'd since forgotten to follow through.

Since the last night they'd gone through the small battle in the temple, Kat had either forgotten about their time of pairing, or she'd chosen to *pretend* she'd forgotten. Whatever was the truth, Adrian didn't know. He equally didn't see that knowing would make any difference. Kat had never again wanted to join with him. She'd not even been open to the idea.

He supposed that with so much time having passed since then, he shouldn't still think about it, but he did. Despite how many years had passed, his memory hadn't forgotten how good it had felt to be joined with her. He'd had a small taste of extreme pleasure before it had been ripped away. That Kat didn't seem to remember the physical joy they'd shared made it just that much harder for Adrian. It had been wonderful being that close. At the time, she'd seemed to have enjoyed it as much as he had. He wished she'd wanted to try again after realizing she had no memory of it. She hadn't.

There had been many times that Adrian had admitted to himself that he wished he hadn't paired with Kat. He didn't like that being the truth. He wished he felt differently. It wasn't just the physical joining that was missing from their pairing. Although they'd embarked on a form of friendship, that had never fully developed either. Sometimes Kat seemed to regard him as just a necessary thing in her life. They were paired. Now they had to remain together for their whole lives. She often acted like she accepted that, and like she accepted *him*, but she equally emanated that she wasn't happy about it.

Adrian once again considered the unfairness of their people having to pair to one person for life. After Isabella had paired with Trent, he'd supposed it wouldn't matter who he paired with. The person he'd most wanted to be with had already found the person *she* wanted to be with. It had seemed irrelevant who Adrian found as a replacement. Since that time, he'd grown to regret having been so quick to give in to Kat's request to pair. It was rare that he regretted anything, but in that, he did.

On the night of the last battle between Kat and Isabella, it had become evident that Kat hadn't been controlling herself for some time. Something else had been pulling her strings like she was a puppet, guided to say and do things that she wasn't fully aware of. When that had been over, Kat hadn't even known she *had* paired with Adrian. That had almost broken Adrian's heart. He hadn't particularly wanted to pair with her, but something about her not even knowing that he had took his sadness to a level he'd never experienced before.

Despite the odd circumstance of them being paired without her conscious knowledge or consent of it, they had remained paired. In the modern world, it might have been a reason to divorce or declare a marriage annulled. In the ancient village, there was no such thing. They'd paired for life. There was no changing that.

In their bed, Adrian continued to lie quietly. He wished so many things were different between him and Kat. He wanted to once again share the physical pleasure he'd experienced for only a short period in his life. He wanted to reach out and touch the warm skin beside him. Sadly, he didn't dare.

CHAPTER 5

"You are up early," Adrian said to his daughter, Esmeralda, the next morning. Occasionally, when he looked at her, he wondered who she was. While he loved her as his child, sometimes she perplexed him. There were some aspects of his nature in her, but there were far more of Kat's. He'd often questioned how he truly felt about that.

Esmeralda looked at him and gave a small but sad smile. She accepted he was her father but saw that as no reason for him to question anything she did. She knew it wasn't right for her to feel that way. Her closest friend, Cesare, had informed her many times that her father was a good man, and she should appreciate him. Thinking about that, she broadened her smile in an effort to at least appear appreciative and happy.

"I am meeting Cesare," she said. "He is beginning his work with the tailor this morning. I said I would dine with him before he goes there."

Kat heard the conversation and couldn't help but provide her opinion.

"You do not need to do everything he wishes you to, Esmeralda," she said without hesitation. "You are separate people, not one."

Esmeralda glanced at her mother. She knew the two of them were more alike than she and her father. In some ways, her mother was a kindred spirit. She, too, seemed to have within her a desire to be free of convention and expectations of others around them.

Despite the similarities in their natures, Esmeralda had long before conceded that there was something odd about her mother. Her father may not have been in any way exciting, but at least he could sometimes make her smile in his efforts. Her mother was far more serious. Esmeralda couldn't remember one time that her mother had made her smile or even *tried* to make her smile.

"I do know this, Mother," she replied. "Cesare is my friend. I like him, and I will support him when he wishes to have my support."

She turned away from her mother and smiled at her father again. Sometimes doing so helped her to reset from the level of seriousness and discomfort she felt in her mother's presence.

Nothing more was said as she walked out of the small home. Every day that she closed the door behind her, she felt herself breathe easier. For as long as she could remember, she'd felt the tension within the walls of the structure. She knew it wasn't normal in the village. Other people who were paired seemed happy with each other. Her mother and father never had.

"Thinking, thinking, always thinking," she heard a familiar voice say.

When she turned, Esmeralda saw Cesare walking toward her, his face full of a grin. She couldn't stop herself from smiling back at him. In his presence was the only time that she felt like she could fully be herself and be relaxed. It was also the only time that she felt she was truly at peace in her soul.

"How are you this fine morning, my blue-black friend?" she heard him ask.

It was a friendly reference he often made to the color of her long hair. He wasn't the only one who'd ever commented on her hair color, but he *was* the only one who referred to it with affection.

"I am very well, my *golden* friend," Esmeralda said in reply, making him chuckle.

When he reached her, she reached up and messed up his previously tidy golden locks. As she expected, he, in turn, messed up her black mane, making them laugh together. Although it was a childish thing, they'd been doing it for so long that it had become a habit that was both annoying and comforting to both of them.

As they turned and began walking to the large village dining area, Esmeralda looked at him.

"Are you excited to be embarking on your trade today?" she asked and saw Cesare nod in response.

"I am," he said. "You know that I have wished for a vocation for much time. I am not sure yet if it is what I shall make my permanent trade, but I am eager to begin and to find out."

Although she didn't like to, Esmeralda felt envious. She thought that she, too, should be looking at options for ways to contribute to the village. It was difficult. Her mother wasn't approachable for such a conversation, and her father was so easy going that he hardly seemed *able* to have such a conversation.

Unconsciously, as she pondered her dissatisfaction, she sighed out loud.

Hearing the sound he'd often heard before, Cesare stopped walking and turned to face her.

"What is it, Esmeralda?" he asked, genuinely concerned.

The two of them had always known each other. Over their lifetime to date, he'd seen her despondency many times. He didn't understand it, but he'd grown able to accurately identify it. Sometimes it worried him. Other times, he did what he could to try and pull her out of it and then waited for his effort to work.

Esmeralda looked at him. In many ways, she found him an odd-looking person. His golden hair color was a stark contrast to that of anyone else in the village. She supposed that was part of what made them so close. In that regard, she was the same - the odd one out.

"I wish to find my trade also," she said to him. They were words she'd said many times. She was never sure if she truly believed them, even though they were thoughts from her own mind. "I do not know what to try."

Cesare smiled at her, moved to her, then put his arm around her shoulder, prompting her to begin walking with him again.

"You will know when it is the right time to," he said confidently. "Just as your mother and father knew, and my mother and father knew, you will know also."

After entering the large dining area, they sat at one of the long wooden tables and began selecting items to eat. When their plates were sufficiently full, Esmeralda turned and looked at him.

"Sometimes, I am not sure if my mother and father *are* both happy in their trade," she said.

Cesare looked at her with no attempt to hide the curiosity he felt about the statement.

"Your mother and father both work in the mill," he said and saw her nod. "Why do you think they are not happy there?"

"I am not sure," Esmeralda replied. "There is something about them that always seems unhappy."

"That may not have anything to do with their work in the mill, Esmeralda," Cesare said quietly. He'd grown up seeing Kat and Adrian together. It had never escaped his attention how different their relationship seemed compared to the one that his mother and father shared. "Perhaps there is something else that makes them unhappy," he said before wondering if he should say such a thing. "Or perhaps they are not unhappy at all. Everybody shows their happiness in many different ways. Look how happy I am!" he said, frowning in an attempt to hide his regret at saying anything about her parents.

Esmeralda grinned at him. She didn't feel happy, but she did know when he was trying to make her smile. It was rare that anything produced true happiness in her, but she appreciated that she could at least *pretend* to be happy. It was another thing about Cesare that made her truly pleased to be able to call him her close friend. There was a goodness about him that she loved. His good nature produced in her a feeling of being safe and accepted. In that way, he was like her father.

Thinking about her parents again, Esmeralda found herself wondering about their pairing. She'd never asked either of them how they'd come to be paired, and neither of them had ever talked about it. All she could judge the success of their pairing by was how she viewed other paired couples in the village. Day after day, week after week, month after month, every time she saw others, they looked happy to her. Whenever she looked at her mother and father, they never did.

She fought to push her serious thoughts away from the forefront of her mind. It was never an easy thing for her to do. She didn't know if it was due to a lifetime of influence by her always-serious mother or if it was something naturally inside of her. What she did know was that she was rarely as happy as everyone else seemed to be. Their difference in happiness levels was an ongoing source of wonder for Esmeralda when she tried to study her friendship with the golden boy.

Turning to look at him, she saw him smile at her. They weren't at all alike as people. She thought it was very fair to believe that she and Cesare were complete opposites, both inside and out. Regardless, he was the person she'd always felt closest to. He was the one she trusted fully, and the one she felt she could most easily relax around.

She smiled back. Smiling was an activity that didn't come naturally to her, but over their course of a friendship, she'd developed the skill to try and make it more of a normality.

"You are important to me," she heard him say to her.

All she could do was try to smile again and nod.

CHAPTER 6

"Isabella!" Elder Rhys exclaimed when he saw her enter the large exterior doors of the temple after the morning dining. It was no surprise to the ancient that she was there. She'd been training with him inside the depths of the large building since the last battle years earlier. In more recent times, her frequency of visits had lessened, but he continued to sense her dedication to learning.

Isabella smiled at the ancient. Sometimes she had to remind herself that he'd told her he was more than 600 years old. He hadn't appeared to age over the time that she'd known him, and she'd never been bold enough to ask how long an ancient was expected to live.

"Elder Rhys," she said as she neared him. It was a pleasure to be able to be around him so easily. During the periods of the build-up to both small battles, something had made close vicinity to him deeply painful in her body. It had been one of many things that had made no sense, but with it having happened both times, it was something neither of them could ignore.

"Are you here to..." Elder Rhys began to ask until he sensed someone approaching from behind him. When he turned, he saw Elder Scott walking toward them.

"Isabella," the elder said as he nodded at her. "Good morning to you."

"Good morning, Elder Scott," Isabella replied, smiling at him. She said no more as she and Elder Rhys waited for the elder to pass by and exit the building. When Elder Scott had left, she returned to her conversation with the ancient. "In response to your unfinished question, Elder Rhys, no. I have come in only to check on you."

"Me?" the ancient queried. "Why so?"

"I do not know," Isabella replied cryptically. "I woke with a very strong need to ensure your safety."

Elder Rhys blinked in surprise at hearing her words. If anyone else had said them, he would have instantly laughed them off, disregarding them as silliness. When Isabella said such things, he knew he shouldn't disregard them. He'd learned that a great part of the growth of Isabella's powers was her intuition. Not only did she possess an extraordinary level of it, but it was also rarely incorrect.

"Come with me," the ancient said and saw her nod.

The two of them quietly walked through to the room he used for private meetings. When inside, he closed the door and invited Isabella to sit.

"Tell me," he said, prompting her to expand on what she'd already said.

Isabella shook her head slightly.

"I cannot, Elder Rhys," she said. "When I woke this morning, I had feelings that I cannot explain. I had no conscious thought in my head. I did not hear any words. I did not see any vision. I woke, and I felt very strongly that I needed to come here and ensure your safety."

As Elder Rhys studied her face, he could see her concern for him. It both pleased and worried him.

"Your instinct has proven many times that it is always correct," he said.

"Yes, I believe it is," Isabella said as she nodded. "What could it mean? What could have made me feel such a thing? I have always received warnings in the form of visions of the night or voices in my head. This feeling seems very different to me."

Elder Rhys nodded. "As you describe it, it does sound different," he replied. "It may, however, prove to mean nothing."

"You do not feel anything?" Isabella dared to ask him. When he shook his head, she felt a familiar feeling of desperation begin to flow over her. "You do not sense any danger?" she further asked.

Hearing the sliver of panic in her voice, Elder Rhys studied her face. Since realizing that Isabella was a chosen one and destined to become an ancient in the future, he'd known he should never dismiss anything that she said to him.

"Your belly?" he asked, curious. One sure sign that trouble had previously been about to strike in the village had been the golden glow that had begun to show on Isabella. "Has it begun again?"

Isabella subconsciously placed both hands over her belly. She took a moment to focus and concentrate on how her body felt before she shook her head.

"No, I do not believe so," she replied. "I am not uncomfortable being this close to you, and I do not feel the warmth. No golden glow has shown."

The two regarded each other for a long time in quiet contemplation. Isabella had undergone much training since the last battle. Nothing had so far presented itself as a threat again, but she, Trent, and Elder Rhys all expected it to happen.

"Perhaps it is nothing, Isabella," the ancient said to her. In truth, he wasn't sure. He did believe that sometime in the future, a threat was going to present itself. There was no way to know when that would happen. It could be many more years in the future. It could be later that day. Until a sign came, there was no way they could ever be completely prepared for it. "Could it be something else that is happening within you that has affected you on waking this morning?"

Isabella took a moment to consider his question. After a long while, she shook her head.

"No," she replied. "What else could make me wake with such a thought?"

Elder Rhys smiled sadly and leaned forward.

"Could you again be with child, Isabella?" he asked and instantly saw the look of surprise on Isabella's face.

"I…" Isabella began to reply, feeling her face become heated. "No, I do not think so, Elder Rhys. It has been many years since I was with child. I … I have come to accept that there shall not be any more."

Elder Rhys nodded. He'd suspected the same. His mention of the possibility had been purely to distract Isabella. Having watched her grow from an infant and having spent more time with her in recent years, he knew that she could focus on one thought for many days and nights. He didn't want that for her.

"Very well," he said, smiling. "I am sorry, Isabella, but I do not know what has driven you to come to me this morning. I do believe that you and I can find peace in the discovery that you are able to be this close to me without experiencing pain. That is a good sign. We know that the pain comes when your body is preparing for a battle."

"Yes," Isabella replied as she nodded. "It does not seem to be the same as that. Perhaps it is nothing." She paused for a long while before continuing. "I feel that this may be a good time for me to meditate. May I? Will you join me?"

Elder Rhys nodded and stood. Together, the two of them walked to the meditation chamber that was reserved only for ancients. It was one of the few rooms in the temple that was kept not only locked but also hidden. Only the ancients could see the door in the wall in which it resided. To all others, it was just a wall.

Although she had been confirmed as a future ancient, Isabella had not been shown how to use her growing power to enter the door. She knew where it was, and it had been accepted by all of the village ancients that she was welcome in the room. She was in training that would last many years. Acquiring time to sit in the ancients' meditation room for long periods was something that was seen by all as necessary. It was a focused point in the village where the feeling of power was the strongest. Ancient Rhys had learned that in his initial training, as had all of the other village ancients. Whoever had built the temple had done so with that specific location as a center of power.

How the ancients unlocked the hidden doorway continued to be kept from Isabella. She didn't mind. Her training was ongoing. There had been days when the physical, emotional, power, and mind training had left her exhausted. She was very happy to learn whatever she was required to, whenever she was required to. What the ancients deemed her not ready to know, she accepted she would learn in time.

As always, when Elder Rhys did whatever he did to reveal and open the hidden doorway, Isabella looked away. She respected the processes being taught to her - all processes, including those shared with her and those kept from her.

Once in the room, she knelt on one of the rectangular mats that were permanently spread out on the ground. Placing her hands on her knees, closing her eyes, and deepening her breathing, Isabella finally began to feel calm once more.

CHAPTER 7

Elder Scott walked out of the temple feeling his usual cheerful self. Between the temple and the dining area, he stopped and talked to people. As always, the air was warm and fresh, and the population of the village seemed in good spirits.

For a few minutes after he sat at one of the long dining tables in the vast dining area, he enjoyed tasting the delights of the cook's morning creations. For those few minutes, his consciousness was his own. His thoughts were simple, centered around people he'd already seen and interacted with that morning, and people he'd known in his past.

While his consciousness was clear and of his own free will, he took some time to think about Kathleena. They'd been paired for many years before she'd passed to go forward on her next journey. While Elder Scott appreciated that everyone in the village must pass and go on another journey when it was their time, he still experienced many moments when he deeply missed Kathleena. He missed her smile, he missed her laugh, and, most of all, he missed the way he'd always felt when he'd been in her presence.

There was little he found dissatisfaction in when it came to the way the village lived and worked, but the rule about pairing only once was something he did question often. His Kathleena had passed. Now he was alone. It was standard and normal, but he did sometimes wish that he could have a chance to live through a second pairing.

Discouraged with his thinking, he attempted to push the thoughts from his mind. It wasn't right to question how things were done in the village. They'd always been done so and nobody else questioned the rules or ways that had been adhered to for centuries.

The consciousness of Elder Scott switched off. It was as instant as a modern-day light switch being flicked. One moment, he was fully his true self. A moment later, something else had taken over his mind. One consciousness never interacted with the other. On some level, the elder could move through his day as if he were himself, while something entirely different was controlling him.

The times when his true self was quiet and still, and an entity took control of his body, Elder Scott never remembered. To him, he was living every day exactly as he had done on each of the many days he'd been in existence since his birth.

Looking around the dining area, his eyes fell on the younglings, Esmeralda and Cesare. He smiled to himself. They had both reached an age to pair. Elder Scott made a mental note to talk to Elder Rhys about that possibility. A time was approaching when there would be several pairings taking place, but theirs would be the most important.

His authentic consciousness regarded the young people as a couple in love. He could remember how it had felt when he'd been in that stage with Kathleena. It had been a glorious time. They'd been young enough to experience the initial feelings beginning, but not yet at the time when life would become serious once children started to arrive.

His authentic consciousness was saddened that he and Kathleena had only been blessed with one child. That child was now happily paired and had children of their own. There was so much potential in the pairing process, but, at the same time, also reason for heartache.

The authentic consciousness of Elder Scott disappeared again, replaced by another. The entity inside of him continued to watch Cesare. The golden child of Isabella was someone who had to be monitored carefully. The entity suspected that Cesare was already developing powers, even though the youngling wouldn't yet know they were present. He was a threat, but not as much of a threat as his mother was. Isabella was the entity's ultimate target. If ever the entity was going to succeed, Isabella needed to be removed from the village forever.

Disturbed by the attention it was giving to the golden child and his mother, the entity shifted its gaze to Esmeralda. Looking at her only ever made it smile.

She was its seed. Through Antonio's consciousness, the entity had worked its charm on Esmeralda's mother, Kat. Even with eighteen years having passed since then, the entity could feel glee as it observed its offspring. It still didn't think Kat had any idea that Esmeralda had been created from Kat's time with Antonio. Wiping her memory of all that she'd done during that time had ensured that. As far as Kat and anyone else knew, Esmeralda was the product of Kat and Adrian. The entity had no concern that anyone would ever suspect any different.

From afar, the entity had watched Esmeralda grow inside of Kat. It had then watched her grow since she'd been born. Silently, it monitored her all the time even though she didn't know it. It waited patiently for her to reveal she had powers growing inside of her. As yet, the entity had felt none. There was a slight concern over that. It didn't see it could be possible that she *wouldn't* have powers, but them taking so long to reveal themselves was unexpected.

As it watched how she looked at Cesare, the entity was pleased overall. It trusted that Esmeralda's powers would grow quickly once they started, and they would be strong. It wouldn't be long. The entity just had to be patient.

Silently, the entity returned the consciousness once more to the real Elder Scott. As far as the elder was concerned, he'd been sitting there with his own thoughts as he looked around the room. There was no feeling in his mind that something had just replaced his consciousness with its own. There was no indication whatsoever in Elder Scott's body or mind that he'd momentarily been pushed aside and shut down.

Looking down, he saw he still had a little food to consume. Happily, he ate what was left on his plate before standing, going to wash, dry, and put away his dish, and then walking out into the glorious sunshine once again.

CHAPTER 8

Isabella spent many hours in the ancients' room of meditation. Although she'd been taught how to master such control of her mind years earlier, there were still days when she felt it was a challenge. There were so many aspects to it that left her exhausted.

In her body, she thought that sitting in one position for so long shouldn't have been difficult. Years on, she continued to find it hard to sit still and keep her legs happy that she wasn't moving. Compared to the average age of the villagers, Elder Rhys had told her that at her current age of 42, she was still very young. Whenever Isabella stood up after sitting for many hours, she questioned that. That aspect of her meditation she could laugh off, knowing that it would only be a few minutes of discomfort before her legs bounced back to feeling normal again.

It was in her mind that she always felt the most tired after such a long period of meditation. It had taken her many months of working on her focus before she'd finally been able to reach the place of consciousness that she needed to.

She was thankful for the patience of Elder Rhys. Despite Isabella's constantly active mind trying to fight and make her think of many things at once, the ancient had worked with her until she'd found the ability to tune out to the simplicities of daily life.

Since mastering the ability to control her thoughts completely, Isabella had begun to enjoy the sense of calm she felt after meditation. The process left her exhausted, but it also left her mind at rest. Having always been someone curious and analytical, the calm that meditation left her with was more than welcome. It was needed. It helped her to stay balanced within her body and her heart. It helped her to stay focused within her daily routines. It helped her to feel complete and happy in her family and home.

Although there had been no further threat to the village over the previous eighteen years or so, the possibility was always there, sitting just below Isabella's full awakened state. That was something that she, Trent, and Elder Rhys had talked about in-depth in the months following the last battle. As time had passed, the frequency of the talks had lessened, but the seriousness of them had not. Whether talking about it or not, Isabella never completely forgot about it.

Feeling it was time to leave the temple and move on with other aspects of her day, Isabella looked around the meditation room. To the far left of her sat Elder Rhys. She didn't know how he did it, but she knew that he could sit as he was for many more hours than she could. From her initial questioning of him about it, Isabella knew it was the strength of his mind that provided him with that ability. He could maintain focus on his meditation for incredibly extended periods. He could also stand up afterward with no more discomfort than Isabella felt after only a few hours. That was one of the biggest surprises, given that he'd often told her he was more than 600 years old.

Seeing two other ancients had entered the room and were in deep meditation, Isabella smiled to herself. She hadn't even noticed them enter. That was a great thing. It meant that she had been as deep in meditation as she needed to be. She wasn't always successful in getting to that place in her mind. She was always pleased when she realized she had.

With the positive thought in her head, she stood as silently as she could. For the few minutes that followed, she reached down and massaged her thighs in an effort to help them wake up. Once she felt her limbs fully alert again, she crept quietly to the exteriorly-hid doorway and walked out.

When she stepped out into the sunshine, she wasn't surprised to see her daughter, Alessia, sitting on one of the large square stones near the temple entrance.

"Mother!" Alessia exclaimed when she saw Isabella exit the temple structure.

Isabella smiled at her daughter. Raising children had proven even more rewarding than she'd guessed it would, but Cesare and Marco had always been independent. Both were loving and respectful, but they had natures that made it normal for them to be gone and out of Isabella's sight for most hours of every day. Alessia was different. She'd always wanted to be close to Isabella. At first, it had proven a challenge for Isabella as she'd indulged in training for several hours each day. She'd often appreciated that her mother, Crisiana, had always been happy to watch Isabella's children when they were young so that Isabella and Trent could train for as long as they needed to.

With the children now being older and the training having lessened, Isabella found each of her children had fallen into an unspoken schedule. The boys looked after themselves. In contrast, every day, Alessia waited around for her mother to finish whatever it was that she did inside the great temple structure.

"Daughter, you need not wait for me," Isabella said, delivering the familiar speech. "Where are your friends?" she went on to ask, already anticipating the answer that would come.

Alessia smiled.

"They are with their families," she said.

She knew her mother worried about the lack of time she spent with other children. There was no real reason why she felt drawn to be close to her mother. It was as it had always been. Inside of her, Alessia felt a much different connection to her mother than she did to anyone else. Sometimes the feeling was overwhelming, but she'd taught herself not to show the feeling to anyone else. To all around her, she presented the look of a child who was happy and carefree. Her exterior successfully hid other things that she felt going on inside of her.

Seeing her daughter's smile, Isabella said nothing more. She took Alessia's need to be close as a form of shyness. Isabella understood that. She'd been similar in her youth. Regardless, she hoped that it wouldn't be long before her daughter found the confidence to be at least a little more independent.

CHAPTER 9

Esmeralda moved through her day as she always did, with the exception of not having Cesare by her side. For as long as she could remember, the two of them had spent most of every day together. It had begun very early on, while Adrian and Isabella had spent time together. While the years had passed, Cesare and Esmeralda had developed their own schedule of time spent together.

As hours passed between the morning meal and the evening meal, now and then she walked past the location of the tailor. When she did, she caught Cesare's eye. Although the day was different with them not doing things together, even just seeing him smile at her briefly felt like a necessity to her. She didn't stop and talk to him, seeing him listening to all that the tailor elder was telling him. Talking to him wasn't something she required. She just needed to see his face and bright golden hair now and then.

At the evening meal, Cesare approached where she sat and grinned at her as he sat beside her.

"How has your day been, Esmeralda?" he asked. In truth, he felt like something had been missing all day too. There had been so few days in their lives when they'd not spent all hours of daylight together. It felt anything but normal not to have her by his side.

Esmeralda produced a smile for him, as she knew he'd want to see. Although she projected a false façade on the outside, she never lied to him with words.

"I have found it strange to not be with you today," she said in full truth.

Cesare's smile widened. He liked her honesty whenever she spoke. She didn't always say words that others would consider positive, happy, or even right to say. Regardless, Cesare did love knowing that she was always honest whenever they talked.

"I have found it strange also," he reassured her. "I have learned much today, but I felt best at those moments when I saw you in the distance."

"You did?" Esmeralda asked. "I did not wish to interrupt your training."

Cesare laughed softly and nodded. "Esmeralda, you and I have always spent our days together. It felt *very* different without you beside me today."

"How will we play now?" she asked quietly.

To anyone else who might have heard the question, they could have assumed she was talking about child's play. To Cesare, there was no confusion about what she referred to.

"After we dine," he said, grinning. "I believe this day will be the day that I win."

Although she rarely felt happy, Esmeralda smiled a true smile.

"We shall see," she said. "Tell me about your training today."

Cesare laughed again.

"I know your tricks, my blue-black friend," he said as he studied her face. "You think you can distract me so that I do not play as well as you know I can."

"Not at all," Esmeralda teased him. "You do not need to be distracted for me to win."

The two of them said nothing more, silently eating their meal until their plates were clean. After taking the time to wash, dry, and put away their dishes, they walked out into the warm, still air.

CHAPTER 10

As they had done almost every evening since they'd been nine and ten years of age, Cesare and Esmeralda walked to the great temple then made their way along the length of it. Neither knew why they'd always been drawn to the spot behind the temple. Neither knew it might have been the exact location that Esmeralda had been conceived. Why it would make sense for her to be drawn to the spot she'd possibly been created, it was hard to know. As with so many things about the village, it just was.

When the two of them reached the spot they both felt most at ease in, they found their usual places, facing one another five large footsteps apart. With the location so secluded, they knew they didn't need to worry that anyone would come across them. They'd never seen any other villager in the small area over the years they'd been going there.

Cesare watched her face and smiled at her as he began moving his feet. It was rare that they took their play seriously. Most of the fun came from them teasing and taunting one another. That, neither ever tired of.

"It shall be my win this evening, my blue-black friend," he said while delivering her a broad grin that spoke of his eagerness to play.

While he spoke, Esmeralda lifted her right hand. She grinned back at him as she began to summon the familiar power she'd experienced most of her life. Slowly, at just the pace she wanted it to, a small ball of blue flame began to emerge and then grow. She played with it as though it were a ball, tossing it a little way into the air and then catching it again, over and over.

As always, Cesare felt entranced by the sight. He had to shake his head in an effort to not feel hypnotized by it before he raised his own hand. Although he knew she could take that moment to strike at him, he equally knew that she wouldn't. The opportunity was always there as the two of them readied to play, but it was an opportunity she never took. As his golden flame appeared, Cesare watched her wait patiently, her blue orb of flame gently being thrown up and down.

The warmth of the golden flame in his hand was reassuring to Cesare. He was well used to it, having summoned it the first time when he'd been only eleven years old. Knowing even at that age that what he could do wasn't normal, he'd mostly kept the knowledge of his skill to himself.

There was still only one person he fully trusted with his secret, partly because of their friendship, and partly because she'd found out on the same day that she could do the same thing. Even his mother and father he'd kept the odd behavior from, suspecting it was something neither of them would understand.

As he began to mimic Esmeralda's action by tossing the small ball of golden flame up and then catching it again, he watched her face. Even though it was a game that had been going on for many years, neither of them had ever suggested they go an evening without it. Whatever drove them to have the ability to do such a thing, it was something that both had. It was yet another level of oddness that they had in common, further securing their strength as friends.

"You feeling stronger today, Golden Boy?" she teased him.

It was when they played their private game that Esmeralda could almost feel completely happy. There was something fulfilling about the feeling of coolness her blue flames gave her. There was also something addictive about sharing the experience with her close friend.

While she watched him mirror her movements, throwing the ball of golden flame up and down, Esmeralda took a moment to reflect on how long they'd been playing the particular game together.

She could still remember the day that she'd discovered her ability. She and Cesare had been right where they currently stood. Very early on, the two of them had been drawn to the location, mainly because it was a quiet place where nobody else ever seemed to go. When they'd been that young, they'd both preferred to not be the two odd children in the large population of the village. In their quiet spot where nobody else seemed to go, they weren't the rare two in a great many. When they were alone like that, they were the *complete* population - not the odd ones out, but the entire *normality*.

On that day, they'd been playing a form of tag, running around innocently. Esmeralda could still remember how much she'd wanted to feel the same level of happiness that her friend always seemed to exhibit. Something about the state of her mind, and how her thoughts changed, had coincided with her right hand beginning to feel cold.

At the moment that she'd raised her hand to look at it, she and Cesare had both seen the blue tinge appear over her skin.

"What is that?" he'd asked her, moving closer as if intrigued by what he was seeing.

"I ... I do not know," Esmeralda had replied. It was her first time seeing the odd color on her skin. "It feels funny."

Cesare had moved closer still. When he'd reached out with his hand to touch hers, she hadn't stopped him. As soon as his skin had connected with hers, Cesare had felt the coldness of her hand.

"You feel different," he'd said to her as he'd pulled his hand away.

"So do you," Esmeralda said to him, aware that when their hands had made contact, she'd felt an incredible heat from his skin.

"I do?" Cesare had asked, rubbing one hand with the other.

For a long while, both had said nothing more, absorbed in the feelings they were experiencing apart but yet together.

The more they'd concentrated, the more they'd both felt new things. When Esmeralda had upturned her palm, out of the blueness of her skin had begun a small ball of what looked like a flame. It had startled her, almost embarrassing her, until she'd looked at Cesare.

Cesare had repeated the action he'd seen her do. He hadn't expected anything to happen when he did. Copying her movement had been his way of reassuring her that she was alright. Even at that young age, he'd perceived how little happiness Esmeralda seemed to have within her. The discovery had made Cesare eager to help her to feel better about her life.

On mirroring the way she'd moved her hand, he'd grown aware that his hand had begun to heat up. When the warmth had increased to the point of it being impossible to be normal, he'd shifted his gaze to it. As he and Esmeralda had watched, almost exactly the same thing that had happened in her hand then happened in his. Both had stared, moving their sight between his hand and hers.

"What is it, Cesare?" Esmeralda had asked, curious but not fearful.

"I do not know," he had answered, looking right into her eyes. "They are not the same. Yours is blue, and mine is…"

"The color of your hair," Esmeralda had finished.

When she'd noticed his surprise as he looked at her, she'd seen his gaze shift upwards.

"Like yours," he'd said, momentarily confusing Esmeralda with his meaning. "This is yellow, like my hair. Yours is blue, like *your* hair," he'd gone on to say as he'd pointed at her head. "But what does yours feel like, Esmeralda? Mine feels very warm."

"Cold," Esmeralda had replied, refocusing on the sensations flowing through her hand. "It is cold, but it is nice. It does not hurt me. I like it."

The two of them had remained still for a long time, both feeling a sense of wonder. It was a new thing that not only had happened but had also occurred for both of them at the same time.

"Why are we seeing this now? Together?" Esmeralda had finally asked. "Does everyone do this?"

Cesare had shaken his head. "I have never seen this before," he'd said. "Shall we tell anyone?"

Esmeralda had hardly needed to think before answering his question. She'd known, without any doubt, that she wanted to keep what was happening a secret from everyone else. It was a strange thing to see and experience, but it was also something that she felt was right. Having seen him waiting for her answer, she'd shaken her head.

"Let us not," she'd said. "It is something that you and I are sharing together. I would like for us to keep it for just you and me. What say you to this?"

When Cesare had nodded, Esmeralda had felt a new level of closeness to him. Although they'd both been young children, she'd felt more mature than the other children in the village. What she and Cesare had experienced was one more thing that separated them from everyone else.

At that moment, Cesare had given consideration to his mother and father. He'd never had any desire to keep anything from them. As he'd focused on the feeling that the golden flame was providing to him, he couldn't see any harm in doing so.

"I shall say nothing," he'd reassured her. "How do we stop it?"

On hearing his question, Esmeralda had focused on her hand and willed the ball to disappear. It had taken several minutes, but she was successful. One instant, the blue flame had been visible. The next, it had disappeared, as her skin changed in color and returned to its usual temperature.

"How did you do that?" Cesare had asked after he'd watched what she'd done.

"Think about it going away, Cesare," Esmeralda had replied. "Think hard. Imagine that you are wishing it were not there at all."

It had taken Cesare much longer to make it happen. When he had, he'd grinned at her in such a way that had almost summoned happiness in Esmeralda.

"It worked!" he'd exclaimed, excitement evident in his voice. "I did it!"

"Why do you think we did that?" she'd asked.

"I do not know," Cesare had replied. "We do not know if we can do it again, or if it was only one time, but it is getting late. I must get home, Esmeralda."

"You will not say anything?" Esmeralda had asked, suddenly finding herself uncertain if he would keep their secret.

Cesare had moved closer to her and placed a hand on her arm before leaning in and speaking quietly.

"You have my word," he'd said. "I do not know what it is. I have no need to tell anyone of this, Esmeralda." After a long period of her looking at him with uncertainty, he'd spoken again. "Come. I shall walk you to your home."

The two of them had remained silent as they'd made their way to the small house Esmeralda lived in with her two parents. Once outside,

Cesare had reassured her again that he would not say anything. After he'd walked away, Esmeralda had entered her home. She'd known she wouldn't have to hide anything from her mother since it was rare for her mother to ask anything. Esmeralda had anticipated more of a problem in dealing with her father. On that evening, even he had appeared oblivious to anything having changed in Esmeralda, for which she was glad.

After that day, Cesare and Esmeralda had experimented with summoning their respective flames on their hands. After mastering those skills, they'd begun to play around with the two flames, making a game out of it. It was something neither had ever shared with anyone else. Neither had spoken of the strange things they could do, and they'd never indulged in summoning the strange orbs of flame when anyone else was around. Despite how many years had passed since that first day it had happened, it remained the biggest secret either of them had.

"You are distracted," Esmeralda heard Cesare say, breaking her out of her reverie. "What are you thinking about?" he went on to ask.

Esmeralda tossed the blue flame up and down once more, increasing the intensity with which she looked at her close friend.

The passion Cesare could see on her face told him she was about to move. He readied himself without waiting for her to answer his question. He knew when she was past being able to converse with. The way she could go from being regularly conversational to being in a place ready to strike always amazed him. They were only playing, but the way her face changed made him feel like she took it all far more seriously than he did.

The game they'd created out of their strange abilities was purely made of moves to strike each other. There were no absolute rules. Early on, they'd discovered that if they threw the flames at each other, they were mildly struck, but without any long-lasting pain. When Esmeralda's flame hit Cesare, he was momentarily overwhelmed with feeling an intense level of cold that was strange to him. When Cesare's flame hit Esmeralda, she felt a level of warmth she found uncomfortable but not painful.

For a while, they'd experimented just with the feeling of each other's orbs of flame hitting each other. It had been interesting, but not harmful. Over time, the game had changed.

Cesare watched her eyes. He knew the only way to gauge what she was planning was to watch the way her eyes flickered just before she threw an attack. It had taken him a long time to work out how he could tell what she was about to do, but he was confident he had.

Seeing the movement of her eyes and the flick of her wrist, he quickly cast his flame in anticipation of where it would hit and deflect hers. In his mind, it always looked straightforward. In reality, it was rare that his calculation adequately met hers at all.

Esmeralda felt the power flow through her as she let the ball of blue flame fly. She, too, had trained herself to watch the moves of her opponent. Even after all of their years playing the small game, she still didn't think that he understood what really happened. She could always see him anticipating her move. Having observed and studied him so well, it was always in that final moment that she changed her strategy.

The blue flame bypassed the golden one that had been set free. As was usually the case, Cesare felt the cold hit his right side, under the arm that he'd raised to release his own flame. The cold striking him made him cringe, but then he smiled at her.

"That was just luck," he called out to her.

"Was it, Golden Boy?" Esmeralda teased him. "Luck? Or skill?"

Cesare grinned even wider before encouraging her on. The cold hitting him was uncomfortable. It was never enough to make him want to stop playing.

"Again," he said, bringing up his hand again.

It had taken time for them both to be able to summon more than one ball of flame on any given day. After so many years of practice, both could now summon the orbs at will.

He watched as Esmeralda accepted the challenge and summoned another blue flame into her hand. They weren't truly competitive toward one another. It was childish fun that had continued even as they'd begun leaving their years as children behind them.

Before Esmeralda's face had struck its serious and intense pose, Cesare let his ball of golden flame fly. His objective was to hit her body with it. He was glad when he saw her counterattack straight away.

Midway between the two of them, they saw the blue and golden orbs of flame collide. The result was a blinding light. It wasn't large, and it made no sound, but the brightness of it was something neither could look at comfortably.

"I think that was mine," Cesare teased Esmeralda.

"I think not!" she counter-teased. "Only one of us has been hit, and that is you. Therefore I have won again, Golden Boy."

Cesare smiled at her. In truth, he wasn't someone who needed to win at anything. He liked their little game, but the thing he enjoyed most about it was that it seemed to engage his friend in a way that she didn't engage with anything else. It was rare that Esmeralda exuded anything close to happiness. When they played, her mood seemed to at least edge closer to it.

He bowed but said nothing, just glad she was smiling.

CHAPTER 11

Trent spent many hours each day in the large garden that provided food for the entire village. Although he'd never had any experience in gardening when he'd grown up, since arriving in the ancient village, he'd come to love it. The more years that passed, the less he thought about his previous life in modern times. The consistent consideration when he *did* think about it was that he had no regret about having left it behind.

"You are smiling," he heard Isabella's voice say from behind where he crouched, bent over to thin carrots.

When he stood and turned to face her, he couldn't help but grin.

"How could you know that, my beautiful Isabella, if you could not see my face?" Trent asked, intrigued about her ability to sense things in other people.

Isabella laughed. "I did not. It was only a guess," she said, happy to be near him again.

As she moved closer, she was pleased as his arms naturally opened and welcomed her into them. There was never a day when they didn't see each other. Regardless, during her day, she still felt the pull to go and see him in his workplace on occasion.

"Alessia was looking for you earlier," Trent said after kissing her gently.

"Yes, she found me when I left the temple," Isabella replied. "I know she is young, but I feel she may be ready for an occupation."

Trent nodded. As much as he loved his daughter, he'd often wondered about her lack of independence or desire to be away from Isabella.

"Where is she now?" he asked.

"I told her I must speak with you alone," Isabella replied.

"Oh? What is it?" Trent asked, instantly concerned.

Isabella grinned. "It was merely an effort to encourage Alessia to find a friend to enjoy time with rather than spending time with me," she said. "However, I *do* have something to tell you."

Trent pulled her closer to his chest and kissed her again. Whenever Isabella announced she had something to say, he could never be sure if what was to follow would be serious or suggestive. With her, any conversation they shared could go either way.

Isabella leaned in close to his ear. "In our bed this evening, I shall like..." she started to say. Just as she did, words appeared in her head, making her shudder and pull away from Trent.

'The time of Isabella is almost up,' a male voice said in her mind. 'She and her son will soon no longer be in my way'. She waited to hear if anything more was said. There was only silence.

Trent saw her facial expression as she took a step back from him. He recognized the glazing over of her eyes. He also knew it would be useless to ask her a question at that moment. Instead, he focused on her face and waited as he tried to remain calm. It had been a long time since any conflict had happened in their life together. While he accepted that it was likely going to happen sometime in the future, he hoped the time hadn't come yet.

Isabella felt her consciousness return to normal. Although she'd continued to be awake, her concentration had shifted when she'd heard the voice. The words had been few, but they had been powerful enough to command her attention.

Refocusing on Trent, she saw how serious he looked. While she never wanted to cause any concern in him, she once again appreciated just how much he loved and cared for her.

"A voice," she said, seeing him waiting. "It was a man's voice, saying..." she started to repeat as she felt a shudder pass through her body. The reference to herself was worrying enough. The voice, having gone on to mention her son, managed to push aside any worry, replacing it with anger and a desire to fight. She looked into Trent's eyes. "It is beginning, but it is not only me they wish to hurt this time, Trent. It is also Cesare."

Trent was startled. In all the conversations he'd had with Isabella and Elder Rhys about the possibility of the entity returning, they'd never discussed the children being involved.

"Cesare?" he asked in his surprise. When he saw her nod, he asked for clarification. "What was said?"

"The voice said that my son and I will no longer be in their way," Isabella said as she studied Trent's face.

"No more was said?" Trent asked but only saw Isabella shake her head in response. "We must go and speak to Elder Rhys."

Isabella nodded. "Yes. He is still in meditation at present. When he has completed his time of peace, I shall go and see him. I shall ask him for his guidance."

"*We* shall go and see him, Isabella," Trent said. "Whatever may be coming, you shall not prepare for this alone. I may not have the same powers as you do, but I have learned enough to be able to help."

"Yes, it was a surprise before when you showed your abilities," Isabella said, nodding. "What you have been able to learn will be of surprise again, I am sure."

Trent nodded and pulled her close to him, wrapping his arms around her and holding her tightly.

"Whatever may be coming, we will be prepared for," he said. "It will not hurt you or our children."

Isabella tightened her hold around his body as she nodded. His choice of words evoked in her a concern that he'd mentioned her not being hurt, and their children not being hurt. He hadn't mentioned the possibility of *him* not getting hurt. She pulled away from him and gave a sad smile, not wanting to think about that possibility.

"You must return to your carrots," she said, making Trent grin at her. Behind the smile, she could see the seriousness of his concern. Regardless, neither of them turned away from the effort to appear happy.

"I can think of far more pleasurable things than carrots, Isabella," Trent said, his voice low. "You did not finish the sentence you began earlier. How shall I be able to concentrate on carrots when my thoughts will continue to wonder what you were going to say?"

Isabella laughed before she took a step closer, reached up, and kissed him on his lips.

"You shall be able to," she said, not answering the bigger question. "I shall go now and bathe while I wait for Elder Rhys to complete his meditation."

Trent gave her a mock look of disbelief before just grinning at her. She knew that any mention of her bathing in the warm pool of the village stirred him.

"Be off with you before you tempt me to join you," he said with affection.

Isabella grinned before pulling away and beginning her walk up the path from the garden area. As she walked, her mind left the place of trying to appear happy. The words that she'd heard still lingered in her mind. They were few, but there had been no doubt about their meaning. Yet again, something was coming for her.

What she tried to focus on at that moment was the voice. She'd experienced the entity's words in her head previously. On both occasions, she'd gone on to hear the person in reality. The voice she'd just heard had sounded familiar, but she knew it wasn't Kat's. It also hadn't sounded like Antonio - the man previously used by the entity for an attack strike. She also guessed that whoever - whatever - the voice belonged to, it either hadn't known she could hear them, or it had intentionally planted the words in her head.

She took a moment to consider that possibility. Would it purposely alert her to such a thing? Not if it intended to strike against her, she didn't think. The other possibility was that it had decided to start a game of making Isabella worry about things when she didn't need to. She couldn't be sure either way, but she thought it was more likely the former than the latter. Something had decided it was time to work towards eliminating her from the village, and it wanted to take her son as well.

Considering the possibility of anything happening to any of her children, Isabella's feet began to move faster. She was glad when she saw nobody else was in the area around the pool. Removing her shoes, she stepped into the warm water and dived under before rising, casting her hands through her long red hair. Once she felt refreshed, she sat on the ledge that ran along the inner edge of the pool, underneath the waterline. Although it had been a favorite spot for her and Trent many times, she appreciated that she could sit alone in the warm water and focus on more serious things.

For almost two decades, she had been waiting for another attack on her or the village. The time could be drawing nearer when it would happen. She took a moment to wonder if she was ready for it. She'd felt prepared in the first years of training after the last attack. During those years, she and Trent had both received training in various aspects of using powers to create and fight with the golden flames.

Experiencing a moment of panic about whether she was suitably ready for what might be to come, she lifted her hand just clear of the water and focused. Seeing the skin on her hand begin to change to a golden color was reassuring. She subtly smiled then once again submerged her hand under the water. She'd never summoned a golden flame when out in public, and she had no desire to at that moment. She'd felt the power begin in her and seen the starting stage of it. That was enough for her to feel reassured of her skill, at least for that moment.

Closing her eyes, she leaned back and let the warmth of the sun flow over her. Despite having never lived anywhere else, she never tired of feeling the warming of the sun and the water as she listened to the nearby waterfall flowing into the pool. Behind the waterfall was a cave that housed the great source of golden power. She'd seen it once when Trent had passed from his future to their current time. She'd never seen it again. Glancing at the waterfall, Isabella didn't know how Elder Rhys had parted the water or enabled her and Trent to walk over the top of the pond to enter the cave. It was just one of many magical things that she was yet to be trained in.

As she indulged in the simplicity of warmth, Isabella's mind remained busy. After a long while, she climbed out of the pool then moved to one of the long warming stones to dry. Lying down, she cast her mind to her oldest son. She assumed Cesare was the son who'd been referred to by the voice that had spoken. Was she safe in making that assumption? Neither of her sons had ever shown they had anything mystical or powerful inside of them. So far, Elder Rhys hadn't mentioned that Cesare was destined to become an ancient. The only reason Isabella thought he might be was because of his hair color. It was the same color as the large rock behind the waterfall. That couldn't be a coincidence. To her, it had to *mean* something. What, she didn't know.

Casting her uncertainty aside, Isabella found peace in her mind once more as she let the warmth of the sun and the stones do their job of drying her. After a long while, she sensed Ancient Rhys ending his meditation.

Calm in her mind and her soul, Isabella stood and made her way toward the garden to ask Trent to join her.

CHAPTER 12

Alessia watched her mother and father walk into the temple together. She'd seen Isabella at the village garden. She'd also seen her go to the pool to bathe and then dry out. No matter where her mother went, Alessia found herself drawn to watch her. She didn't think it was a usual thing for any child to do, but for as long as she could remember, she'd felt a need to ensure her mother's safety. The need didn't come from any conscious thought. It was just something natural inside of her.

Alessia had heard the strange words in her head. As she had, she'd seen her mother's reaction at the same moment. She'd also seen her father's reaction to whatever her mother had just experienced. It certainly wasn't the first time Alessia had heard voices in her head, but it *was* the first time that it had looked like someone else might have heard them at the same time.

Quietly, she remained still until her parents were out of sight. As always, Alessia wouldn't say anything to anyone about what she'd heard or what she felt. She didn't understand what was inside of her that made her able to hear the odd conversations that she did. She equally had no desire to share her knowledge with others. Not only did she suspect it wasn't right that she could hear conversations that she knew had nothing to do with her, but she also felt very embarrassed by it.

What she'd heard earlier had made her wonder if it *was* a conversation that had nothing to do with her. The voice had talked about her mother and one of her brothers. That concerned Alessia slightly. She tried to push her concern aside with the confident belief that her mother had also heard the words. Her mother had heard them, and she'd appeared to have shared them with her father. Knowing they would react however was best left Alessia feeling a little soothed. Most things she heard in her mind, she disregarded. There had been many things that she was sure she should never have known, especially since she was only fifteen. All those things she filed away, hoping that she'd never hear them again.

Turning away from the temple, she saw a friend and began to walk toward her. At many moments throughout any day, Alessia felt older than the other children of the village. In her heart, she didn't want to spend time with them. Her true desire lay in ensuring the safety of her mother, her father, and her brothers. Feeling it was wrong of her to want to do that, she'd had plenty of moments when she'd pushed herself to appear more childlike than she felt.

"Alessia!" she heard her friend say.

Alessia smiled and greeted her friend before shifting her mind into that of childish play. She never quite fully succeeded in tuning out to the serious thoughts she heard each day and night, but she was confident in her ability to hide it from other people.

As she and her friend ran off together, she closed off her mind. It was something she'd tried to do a great number of times since she'd realized she could hear the thoughts of others. It had taken many years of her trying before she'd finally begun to feel it was something she could grasp.

Focusing on putting up a wall around her mind, all voices halted. It wasn't a perfect process. It took intense concentration and focus to put the wall up, and it took even more to hold it there. She maintained hope that one day she'd be able to put the wall up, and it would stay up, enabling her to live in silence. She also accepted that day might be a long way off.

CHAPTER 13

Elder Rhys sat quietly as Isabella relayed to him the words she'd heard in her head. There were so many things that surprised the ancient about what he heard her say. In the past, he'd experienced times when he could see and hear the same things in his head as Isabella had seen and heard. As she spoke, he realized it had happened only to her and not him. The other surprise was that it had happened at all. They'd been expecting it for many years. That didn't stop the apprehension that came from knowing it could be about to begin all over again.

"Do you think it means something is going to happen soon, Elder Rhys?" Trent asked.

Although they'd prepared for such an event since the last one, most of his training had been completed more than a decade earlier. Isabella had continued to train with the ancients because she was expected to become one. Trent's training had involved only skills he might need to fight if an entity showed itself again.

Elder Rhys nodded. "It is something that we should prepare for," he said. "You did not hear the voice specifically say 'Cesare', Isabella?"

Isabella shook her head. "No. It referred only to my son. I do not think it would be Marco," she said, looking from the ancient to Trent. "He holds nothing of value to whatever it was that was speaking."

Trent studied her face. "We do not know that Cesare does either, Isabella. Our assumption of that is based purely on the golden color of his hair. The assumption we have always made could be the same reason the entity might make the *same* assumption."

"It is true," Isabella replied, nodding. "Whichever of our sons it intends to hurt, we must prevent it from doing so."

"Isabella," Elder Rhys said, slightly startled by her words. "*Whoever* it intends to hurt, we must prevent it from doing so. You are no less important than your children."

Isabella remained silent. In her mind, she argued with his last statement. In her voice, she kept quiet. She didn't at all regard herself as important as any of her children. Regardless, she did appreciate the value that Elder Rhys had always seemed to place on her.

"What shall we do?" Trent asked.

"All we can do is wait and see what happens," the ancient replied.

"Each time we have gone through this before, something has happened to give us a warning. I do not see why this time would be any different," he said before turning to face Isabella again. "You do not have a glow? You do not feel discomfort being this close to me?"

Isabella shook her head.

"No, Elder Rhys," she replied. "There is nothing similar to before. It is only the words that have caught my attention."

"What if it is *not* the same as before?" Trent asked. "Two times now, this thing has attempted to attack Isabella, but each time, she's known something is going to happen. Would it not be fair to assume that the entity will be less obvious next time? Would it not work harder to try and keep from Isabella whatever it is planning?"

Elder Rhys nodded in agreement.

"You may be correct, Trent," he said. "We cannot anticipate what it is planning, if anything." He looked at the couple for a long while before continuing. "Shall we train?" he asked, directing his question at Trent. "It has been quite some time."

Trent nodded. "Yes, I would feel better if we do."

Elder Rhys stood, indicating to the couple to do the same. Without speaking further, the three of them walked through the temple to a large area in the rear. Once again, it was a room that was only accessible to ancients. To anyone else who lived in the temple, or even just passed through, they knew nothing of it.

Once inside, Elder Rhys stood off to the side and encouraged Trent to exercise what he'd learned over the years. As the ancient watched, he saw Trent raise his hands in preparation to summon a golden flame.

Trent concentrated on his hands. Despite how much training the three of them had done together in the first few years following the last battle, summoning power was still something he found difficult. Initially, he had needed an ancient soul of a friend of Elder Rhys to help him. That had been difficult enough. Since the old soul had moved on, Elder Rhys had encouraged Trent to still try and summon the flames. After Trent had forced himself to believe that he also had some form of powers within him, he had begun to be able to do what he was training to do.

As he attempted the summoning after so long of not having done so, he felt frustrated. He felt it had been too long since he'd actively trained. Although he'd eventually overcome the disbelief that he had any powers, so much time had passed that he'd lost the belief once more. He was both saddened that he had lost any power it had begun to look like he had, and angry at himself for not having continued to practice in recent times.

Isabella watched him for a long while. Over their years together, she'd learned to accurately identify his moods and emotions. She could sense his current dissatisfaction. After she felt his mood darken towards wanting to give up trying, she moved to him and placed her arms around him.

"We found each other through destiny, Trent," she said quietly near his ear. "It was not only me who did that. It was you also."

Trent understood what she was saying. He'd heard the words before. It was her way of reminding him that he did have it within him to do what he needed to do to secure their long and happy future together.

As Isabella removed her arms and took several steps backward, she watched as he tried once more. She was pleased when she saw the small flame appear over the palm of his hand.

"Now the other one," Isabella said as she raised both of her hands.

Trent watched her as she easily summoned a golden orb of flame into each of her palms. The sight drove him on to concentrate on his other hand. Maintaining eye contact with her, he felt a second golden flame leap into life over his palm.

"A third," Isabella challenged him as she moved one of her flames over and into the other, forming one larger orb over her hand.

Trent's focus was captured as he did the same. It took longer for him, but he achieved it. With thought and focus, he was able to create a much larger ball of golden flame over one hand before he concentrated on the other hand and summoned another.

Elder Rhys watched the two of them. It was good that Trent could carry out the action. It was not so good that he still seemed to need an external person or soul to urge him on. If another battle were in their near future, the ancient would prefer Trent could fight under his own focus. As he continued to watch Isabella and Trent, Elder Rhys tried to maintain hope that whatever was being planned without their knowledge, the plan wouldn't be put into place for a very long time yet.

Briefly, the ancient thought back to a time when he'd felt ready to give up on his living self and let himself pass to go on his next journey. As he watched the two people before him, he was glad he hadn't given up on his life that easily. The two people in front of him needed him. They showed that to him every time he saw either of them. When his time came, he would be glad to move on with the next part of his journey. Until then, he would remain right where he was, doing whatever he could to protect the village and all of its inhabitants.

"Connect!" Elder Rhys called out to them.

Summoning the orbs of golden flame was only one part of what they needed to be able to do. The other was using them to fight against someone else.

Isabella kept her eyes focused on Trent's as she used her full control to raise her golden orbs into the air. Using her mind, she moved them upwards at a slow pace before making them hover above and away from her.

Trent watched the orbs. His role was to hit Isabella's golden flames accurately with his own. It was an odd form of target practice, but one he appreciated was necessary.

Focusing, he raised one hand and took aim at one of the orbs Isabella had released. When he felt sure he was aiming correctly at it, he let his orb fly. Moments later, the two joined midair.

"Good," Elder Rhys said. "Now, moving and faster."

Trent nodded and watched as Isabella connected telepathically with the orb still floating. Before him, it began to move around in a jerky motion, slowly at first and then gradually picking up pace. He studied it, trying to anticipate its move.

"Instinct, Trent," he heard Elder Rhys say.

Trent instantly let his last orb go, throwing it with force. He'd hoped he would be able to hit the moving ball of flame. He hadn't.

"Again, Trent," Isabella said to him, prompting him to take time to produce another ball of flame into each of his palms.

When he'd summoned the flames, Trent watched the slow-moving orb again. Without as much analysis, he threw his two orbs one after the other, using only his gut instinct for guidance.

All three watched as both orbs connected with the one Isabella had sent upwards. It was a source of pleasure for Isabella, relief for Elder Rhys, and pride for Trent.

"You have done well, Trent," the ancient said. "You must practice more, however."

Trent nodded.

"I shall," he said. "If a battle is to come, and it is similar to the previous two, I will be ready to play my part."

"Good," Elder Rhys said. "Last time, it was unknown to the entity that you had the ability to fight like this. Next time, it will be of no surprise."

"Shall we continue?" Trent asked, determined to hone his skills more.

Elder Rhys was pleased. "Continue," he said as he nodded.

Isabella and Trent worked together to simulate different scenarios of attack. Their orbs coming together only resulted in the golden flames dissipating midair. They knew they couldn't replicate the battles between the golden flames and the blue they'd seen previously. It didn't matter. What they needed to gain confidence in was working together, using the golden flames to attack.

After a long while, Isabella turned to face the ancient.

"We shall return to our home now, Elder Rhys," she said. "May we come again tomorrow?"

Elder Rhys smiled and nodded. "You may."

Although happy with his progress, Trent was equally glad to leave the temple. It seemed like so little energy should have been spent summoning small orbs of flame and throwing them. In truth, it left him exhausted.

CHAPTER 14

At the evening meal, Isabella was pleased to see Adrian. Day to day, they still saw one another, but they spoke together as friends less often than they had before both had gone through the pairing process.

"Isabella!" Adrian exclaimed when he saw her approach with Trent by her side. "Tell me what you have been doing."

Isabella grinned and gladly sat beside her lifelong friend. It was noticeable that Kat was nowhere to be seen. Isabella tactfully didn't mention or ask about that.

"You know I do not have anything exciting to tell you about, Adrian," she said, continuing to smile at him. "I would much rather hear about your work."

Adrian smiled sadly. There were aspects of his life that he was unhappy in. The safest topic of conversation that he could share with Isabella was his work at the mill. He felt happy that she wanted to hear about his day but sad that the conversation was so often censored.

"It is well," he said as he saw his daughter enter the dining area.

Seeing his attention shift, Isabella moved her sight to see what he was looking at.

"They continue to be good friends," she said. "Esmeralda means as much to Cesare as you have always done to me."

Adrian looked at her and nodded.

"I do believe you are right, Isabella," he said. "You and I did spend time together like they do now."

Isabella could hear the sadness in his voice. It broke her heart knowing that he'd been so cheerful when they'd been younger. She placed a hand over his on the table and squeezed it.

"Although we do not spend as much time together now, my feelings for you as my friend have never faltered," she reassured him.

Adrian squeezed her hand back.

"Thank you," he said before leaning forward so he could look around Isabella. "Trent, how goes your work in the garden?"

Trent happily talked about the latest aspects of knowledge he'd been gaining regarding the growth of food for the small community. It had been many years that he'd been working in the garden. Despite how much he'd already learned, he knew there was still a great deal more that he was to be taught by the elders who managed the garden area.

As the men on either side of her talked, Isabella watched her oldest son and Adrian's daughter. They were a distance away, huddled together as they ate. It had been that way for many years but always made Isabella smile. She had uncertain feelings about Esmeralda, but she knew that the young lass with the blue-black hair made Cesare happy. Despite a hint of uncertainty about whether Esmeralda had inside of her any of Kat's ability to be easily manipulated by the entity that had used her mind and body twice, Isabella had long before decided she would accept Esmeralda as her own person. She might have been born from Kat, but she wasn't her.

'They must be paired,' she heard in her head. The voice was the same as she'd heard earlier that day. It was an odd thing to hear. It had no context, making Isabella wonder if she was hearing snippets of larger conversations. It made no sense why that would be. It equally made no sense that whoever the voice belonged to fully *intended* for Isabella to hear.

CHAPTER 15

Antonio sat in the large dining area with his Ariana by his side. In the distance, he could see Esmeralda. When he looked at her, he felt confused. There was a slight memory inside of his head that was centered around him and the young woman, Kat, having joined. There was also a faint recognition that the young woman who was Kat's daughter might also have been created from his seed. It made no sense. Kat never even looked at him.

Since the night in the temple, when he'd woken up from what felt like a long dream, he'd felt like he was two different people. He had memories of his life with Ariana and their children. Those memories made sense. The ones that didn't make sense were the ones that showed Kat as part of his life. He also had mixed memories about Crisiana - a woman he'd grown up with from childhood. He knew he'd hardly spent any time with her since they'd been very young. The memory in his head was more recent, and disrespectful to Ariana.

"Are you well, Antonio?" Ariana asked.

She'd seen his face express confusion many times in their years together. Only a few times had she asked him about what he was thinking in those moments, but he never seemed able to give her any clear answer.

Antonio turned his head and focused on her. She was the one person in his life that he loved and knew was constantly there for him. They'd been together for a great many years, but they still enjoyed each other's company.

Looking at her, he saw a hunger in her for intimacy. The look fueled him. All other thoughts were forgotten.

CHAPTER 16

The entity within Elder Scott was growing impatient. It wanted control of the village, including the people and the power that lay within it. In its form, the entity had no concept of time. All it could judge anything by was how it saw the people of the village grow and age. How they did that, it had no concern for. Only two people out of the entire population were important as far as age went.

Residing within the elder, it had waited many years for Isabella's child to grow, and for its own offspring to grow. Putting its own seed in danger was of little consideration. It had been feeling the powerful strength of Esmeralda grow since she'd been in Kat's womb. Although she'd not exhibited any powers outwardly yet, the entity was hopeful that she would soon.

Testing her abilities, it reached out and attempted to see into her thoughts. As always, the attempt was a failure. It continually dismayed the entity that whenever it tried to see into Esmeralda's mind, there was nothing there. It made no sense to be the case, but that's how it was. As time continued to pass, the entity did experience some hesitation about whether she *was* going to grow into her powers or not. It supposed it didn't matter. The plan had developed and changed over many years. At first, the entity had intended to use Esmeralda to fight Isabella. The problem with that plan was that Isabella's golden son was likely to be as strong as she was. If the two young people were of the same power level, the fight might not be won in the favor of the entity.

The current plan was to encourage the pairing of Esmeralda and Cesare. Their powers could offset each other, but what could a being that had the combined powers of both be like?

Inside of Elder Scott, the entity looked around. Seeing Esmeralda and Cesare in the distance, talking closely as they always seemed to do, it nudged its host.

Elder Scott finished his meal and stood before going to wash, dry, and put away his plate. As soon as he had, he experienced a strong inclination to go and talk to Elder Rhys.

"You wish to talk to me?" the ancient asked him when they came face to face inside the temple.

Elder Scott nodded and smiled.

"Yes," he said. "I have been watching Esmeralda and Cesare. I believe it is time for them to consider pairing."

Elder Rhys was surprised by the statement. Elder Scott knew, as everyone did, that it wasn't the elders who made such decisions in the village. It was the ancients, which Elder Scott was not.

The ancient considered his response before saying anything. It was the first moment that he noticed something different about Elder Scott. Although startled, it wasn't a moment he wanted to show his wariness in.

"They are a worthy couple for consideration in the pairing process," Elder Rhys said, nodding. "Am I correct in assuming you believe they should pair to one another?"

Elder Scott nodded his head with enthusiasm.

"Yes! There is no greater pairing match for either of them," he exclaimed.

Elder Rhys nodded again while watching the face of the elder in front of him.

"I shall talk to their mothers and fathers, and to the ancients," he said. "Thank you for this suggestion, Elder Scott."

As the ancient began to walk away, the entity inside of Elder Scott felt angry. It had wanted a far better and more instant response. The lack of speed or understanding of the importance of the match only fueled the entity in its belief that all ancients had to be destroyed. They stood in the path of progress and advancement. The villagers saw them as some kind of rulers or saviors. They were neither, but as far as the entity was concerned, the ancients did have far too much power.

Feeling that its anger was causing stress in the body of its host, the entity retreated its presence and enabled that of Elder Scott to move into the mind's forefront. The idea of Esmeralda and Cesare pairing was a seed that had been planted. The entity forced itself to sit back and wait in an effort to prevent itself from reacting without planning and thought.

Elder Scott felt his alertness change. It happened so often that he didn't regard it as anything important to worry about. It was most likely a part of getting older. Although he didn't particularly remember walking into the temple, that was where he lived. Quietly he made his way to his bed-chamber to lie down and relax.

As he lay down on his bed, he let his mind cast back to his life with Kathleena. He'd been thinking about her more and more in recent times. He wasn't sure why. She'd passed on to move on with her journey many years earlier. Recently she'd been on his mind often.

He smiled as he remembered what she'd looked like and how she'd sounded when she spoke. Thinking about her was a happy thing for him to do. He didn't know why, but sometimes he felt like his body was unhappy about something. It made no sense, but he'd felt his heart beating at an abnormal speed and power on different occasions. Lately, it had started to happen more often. The more frequently he felt his body tense, the more often he felt the need to lie down, breathe deeply, and remember the happy times with his beloved Kathleena.

CHAPTER 17

Isabella and Trent sat together on a grassy area of the village. It was an area they'd grown familiar with when Trent had first arrived. Although it was a wide-open space, when Trent had been in the future, there had been no concern about anyone in the village seeing him as he'd pitched his pup tent and slept there. Now that he was back in the same time as the villagers, there was no hiding from anyone as he and Isabella sat in the vast area.

"Do you feel prepared for whatever is to come?" Isabella asked him.

She'd chosen the area to sit because it was one place that was so open, it would be impossible for anyone to listen unless they walked up to where the pair sat on the ground.

"Do *you*?" Trent asked her back. "The hardest thing for me is this unknowing. Could we be imagining that something is going to happen when it is not?"

"You do not believe I have heard what I have?" Isabella asked, surprised.

Trent shook his head, horrified at her having thought such a thing.

"No!" he exclaimed. "Oh, no, Isabella, of course I do not doubt what you have heard. My uncertainty lies in whether we are *interpreting* the instances correctly."

Isabella nodded.

"Yes, I agree," she said. "We must believe something is coming, Trent. If we maintain that belief, we will continue to prepare. If nothing comes of it, what of it? We shall have completed more training for no purpose. That matters not. Better that than we not be prepared if something *does* happen."

"Yes," Trent agreed, nodding.

Feeling like his mind had been overloading with worries since hearing about the voice speaking in Isabella's head, he turned his thoughts to her face. When he'd studied her for as long as he could stand, he leaned forward and kissed her.

Isabella instantly reacted. They didn't share themselves with each other often enough, with their lives being full of many other things. As her lips caressed his, she felt his tongue push into her mouth. The feeling electrified her, making her groan.

Trent smiled at the sound. It was difficult not to move forward with some level of intimacy, particularly when she sounded like that.

"You must be quiet, Isabella," he whispered, smiling at her as he gently pushed aside some hair from her cheek.

Isabella's response overrode his words. While she wouldn't be overtly sexual in front of others, she didn't hesitate to move her head toward him again, then plunge her mouth onto his. She had no desire to stop the feeling of excitement rushing through her body.

Trent wanted to stop what they were doing out of respect for the village and its ways. It wasn't easy to put that thought into action. The way her tongue was moving against his was too delicious to turn away from.

Eventually, his appreciation for discretion got the better of him. He pulled back, sincerely wishing he didn't need to.

As Isabella's confusion cleared, she grinned at him.

"You are very good at keeping me from doing things I should not," she said, teasing him.

Trent laughed out loud.

"It is not easy for me to do, as you well know!"

CHAPTER 18

Every night, as Esmeralda lay in her bed, her mind wandered into a realm of thinking about the life that she lived. Why she questioned it all so much, she had no idea. It was a part of who she was, and she accepted that.

She'd always felt she was different from everyone else in the village. That feeling never went away, but she'd accepted her differences due to Cesare highlighting his own. Their friendship had always guided her to stop doubting who she was as a person. While she knew that the general population looked at her with curiosity, she understood that what they saw wasn't necessarily who she was. Cesare had helped her to see and believe that.

He'd always had the opposite problem. From a very young age, he'd shared with Esmeralda that it was uncomfortable for him in the village sometimes. People seemed overt in their attention to him, treating him like he was some unique source of wonder. As he'd gotten older, he'd found the strength to keep away from people he knew acted that way towards him.

In explaining how different he felt, he'd helped Esmeralda to not think about her differences so much. They were close friends. While she didn't share everything with him, she knew that she *could* if she wanted to. That meant a lot to her. Neither of her parents had inspired any desire in her to talk to them about anything that was bothering her. Her father was friendly but often unhappy, even though he continued to try and cover it up. Her mother was unfriendly and unapproachable.

She was thankful that she and Cesare had been drawn to one another as children. Although she knew it was mostly due to her father and his mother being so close, Esmeralda believed it was also due to much more than that. Both being unique, they were kindred spirits, of a sort. Their uniqueness made them similar and able to understand each other.

The only thing she regretted never having shared with Cesare was the ongoing feeling that something was trying to push into her mind and her thoughts. She didn't know why she'd come to that conclusion about what the sensation represented. She'd never heard of anyone being able to read another's thoughts. Regardless, she had a very strong intuition that it *was* happening.

When she'd first felt the sensation, something had happened inside of her mind. Instantaneous, natural, and beyond her control, it had felt like a wall had been quickly erected to protect her thoughts. Since that first time, for the most part, it had continued to be a natural occurrence. On the odd occasion, she'd felt the sensation of someone trying to look into her mind, and she'd quickly raised the invisible wall herself.

It was the only thing she'd fully kept to herself and not shared with Cesare. For a moment, as she lay in her bed, she wondered if she should. She suspected he wouldn't understand, and it seemed like something that would be too hard to try and explain anyway.

The hardest thing about not sharing such a big thing with him was that it made Esmeralda question their friendship. She regarded him as her close friend. She believed he felt the same way. He was nineteen. She was eighteen. She'd heard recent talk about it being time for new young people to pair. She wondered if they would be expected to. She suspected not. Her father had been close friends with Cesare's mother, but he hadn't paired with her. More than once, Esmeralda had questioned if her father would've been a much happier man if he had.

CHAPTER 19

Alessia felt overwhelmed. Inside her head, she could hear the thoughts of many. Most didn't matter. The less important, she fought to push aside and make quiet. In contrast, when she heard anything about anyone in her family, she did take notice.

Although she never repeated anything that she heard, she was aware that there were three voices in the village who often spoke to one another, but only in the silence of minds. The topic of their conversation was often Alessia's mother, her brother, and her brother's friend, Esmeralda.

In recent times, she'd heard the voices talking about Cesare. At first, they hadn't specified he was the one they were discussing. Now that they'd begun mentioning Esmeralda into the same conversations, Alessia had no doubt it was him and not their brother, Marco, who was the subject of their talks.

While there were things being said that were mildly concerning, she was intrigued by the whole thing. Her family was quiet and peaceful. They'd never hurt anyone - *nobody* in the village ever hurt anyone. The only reason that Alessia could imagine someone was focused on her mother, her brother, and Esmeralda, was that they were different.

None of the three outwardly exhibited it, but Alessia knew that they each held the same skill. In her head, she'd seen Cesare and Esmeralda make a game out of their ability to summon bright lights from their hands. She'd also seen her mother and father do the same thing, but she knew it wasn't a natural thing for her father. He was trained in it but needed external assistance with it.

How they could do it, she had no idea. She hadn't seen anyone else in the village do such a thing, and she was equally sure that she couldn't do it herself. It was just one of the many intriguing things she'd seen during her fifteen years of life that she had no explanation about. Whatever it was that they did, and however they did it, they kept the knowledge mostly to themselves. Alessia knew that Cesare and Esmeralda played their little game with it, but neither told anyone else about what they could do. She also knew that her mother and father shared the knowledge with the ancient, Elder Rhys, but nobody else.

As she pondered why she had the ability to hear so much around her, she heard the now-familiar voice begin to talk again. In her mind, she crouched, silent but listening so she could hear, but they wouldn't know she was.

'The plan is in motion. I will push for Esmeralda and Cesare to pair. She is my seed. She must be protected and encouraged to make even stronger seed with the boy of gold.'

Alessia remained still and silent in her mind. She waited for the conversation to expand. It didn't. Although it had been short, it had provided some new things to think about. Someone wanted her brother and his friend to go through the pairing and create new life. Although unfamiliar with the process, Alessia was old enough to know that the purpose of pairing was to produce more children for the village. It was hard to imagine her brother doing such a thing. He was older but didn't seem old enough for that.

The intrigue was strong, but the need for sleep was stronger. Alessia drifted off, forgetting everything.

CHAPTER 20

When Isabella woke in the fading darkness of the next morning, she was relieved that she'd once again enjoyed a peaceful night. Nothing had presented as a vision of the night, and no words had called out to her. While part of her wished that whatever was coming would just get on with it and happen, she found peace in the hope that it might not happen at all.

Turning her head, she looked at Trent. The room was dark, but she could see his profile. Knowing nobody else was up, she felt bold. Reaching out, she placed her hand over him. Straightaway she felt him grow to her touch. Feeling him grow as he became aroused was something she'd never tired of. Although not sure if he was awake or not, she took her time, stroking the length of him.

Trent felt her hand and teased her by lying still and pretending to be asleep for as long as he could. When he couldn't stand the thought of her missing out for any longer, he subtly lowered his hand to touch her in return. After a few minutes, he felt her turn onto her side, fully facing him. He mirrored her action and pulled her close.

No words were said as Isabella lifted one leg and placed it over his hip. She didn't need orgasm or release. What she was hungry for was the beautiful feeling of him filling her up.

Trent remained still as he felt her push against him and then enclose him. Even without hardly any stimulation from him, he could feel she was incredibly wet. The moist warmth was like a level of bliss he'd only experienced since finding her. He'd had many lovers in his previous life. The connections he'd had with them in no way compared to the connection he continued to feel with Isabella, even after two decades.

Isabella moved her hips, enjoying the feeling of him inside her. When she was ready to give control to him, she pulled him with her as she moved to lie on her back.

In response to her unspoken request, Trent happily obliged, moving over her and settling between her thighs. Before entering her, he rested his weight on her and kissed her deeply. The taste of her lips increased his hunger, prompting him to pull away and move down her body, teasing her with a delay till the pleasure of joining.

As Isabella focused on the feeling of his tongue tasting her, she fought to remain quiet. It was a pleasure they'd indulged in less often since they'd become parents. Most of the time, she enjoyed their joining too much to want to devote any time to what Trent was currently doing. Concentrating on the delicious feelings flowing through her, she was quickly overwhelmed as she reached a deep and powerful orgasm.

Feeling her shimmering under his mouth, Trent smiled. Pleasuring her that way was something he'd veered away from. When Isabella wanted pleasure, she didn't usually let him give it to her orally. He was pleased she hadn't pushed him away. It was a joy to him and fueled him on, making him grow harder as he moved up her body, kissed her lips, then welcomed her hips rising to meet his. As he slipped inside of her, he maintained control, remaining slow as he moved in and out of her silkiness. Focusing on the softness of her lips on his, he subtly moved his hips until he felt her climax again from his movements. As Isabella's body clenched underneath him, he could hold back no more. He fought to maintain quiet as his body tensed in blissful joy.

Isabella held him close while both of them relaxed. When she felt him begin to raise his head, she gently but firmly guided his head back into her shoulder before she began to stroke his back. She'd always loved the feeling of him inside of her, even after they'd both reached that magical place. It was nice, being joined with him, but it also felt like a blessing.

Trent remained still, focusing on the feeling of her hands stroking up and down near his spine. He was in constant wonder that even after two decades of having been paired with her, he could still feel so much passion for her. He didn't know how many people truly felt that way about their partner after so long.

After a long while, he moved his upper torso back from her, maintaining the join with the knowledge that it was important to Isabella. Supporting himself on his elbows, he leaned down to lightly kiss her lips, over and over. Each kiss he gave, he felt her eagerly accept. He lay like that, unmoving in any other way until he heard movement coming from where their children slept.

As he moved out of her, Isabella felt the same instance of loss that she always did at that time. When they were connected, they were one. There was nothing else like that feeling. Regardless, she welcomed Trent pulling her close to his chest as he lay back on the bed.

It was a soothing comfort, having him by her side every night and every morning. When she thought about the possibility of something inside the village wanting to hurt either of them or anyone else, Isabella worried. Something inside of her had been able to deal with whatever the strange thing was that had come out of Kat and Antonio previously. Despite her previous success, she maintained concern about Trent or any of her children being hurt in any way. She'd seen the way her father passing on had affected her mother. Even though Crisiana had put on a happy face since then, Isabella still sensed the sadness in her from time to time.

Life without Trent was something Isabella couldn't bear to imagine. He was her soul mate. She needed him.

"What are you worrying about, Isabella?" she heard Trent whisper from beside her. "Your body has grown tense."

Isabella lifted her head from his chest and looked at him. With the room growing lighter, she could see his face clearly. It was such a handsome face, even after them having aged so much. Each time she looked at him, she still felt compelled to kiss his lips.

Trent welcomed her kisses but didn't let her distract him. Whatever she'd been thinking about, it showed greatly in her body.

"Tell me," he said quietly.

"I was thinking about what may be ahead for us," Isabella said. "I do not want anything to happen to you or Cesare or Marco or Alessia."

Trent raised his hand and ran his fingers through her hair. The color and silkiness of it had never changed over the twenty years they'd been together. He continued to be in awe of her and the other women in the village. They didn't age at the same rate as the women he'd known in the big city he'd left behind. He briefly wondered if the women of the city knew just how much healthier they might be if they lived a far simpler life with less stress.

Noticing his thoughts had gone off on a tangent, he refocused.

"Together, you and I will not let anything happen to any of us, or anyone else," he said. "We *will* be ready for whatever is to come." When he heard no reply, he turned to his side, facing her and kissing her. "Please do not worry so much, Isabella."

Isabella nodded and kissed him back.

"I shall try not to," she reassured him, knowing full well that turning off her thoughts was much more difficult in reality than intention.

CHAPTER 21

When Isabella and Trent went to the morning dining, they were both surprised to see Kat sitting beside Adrian. Although paired, the two of them rarely seemed to spend time together outside of their home or the mill.

"Good morning, Isabella and Trent!" Adrian said in his usual cheerful manner as they sat near him.

Trent and Isabella returned the greeting. It was noticeable that Kat didn't turn to face or greet them. Despite Kat's ongoing persistence in not investing any time into the friends of the man she'd paired with, Isabella refused to be the same.

"Good morning, Kat," she called around Adrian. In response, she saw Kat turn her head, begrudgingly return the greeting, then return to her eating. Isabella returned her focus to her friend. "How are you today, Adrian?"

As always, Adrian felt dismayed at the lack of interest Kat showed toward Isabella. He understood the discomfort of many years earlier when he hadn't hidden that he'd wanted to pair with Isabella. So many years had passed, it made little sense to him that Kat would continue to act in such a way toward Isabella still.

He knew there was no point in dwelling on the lack of happiness Kat exuded or shared with him. As usual, all Adrian could do was keep a smile on his face and continue being friendly toward everyone.

"I am well," he said to his lifelong friend. "The mill has been very busy, which makes the days go faster. I have less time to think about things at these times."

Isabella watched his face as he spoke. She felt like there was a hidden message in his words, but she had no idea what it was.

"Do you need to talk?" she whispered to him. She was glad to see him nod slightly in response. "I shall walk with you toward the mill when we finish here."

Adrian nodded again. He was thankful she had accurately sensed his mood. He wasn't surprised by that. Isabella had always been able to read him very well.

Through the meal, nothing serious was discussed. When finished, Kat stood and left, not giving Adrian even a glance. It was something he was well used to. No matter how many times they saw it, Trent and Isabella felt surprised and saddened by it.

Sensing Adrian's need to talk to his friend, Trent kissed Isabella's cheek before standing, placing a hand on her shoulder, and looking at both of them.

"I shall go to the garden," he said. "I will see you later."

Isabella and Adrian watched him walk away before they turned to face one another.

"He is a very good man, Isabella," Adrian said wistfully. "I am envious of what you have."

Isabella reached out and placed her hand on his.

"I am very blessed," she said. "You are a very good man, also, Adrian."

"I used to think so," Adrian said, his head dropping as he looked at their combined hands. "I confess that I often think I will never be happy being paired with Kat. I find myself wishing I never had." He looked up, directly into Isabella's eyes. "What kind of man am I to feel this way? It is not right."

"Oh, Adrian, I do not agree," Isabella reassured him. "You have been a good man to Kat and a good man to Esmeralda. Please do not doubt yourself because of the way that Kat is. That is no reflection of you. It is only a reflection of *her*."

Adrian smiled sadly at her. He held many regrets but hated that he did so. Even at the ages they were, he still now and then wondered how things could have been if they'd paired together. It was wrong to think about such a thing. Isabella was very happy in her pairing. He'd never deny her that happiness. He just wished he could find it himself.

"I shall be happy again, Isabella," he said, not sure if he believed his own words. "I feel like this sometimes, but it does not last for long."

Isabella leaned toward him and pulled him into her arms.

"I am always here for you as your friend," she said. "Please talk to me *always*."

When she pulled away, she saw Adrian's eyes beginning to water. It was a sight that made Isabella feel like her heart was breaking. A moment later, she found herself wanting to ask him if he'd noticed anything different about Kat lately. Isabella was curious to know if Kat's belly had started to glow blue again or if her mood had changed. Isabella remained quiet. She suspected that even if Kat had gone through any such changes in recent times, it was entirely possible that Adrian wouldn't know. If she asked, that possibility would be highlighted and could make Adrian feel worse.

Isabella kept her questions to herself. If Kat were undergoing any kind of change at the mercy of the entity again, all would know soon enough.

"Come," Isabella said, standing and holding out her hand. "I shall walk you to the mill."

Adrian nodded, smiled, stood, and wrapped his hand around hers. He appreciated the moment as he squeezed her hand and then released it. It was fortunate that he had such a good friend. Unfortunately, having Isabella by his side did nothing to change the unhappiness he felt in his life with Kat as his paired partner.

CHAPTER 22

After walking her friend to his workplace at the mill, Isabella made her way back to the kitchen. Despite all that she undertook during the day with training, meditation, and spending time with Trent and their children, she'd resumed helping with the fetching of items for different people around the village. It wasn't needed with there being another generation who could help with such things, but it was something that Isabella enjoyed. It provided easygoing times among the serious.

As she approached where the cooks were working, Cook Joan called out to her and smiled.

"Miss Isabella! Are you here to help?" she asked.

Isabella grinned at the cook, noting how little she'd changed over the years even though she was much older than Isabella.

"Yes, if you require me, Cook Joan," Isabella replied. "Is there anything that I can fetch for you?"

The cook smiled, nodded, and moved to pass a basket to Isabella.

"Yes, please," she said. "Can you please gather the carrots? As many as you can fit into this would be ideal."

"Of course," Isabella said before sensing someone at her side.

When she turned around, she saw her daughter.

"May I help, Mother?" Alessia asked. She knew it was an innocent question. Behind the innocence of the words was a growing concern for the safety of her mother and Alessia's need to monitor Isabella.

Isabella saw Cook Joan wink and nod.

"Your youngling is eager to take over your role, Isabella," the cook teased. "Perhaps it is time you let her."

Isabella grinned at the cook before responding to Alessia.

"You may," she said, once again wondering why her daughter preferred to spend time with her than with her friends.

As the two of them walked out into the sunshine, Alessia could hear her mother's thoughts. In truth, she could hear the thoughts of many, but she was slowly learning to control how many of them could invade her mind at any one time. She'd also taught herself how to focus on the ones that she wanted to and ignore the rest.

"It may be time for me to take on a vocation, Mother," she said.

Isabella stopped walking and turned to her daughter. The words were similar to what she and Trent had spoken about a short time before. It wasn't quite enough to make her wonder about the coincidence, but it was enough to get her attention.

Resuming her walking, Isabella responded.

"It is usual for us to begin a vocation when we are past eighteen, Alessia," she said.

"Yes, but I do not care for play, and I feel that I can be of *value* doing something," Alessia replied.

Isabella considered the suggestion. She'd never seen anyone want to begin working at such a young age. It was neither expected of young people nor usually wanted by them.

"What would you like to do?" she asked.

"I do not know," replied Alessia. "I could do this. I believe you enjoy fetching things for the cooks."

Isabella laughed softly. "I have done it many times. I never knew where I should belong in the village until Cesare, Marco, and you came along. Then I knew that my place was as a mother."

Alessia knew from years of hearing her mother's thoughts that there was a much more important role that Isabella played in the village. Although Isabella's words didn't paint the full picture of her place in the community, Alessia didn't question or correct her.

"I shall find that place also," she said. "That is many years away."

"Yes, it is!" Isabella exclaimed with affection as the two of them entered the vast garden area.

When they approached the lengthy area where carrots were grown, mother and daughter both saw Trent look up, smile, and move toward them.

"The two most beautiful young women in the village have come to see me," he said, teasing them. "How fortunate am I?"

"Father!" Alessia said in a mock telling-off.

Trent chuckled. His daughter was usually very shy and timid. As a result, he didn't often tease her in any way, preferring to let her dictate how and when the two of them shared conversation.

"What can I get for you?" he asked, directing his question at Isabella.

As he looked into her eyes, it was difficult not to think about their morning wake-up pleasure. Trent fought to keep focus as he listened to Isabella's reply.

"Cook Joan would like as many carrots as you can fit into this basket please, Trent," she said, also in danger of replaying parts of the morning in her head.

As Alessia caught the initial thought pattern of her father and mother, she quickly put into practice her growing art of switching off hearing their thoughts. With her ability, she'd already learned much about the act of joining between a couple who were paired. After the first few times that she'd been made witness to such thoughts, she knew it was wrong to hear them. Those thoughts had been the first that she'd wanted to never hear again.

While Trent was away gathering the produce, Isabella turned to her daughter.

"I see no harm in you doing this if you wish to," she said. "It is not an official vocation. You can do this now, and later choose to work somewhere if you wish."

Alessia smiled. She knew her mother didn't like her spending so much time so close by. The knowledge didn't hurt Alessia in any way. She understood that her mother wanted her to be independent, as was expected of everyone. There was nothing to feel hurt by in knowing her mother didn't want her by her side all day, every day.

"I can?" Alessia asked.

"Ask your father and see what he thinks, but you have my blessing to do this each morning," Isabella replied as she saw Trent returning.

Passing the full basket to Isabella, Trent could tell something was on his daughter's mind. Her face rarely looked animated. When it was, something important was coming.

"Father," Alessia began. "I shall like to do this job so that Mother does not need to."

Isabella chuckled. The reason wasn't exactly correct, but she didn't say anything to dispute Alessia's words.

Trent looked from one to the other.

"You wish to do as your mother has done, and do the fetching in the mornings?" he asked for clarification. Seeing both women before him nod, he was surprised but pleased. "I think that is a good idea," he continued.

Alessia grinned again. In truth, she had no interest in doing such a job, but she knew that in appearing to want to, she could help her mother to focus on more important things. It also would help to reduce her parents' concerns that she wasn't growing independent. They'd never know about her ability to monitor them even from a distance.

"Thank you," she replied to both. "Shall I take this back to the cook?" she asked, reaching out her hands.

Isabella released her hold on the basket of carrots, allowing Alessia to take it.

"Return them directly," Isabella said. "Cook Joan is waiting for them."

Alessia smiled and nodded before turning and resuming her walk back to the village kitchen. On her way, she could sense a feeling of relief in her mother. She was glad. She knew something was changing in the village, and somehow her mother was at the center of it. If Alessia could help lessen Isabella's worries, even by doing something so trivial as fetching things for people, she was happy to do so.

When Alessia was out of sight, Trent moved forward, pulled Isabella into his arms, and passionately kissed her. There was no surprise in Isabella's response. Trent couldn't remember one time when she'd turned away from their lips coming together.

Pulling away, he saw her face. It was alight with the passion that she'd maintained for as long as they'd known each other.

"You are so beautiful," Trent couldn't help but say to her.

"As are you," Isabella replied, grinning while also looking a little shy.

Feeling her face blush, she experienced a moment of youthfulness. She could still remember how it had been when she'd first met Trent, and how it had felt when they'd shared their first kiss. For her, it had been the first kiss of her life. Remembering, she unconsciously raised a hand and lightly touched her lips with her fingertips.

Trent saw the motion and felt his heart skip a beat at the sight. It could have inspired sexual desire in him. At that moment, what he felt was the deepest love for her.

"You must work," Isabella said, breaking the thoughts of both of them.

Trent nodded and grinned.

"I must," he said before kissing her and turning away.

CHAPTER 23

After leaving the garden area, Isabella felt drawn to go to the temple. She lived by no set schedule, but when she felt the temple call to her, she knew she had to enter it.

"Isabella," she heard Elder Scott say to her as she walked through the great outer doors.

Turning to see him, she experienced an instant feeling that she didn't like. It made no sense. She'd known him all of her life, even though not at the same degree as she'd come to know Elder Rhys.

Pushing her negative feelings aside, she forced a smile onto her face.

"Elder Scott," she said. "Good morning to you."

"Have you come to see me?" the elder asked.

Isabella shook her head. "I have not," she replied, not expanding on her answer. "Thank you."

Elder Scott studied her face. For the first few moments, he was himself. Before he could walk away, his consciousness switched off, and another switched on.

"I have been meaning to talk to you about the possibility of Cesare pairing with Esmeralda," the entity said through the voice of Elder Scott.

Isabella was surprised at both the content of the words and the tone of his voice.

"I was not aware that they had asked to be paired," she replied, focusing heavily on Elder Scott's face. "Did they come and speak to you?"

"No," Elder Scott replied. "It is time, however."

"They are still young," Isabella said, cutting short the elder's words. "Cesare is only nineteen. Esmeralda is only eighteen."

Inside of Elder Scott, the entity felt anger. Always, Isabella was in the way of anything it wanted to do to take the ultimate power of the village. The anger she evoked in it made it want to reach out, right where it was, and use the hands of Elder Scott to squeeze her neck until she couldn't take another breath.

"They are in love, and we are due for new pairings to take place," the voice of Elder Scott said.

Isabella felt a range of emotions during the conversation. She'd always respected Elder Scott. Although he wasn't an ancient, he had listened and provided her with advice on many occasions. She'd never had any reason to not trust him - until now.

"Thank you, Elder Scott," she diplomatically said. "I shall speak with Cesare and Trent about this when we are in our home this evening."

Incensed by her lack of bending to its will, the entity removed itself from the consciousness of its host. When it did, Elder Scott felt a renewed sense of energy. Without saying anything, he gave Isabella a smile and walked past her.

Isabella turned and watched him leave the temple. She couldn't be sure, but the way Elder Scott had looked when he'd spoken reminded her of the nights she'd seen Kat and Antonio move from being under the influence of something else to regaining their clarity. The possibility of it happening to Elder Scott worried Isabella.

Eager to express her concerns, she continued into the temple to seek out Elder Rhys. When she found him, he smiled at her and welcomed her to sit in the small room he occupied.

"Are you here to meditate, Isabella?" he asked, glad to see her before he noticed the look on her face. "What is it?"

For a moment, Isabella felt uncertain about whether to voice her thoughts. They were fleeting, and she had nothing to assess Elder Scott's behavior against. Did she have the right to suggest an elder of the village wasn't acting his usual self?

After a long period of contemplation, she spoke.

"Have you noticed anything different about Elder Scott?" she asked.

"Elder Scott?" Elder Rhys questioned. When he saw Isabella nod, he continued. "No," he said. "Have you?"

"I am not sure, Elder Rhys, but when I saw him at the temple entrance a short time ago, something seemed different," she said.

"Different? How so?" the ancient asked.

"He..." Isabella started to say. Before continuing, she ran the conversation through in her memory. Had she misconstrued the look and sound of the elder? She didn't know. "He had a similar look about him as Kat and Antonio had..."

Elder Rhys was surprised at what he heard her say. Despite his surprise, he knew not to dismiss any observations or feelings that came from Isabella. Her intuition had so far been impeccable.

"Are you sure?" he asked. "Can you tell me what exactly you saw and felt when you saw him?"

"No, not exactly," Isabella replied, shaking her head. "He suggested to me that Cesare and Esmeralda should be paired. It surprised me, but I told him I would talk to Trent and Cesare about it. When I said that, he seemed ... he seemed to wake up, just like Antonio and Kat did that night."

"Oh, dear," the ancient said. "It does seem like another sign, does it not?" he asked and saw Isabella nod. "He has spoken to me about your son going through the pairing process, and it surprises me that he suggested it. It is not the way of our people to try and create a pairing."

"I told him Cesare is only nineteen," Isabella said.

Elder Rhys nodded. "And Esmeralda is only eighteen. They are both before the time we would like people to pair."

Both sat for a long time, facing one another but silent. There was much to think about for both of them.

"Isabella, I would like you to increase your training," Elder Rhys finally said. "There are still so many aspects that you need to learn."

Isabella nodded. "Of course," she said. "For a possible battle?"

"Not only that," Elder Rhys replied. He didn't want to tell her about a feeling he'd been starting to have. Although he was determined to fight and remain alive for her as long as he could, he couldn't deny to himself that he felt like his time was coming to an end. "Many aspects of being an ancient, you have learned. I feel it will be best if you learn as much more as you can."

"Very well," Isabella said. She could feel a sense of sadness coming from the ancient in front of her but didn't question it.

As Elder Rhys stood, Isabella did the same.

"Come," he said. "I believe one of the chickens passed this morning. It is a good time for you to practice the farewell ceremony to send it on its next journey."

After walking together to retrieve the lifeless body of the dead chicken, Isabella followed Elder Rhys back to one of the hidden rooms in the temple. Inside, over the period of the afternoon, she worked to encourage the body and soul of the small animal to leave the current world and move on to the next. The first time she'd done it, she'd felt a strange feeling flow over her when she'd succeeded in her attempt. Seeing a lifeless body in front of her, then witnessing only a golden orb moving around and disappearing, leaving nothing behind, had reminded her of when she'd seen her father's body go through the process. In subsequent times, she'd found herself in awe of the process. She had no idea how it was done. It just was.

Elder Rhys watched Isabella in her efforts to send the small being on its next journey. He knew that it was less effort to do so with a chicken, but he didn't share that with her. Whenever he'd sent a person on their way, it had taken something out of him physically, leaving him exhausted. Even he didn't know how it worked. What he showed Isabella in her training was exactly what he'd been shown in his own, hundreds of years earlier. He knew it was somehow connected to the magic of the golden stone. *How* it worked, he'd never questioned.

When he saw the body of the chicken disappear, he was pleased. It was only a tiny being, but it was on its way to the next journey it had to take. More than that, Isabella had performed the process with perfection. It pleased Elder Rhys, seeing her progress in the many different aspects of becoming an ancient. She had many years to go before she would assume that title, but she already had great power in her. He believed she had no idea yet just how powerful she was going to become.

"You are progressing nicely," he said when she turned to look at him. "The day grows late, however. Tomorrow I would like you to spend time in the great library, reading before your meditation."

"Yes, Elder Rhys," Isabella said, intrigued. Usually, the ancient invited her to try different things. It was new for him to direct her with such forwardness.

"Very good," Elder Rhys said, beginning to walk toward the door. "Go now. I shall see you tomorrow."

He said nothing more as they walked out of the hidden room, and he turned and walked away from her.

Isabella still felt intrigued as she walked outside. The evening was only just beginning with the sun still out but certainly on its downward path. Breathing in the warm air, she made her way to the warm village pool. It wasn't the same as meditating in the ancients' meditation room, but it was certainly therapeutic in letting Isabella's mind rest.

CHAPTER 24

As Esmeralda sat close to Cesare at their evening meal, she wondered if she should tell him about the feeling she'd had that someone was trying to read her mind. It seemed like such an unlikely thing to be able to be real, but she couldn't shake the feeling that it was indeed happening.

She'd never heard of any such thing in the village. Did that mean it *couldn't* be true? If it wasn't what was happening, what had been causing the odd sensation that made her think that? She wanted to share her feelings with someone. There was only one person that she could express such things to, but even to him, she was unsure she wanted to. She valued his friendship. Although she knew he'd always accepted everything he knew about her, would he accept if she talked about something that might not be real?

Cesare sensed her confusion as she sat beside him, eating. He could read her body language during indecision as well as he could read it during times when she was about to share something with him. When he'd waited long enough, he turned to her.

"Trust in me, my friend," he said quietly. "I can sense that you are mindful of something that you are not letting go of. If you need to speak of it, please do. I shall not repeat it to anyone."

Esmeralda looked at his face. It was a face she knew so well, having seen it almost every day of her life.

"I do know that you would not tell anyone, Cesare," she said.

"Relieve yourself of what is weighing you down, Esmeralda," he replied, encouraging her to continue speaking.

"I..." she started to say.

Just as she was about to tell him about the feeling she'd been having, it came on again. Through the clarity of her mind, she could sense what felt like a fuzzy area that a wall instantly went up around. She'd been attempting it so long that the wall went up by itself. That pleased her but also scared her.

Cesare watched her face and saw her eyes go blank for a moment before she seemed to clear whatever had happened.

"Do you ever feel..." she began to ask before once again questioning her decision to share her feelings. After a further moment of contemplation, she moved forward. "Do you ever feel like someone or something is trying to read the thoughts inside of your head?"

Cesare was surprised by her question. He hadn't tried to guess what she'd been about to say, but what she'd asked was well beyond his thinking.

"I have never had that feeling," he said quietly as he leaned in closer to her. "Do you feel that someone is trying to learn what you think in the quiet of your mind?"

Cesare watched Esmeralda nod, her face full of confusion, analysis, and doubt. He found himself intrigued by her words.

"What does it feel like?" he asked, curious. "What makes you think that is what is happening?"

Esmeralda took a moment to try and think of the words that would adequately explain what made her believe what she'd said.

"It is difficult for me to explain it, Cesare," she said. "Sometimes, it feels like something is trying to get in. I cannot tell you exactly why that is what I have thought the feeling is. It is just a feeling that I have."

Cesare nodded. He knew Esmeralda well. He knew that she rarely talked of things that weren't important or weighing on her. She wasn't often happy, but she also wasn't untrue when she spoke. When she talked, she meant what she said.

"How long has this been happening?" he asked.

"For as long as I can remember," Esmeralda replied, seeing the look of surprise on Cesare's face. "It has always been there."

"You only speak of it now," he said and saw her nod. "Why now?"

"It is something I have grown used to," she said. "I live with it as it is normal for me, but lately, it has felt stronger. Sometimes I feel like something very much is trying to push into my thoughts."

Cesare found the entire conversation interesting. That there was something new to learn about his closest friend was intriguing in itself, away from the curious situation she was talking about.

"How do you deal with it?" he asked.

"A long time ago, I taught myself to put an imaginary wall up around my thoughts," Esmeralda replied. "I am not sure how I did it. Now, it comes naturally. I believe my mind does it automatically when it feels the sensation."

"Then all is well?" Cesare asked, beginning to feel unease as he considered someone might be somehow trying to hurt his friend. "*You* are well?"

Esmeralda heard the caring tone of his voice. It was something she was used to and greatly appreciated. When others in the village had looked at her as if she were too different for them to consider one of them, Cesare had held out his hand to her and reassured her she was as valued as anyone else was. He'd always made her feel safe and accepted.

She smiled as much as she could.

"I am well," she reassured him. "I ask the question only to determine if this happens to others."

"I am glad that you have asked me," Cesare said. "If we do not share such things with each other, we do not know if we are the only ones experiencing it."

"Like our flames?" Esmeralda asked, remembering again the day they'd both discovered what they could do.

Cesare nodded. "Yes, just like our flames."

The two sat in silence as they continued to eat their meals. When finished, they stood, washed, dried, and put away their dishes, then walked out into the warm air of the early evening.

"I do not feel like playing this evening, Cesare," Esmeralda said.

Cesare turned to her and studied her face. It wasn't the first time that she'd removed herself from their nightly activity, but it was a rare enough occurrence to always worry him. Out of his concern, he moved forward and wrapped his arms around her. It wasn't their first hug, but he felt she needed it.

Esmeralda welcomed the closeness of him. When she'd been very little, she'd received such affection from her father. In more recent years, he'd backed away from it. Her mother, in contrast, had never been affectionate. Whenever Esmeralda tried to summon a memory of Kat hugging her, she could find none.

Wrapping her arms around Cesare, she clung to him. Physical touch was something she wasn't used to. Whenever he offered it, she welcomed it.

Cesare held her close. It wasn't something they often did. When they did hug, he could feel how much she'd missed out on that kind of affection from her family. It saddened him. Even though he didn't need or want any such affection from his own mother or father, on occasion, he was still subjected to it. It was yet one more thing that made him grateful for the parents that he had, and sad for the parents that Esmeralda had.

"Come, my blue-black friend. I will walk you home," he said as they pulled apart. "You get a reprieve from our play this evening, but only because I know that tomorrow evening I shall be the victor."

Esmeralda smiled at him as best she could, knowing he wanted her to. She felt confused and sad about so many things. Knowing that she felt like that so often compounded the feeling. Other people around her were always so happy. She was sad, and then she was sad about being sad. Sometimes she wondered if the sadness would ever truly go away for her.

When they reached her home, Cesare wrapped his arms around her once more.

"I shall see you in the morning?" Esmeralda asked and felt him nod against her head.

"You shall," Cesare said as he pulled away. "Sleep well, Esmeralda."

Esmeralda watched as he turned and walked away. Although she always knew she was going to see him the next day, sometimes when he left her, she felt an intense emptiness inside. She disliked the feeling, but she didn't know how to make it go away.

Upon entering her home, she saw her mother and father. As usual, they were not speaking to one another. They could be in the same room for many hours and never seem to regard each other at all. Esmeralda found it difficult to watch. At her age, she understood the importance of pairing to the village. She continuously wondered how it had come to happen between her easy-going father and her never-happy mother. Had they always been like that? Had they paired, never talking to one another? She couldn't comprehend how it could be. Even when she was with Cesare, they talked.

Seeing her father look up and smile at her when she walked in, Esmeralda did something she rarely did. Walking up to him, she wished he would hug her. She was glad when Adrian correctly anticipated her need. He said nothing. He asked nothing. For that, she was glad.

CHAPTER 25

As soon as Cesare entered his home, he could sense something was different. The looks on his mother's and father's faces told him to expect something was going to be talked about, and it was going to be serious. After closing the door behind him, he turned toward them and waited.

"We must talk," Isabella said to her oldest son. When she saw him nod, she pulled out a third chair at the table she'd been sitting at with Trent. "Sit."

Cesare did as he was instructed. His mind was active, trying to think about what he could have done wrong to incite his mother's seriousness. Both of his parents were generally happy and playful. When they weren't, he knew to be prepared for anything.

Trent looked at his son. Out of all the things that had surprised him about moving from modern times to the time of the ancient village, Cesare was one of the biggest surprises. Trent had never thought he'd be a father. It had never been something he'd visualized in his life. As he looked at Cesare, he felt surprised that he could have come from Trent's genes, but he also felt pride.

"It was suggested to me today that you and Esmeralda may wish to pair," Isabella said in all honesty.

Trent looked at her, pulled sharply from his previous thoughts. He almost laughed at the straightforwardness of her statement. Sometimes she was subtle. Other times she most certainly was not.

Cesare wasn't often stunned into silence, but that was exactly what hearing his mother's words did to him. He and Esmeralda had never talked about the pairing process at all. They'd neither mentioned the possibility of them pairing with other people nor pairing with one another. He was curious about who could have said such a thing. Seeing his mother and father both waiting for a response from him, he finally spoke.

"I do not understand," he said, looking from one to the other. "It has been *suggested* to you?"

Trent watched his son's face. The surprise on it was evident.

"This is not a conversation that you have had with Esmeralda?" he asked. When he saw Cesare shake his head, he was as confused as he could see his son was. "Neither of you have spoken about the possibility with anyone else?"

Cesare shook his head again.

"I cannot speak for Esmeralda, but she has never spoken of such a thing to me," he said. "I do not believe she would have talked about something so private to other people but not to me. It would not … no, I do not believe that could be true."

Isabella listened and assessed her son's statements. Her intuition told her that he was being truthful. The discovery heightened her wariness about Elder Scott. He had been the one to mention the pairing. She'd wondered about his intention then. Now that she had confirmation that the idea hadn't come from Cesare and Esmeralda, she felt her suspicion grow further.

"Do you feel it will be something you and Esmeralda will wish for in the future?" she heard Trent ask. She understood his intent. The conversation had been embarked upon for an entirely different reason, but while it was active, there was an opening to find out how their son felt. "You have not discussed it, but do you think of her as a future pairing partner?"

Trent watched his son's face as he considered the questions. He could see that Cesare appeared more confused by the questioning than embarrassed by it. Trent waited, letting the young man process his thoughts for as long as it would take.

"I…" Cesare began to say. Pushed to consider the idea, he made himself consider it for a few minutes. So far, pairing hadn't been something he'd given any thought to. He was only nineteen. He'd just begun his work with the tailor. He didn't feel ready for such a thing. "I did not know this happened this early," he finally said. "I have not considered it." He paused again, wanting to give an answer. "Esmeralda is my friend. How could I know?"

As Isabella saw the uncertainty in her son, she was reminded of the time before she'd met Trent. She'd been in the same position, wondering if she and Adrian were to be paired. They'd been such close friends then. They still were, but they'd spent many more hours together then than they ever had since she'd paired with Trent. It had been a confusing time for her and Adrian. She completely understood that being asked such a question could produce the same confusion in Cesare.

"Who has said such a thing?" Cesare asked, still surprised. "I have not spoken of this to anyone. I do not believe Esmeralda will have spoken of this to anyone. How could anyone think such a thing?"

Trent watched the faces of Isabella and their son. He knew Isabella's questions had flowed on from her having experienced an odd exchange with Elder Scott earlier in the day. Since she'd told him, Trent had decided to take more notice of the elder whenever he next saw him. The two didn't often cross paths. Regardless, Trent would keep an eye on the elder. Whatever it was that had tried to attack Isabella in the past had the ability to insert itself into the bodies and minds of others. He assumed that Elder Scott was as likely to become a host as Antonio and Kat had been.

Isabella had no desire to answer her son's questions. Her feeling about Elder Scott was only that - a feeling. So far, she'd had no symptoms that suggested something was going to happen, other than that feeling and the voice that she'd heard only a few times. It was too soon to know for sure if there was anything to worry about.

"It is of no concern at the present time," she said. "Your father and I simply wished to know if it was something you were considering."

"No, it is not," Cesare said, studying his mother's face. "We have never discussed it. I do not believe it is something either of us has considered or will consider in the near future."

Isabella nodded. "Very well," she said, dismissing the conversation.

Cesare knew when he'd been dismissed. Quietly, he left the table, his emotions mixed. While he'd never talked to Esmeralda about pairing with her, had *she* talked to someone about it? Before the conversation they'd had over their evening meal, he would never have thought she'd keep something so important from him.

That conversation had surprised him. Not only had something been happening to her that she'd kept from him, but she'd implied she'd kept it from him for a very long time. For a moment, he wondered what else she'd not told him.

He felt confused. He'd grown up beside Esmeralda. During their life as friends, he'd known of her inner turmoil and unhappiness. He'd watched her go through different emotions and stages in her life. There had been many things he'd seen her become upset or morose over. Despite her moods and her sometimes dark thoughts, the one thing he'd never doubted was her honesty with him and her openness.

Now he doubted both.

CHAPTER 26

As Trent and Isabella lay in bed, holding one another, Trent worried about her. To many, the small things that had begun to happen around Isabella might not have captured their attention. To Trent, they very likely meant something.

"What would you have done if Cesare had said he and Esmeralda *had* been talking about going through the pairing?" he asked, curious.

Isabella took a moment to think about the question. In truth, she hadn't asked about the pairing of the young friends because of the possibility.

"I did not think they had embarked into that conversation," she said. "If he had said it was something they were discussing, I am not sure how I would have advised him."

"They are both very young," Trent said. Even though in the world he'd left behind, eighteen and nineteen were ages that people *did* marry, he hadn't heard of anyone pairing so young in the village.

"Yes," Isabella replied, cuddling further into his chest. "I did not feel ready until I met you when I was twenty-one. I believe twenty is the age it is suggested. Cesare is not far off that age, but Esmeralda has another two years. I trust he will tell us when the time is right for him, and for her if she is his intended."

"They are always together…" Trent started to say before thinking about how things were in the village prior to his arrival.

As if understanding where his thinking had been going, Isabella spoke after she raised her head and kissed him lightly.

"Yes, as Adrian and I were before I met you," she said. "We were as close as Cesare and Esmeralda are now, but I did not feel certainty about pairing with him when he spoke of it."

Trent knew he didn't need to ask if she'd ever regretted not pairing with her lifelong friend. Since the day Trent had met her, Isabella had been open about how she felt about him, just as he'd been open about how he felt about her. He knew she sometimes experienced sadness over how Adrian's life had played out, paired with someone he wasn't happy with.

Thinking about Adrian and Kat, Trent focused on the latter. Day to day, he hardly saw Kat. Even during the times when Adrian dined with

Isabella and Trent, Kat was rarely seen. Where she went and what she did, Trent had no idea. He wasn't even sure that *Adrian* knew where she went and what she did. At one level, it didn't matter. Knowing that she'd easily been manipulated by an odd entity in the past placed some emphasis on wanting to know what she did, and with who.

"You are thinking too much," he heard Isabella say. Her words made him smile. He never fully turned off his thoughts to the strange instances of the village. For her, he happily tried to smile the thoughts away.

"I was," he said as he turned and nudged her onto her back. "I think it must be time for sleep," he said, teasing her before he plunged his mouth onto hers, kissing her passionately.

Feeling her body relax underneath him successfully put his own worries to rest - at least for the moment.

CHAPTER 27

As Elder Scott slept, the entity that resided deep within him was active. It was growing impatient. Although it had committed to waiting until the golden child of Isabella was old enough to join with the entity's own offspring, time seemed to be moving too slowly.

All it wanted was to seize the power of the village. It wasn't too much to ask. There were so many aspects to what it wanted and how it could get it. Standing in its way, most of all, were the ancients. Getting rid of them was a priority. They had the ability to sense the entity's presence in others. Although it had been successful in surprising them with its presence spreading over Kat and Antonio previously, Isabella had proven able to sense things that the entity wasn't aware she was sensing. That caused a deep frustration in it.

Getting rid of Isabella was most essential, but so was getting rid of her golden offspring. They were both anticipated to be the most powerful of the village in the future. Perhaps they were destined to become that, but their destiny wouldn't play out if only the entity could twist the ways of the village and inseminate Esmeralda with Cesare's seed. The being that would be created from their joining would be strong enough to eliminate Isabella and Cesare once and for all. After that, the entity could work just with Esmeralda, letting her know she was a part of it, and using her to help it in its quest.

In its thoughts, the entity smiled. It was a good plan - eliminate all other ancients, get Esmeralda and Cesare to join, then wait and guide their offspring to slaughter the newest ancients-to-be.

In its impatience, it began thinking about anything it could do in the present moment. It had long before assessed who in the village was malleable. There was no joy in completing those assessments. The villagers, as a whole, were strong people. Their bodies and minds were kept in the healthiest of states. There were still only two minds that the entity could easily get into - those of Kat and Antonio. That wasn't ideal. The entity suspected that both were constantly watched and monitored by Isabella and the ancient she spent time with.

Elder Rhys - that was who needed to be removed first, the entity acknowledged. He'd been seeing much of Isabella. The entity wasn't certain what was going on there, but it suspected they were always preparing for its return. It found satisfaction in knowing that they didn't know it was within someone who was a part of their lives. In that way, Elder Scott was the perfect host. Elders were revered in the small community. Nobody would suspect he was anything but good and pure.

With its impatience growing to a level that made the entity reactive rather than strategic, it began working its magic to enter the consciousness of Kat and Antonio. It didn't want Isabella to sense any change in them, but they could both be instrumental in at least eliminating one or more of the ancients of the village. That would make everything else far easier, especially if they could rid the community of Elder Rhys. As far as the entity was concerned, that particular ancient had far too much input into too many villagers' minds and hearts.

Feeling the connection complete with its two puppets, the entity turned its efforts to Esmeralda. It wanted her to want to pair with the golden boy as soon as possible. As always previously, when it tried to enter her mind, all it found was a wall. As always, the discovery angered it profusely. It wanted her strength - but not against itself.

CHAPTER 28

Esmeralda woke in the night. Around her was complete darkness, indicating it was nowhere close to sunrise. She'd felt exhausted when she'd gone to bed, expecting she would have an uneventful and constant sleep. Waking when she knew she hadn't slept long enough always added to her despondency.

As always, when she'd woken before she should have, she focused on her thoughts. As always, in her mind, she experienced that same familiar feeling. No matter what had driven her to wake at that moment, she was under the impression that something had just attempted to do something to her mind. She supposed she should have felt scared at the prospect. Instead, the increasing feeling of her head being invaded caused anger in her. Whoever it was - *whatever* it was - that was trying to push into her thoughts was increasing its efforts. What did they want? She knew nothing. She had no secret knowledge about anything…

That wasn't quite true, she realized. She had a secret that she shared with Cesare. Both of them had their ability to play their little game, summoning, playing, and striking with the small orbs of flame. It was such a small thing to both of them, but both had felt it was something they shouldn't share with others. Was that due to a childish selfishness of wanting to have something nobody else had, or was it because they each knew that something unpleasant could come from the knowledge being made public?

She pondered that possibility. Maybe it was just her intuition that held the secret inside. Maybe whatever was trying to get into her mind as often as it was, wanted that precise secret.

Frustrated by her mind thinking so much, she turned over onto her other side and closed her eyes again. She was old enough to know how the value of sleep affected her. It was hard enough to remain positive day to day. When she had nights of interrupted sleep, she felt even worse in the mornings. While she was thankful to have Cesare close by to at least try and cheer her up, she wished that she could find happiness in herself without having to rely on him.

At the edge of her mind, she felt another moment that made her think something was trying to get in. She shook her head in the frustration that was compounding by the minute. As hard as the effort to enter her head was, her head fought harder to keep it out. She supposed that in itself should have left her exhausted. It didn't. All it did was increase her wakefulness.

"Leave me alone!" she said out loud, whispering but with force.

Surprisingly, saying the words with her voice resulted in Esmeralda feeling the sensation lessen. She forced herself to take deep breaths, slowly in and slowly out. Focusing as she was, she felt the muscles around her body relax, letting go of the tenseness they'd felt moments earlier. Her mind moved from the chaotic state it had just been in to one of emptiness. A void was created, pushing from her mind any thoughts. Without intention, she'd done as she'd done many times before and moved into a state of calm meditation.

Finally, the body and the mind of Esmeralda found peace again, allowing her to fall into her much needed slumber.

CHAPTER 29

Cesare woke early with the conversation of the night before on his mind. Although he truly believed that Esmeralda hadn't even thought about them pairing, let alone spoken about it, there was enough uncertainty in his mind to cause in him some anxiety. She was his closest friend. He never wanted to hurt her or doubt her, but he *did* feel doubt.

For a moment, he considered avoiding her that morning. There had been rare moments when they'd not seen each other at or for the morning meal. Thinking about the possibility, he was saddened by the thought. He was also angry at himself for having *considered* such an idea. Throughout their years as friends, he'd always made sure he was there for her whenever she'd needed him. He didn't know what was for certain with regards to the pairing question. What he did know was that she had something much deeper going on, and she'd told him about it. If she'd held onto that for as long as she had and then told him, she must have very much needed him to know.

He climbed out of bed. Even though it might be uncomfortable facing her if there was any possibility she'd been talking about the two of them pairing, he still had to be there for her.

Before he walked out of his family home, he saw his father approach him.

"Are your heart and mind at rest, Cesare?" Trent asked.

Cesare nodded but didn't pretend to smile.

"They are," he said.

Seeing his father's look of acknowledgment, Cesare walked out into the dim sunlight. It was far earlier than he usually left his home, but he needed an escape. Knowing no other villagers would be there so early, he walked in the peaceful silence to the village pool.

As he waded into the warm water, he felt a familiar calm flow over him. It had been much needed. His mother asking him such questions so soon after Esmeralda had shared the secret she'd held from him for so many years had caused a feeling of chaos in what was usually a calm soul. He didn't like the feeling of uncertainty that was growing within him.

Relaxing back to lean against the pool wall, he closed his eyes. Although unable to pinpoint exactly what was coming, he felt like change *was* coming for him. He wished he could feel positive about that. He didn't. Although he had no idea what was going to change or how it was going to happen, the feeling was building and intensifying.

Looking around to make sure nobody could see, he raised one hand out of the water and quickly summoned a small golden flame onto his palm. There was reassurance in its warmth. The physical aspect of it calmed him, while the knowledge of it being a secret that only Esmeralda knew about gave him some strength. She had kept a secret from him, but he equally kept his secret from everyone else. Was it any different?

Not wanting to risk anyone seeing what he'd created in his hand, he used his mind to extinguish it and let his hand relax under the water again.

After a short time more, he climbed out and lay down on the drying stones. It was a different level of warmth they provided, heating his back first and then his front when he turned over.

When he was adequately clean and dry, he began his walk to where he knew Esmeralda would be. It might not be comfortable, but he would never let her down.

CHAPTER 30

Alessia lay in her bed for a long while. It had been an odd night of sleep. Although she could hear the thoughts of many during her waking hours, her mind continued to work through her visions of the night. Usually, upon waking, she could remember conversations and scenes that her mind had experienced through the nighttime hours. The night she was waking up from had been particularly busy and somewhat worrying.

While she saw and heard interesting thoughts and silent speeches that came from her oldest brother and his friend of many years, of more interest was another person trying to read *their* thoughts. Alessia had been sensing the occurrence more and more frequently. She didn't know who or what it was, but she could clearly see an attempted connection between the strange being and Esmeralda, in particular. Alessia's concern over that was lessened by the fact that she could equally visualize Esmeralda's mind closing itself off to the effort. It was an intriguing thing for Alessia to watch and sense - something attempting to get into Esmeralda's mind. While Alessia's mind took her there without intention, and Esmeralda's mind either didn't know she was there or didn't mind, it most definitely did continue to reject the effort of whatever or whoever else was trying to get in. Knowing that made it easier for Alessia to relax and not worry about it.

She'd also sensed the same thing trying to get into Cesare's mind. With that effort, it had succeeded to a degree but had appeared to remove itself when it had found nothing of interest. While visualizing what had been going on, Alessia had been able to sense the dissatisfaction of what was trying to get into her brother's mind. Whatever it had been seeking, it didn't appear to have found.

The strangest thing of all, for Alessia, was the knowledge that although she could see into the minds of so many, nobody could see into hers. Of that, she did not doubt. Everyone who knew her viewed her as quiet and hardly thinking at all. While that certainly wasn't true, she liked them thinking that. She liked that nobody knew how much she constantly had to see, hear, and feel. The words, thoughts, and scenes that emanated from the minds of others into her own were sometimes unbearable, but she continued to teach herself each day how to be selective and not let too much in.

The thoughts of most, she knew she needn't dwell on. They were innocent and mostly about the day to day aspects of the village and the villagers' work. Now and then, she'd been subjected to thoughts that she regarded as hugely private. Those thoughts, she'd worked hard to instantly jump out of, and lock her mind against.

The only thoughts that presently held her attention were the ones surrounding her mother, father, and oldest brother. Indirectly, she'd made Esmeralda part of that group. She knew Esmeralda, having watched her as Cesare's friend for as long as she could remember, but that was a side aspect from the intrigue of knowing something or someone else had a particular interest in the young woman with the blue-black hair.

While Alessia hadn't yet seen anything to push her to declare her ability to anyone, she was committed to continuing to monitor all that was happening. If something caught her attention that looked vital, she'd share it with her mother and father. Until that day came, she'd keep everything to herself, safe within her mind.

CHAPTER 31

Cesare stood at his usual spot, waiting for Esmeralda to emerge from her family home. He felt uncomfortable but didn't want to. He had to keep reminding himself that nobody had said Esmeralda had talked about any desire for the two of them to pair. His mother had said *someone* had suggested it as something wanted. The words she'd used hadn't absolutely indicated that Esmeralda had said anything at all.

When he saw the door open, Cesare put on the best smile that he could. Seeing her, he didn't know what kind of mood she was in. That never truly showed itself until they'd been in each other's presence for at least a few minutes. She was as good as he was at plastering on a fake smile to cover up any negative thoughts that might be simmering internally.

As she approached him, he looked closely at her face. There was nothing different about her.

"Are you well, Cesare?" Esmeralda asked. "You seem concerned about something."

The way that he was looking at her unnerved her slightly. She'd thought she knew all of his facial expressions and body stances. Even though he'd been waiting for her, just as he usually did, something *wasn't* usual.

Cesare studied her face further before replying.

"Yes, I am well," he said.

For a moment, he considered not saying anything to her. Another moment later, he changed his mind. If he didn't speak, it could fester. He knew he didn't want that to happen between them.

"I would like us to talk alone," he said, instantly seeing the surprise on her face.

Esmeralda nodded. She felt nervous, as if something not good was about to happen.

"Of course," she said before watching him begin to walk toward the spot where the two of them usually played their private little flame game.

When they reached their location and were both sure that nobody could see or hear them, Esmeralda watched him while waiting for him to speak.

Cesare played questions and words over in his mind. What was he so worried about? His mother had asked him one or two questions. It was nothing to be concerned about or even give thought to. Regardless, he knew it would be on his mind if he didn't speak.

"Esmeralda, we are good friends," he started to say. Seeing her nod with a confused look on her face made him realize he hadn't said anything she didn't already know. He took a moment to consider how to ask the question he wanted an answer to, without seeming accusatory. "My mother and father asked me last night if I'd thought about the pairing process yet," he said.

Esmeralda was surprised by the declaration but only nodded and waited for him to continue.

"I… I am uncertain if you and I are destined for that," Cesare said, stumbling forward in his words. "What are your thoughts?"

"Cesare," Esmeralda said, wondering from where the subject had emerged. "The pairing process is something that my mother and father *have* talked to me about, but I do not consider myself old enough for it yet." She paused and watched his face, wondering if he would be relieved or upset by what she'd said. "I have no thoughts about you and I being destined for becoming paired, as I have no thoughts about being paired at all. I am sure the day will come when I give thought to that, but that day is not yet here."

She waited in silence, wondering how he was feeling. Nothing about his stance or facial expression gave her a clue. After a long while, she moved up to him, almost touching his chest with hers.

"Did you *want* me to consider you and I pairing?" she asked out of curiosity. "Is that what this is about?"

Cesare shook his head.

"No," he said quietly, aware that he didn't want to hurt her feelings in any way. "That is, I also had not thought about the possibility. I feel too young also."

"Why do you seem concerned?" Esmeralda asked. "What has driven your mother and father to bring up such a thing? Do *they* wish for you to pair so soon?"

"Not that I am aware of," Cesare said, beginning to feel embarrassed that he'd brought the subject up at all. He should have trusted his gut instinct that had told him that Esmeralda wouldn't have been the source of the subject. "My mother said someone suggested our pairing."

"Who?" Esmeralda asked, a slight panic beginning as she wondered if it could be the same person that had been trying to get into her mind. "*Who* was it, Cesare?"

"I know not," he said. "I am sorry, Esmeralda. I wanted to ask because of what my mother said. I do not know any further details that I can share with you. All I have been able to think about since she asked me about it was whether I was going to hurt you somehow."

In a rare instance, Esmeralda smiled a true smile.

"I do not believe that you could ever hurt me, Cesare," she said. "Neither of us are old enough to worry about the pairing process. We are still young. We still play childish games," she continued, relieved to finally see a small smile grace his face. "We do not need to worry about this. I have never heard of any two people being forced to pair. It is unlikely it will happen to us."

Cesare nodded, feeling the relief settle across his heart, his mind, and his body.

"I am fortunate to have you as my friend," he said.

"And *I* am fortunate to have you as *my* friend," Esmeralda responded. "Come. Let us go to eat and not speak of this again - at least for a long while. Whoever has said such a thing to your mother does not know how we truly feel about each other as friends. It is nothing to dwell on."

As the two of them turned and began walking toward the dining area, Esmeralda felt her panic increase. She fought hard not to show it, but the timing of 'someone' having mentioned such a thing worried her, as did her feeling like someone was intent on reading her thoughts. They were probably two completely separate things. Instead, they felt like they'd compounded onto one another.

She said nothing more that was serious as they ate together. Inside, she realized her turmoil had just risen another level.

While they ate, Cesare felt relaxed. He'd wondered if anything uncomfortable was about to happen between the two of them. He'd been worried about nothing. They'd continue to be friends. They'd continue to be there for each other as they needed to be. Neither of them wanted to change that. Whoever had spoken to his mother had done so with incorrect knowledge. It was a relief, and it was something to smile about.

From across the dining area, eyes watched them. Inside of Antonio was a further division of the entity. As always, it was driven to watch Esmeralda - its offspring. It was determined to guide her to be with Cesare so that another level of offspring could be created, then used to extinguish Cesare and his mother.

As Antonio's consciousness flowed in and out, the real soul of him was unaware, yet again, that it was being used. Now and then, he had snippets of memories of being with Kat, and of Esmeralda being of his seed. As time was passing, he was losing more and more of himself as the entity geared up to use him once more in another fight.

"I shall move on with my day now, Antonio," he heard Ariana say from where she sat beside him.

Turning to look at her, the entity let the real Antonio move to the forefront of his mind. Antonio leaned forward and kissed the woman he'd paired with decades earlier. He knew he'd loved her then and still loved her deeply. He just wished that he didn't keep having periods of time when he felt like he'd lost time. It had happened before, and it was happening again. The worst thing about that was that increasingly longer periods of time appeared to be disappearing on him.

Seeing the look on Ariana's face told him that she had no idea he'd been vacant for the previous minutes. To him, she appeared to have thought he was there with her, listening to her talk. It saddened Antonio. He *wanted* to always be there with her, listening to her speak. Why he had the periods when he wasn't, he couldn't understand.

"Wait," he said, standing up just after she had. When she turned back to face him, he moved forward, pulled her into a bold embrace, and kissed her deeply.

He could tell she was surprised when they pulled apart. He could also see that she wasn't disappointed. They'd had a long period when they'd not been intimate earlier on in their pairing. That period was long gone. Both of them enjoyed their intimacy and could indulge in it openly, with their offspring having their own homes and families.

Offspring. As the thought crossed his mind, he automatically turned and looked at Esmeralda. As his authentic self, he didn't know why he was drawn to look at the girl with the blue-black hair.

"I will see you later," he heard Ariana say to him, drawing his attention back to her.

He smiled in response, hating being so confused.

CHAPTER 32

As Isabella entered the great library in the temple under instruction from Elder Rhys, she was in awe. It wasn't the first time she'd been in the great room. She didn't know why, but it gave her peace. When she'd first begun her training to become an ancient, she'd spent much time in there. In more recent years, she'd visited it less often.

Walking through the hidden door with Elder Rhys by her side, she did as she always had upon entry. Stopping still, she looked upward. On the ceiling were paintings of the most incredible colors. Elder Rhys had told her that they told stories about the village in the past. They'd been painted long before he'd been born. Knowing that he was more than 600 years old told Isabella just how old the village and its walls must have been.

Appreciating the vibrancy of the colors, she also appreciated how much gold had been used across the ceiling. It gleamed in the images that someone had taken time to paint. It also showed in the square-shaped trim that framed each one. It wasn't quite the same as the giant golden stone she and Trent had seen in the cave when he'd passed into her time, but it was still beautiful.

Elder Rhys allowed her the time to be silent and still. He never stayed with her in the great library anymore, but he never left until he'd watched her have that first moment. There were many things about the strength that emanated from Isabella. Those things amplified when she stopped still and just looked at the ceiling in the great library. At those moments, her face took on an appearance of serenity and calm. Those things, Elder Rhys didn't always see on her face.

Having had her fill of the day's first glances around the room and ceiling, Isabella broke herself out of her trance and looked at the elderly man beside her.

"Thank you, Elder Rhys," she said, smiling. "I shall read now."

Isabella watched as the ancient smiled, nodded, then retreated out of the door. Once alone in the vast room, she took her time walking around the walls. Stories were told through images around the top half of each wall. She'd studied them many times but always felt she could read them again and again. There was so much more to read in the room, and she would move on to the ancient scrolls soon enough. Before she did, it was her ritual to interpret what she could from the paintings that moved in a forward fashion clockwise around the walls.

When she reached the image that showed the golden stone she'd seen two decades earlier, she stopped. It was an image that always captured and held her attention. As far as images went, it wasn't complex. The power it exuded as it detailed the golden stone emanating a bright light as someone touched it was invigorating to look at. She'd looked at it many times. Each time, she found herself looking at the person who was touching the rock. It was a man, but who was he? Was he the one who had painted the stories on the walls of the temple? Was he one of the men who had *built* the temple? She'd once asked Elder Rhys about it. He hadn't provided any insight, other than to tell her that she might find her answers within the scrolls.

Allowing herself one more minute to look at that one image, she remembered one reason why she liked it. The figure in it had golden hair - the same color as Cesare's. When she'd first noticed it, she'd been surprised. Nobody that she knew of had ever seen such hair color before he'd been born. That didn't mean it had never before existed, just that the current living villagers hadn't seen anyone with hair like that. When Cesare had been born with his head covered in the golden locks, Isabella had wondered about it but then dismissed her wonder as she'd grown to accept it was what it was. When she'd first visited the great temple library and seen that image for the first time, her curiosity about it had reignited.

Knowing she'd never find any answers or gain any further knowledge from the images on the walls, she turned toward the shelves in the room. In slots were thousands of scrolls, Isabella had guessed. She'd pulled out many of them and read them. She knew that some contained stories of people who had lived in the village and then had passed on. Those scrolls, she'd moved on from fairly quickly. They were interesting, but they provided nothing that captured her.

Walking to the other side of the room, she focused on a second wall of shelves. In those, she knew were the more intriguing scrolls. She'd read four of them in her previous visit. In those scrolls was detailed information about the ancients and the powers they could possess.

Pulling out one scroll she'd previously not read, Isabella walked to the one seat in the room. Settling in, she rested her body as her mind began to absorb details about the golden stone and the golden glows she'd experienced. They were the sources of most intrigue to her. She'd experienced both. She wanted to know how they'd come to be in existence and what their ultimate purpose was.

Two hours into her reading, her mind grew alert as a growing-familiar voice spoke inside her head.

'They are needed to create the next level of being.'

Isabella closed her eyes and focused, trying to determine where the voice was coming from and who it belonged to. Once again, the voice faded before it made her party to whatever conversation it was having. Isabella felt frustrated but resolved she could do nothing - not yet at least.

CHAPTER 33

As Trent worked in the garden, he took a moment to stand still with his face upturned toward the sun. It was something he'd done several times every day over the time he'd been in the ancient village. It was a simple action but made him remember to appreciate the wonderful life that he was living. Basking in the warmth of the sun and the air, it was a form of meditation in itself to close his eyes and enjoy the simplicity of it.

"You look at peace, Trent," he heard a voice say after a few minutes of his tranquil action.

When he opened his eyes, he saw Elder Scott approaching. While he'd had little interaction with the elder during his time in the village, Trent was wary. Isabella had explained it was the elder who had suggested the pairing of Cesare and Esmeralda. With it being unknown *where* he'd formed such an idea when the two of them were under the usual age of pairing, Trent was curious to know what the elder sought.

"Elder Scott," he greeted the elderly man as he reached where Trent stood. "It is not usual to see you here in the garden. What can we help you with today?"

The elder smiled at Trent. He wasn't sure why he felt so inspired to go and suggest the pairing of Trent's son. It had been a growing idea inside of him that he couldn't shake. Never having felt such a strong need for such an action in the village before, Elder Scott was both excited and driven in his quest.

"I wish to talk to you about young Cesare and Esmeralda," he said.

Trent was both surprised and not surprised by the statement. He expected Elder Scott knew Isabella would have told Trent about his effort in making her consider the idea the day before. Most people in the village would have known that Isabella wasn't someone who would bow down to Trent or anyone else. It made no sense that the elder would attempt to sway Trent in an effort to then sway Isabella.

"Oh, yes?" Trent asked, trying to hide his suspicion.

"Yes," Elder Scott said, grinning. "They are very much in love. We can all see that. It would be to the advantage of the village population if they were to pair, do you not agree?"

"My son is not yet twenty, Elder Scott," Trent replied, closely monitoring the face of the man before him. "Is that not the age that pairings are considered for the young people of the village?"

Elder Scott nodded, his smile only slightly fading.

"It is true," he said. "I do believe, however, that when two people are certain that they wish to spend their lives together..."

"Do they?" Trent interrupted. When he saw the elder's confused look, he expanded on his question. "*Do* they wish to pair and spend their lives together?"

"Oh, I believe it is evident that they do," the elder replied, his grin resurrecting once again. "Anyone who sees them can see that."

"It is true that Cesare and Esmeralda are close friends," Trent said, nodding. "Are you sure that means they wish to pair? Has someone *told* you this?"

The grin faltered once more. In truth, Elder Scott had no idea why he thought the young people wanted to pair. He just had the strong compulsion that it must be true, and it must be his job to make sure it happened.

"No," he replied, a feeling of vagueness flowing through him. "I do not..." he began to continue before his consciousness was ripped from him completely.

Trent watched the change in the face of the elder. It wasn't dissimilar to the changes he'd seen on Kat and Antonio during the moments of battle within the temple. Inside, he felt the distinct emotion of dread. Coming to the belief that Elder Scott had an entity inside of him, Trent closed his mind and focused to make sure it couldn't be truthfully read.

He remained silent, clearing his thoughts while focusing on the elder's face and waiting for him to speak again. When Elder Scott did, it was very noticeable to Trent that it wasn't the same person. While the voice was certainly similar, the tone was completely different.

"It is required that the population be inspired to grow," the face of Elder Scott said. "It is the belief of the elders and ancients that Cesare and Esmeralda are destined to be together, so shall be."

Trent nodded, framing diplomatic words so he didn't at all sound like he suspected Elder Scott was not himself at that moment.

"They may well be destined to be paired to one another," he said. "If they are, destiny shall be happy to wait until it is their time. Not only is Cesare only nineteen, but Esmeralda is another year younger still. I do not believe anyone of only eighteen years of age has been forced to go through the pairing, have they?"

The mood of the entity within Elder Scott changed to sullenness. Everything could all be so easy if only there was no objection to what it needed to become the most powerful being. It wasn't powerful enough yet to bring Isabella and all the ancients down, but it would be, if only it could move things forward for its ultimate plan.

Trent watched Elder Scott shake his head and force a small smile onto his face.

"It is the responsibility of all to contribute to the maintenance of the population," the entity said through the face of the elder. "However, we shall wait until the time is right," it continued before walking away fuming.

CHAPTER 34

At their almost-nightly play, Cesare and Esmeralda set themselves up and embarked on their game. As much as Esmeralda teased Cesare about not being as good as her in the small matches they held, she did want him to get good enough to beat her far more often than he did. At different times, she'd wondered if he always let her beat him on purpose. In more recent times, she didn't think he did. They were as powerful as each other in summoning and letting the flame orbs fly. He was just slower in his response to avoid the ones she directed at him.

Her mind distracted, both were surprised when the orb that Cesare let fly swiftly struck Esmeralda's arm. When the initial feeling of surprise had passed, she saw the smile that graced his face. She was happy to see it. In most things, it seemed like he was wiser and better because he was older than her. In their small battles, she knew it was he who could learn from her.

"Well played," she called out to him. "I shall not make it so easy for you again, Golden Boy."

Cesare chuckled and shook his head. Although he knew she was teasing him, he equally knew that she was being truthful. He understood and had long before accepted their differences in level of skill in the small game they'd created between themselves.

He watched as she formed another blue ball of flame on her palm. As much as he enjoyed the warmth of the golden flames he could produce himself, whenever he saw her summon her blue flames, they held his view captive, enticing him with their cool blue.

Esmeralda watched his face and easily anticipated his next move. She wanted him to improve his skills. Although it was only a childish game that they'd invented, as she had begun to feel something that made her increasingly feel uneasy, she'd considered that their game might be useful for something else. She had no idea what the intent was of whatever had been pressing on her mind. She didn't know its intention or if she would ever see it in real life. If she did, was it intending to hurt her in some way, or hurt someone she knew?

Looking at Cesare, she felt a new determination. She would never let anyone hurt him. They might not be destined to pair and live their lives together in the formation of a family. That didn't matter. He'd always been there for her. If any threat was made against him, she would be by his side.

Her chain of thought was broken as she watched Cesare put his hands down and walk toward her.

"You are distracted," he said when he reached her. "Are you still worried about what you talked about earlier?"

Esmeralda almost shook her head. Changing her mind about attempting to cover up her concerns, she nodded instead.

"A little," she replied.

"Could you be mistaken, Esmeralda?" Cesare asked. "I have never heard of such a thing happening among our people."

"I agree," Esmeralda replied. "It is not something I have heard of either but, Cesare, have you ever heard of anything happening like *we* can do?"

"No," he said, shaking his head. "It is true that you and I have the ability to do something I am not sure anyone else can do. It is, therefore, unfair of me to have uncertainty about what you have shared with me."

Esmeralda put a sad smile on her face.

"It is not only you who has doubts," she said. "I have them also. It is only a feeling that I have. I do not know if what I am sensing is real and true. It could be something else, or it could be nothing."

"I do not believe it will be nothing," Cesare reassured her as he placed a hand on her arm. "You would not have such thoughts if there was not something true behind them." He paused as they studied each other's eyes. "Have you considered talking to your mother and father about this?"

The mood was broken. Although Esmeralda knew he didn't fully understand how disconnected her family was from each other, she pulled away in dismay.

"I will not speak to them," she said. "My years of being around my mother have proven to me how little she regards me and how little interest she has in what I am doing or feeling. My father, in contrast, I do believe would be happy to listen to whatever I say, but he would laugh away my concerns. He would not know how to act or to help."

As he had many times during their years as friends, Cesare felt saddened as he listened to her speak. Although he had no interest in spending time with his parents, he was continually thankful that he had them and that he respected them. They'd always been there when he'd needed them, and he knew they always would be. He wished Esmeralda had the same thing. He suspected she would always have the same heartache inside of her because of the coldness of her mother.

"I shall be here for you … always," he said before holding up his arms.

Esmeralda gladly walked into them. Although she'd been honest in saying she was too young to consider going through the pairing process, she did know one thing for certain - she wanted him by her side for always.

CHAPTER 35

The entity came and went in its consciousness, using Elder Scott as its host. Knowing the elder's mind and body wouldn't be enough to bring down an ancient, the entity had also spread its sub-consciousness once again to Antonio and Kat. Although Kat didn't feel it, she was being primed for manipulation all over again. Antonio, on the other hand, was having a harder time accepting the entity taking control of him.

Day to day, as the entity monitored what was happening in each of its sub-hosts, it could feel Antonio's increasing resistance. It added to the growing frustration and anger of the entity. Previously, Antonio had easily been taken over. The entity had guided him for more than two years without Antonio realizing he wasn't in control of himself. Since the last battle, he hadn't been as easy to control.

In its efforts to keep the manipulation going, the entity not only spent more time in the head of Antonio but also did so with increasing power. Although it had no body of its own, the strength it had to use to keep Antonio's true consciousness at bay felt exhausting. The ideal solution would have been to find another host. Every now and then, the entity would reach out and test others. There were no suitable candidates for that in the village. As dismaying as it was, the other villagers just weren't as pliable as Kat and Antonio.

The other source of exhaustion to the entity was its continuing attempts to enter Esmeralda's mind. It had a clear plan for her. Manipulating her was essential for that plan to work. That she could hold her mind so closed off for so long told the entity just how strong she was. That both pleased it and angered it. It wanted her to be the strong being that it had always believed she would be. It just didn't want her to use that strength against *it*.

Periodically, the entity had to re-evaluate what it ultimately wanted and how it was going to take it. The power it wanted was held captive by two aspects of the ancient village - the large golden stone with its veins flowing underneath the township, and the ancients themselves. The former, the entity would never be able to take without removing the latter first.

The combined power residing in the ancients was considerable. Each of them was powerful enough as an individual. Together, they were almost indestructible. The only way to take them all out would be to take one out at a time. As the entity did that, it was hopeful that it could simultaneously seize that ancient's power for itself. If it could layer each ancient's power within its own consciousness, then find a suitable young host to live in, it could easily work toward the second part of its plan - to take control of the golden stone.

It had tried to gain the same power in the future. In that, the entity had failed. Not only had it destroyed itself, but it had also destroyed the entire village and all who resided within it. From that mistake, it had learned before it had pushed its consciousness back in time to try all over again. This time it wouldn't fail. With more patience and determination than previously, it would gain power and take full control while keeping the village alive and receptive to its efforts. Without ancients, it would be ruler, and it would make all of the villagers bow down to it.

In essence, it would become their god.

CHAPTER 36

Elder Rhys lay on his bed in the quiet of the evening, pondering how things might go within the village in the near future. He'd had no visions of the night himself. He'd equally not seen any visions of the night belonging to anyone else. It wasn't enough to alarm him, but it did play on his mind. Previously, he'd had the ability to see the occasional night vision that one villager or another was having, including Isabella. She'd recently told him that she'd been hearing a voice in her head. No visions of the night had accompanied that. It was a source of curiosity for the ancient.

With some foresight into the future, Elder Rhys knew that another strike from whatever - *whoever* - it was that intended Isabella harm might alter the village for good. The villagers had no idea how important the role of the ancients was in sustaining the golden stone that helped them to survive. In front of the general population, even the ancients who openly displayed some of their responsibilities kept most hidden. That was the way it had to be. The ancients hiding their powers away from others helped in hiding who the ancients actually were. Although the village had hardly any history of violence, it wasn't worth the risk to reveal who every ancient was. If one fell, others had to resume their place.

Elder Rhys felt tired. He knew he was approaching a maximum age for an ancient. He didn't fear passing on to begin his next journey. He did fear leaving Isabella, Trent, and the other villagers, before knowing they were safe. He turned over to sleep to ready for another day.

CHAPTER 37

Over the following weeks, Trent and Isabella increased their training. While there was little variety to it, both knew that there was ongoing room for improvement. Isabella was close to perfecting her ability to summon one golden flame after another in short succession. Trent was a little further from perfect in his attempts to do so. He could summon the flames, but it still took him a great deal of time, concentration, and encouragement. If they went into battle, it was possible he'd have none of those to fall back on.

Trent worked hard but couldn't stop his growing nervousness. He didn't want to let anyone down, especially Isabella. The previous battles hadn't hurt her in any way. From Trent's viewpoint both times, it hadn't seemed like she *could* be hurt from such a small battle. The unknown was what would happen if Isabella was seriously hit by one or more of the blue orbs of flame. She'd escaped them so far. Trent hoped she could continue to do so.

Isabella watched him. His face, his body stance, and his words all told her that he felt like he wasn't doing enough. She knew it was hard for him. He didn't naturally have the power in him that she had in her. There had been plenty of times when Isabella had wanted to tell him not to worry about training and instead let her do it all. She hadn't said such a thing. Not only could it have hurt Trent, but it could also impact any future battle they might have.

"Again," she called out to him during their latest training session.

Trent focused on his hands. Having increased their training frequency again, at least reliably summoning a golden flame at will was getting easier by the day. The biggest difficulty he continued to have was firing the golden orbs and accurately hitting ones that were flying around in the air. He knew it might not be something he *needed* to excel at, but he wanted to regardless. He'd seen the strange balls of blue flame emanate from Kat and Antonio. He wanted to be sure that he could hit one if he needed to.

Watching the golden orbs of flame that Isabella had summoned and sent into the air, Trent strengthened his focus on them. He could tell that she was purposely avoiding them having any set pattern. While a small part of him wished she'd make it easier for him, he knew she couldn't.

They were working toward being able to coordinate a counter-attack together. There could be no guessing what any rival blue flames would do, or how they would move.

"Stop thinking, Trent!" Isabella called out to him.

As soon as he heard her words, Trent threw the balls of golden flame. One directly after the other, he watched as they each connected with one of the orbs that had been moving around the room.

"Good!" Elder Rhys called out, pleased with the progress he could see Trent making in his training. "Again!"

Isabella wasted no time in summoning two more orbs and distributing them up into the space above their heads. Almost straight away, she saw Trent summon two more of his own and throw them. The result made Isabella grin. Without any prompting or taking time to think, Trent had hit the targets again.

She smiled at him, pleased. There was a long way to go in the two of them perfecting a counter-attack, but they were well on their way.

CHAPTER 38

Without fail, Kat left the mill at the end of every day with the intention of going to dine, going to bathe, and then going to sleep. She'd been doing the routine for so many years that she never questioned the possibility of living her life in any other way. Only now and then did she stop to sit down and think about who she was and how her life had played out.

As she sat in the warm water of the village pool, she felt nervousness within her. It had been growing and intensifying in recent times. The thing that surprised her most of all was that there was a familiarity with the feeling. Sometimes it felt like she'd experienced it before but couldn't remember when.

She shook her head in an attempt to stop the feeling and the thoughts associated with it. For the duration it took for her to climb out of the warm water and lie down on one of the long drying stones, the attempt was successful. As soon as she lay down and tried to find some enjoyment from the warmth that came from above and below, the nervousness returned.

Generally, she wasn't unhappy with her life. She believed she didn't have the same relationship with Adrian that other women in the village had with the men they'd paired with. That was of no concern to her. Although she could remember some eagerness about wanting to pair in her youth, there was vagueness even in that. She still didn't entirely remember having consented to pairing with Adrian. She equally didn't remember having ever joined with him.

The memories weren't entirely missing. Sometimes she'd see a snippet of one or another in her mind. They were visions that seemed to be centered around her, but she saw them like watching them happening to someone else. There had been many times when she'd believed that if Esmeralda didn't exist - if there was no proof of Kat ever having given birth to a child - she would have found it difficult to consider she'd ever joined with a man. She had no recollection of the process. She had no idea what it entailed or how it had been when she'd been with Adrian that way.

Adrian. That was another ongoing source of thoughts for her. They'd been paired for a great number of years. He'd stayed by her side throughout all of that time, as was the way of their people. She wasn't oblivious to his obvious lack of happiness. He hid it well, pushing it behind his façade of a smile and a cheerful voice. While Kat conceded she didn't know him as well as she should have after so long, she did have the ability to identify when he was attempting to hide his true feelings.

Did he regret having paired with her? That question, she could never answer. Did she regret having paired with him? Sometimes she did. She had no recollection of why she'd agreed to it. She supposed things had been better between them then, but the memories of that time in her life continued to be vague. There was no certainty about what were real memories and what were some odd form of created falsehood in her mind.

'Esmeralda is of age to pair,' a voice suddenly said in her mind. 'You are needed to make this happen,' it continued. 'You are important, Kat. You are needed.'

Kat heard the words. She could've been surprised by hearing them in her mind. She wasn't. Like a modern-day light switch being flicked, that was the moment Kat's true consciousness was ripped away from her, put into hibernation like it was an item that was boxed up and put on a shelf to be used again another day.

CHAPTER 39

Although the days passed at their regular pace, to the entity that Elder Scott hosted, it felt like time was moving increasingly slower. It had already spent too much time waiting for Esmeralda and Cesare to grow. The waiting began to add to the mounting and almost unbearable frustration that it felt.

Now and then, it would attempt to move forward or back in time to try and cheat time itself. It didn't work. It was stuck in the daily grind of village life, just as the villagers themselves were. There was yet more frustration that came from that.

Although the entity continued to try and manipulate all players in its plan for ultimate power, there were also times when it tried to be still. Its own mind sometimes felt crazed in its efforts to consider so many people and the many ways they could help it in its quest.

It also tried to remember its life in the past. There was never success or pleasure that came from that. The entity was sure that it had lived as a human, complete with its own body. It was just as sure that it had been a villager in the village that it now wanted to control. Who it had been, and what role it had played, evaded the entity's mind. Its memory of times past was non-existent when it tried to pull forward any visualization of its previous life. Why that was, it had no comprehension.

Without even knowing why, it was compelled to keep moving forward in its plans. There was a need within the entity that drove it on, no matter how difficult everything seemed at different times. There was a destiny that needed to be upheld. It was sure of that, even though it had no conscious thought about where the idea had come from. It was destined to be the greatest being, and have the greatest following. It was meant to rule. It was meant to have ultimate power over the land, the structures, and all of the people of the village. Why was that? The answer to that question was never known. It was just as it was meant to be. The entity maintained that belief and adhered to the plan that would enable it to make its destiny a reality.

Dissatisfied with the lack of knowledge it could gather even about its own life, the entity scattered its consciousness.

Jumping to Antonio first, the entity could tell that the man's mind continued to fight with attempts of invasion into its actions and thoughts.

The entity pushed its power to dissolve Antonio's true consciousness. It hadn't been as difficult to manipulate him on previous occasions. It was growing more difficult with every attempt the entity made.

Looking through Antonio's mind, the entity could see that parts of its real life were happy. Antonio was satisfied with his work life and his home life. Before the previous battle that his mind and body had been used for, he had experienced a long period of little intimacy with his paired partner, Ariana. Around and since the time of the last battle, their intimacy had not only resumed but had thrived. The entity often sensed the intense pleasure that Antonio experienced. While the entity accepted it as part of who Antonio was and how he lived his life, it was less acceptable with the entity's plan. It wanted Antonio all to itself. There was no room for Ariana as a constant distraction.

The entity focused harder still. If it needed to, it would do something to remove Ariana from Antonio's consciousness. The time for that hadn't yet arrived. In truth, the entity wasn't sure if losing Ariana would make Antonio stronger or destroy him, making him even less susceptible to mind manipulation. It was a risk the entity wasn't yet willing to take. There were only two villagers among the thousands who resided in the community who were malleable at all. The entity wasn't so impatient that it would act hastily in any way that might prove detrimental to its own plans.

At that moment, the entity projected the image of Esmeralda into Antonio. It was an effort to remind the sub-host of its role in her creation. In Antonio's true consciousness, he didn't completely remember his time with Kat. The entity had pushed snippets of images into Antonio's mind, but as yet, the man hadn't fully accepted them.

The entity pushed harder. Although time appeared to be slowing down, it wanted Antonio's mind all to itself. The main players in the village might consider Esmeralda and Cesare too young to pair. When enough time had passed for that to change, the entity wanted its players to be primed and ready, fully under its control.

After one final push about Kat and Esmeralda into Antonio's mind, the entity scattered its view to Kat. In assessing her state of mind, it was pleased. She was as malleable as she had been on the previous two occasions. That pleased the entity. It was the one easy part of its ultimate plans. Kat had very little memory of how she'd been used previously, and the people who knew had collectively decided not to tell her too much about it. That was best for her, for those who knew, and for the entity itself. Manipulating her mind was something that could be done from a clean slate of effort. Her mind was as open in the current time as it had been two decades earlier.

Into her mind, the entity pushed the idea about Esmeralda pairing with Cesare. With its growing impatience to make something happen and move forward *somehow*, the entity shared with her the beauty of a child that could be born from the match. It was a risk, pushing such an image into Kat's mind. The entity knew she wasn't a naturally maternal woman. She'd contributed to the raising of her child, but only with limited effort. For the most part, Kat had left the teaching of Esmeralda to Adrian. It was difficult to know if she could be swayed by the prospect of another generation of her family or not.

As the entity studied her thoughts, it found surprise in where her current thought processes had taken her. She was questioning her pairing with Adrian. She was also wondering why she couldn't *remember* pairing with Adrian. That was not good. If Kat questioned her memories too much, she might do as her daughter had done and close her mind.

It was at that moment that the entity closed Kat's true consciousness off completely. There could be no more subtle suggestion. When Kat threatened to question her memories as Antonio had been, the entity's sub-conscious moved to take her over completely.

The entity was elated. Its sub-consciousness easily moved into Kat's mind, thoughts, body, and feelings. There was no wall to push through. There was no more questioning in her soul about what was real.

Through Kat, the entity could begin to move everyone closer to accepting that Esmeralda and Cesare had to pair. Once that happened, the stronger being would be created. With Esmeralda and the offspring to help it, plus Kat and Antonio in their altered consciousness present at the right moment, the entity would be able to easily take down Isabella, Cesare, and possibly even Elder Rhys all at the same time.

Continuing to smile in its mind, the entity pushed the idea harder into Kat while simultaneously pushing images of memories into Antonio. Time had been passing slowly. The entity was gleeful that with its efforts, time was about to speed up once again.

CHAPTER 40

Esmeralda sat on one of the drying stones near the village's pool. Having bathed and then laid down in the sunshine until she'd felt dry, she looked around her. She'd never seen any place or thing other than what was housed within the large walls she saw every day. On occasion, she'd wondered what was beyond them. She'd never asked if anyone knew.

Although she'd always been dissatisfied and not entirely happy, she didn't have any desire to leave the village even if it had been possible. She had Cesare as her close friend. That wasn't the only consideration she expected she'd have to allow for if she'd wanted to try and leave. In the core of her soul, she suspected that no matter where she went, she would always be herself. The feelings she experienced day to day, week to week, and month to month were deep inside of her. They weren't driven by external things happening around or to her. No matter where she went or what she did, she would always feel the same way.

She cast her mind back to the previous evening and her game with Cesare. Even though they'd been playing their childish game for many years, he never seemed to improve to the point where he could easily succeed in winning. She didn't know how that could be. She supposed she was improving at the same rate as he was, making it impossible for him to ever catch up to her in his skill level. Maybe that was the reason she hit him with her orbs far more often than he hit her with his.

There was no real reason to ponder such a thing. It was only a made-up game from when they'd been very young. She wasn't sure why they still played it or gained satisfaction from it. In recent times, it had felt like the game had changed, moving from childish play to preparation for something more important. She had no idea how that could be. There seemed little that ever happened in the village that could require their assistance in such a way.

"Esmeralda!" she heard her mother's voice call out to her from the path that led to the pool area.

Esmeralda turned, deeply surprised. Kat rarely spoke to her at all, let alone went out of her way to find her. Esmeralda waited, remaining where she sat on the large stone until her mother reached her.

"We must speak," Kat said. All morning she'd felt a strong compulsion to find her daughter and talk to her about the idea in her head.

Esmeralda waited, too surprised by her mother's presence to ask what the conversation was going to be about. As she watched, she saw Kat move to stand directly in front of her. She made no move to sit beside Esmeralda, seeming to try to make herself look far more authoritative in her daughter's life than she truly was.

Kat looked down at the young woman. Sometimes it was difficult to comprehend that Esmeralda had been created and born of her womb. Kat momentarily wished she knew her daughter better. She equally knew that the reason they'd never been close was because she'd not wanted them to be. Esmeralda being born from a joining that Kat couldn't even remember had only resulted in confusion in Kat. Not being able to remember pairing or joining with Adrian had been overwhelming enough without having to think about the small being that had resulted from it.

Shaking her head in an attempt to push aside her brief thoughts of wistfulness and confusion, Kat finally spoke.

"You and Cesare must pair," she said. Why the need for such a suggestion was present in her mind, she didn't know. She only knew it was something that was needed by everyone in the village, and it was needed soon.

Esmeralda didn't like what she'd just heard. It had been surprising enough that Cesare had asked about the subject a short time before. Her mother bringing up the topic as well was enough to push Esmeralda's concern to another level. She stood up to face her mother, initially not sure how to respond. After a long while, she found her words.

"Mother, I do not understand…" she began to say. Her sentence was cut short by Kat's voice interrupting.

"The two of you must pair!" Kat insisted.

Esmeralda watched her mother's face. While the two had never been close, there was something extremely unnerving about Kat's countenance.

"Why do you say such a thing?" Esmeralda asked.

"It is your destiny," Kat replied. "It is the duty of you both for the village and the maintenance of population."

Esmeralda was intrigued. "Yes," she said slowly as she nodded. "I do understand the importance of the pairing process."

"It is settled then," Kat said curtly before turning to walk away.

"No, it is not," Esmeralda said to her mother's back. She rarely argued with her mother. Regardless, she felt very strongly that despite what Kat was trying to do - and *why* she was trying to do it - what she was suggesting was not right.

Esmeralda watched as her mother turned around and faced her again. The look on Kat's face was something she'd never seen before.

"You *will* pair with Cesare," Kat said again, her voice lower, quieter, but leaning far more toward menacing in its tone. "It is your destiny."

Esmeralda was beyond confused and intrigued. That her mother was suggesting such a thing at all had been surprise enough. Her voice changing, along with her face looking like it never had in Esmeralda's presence, compounded concerns even further.

"Why do you want this?" she dared to ask. The question was voiced for two reasons. She did want to know the answer, but there was also something inside of her that wanted to antagonize her mother. "Even if Cesare and I *are* destined to be paired together, as you have said, it is not yet time…"

"It is time when I *say* it is time!" Kat said, her voice rising in volume and depth. "Why do you question me so? I am your moth…"

Esmeralda couldn't stop her emotions from erupting. She'd had eighteen years of seeing how different her mother was toward her compared to how other children's mothers acted toward them. She'd noticed the difference in nature between her father and her mother. Although Esmeralda had little time for her father, she'd never forgotten that it was him who had taught her all that she'd had to learn as she'd been growing up.

"Mother?" Esmeralda asked. "Is that what you were going to say? That you are my *mother*?" She paused a moment as she watched dissatisfaction transform into something far darker on her mother's face. "You have no idea about what that word means. Tell me this - did you ever *want* to be my mother? You have never shown me affection or love…"

She watched as Kat scoffed at the words spoken. The reaction pushed Esmeralda's confidence to another level.

"You have *never* shown me affection or love," she said loudly. "You have never guided me or taught me how to be who I am meant to be. You are many things, but you cannot call yourself a mother to me."

For a moment, Kat could see through the fuzziness of her consciousness. She could see the anger and hurt on her daughter's face. Briefly, she wanted things to be different. As quickly as her true consciousness had appeared and been affected, it was lost again.

"You have a destiny," Kat said, moving forward and placing her face only inches in front of her daughter's. "You *will* fulfill it."

Esmeralda was so stunned by the interaction that she said nothing more as she watched her mother turn and walk away. Feeling even more alone than she usually did, she sat back down on the large drying stone. Although unhappy much of the time, it was rare that her body transformed her unhappiness into tears. She didn't want to cry. At that moment, she couldn't stop it. What began as a desperately needed release of one tear quickly evolved into the breaking of a long built-up wall. When the sobbing came, her strength evaporated.

It was at that moment that the entity felt something change in its existence. A wall that it had come up against hundreds of times over many years suddenly felt very, very open.

Esmeralda fought to control her sobbing. After a few moments, her strength regained. As it did, she realized what had happened.

'Leave me alone,' she said forcefully in her mind before resurrecting the wall around her thoughts.

The entity heard her voice talking to it. There were so many ways to feel about that. Its offspring - the seed it had planted years earlier - had spoken directly to it. That was reason to rejoice. Feeling the wall go back up almost as quickly as it had fallen was reason to be angry again. In the time that the wall had been down, the entity had been so surprised that it hadn't delved in to find anything in the mind of Esmeralda. An opportunity that had so briefly been presented had also been quickly lost.

Another aspect of what had just happened left it at peace. Even if she'd resurrected it as quickly as she had, Esmeralda *had* let the wall fall. She'd done so in a moment of deep despair. The entity was happy. After years of trying, it had finally found a way in.

CHAPTER 41

In his work, Adrian felt content enough. There were many reasons for his happy nature to be challenged in his life, but his work wasn't one of them. Being in the mill distracted him from dwelling on the loneliness he increasingly felt. It wasn't an emotion he wanted to feel. He tried hard to hide it from the people he interacted with day to day. The majority of the village population who saw him believed the false façade he presented to them. The most important person in his life never did.

As was usual during times when he was moving heavy sacks of grains around the mill interior, his thoughts turned to Isabella. He knew it wasn't right that he should still regard her so highly. Yes, they'd been friends all of their lives, but it had also been a great many years since she'd paired with Trent. It was clear to everyone that Isabella continued to be as happy with Trent as she had been two decades earlier.

Even though Adrian saw Isabella most days, he missed her. They were still friends, but the degree to which they'd spent time together when they'd been young had fallen away years earlier. He knew that should have resulted in him not still thinking about her so. He couldn't stop himself. Things could have been so different in his life if only Trent hadn't come to the small village. Although wrong to do so, Adrian maintained the belief that if the population had remained the same without that one person entering it, he and Isabella would now be the couple that had paired.

He took a moment to wonder what that would have been like. Would they have truly been as happy as it was easy to believe they would have? Or could such a move have destroyed their lifelong friendship? The wistful side of Adrian believed the former. The more realistic side of him considered the latter could have been true. With so many years having passed, he could have been just as unhappy after pairing with Isabella as he was having paired with Kat.

Kat. Thinking about her never brought Adrian joy. He thought he'd long before accepted their situation. The fact that he kept having the same thoughts told him that he never had. If he'd accepted it, he'd no longer think about his entire situation as often as he did. Suspecting that Kat was as unhappy as he was didn't help. Two people were in a position that they could have avoided if only he had gone with his gut instinct. So many times when Kat had suggested pairing, Adrian had questioned her reasoning. He'd ignored his intuition not to do it. He'd lived with that decision ever since. Now he would have to live with that decision for the rest of his life.

"You must speak with Esmeralda," he heard Kat say to him.

Having been so absorbed in his thoughts, he hadn't even heard her approach. As he looked at her, he felt his heart pound. He'd just been thinking about how different his life could have been if she wasn't who he'd paired with. It wasn't right that he should have been thinking that, and he knew it.

Forcing himself to focus on what she'd just said, he moved closer to her.

"About what?" he asked, centering his thoughts on the subject of his daughter.

"About pairing with Cesare," Kat said. "They must pair."

Adrian didn't hide his surprise at what she'd just said. He had to think back over conversations he'd had and heard. No matter how hard he tried to find the topic in past talks, he was pretty sure the subject had never been spoken of in any context previously.

"Why would we speak to her about this now?" he asked. "She has only eighteen years behind her."

Kat felt the same dissatisfaction she'd felt during the conversation she'd just had with Esmeralda. Why everyone had to argue about what was meant to be, she just did not understand. It was a simple enough thing to believe and do. Why did it seem like they were all against the idea?

"It is her destiny," she said, just as she had told Esmeralda. "They must pair."

Adrian's skepticism rose. The repetitive use of words caught him off guard, as did the tone being used to say them. As he looked at Kat's face, he felt the hairs on the back of his neck rise as his heart began to pump faster. Even though he hadn't seen such a thing in a great many years, the changes in Kat were familiar to him. He shook his head in disbelief. While he accepted he could be wrong in assessing what he was seeing and hearing, he equally accepted that he might not be. It had been many years since the previous instance of Kat not being herself. In many ways, Adrian suspected it was long overdue to happen again.

"Why do you shake your head?" he heard Kat ask.

When he settled his eyes on hers again, he fought with what to believe. There was no reason to think she was again under the influence of the strange thing that had attacked Isabella previously. If such a thing were happening, not only would Isabella have known, but she also would have shared the knowledge with him.

"This is not something we have discussed, Kat," he said diplomatically to slow down the conversation.

"We do not need to," Kat replied. "It is their destiny."

Adrian groaned. Her continued repetition secured his fear. Kat was once again invaded by the entity that had invaded her before.

CHAPTER 42

At the evening meal, Adrian sat patiently, hoping Isabella and Trent would show. As soon as they did, he felt relieved as they sat beside him.

"How has your day at the mill been, Adrian?" Isabella asked him. When she saw him turn to face her, she noticed straight away that something was not right. "Adrian. What is it?" she asked in alarm.

As Adrian looked at her, he noticed Trent one seat over. The strength of Isabella calmed Adrian. The combined strength of Isabella and Trent helped calm him even more.

"I am afraid..." he began to say before he felt the presence on the other side of him.

Turning around and seeing Kat sitting down, Adrian smiled at her but stopped speaking.

"We must continue to speak of this, Adrian," Kat said, desperate to capture and hold his attention. She'd seen him about to talk to Isabella and Trent when she'd walked into the vast dining area. That was something she was not going to allow.

As he had been many times before, Adrian felt conflicted. He was paired with Kat. Even with his fears, he couldn't shun her, particularly in public like they were. With no ability to decide how to proceed, he nodded but remained silent.

From the other side of him, Trent and Isabella glanced at each other. Trent hadn't noticed the same level of emotion on Adrian's face as Isabella had, but he *did* recognize the level of alarm on Isabella's. He was about to ask her about it when he saw the familiar shake of her head. It was subtle and something that wouldn't be visible to everyone who looked at her. Having seen it so many times over their years together, it was as readable to him as the neon-lit signs he remembered from his previous life.

Without speaking, he nodded at her, showing her he understood. He didn't try and create a false conversation. Instead, he focused on the food in front of him, just as everyone would expect him to.

Isabella played out the same scene, relishing every bit of the food on her plate. She experienced a similar situation to what she'd experienced many times before. Knowing Adrian was deeply worried about something, she found herself simultaneously wanting to hear the conversation between him and Kat, and *not* wanting to hear it. Concern for her friend was justification for listening to whatever was being said. Common manners were justification for doing whatever she could to not hear what the two were talking about.

"It is not the right time, Kat," Adrian finally said. His words were the answer to two scenarios. He didn't regard Esmeralda as old enough to pair. He equally didn't regard dining in the public area as the right time or place to have such a private conversation.

"That is not your decision," Kat said with force.

Her voice was loud enough to reach Isabella and Trent. Neither gave any visible indication they'd heard.

"It is as much my decision as it is yours," Adrian said, the feeling of dread flowing over him immensely. "This is not the time for us to speak of it. Eat, then we shall return to our home and talk of it there."

Although Kat was fuming at his response, she could sense Isabella attempting to listen. She didn't want that. It mattered not at all that the matter concerned Isabella's flesh and blood also. As far as Kat was concerned, she was the only one who would control the young couple.

CHAPTER 43

From across the vast area of wooden tables and seats, Esmeralda could see her parents as she sat down in the spot she usually dined with Cesare. He hadn't arrived yet, but that didn't worry or bother her. Since he'd started his training with the tailor, he had often reached the dining area after she had.

Despite her acceptance of his not being there, the more she looked at her mother and father, the more she found herself wanting him by her side. After the earlier interaction with her mother, combined with the subsequent feeling that something had successfully invaded her mind, she'd spent a long time sitting in the sun, trying to resurrect the full strength of her mind's walls. The combination of the two things happening had left her exhausted emotionally.

Looking over at where her parents sat with Cesare's parents, she forced herself to try and ascertain what was happening. It was difficult to miss the staunchness of her mother. Kat's look of determination to be the one in control was more pronounced than usual, but it was nothing new and certainly nothing unexpected. Of more interest to Esmeralda was the look that her father held. His face was as rigid as her mother's. It made Esmeralda hopeful. It was entirely possible that her mother had tried to sway her father into agreeing to the pairing. If that was the case, the look her father was giving to her mother allowed Esmeralda to consider that her father was going to be on *her* side, not her mother's. She hoped that was the case - desperately.

As much as she always wanted Cesare to be her friend, she had no desire to pair in the immediate future. If her mother was going to push for it to happen, she didn't know what she would do. There were worse things that could be forced upon her. Certainly, the idea of pairing with anyone *other* than Cesare was even less appealing. During her conversation with her mother, Esmeralda hadn't been left with the impression that her mother just wanted her to pair, so much as she needed her to pair specifically with *Cesare*. While it was a worrying thought that her mother wanted it so soon, at least Esmeralda knew she would have him by her side, no matter what was to happen.

"You look deep in thought, my blue-black friend," she finally heard the welcome and friendly voice say.

As soon as she heard it, she turned, stood, and threw her arms around him. It wasn't a usual show of affection for Esmeralda, especially in such an open place as the dining area. Although she hadn't done it with any advance thought, she was glad to be in his arms. There, she felt safe and secure.

Cesare was so surprised that he couldn't help but be instantly worried. He said nothing for a long while, instead choosing to hold her close to his chest. Whatever had driven her to do such a thing, it was serious. Of that, he did not doubt. He teased her a lot, but he knew when it was not a time for such frivolity.

Glancing around briefly, he saw the general population in the area hadn't noticed anything out of the ordinary. When his eyes rested on where his mother and father sat with Esmeralda's parents, Cesare saw the degree with which all four were watching Esmeralda in his arms. The look on Adrian's face, in particular, concerned Cesare. He knew Esmeralda's father was usually happy and smiling. At that moment, Adrian looked anything but cheerful.

Esmeralda clung to him for a long while before extracting herself. Embarrassed by her actions and the way she'd thrown herself at him without thinking, she kept her eyes down as she sat down again. She was glad that Cesare followed her lead, saying nothing as he sat and placed his plate on the table in front of him.

Looking at her, he waited for her to meet his sight. Although it took a long while, eventually he saw her head turn toward him.

"Do you wish to talk now?" he asked her in almost a whisper.

Esmeralda shook her head but could not speak. So many things had been happening that she felt the threat of losing control of her emotions. With having felt the presence of the invader in her mind when she'd experienced her emotional pain, she knew she had to remain mindful of how she was feeling. It had happened only once. Once was more than enough.

Cesare reached over, placed his hand over hers, and squeezed it. It was a small gesture, but it said how much he fully intended to support and be there for her, no matter what had happened.

Esmeralda was thankful for his presence beside her. She wasn't sure how comfortable she would be talking to him about how much her mother had affected her earlier. Generally, she didn't like to show emotion. Although that was normal for her, she knew that she did have to talk, and Cesare was the only person she fully trusted to do so with.

Squeezing his hand in response, she gave him a small smile before turning back to her plate and resuming her meal. They would talk, but she would wait until she was sure nobody was around - in person, *or* in her mind.

CHAPTER 44

"Your mother said that to you?" Cesare asked for clarification after Esmeralda had relayed the words Kat had said earlier. The two of them had remained silent as they'd finished their meals and made their way to their special spot in the village. "You think she wishes to push for us to pair *now*?" When he saw her nod, he understood the degree that his friend had been upset. "It is similar to my mother asking me about this the other night."

Esmeralda nodded again.

"Yes," she said. "I may be wrong, Cesare, but something is happening. I do not understand any of this. People wish for you and I to pair, even though we are much younger than is normally the pairing age. Then there is this *thing* constantly pushing into my mind..."

Cesare looked at her in surprise. "You did mention this before," he said. "Why do you seem more upset by it now? Has something further happened?"

Esmeralda sighed. She'd not yet shared with him the experience she'd had earlier that day, having wanted the two of them to focus only on the strange occurrence with her mother.

"After my mother had spoken to me so, I... I cried. When I did, I could feel it enter my mind," she said. "Usually, I can keep it out even though I feel it trying to enter. This time, when I was not concentrating, I could *feel* it enter here, Cesare," she continued as she used one finger to point at her temple. "When I realized what was happening, I closed my mind again, but it did get in this time. That scares me. I do not know what it seeks, but it is persistent. There must be something that it wants from me."

"Or needs," Cesare said, thoughtful. "What could you have inside your mind that it could use? You are no different except for the summoning skill that we both have. Do you think that is related to this?"

"Yes, perhaps it is," she said, nodding in agreement. "Have you felt it also? The feeling of someone or something trying to get inside your thoughts?"

Cesare considered the question for a long while before he shook his head.

"I do not think so, Esmeralda, but what does it feel *like*?" he asked.

"Can you explain the sensation to me? Why do you think *that* is what is happening when it is?"

Esmeralda had tried to answer the same question before. It wasn't an easy thing to analyze and speak of. The belief came purely from her intuition. She didn't know how to explain to someone else how to assess if the same thing was happening to them.

"I cannot give you any indication of how to feel this, Cesare," she said. "I cannot even explain to you how I know this is what is happening. I ... I just *know*."

Cesare nodded before moving closer to her and encouraging her into his arms again. Although he couldn't support her by going through the same thing as she was, he could ensure she knew he was there for her however else she might need him.

Esmeralda welcomed the hug again. Being so physically close was becoming increasingly regular between them, for which she was appreciative. She'd been starved of physical affection her entire life. It felt good to have it open to her as often as it presently was.

"I will not let anything happen to you," Cesare said.

He knew as well as she did that it wasn't a promise he could absolutely keep. If something was entering her mind, he had no way to stop that from happening.

CHAPTER 45

Like a puppeteer pulling strings to sway a marionette to do and move as he wished it to, the entity had spent its day trying to manipulate the major players in its game. The main difference between it and a puppeteer was the level of exhaustion the entity felt from its efforts.

Although Antonio was mostly under the entity's spell, there had been times when it had needed to push harder at Antonio's mind. The more time that passed, the more resistance the man was giving. The entity could tell that it was losing its grip on Antonio, and it was happening far too quickly. It made the entity want to move ahead faster in its plan. It had wanted to wait and see the young couple pair and create a being with the next level of power. As the entity observed the disharmony beginning between its players, it had to concede that it might need to find another way to get what it wanted.

In contrast to Antonio's growing resistance, the sub-consciousness inside of Kat's mind was proving far more rewarding. As she had been previously, Kat was again easy to manipulate. She'd hardly noticed that her consciousness had been pushed aside in her mind. At the very first suggestion that she make the pairing happen, she'd gone to work, talking to Esmeralda and then Adrian. While the result hadn't helped the entity in any way regarding the pairing, the entity *was* pleased that Kat had played her part so well. It was also pleased that the way with which Kat had talked to Esmeralda had, in turn, provided the entity with access to Esmeralda's mind. It had been access with not enough time, but it had been access regardless. That had made the push into Kat's mind a success in itself.

The entity took time to consider options. Kat was always going to be a major supporter as one of the entity's sub-hosts. Even though she'd been through the meager battles twice before, there was no doubt that she would go through it and fight for the entity again. She was malleable, making her a sure bet in any fight.

The uncertainty lay with Antonio and Esmeralda. The former could very well not be available at the moment he was needed. The latter was a very big work-in-progress. The entity now knew one way to get Esmeralda to open her mind. That didn't mean it was going to be able to do it on demand. She'd been in a fragile place emotionally. Even sending

474

Kat to work on her again might not produce the same result a second time around.

It was hard to remain calm and not rush ahead, but the idea of the creation of a more powerful being was like a drug to the entity. As unlikely as it seemed that all the pieces of the entity's plan would fall into place, it couldn't let go of the idea that all it had to do was get Esmeralda on its side, then wait for her offspring to join the fight. It would then be easy to extinguish every ancient from the village - and every ancient-to-be.

The entity had planted the seeds of its plan into the minds of who it could. The best thing it could immediately do was wait at least a day or two and just watch what happened. Without her awareness, Kat was already helping the entity in its plan. If the entity backed off, there was a chance Antonio would relax and fall back into line as well. Quietly, it sank backward from the forefront of Elder Scott's consciousness.

Elder Scott blinked, thinking about what a glorious day it was. Around him was sunshine, warmth, and the hum of happy people. He walked on, smiling as he considered he was truly blessed in the life that he lived.

CHAPTER 46

When Esmeralda walked into her family home after her evening time with Cesare, the tension was immense. It had never been a home of happiness, but the air felt even thicker than usual.

When she looked at her father, she saw him give her a sad smile. That was not surprising. It was a facial expression she'd seen on him most days of her life. Although she didn't often feel the need to be forward in showing affection or love toward either of her parents, at that moment, she felt sorry for Adrian. She'd never connected with him as completely as she did with Cesare, but she'd never been treated badly by her father either.

She knew he was a kind man and a good man. Cesare had helped Esmeralda to appreciate that through the telling of stories involving Adrian when Cesare had been a small child. Her friend had, on many occasions, shared fond memories of how Adrian had played with him and talked to him over Cesare's early years. The stories had been told in an effort to help Esmeralda think more highly of her father. Sometimes it had worked. Other times it hadn't. She didn't regard anything as being wrong with her father. She just hadn't established with him the same level of rapport that she knew other young people had with their parents.

In feeling momentarily sorry for her father, Esmeralda moved to him and placed her arms around him. Although it was a move to help him feel better, feeling his arms move around her made *her* feel secure too. The two remained together for a long while, not saying anything before Adrian pulled away and looked at her.

"Are you well, Esmeralda?" he asked quietly.

The tone of his voice reminded Esmeralda of the kindness he had always shown her. No matter what degree of coldness her mother treated her with, her father had at least always tried to show her love, even when Esmeralda hadn't been fully accepting of it.

"I am," she said, nodding.

"Do not worry," Adrian said as he reached out and squeezed her hand. "I have been told of what is wanted by your mother," he whispered as he briefly glanced over toward where Kat sat. "If you do not wish for the pairing, I shall not agree to it."

"Thank you," Esmeralda replied.

"You must be honest with me, Esmeralda," Adrian continued. "*Is* this something you do not want? Is it something that you wish me to *prevent* from happening?"

Esmeralda nodded.

"Yes, Father," she said. "Cesare is my dear friend. Neither of us wish to go through the pairing process with each other - or with anyone else."

"It is understandable," Adrian replied. "I do not know what your mother is thinking, however please know that I will fight for *you*."

In her relief, Esmeralda released a long, deep sigh. Nodding again and giving her father another sad smile, she leaned in and briefly gave him another hug. They weren't completely connected as father and daughter, but it felt good to know he was on her side.

Adrian watched as she moved away. He hadn't been entirely truthful with her when he'd said he didn't know what Kat was thinking. Full honesty would have had him say that he believed Kat was under the influence of someone - some*thing* - completely other than herself.

Over the following two days, Alessia felt the thoughts and voices in her head increase. Although they pressed on her in ways she'd never before experienced, she continued to keep the issue to herself. Through her mind, she could see and hear everything that everyone around her was thinking, seeing, saying, *and* intending. She felt pressure from it all bearing down on her mind, but she also felt like she was in a rare and powerful position.

From her mother and father, she knew they were doing a level of training she'd never known them to do previously. Through their conversations with each other, and with the ancient, Elder Rhys, she had comprehended that Isabella and Trent had both undergone intense training before she'd been born. Those years had ended, and their training had eased after Marco and Alessia had been born. Now the training was increasing again. From the thoughts and visions she was receiving from each of them, she knew they perceived a threat was coming. In that, they were right. Regardless of knowing they expected something that was indeed coming, Alessia did not confirm their suspicions. She could see they were in a good place, and they were focused. She wouldn't speak and possibly disrupt that.

In another part of her family, Alessia could perceive what was happening with her oldest brother and Esmeralda. The intense sadness of Esmeralda had reached Alessia, as had the brief moment when the entity had succeeded in getting into Esmeralda's mind. It had been almost overwhelming for Alessia to experience the sad moment of Esmeralda's, followed by the anger Esmeralda had experienced immediately afterward.

What Alessia had seen and felt through Esmeralda's thoughts had been simultaneously broadcast to her with what was coming through from the entity itself. The clarity that Alessia could see and feel from all angles at the same time was the equivalent of watching a modern-day movie that was clever enough to show the emotions and thoughts of all characters to viewers simultaneously.

For a moment, she focused on what she'd learned and grown to understand about the strange entity that seemed to be invading the minds of so many. It wanted power. Of that, she had no doubt. It also saw members of her family as the ultimate way to get it. It knew about the strength of her mother. It *thought* it knew about the strength of her brother. In that, Alessia knew better. She'd perceived that the power and strength of Cesare had been greatly overstated by the entity. It was a guess on the entity's part, based on the color of Cesare's hair and the lack of easy ability to get into Cesare's mind.

Alessia focused on her brother. His thoughts easily reached her mind. During most of the day, they were not personal. He was learning a trade. He was surprisingly focused on that when he was with the trade elder. It was rare that his mind went elsewhere during those times. In the mornings and evenings, his mind was elsewhere. Alessia had experienced many thoughts from him, and almost all were centered around Esmeralda. He loved her, even though he didn't seem to know it. Although young, Alessia understood about love. She'd experienced it through a great many people's thoughts and feelings that had flowed through to her. For most, it was a mutually wonderful thing. For a few, it was the source of unhappiness.

In her brother, she sensed it between Esmeralda and Cesare. She also sensed it wasn't a love like the paired in the village shared. No, between them it was a love of friends, yes, but it was also the love of family. That was one of the most intriguing things that Alessia had discovered about her brother and his friend. They weren't related, but the love they had for one another *was*. She knew that. She also knew that they *didn't*. They were equal in thinking of each other as the closest of friends. They were also equal in not realizing there was something more between them.

Alessia was aware of the current plan of the entity to try and get Cesare and Esmeralda to pair. The plan was not going well, and she was glad. The thoughts of the people told Alessia they all considered Esmeralda and Cesare too young to pair. Because of that, it would not happen. While Alessia was relieved of that, there was something more behind them not pairing. She didn't know what - whatever the reason was, nobody had thought it or shared it with anyone else.

In all, she found it all intriguing. It was exhausting, having to listen to so many people for so many hours of each day. Regardless, she did appreciate that she had the strange ability to hear and see so much. It was messy, and it was not common for people to be able to do, but with all that was going on, she knew she was in a safe place. The entity was trying to manipulate people through their thoughts. Alessia could see it was succeeding in some aspects. She could also see that it was failing in others. It was getting frustrated at its failed efforts. In particular, it was angry that it had once succeeded in reaching into Esmeralda's mind, but it had not been able to since.

That was the biggest aspect that made Alessia realize just how powerful *she* was. She'd never had to reach into people's minds. For her, the reverse happened. The thoughts of everyone reached into her mind constantly - even those of Esmeralda - *and* the entity itself.

CHAPTER 48

Elder Rhys felt his expectation of something bad coming change into anticipation. His thoughts about what *might* happen at some time in the future had changed. There was no longer just a possibility of an attack. That uncertainty had converted into absolute certainty. It was coming, and it wasn't only coming for Isabella.

In his heart, Elder Rhys knew the attack was going to be extended to himself. He tried to be at peace with that. He'd been ready to move on to his next journey for a very long time. The only aspect that left him hesitant and regretful about what might happen was him leaving Isabella before he felt she was ready to be left alone as a future ancient.

Having watched her grow as a child hadn't provided Elder Rhys with any more feeling toward her than he had toward any other child in the village. When so young, it was impossible to know who was intended to be an ancient and who wasn't. It had always been the way among their people. Some were destined to have powers within them. Some weren't. Those who possessed that destiny only showed the beginning of their powers growing when they became young adults.

Elder Rhys had enjoyed the journey he'd seen Isabella on since her powers had begun to grow. She'd embraced them just as she should. Inside of her was neither complacency nor eagerness that the ancient knew could be a danger if too intense. He'd seen the result of people wanting too much, and their willingness to hurt others in the process. There was no such thing in Isabella's nature. Elder Rhys was thankful for that. He had full knowledge of how powerful she would become. If she'd also possessed greed and malice, that power could have become destructive.

Over his long lifetime, he'd established with many villagers a level of rapport that he'd enjoyed until their time of passing. There was always sadness in someone being removed from his life, but he understood it was only the start of a new journey for them. That made it easier for him to keep going, day after day, even as he saw those close to him cease to breathe and enjoy all that life had to offer.

As he considered that something was coming in an attempt to cause destruction in the village again, he knew he was ready to pass. He wouldn't hurry the moment it would come. He was committed to seeing

Isabella through her journey of ancient training for as long as he could. If his time came to an end during whatever battle was being planned, he was at peace with that. So many friends and family had lived and then passed during his lifetime. He was ready to see all of them again.

Lying back on his bed, he closed his eyes and readied for sleep. Perhaps it would be sleep that lasted for the night. Perhaps it would be sleep that lasted forever. He didn't know which it would be, just as he never knew. It had been a long time since he'd experienced any vision of the night - either his own or that of another. That was not usual, but he did not question it. His time was approaching. He did not mind if his final times were free of such happenings in his mind.

After yet another weary day, the ancient finally fell into a deep slumber, his mind completely at rest.

CHAPTER 49

As hard as the entity tried to remain calm and silent in its thoughts, two days was enough to let pass before it needed to take action. It had no set plan, but it knew that *something* needed to happen that would take it closer to its goal.

The minds of Antonio, Kat, and Esmeralda had been left in peace. Kat had continued on her path of trying to convince people to let the young couple pair. She'd also continued to be unsuccessful in her campaign. The entity was equally glad of her efforts and angry that she continued to fail. Getting Cesare and Esmeralda to pair and produce the powerful offspring that the entity wanted for its own use just did not seem feasible. Perhaps it could happen over the original timeframe the entity had planned, but the original timeframe was too long. There was no more patience. The entity wanted control. It wanted power. It had waited enough. Somehow it had to move things to the next level.

No matter how things had changed as far as the timeline went, the first step in gaining ultimate control remained the same. The ancients had to be extinguished, one by one. Being hosted in an elder's body and mind, the entity didn't know who all of the ancients were, but there was one who had always shown his position. Elder Rhys was the face of the ancients in the village. In all major decisions and events, he was the one who held and showed the ultimate power. In being that person, he was the obvious first ancient that needed to be slaughtered. Once he was gone, another would have to come forward. It was just the way of the village. There *had* to be a front face for the ancients. If that front face was no longer living, *another* would have to reveal themselves.

The entity smiled inside the chaos of Elder Scott's mind. It was a good plan. Taking down the ancients one at a time would take time, but nowhere near as much time as waiting for the young couple to pair and produce offspring. Once the entity had used its host and sub-hosts to kill off the ancients one by one as they revealed themselves, its next stage of taking power would be easy.

It took time to reflect on the possible ways to move forward. Elder Rhys was often in the company of others. Taking him down wouldn't be easy, but at least the entity's primary host, Elder Scott, *was* an elder. He resided within the temple walls. It would never be suspicious to be within such close vicinity to the well-known ancient. The difficulty would be finding a moment when Isabella wasn't nearby. The entity knew she was an ancient in training. She had to be taken down too. Could the entity strike both at the same time? Alone - probably not. With its sub-hosts - quite possibly.

The entity took its time considering the likelihood of success in that scenario. Kat was primed and ready for another battle. There was nothing about her that caused concern. Antonio was on the cusp of being lost, but so far still had quite a high level of receptivity within him. If he was going to be used, it would have to be soon. Waiting too long could result in Antonio being lost to the entity altogether.

In its consciousness, the entity continued to reach out to its players. As usual, the only one it failed with was Esmeralda. While that angered the entity, it resolved to let her go as a consideration. It had always believed she was going to have incredible inner strength. That belief had proven to be correct. Unfortunately, she was too strong for it to be able to manipulate her mind. If it was going to use her for its cause, it would have to find another way.

As it thought about Esmeralda, it experienced a run-through of her life so far. With the entity's past being hidden within its mind, it didn't know if it had been a father in real life. Had it lived as a normal villager within the tall village walls? It had always assumed it must have. If it hadn't, why would it have been driven in need to be there at all? No, it had to continue to assume that it had lived among the villagers at some stage. If that was the case, it was just as likely that it had paired with someone and gone on to have offspring of its own.

Although rarely sentimental in any way, the entity considered that it would have been nice to have at least some memories of its life as a human. Even if they'd been few, that would have been nicer than having none at all. Perhaps there was someone it had loved previously. Maybe it had been a deep love and fruitful in the creation of children, but did it really matter if that were the case or not? What it *could* remember were all the moments in Esmeralda's life.

From her moment of conception, it had watched her. It had seen her in Kat's womb. It had seen her be born. It had experienced the joy in feeling the power she had within her, and seeing her face for the first time. It knew she hadn't been happy in her life, but if anything serious or harmful had ever been likely to happen to her, the entity was sure it would have stepped in to help her however it could have.

Although it had initially made her for the same purpose it was on at the present time - to create a being more powerful than others in the village - it realized it had grown to love her, just as any father loves their child. She was different from everyone else with her blue-black hair and her sad nature, but she'd been created from the seed it had planted within Antonio. She was a part of the entity. For that, it was deeply grateful.

485

CHAPTER 50

Unknown to each of them, Isabella, Alessia, Kat, and Antonio all woke at precisely the same moment in the middle of the night. Not one of them knew why as they'd each sat up and opened their eyes with the feeling that something important was about to happen.

As Isabella tried to focus her mind through the fogginess of sleep, she searched inwardly for anything solid to grasp on to. Despite her efforts, there was no vision of the night in her immediate memory. There was no voice calling out to her or perception of anyone talking to anyone else. There was nothing for her to pinpoint, but she knew in the core of her soul that something was seriously wrong.

"Isabella?" Trent asked as he woke and saw her sitting up. "What is it?"

Isabella turned to where he lay. The darkness of the room prevented her from seeing him, but she was grateful for his presence. Reaching down with one hand and finding his chest, she felt safe but also incredibly disturbed.

"Elder Rhys," she said as she began to climb out of their bed. "He is in danger."

"How … how do you know?" Trent asked, beginning to move also.

"I … I do not know how, Trent, but we must go … quickly," Isabella said as she put on her shoes and began to walk towards the door. Once there, she let him catch up to her before she opened it and the two walked out.

"Where is he?" Trent asked.

"I am uncertain," Isabella replied, increasing her walking pace. "When we are in the temple, I will know."

Trent asked nothing more. They'd been expecting something was going to happen. It was entirely possible that the moment they'd been anticipating had arrived.

In the quiet of his mind, he tried to concentrate on his hands. In training, it had grown easier. There was always a period of time before he even began training when he could slowly focus and build the strength to summon the orbs of golden flame. Doing it with such advance knowledge and thought in training was far different from being able to summon it under pressure for a fight.

Despite his doubts, he was pleased as he felt his palms grow warm. It was a good sign. Trent and Isabella were on their way to check on Elder Rhys, but as always, it was Isabella that Trent most wanted to protect. He'd do what he could to prevent the ancient from being harmed, but Isabella would always be his primary focus.

When the two of them reached the temple, Isabella took a moment to stop and concentrate on her feelings. She saw no image, and she heard no sounds, but she knew Elder Rhys was within the bed-chamber he resided in within the great structure. Although she'd never seen it or been told where the room was, she confidently let her intuition guide her.

Trent remained quiet as he followed her lead. Whatever was happening, he had full faith that Isabella could find that out and act accordingly. He felt apprehensive that they might be entering another time of battle, but he also felt more prepared. They'd both been training for the moment when the entity would try again. If that moment had arrived, they were ready.

He fought to clear his mind again. Although thoughts wanted to invade, Trent knew that focus was the most important thing for him if he wanted to be able to summon the golden flame at will and help Isabella in any battle that might ensue.

CHAPTER 51

Waking as sharply as she had, Kat shook her head as she sat up in her bed. The fogginess within her mind was great, but as quickly as it was there, it was gone. The room's darkness told her it was nighttime and time for her to be asleep. Usually, when she woke in the night, she would naturally turn over and try to return to sleep once more, just as anyone would. The idea of trying to slip back into slumber was not an option at that moment.

Something was happening that she was meant to be a part of. She didn't know what it was or why she thought that but the idea was in her mind and she couldn't turn away from it. She waited only a few minutes before she climbed out of the bed she shared with Adrian and readied herself to leave. She cared nothing for the man in her bed or her daughter in the next room. There was something she had to do. Even with no comprehension about what that was, she walked out, following an unheard instruction telling her where she needed to be.

Although he'd said nothing to her, Adrian had sensed Kat's waking. He'd remained silent and still, waiting to see what she did. Her recent actions and words had left him suspicious she was under the spell of an entity yet again. Of that, he had no proof. Nothing had happened like had happened previously. As far as he was aware, Isabella had not experienced the golden glow over her belly again. She'd also not mentioned seeing or hearing anything in her mind. It confused Adrian. Was it happening again, or was Kat doing something different?

Determined to know either way, Adrian waited until he heard the door close softly and then climbed out of bed to dress. He didn't want to alert Kat to his presence if he followed her. He equally didn't want to lose her. If they were all about to experience a repeat of what had happened twice before, he suspected she would be headed to the temple. Why that seemed to be an established scene for the small battles, he did not know. He supposed the reason did not matter. He just had to move quickly but quietly and see where she led him.

Once outdoors, he looked around. In the distance, he saw Kat quickly moving in the direction of the temple. By that, he wasn't surprised. The speed with which she was walking, however, surprised him greatly. If he wanted to see where she went once she entered the great temple, he knew he'd have to begin almost a run to catch up to her.

Doing his best to remain as quiet as he could while he increased his stride and pace, his mind shifted to Isabella. It saddened him to realize that his concern still lay more with her than with the woman he'd paired with so many years earlier. It wasn't right that he should feel or act in such a way. It should have been more natural for him to worry about Kat. Whatever she was walking into, she should have been at the forefront of his mind and heart, but she wasn't.

By the time the entrance to the temple came into view, Adrian had moved to an easier distance from Kat. He watched as she moved through the large outer doorway. Knowing the interior of the large structure was like a maze, he moved forward in a desperate attempt to see where she went once inside. From there he crept, propelling his feet forward despite the growing apprehension and fear within him.

He tried to maintain calm, in his heart suspecting why Kat had entered the temple, what she intended to do, and who she intended to do it to.

CHAPTER 52

The instant alertness that Antonio experienced on waking in the dark surprised him. Waking in the night was a regular occurrence for him. Waking up to the degree that he had was not regular at all. His curiosity about it didn't help in his effort to try and get back to sleep. One part of his mind wanted to slip back into slumber. A greater part forced his wakefulness further, making him want to not only be awake but also get out of his bed and leave his home.

While actively thinking that he wanted to go back to sleep, he did as he was compelled to do. No matter how strong his desire was to not do it, he moved forward with dressing, slipping on his shoes, then walking out of the home that he shared with his beloved Ariana.

His consciousness mixed, Antonio found himself highly confused. Even as he thought one thing, he did another. It made no sense. He felt like he'd lost control of his body, his head, and especially his decision-making ability. He didn't even have any conscious thought about where he was going, let alone why.

While pondering what was happening to him, his feet continued to walk forward, one step at a time. It was a long walk from his home to the temple, but he naturally moved there without any conscious thought.

When he arrived at the large exterior doors, he hesitated. Through the fuzziness in his mind, he thought he'd once been there before. It was one of those moments when he thought he'd done something, but his memories were scattered. At the same time, he knew that while he'd never set foot inside the great village temple, he actually *had*. It made no sense. He had two sets of memories, but that wasn't possible. Only one could be true. The other must surely have been a dream.

He momentarily considered he might have been currently *in* a dream. Was he lying in his bed with Ariana at his side? It was a possibility, and yet he knew it wasn't the truth. He *did* have two sets of memories inside of his mind, and he *was* walking into the temple, even though he had no recognizable desire to want to.

As he passed through the doors, he thought to himself that something was wrong, and he must talk to Ariana when he got home. That was the last glimpse of Antonio's true consciousness that he saw and felt before the entity closed it down completely.

Embraced fully as the entity's sub-host, Antonio felt strong as he walked through the maze of hallways and doorways in the temple. He didn't like the structure, but he knew it was where a killing was about to take place. He was a part of that. It would be his hands that produced a final blow to extinguish the life of another.

Gleefully, the body of Antonio smiled and rubbed his hands together. He'd been in the same position before. Something had gone wrong then. Now he had a second chance to succeed.

The mind of Antonio continued to be scattered. Although his true consciousness had been moved aside, even with the forceful push of the entity, he felt erratic in his thoughts and desires. He knew that when he'd been in the temple previously, he'd worked with Kat to try and attack Isabella. That time grew vivid in his mind. They hadn't succeeded, but the time would come when they would try again. Next time they would be prepared.

At that moment, Antonio understood that Isabella wasn't who he was going to attack that night. Instead, it was going to be an ancient - a being with incredible power. That worried Antonio not. He was happy to kill.

CHAPTER 53

Having heard his mother and father get up in the night and leave the house, Cesare's curiosity was piqued. It seemed like something neither would ever do, but they'd been so quiet in their actions that he was left wondering if they had done it before, and more than once. After the door closed behind them, he remained in his bed for a long while, wondering if they would be back at any moment. He waited and waited. When it didn't look like they were going to return immediately, he quietly extracted himself from the home and stepped outside.

"You have been woken also?" he heard the familiar voice say.

Turning toward it, he saw Esmeralda.

"You also?" he asked her and saw her nod. "I woke because my mother and father have left our home."

"As have mine," Esmeralda said, her voice full of surprise. "What do you think they are doing?"

"I know not," replied Cesare. "I do not know where they have gone."

Esmeralda took a moment to focus her mind. Locating people or trying to read their thoughts was not something she'd tried before, but the effort paid off.

"They are in the village temple," she said, immediately turning to begin walking toward the structure.

Cesare reached out and grabbed her wrist.

"Wait," he said, halting her in her progress. "Should we go to them?"

"Yes, of course we should, Cesare," Esmeralda replied. "They could be in danger."

"Danger? Why would you think such a thing?"

Esmeralda pulled her wrist away from his hand before moving up to him. Before speaking again, she placed her arms around him and rested her head on his chest.

"I feel it," she said quietly before pulling her head back to look at his face. For a moment, in the light of the fire torches that lit the area, she thought he looked handsome. It was a fleeting thought and a surprising one. "I feel that they are approaching danger, and you and I must provide assistance."

Cesare thought she sounded extreme in what she was saying but nodded.

"Very well," he said, prompting them both to turn and resume their walk toward the temple.

When they reached the doorway, both stopped.

"I have never been in here," Esmeralda said, a feeling of darkness beginning to flow over her.

"Nor I since I was very young," Cesare said as he held out his hand to her. "Come. You can feel they are here, can you not?" he asked and saw her nod. "Focus on that. Lead the way, Esmeralda."

His encouragement touched her for a moment before she nodded again and turned her mind off to everything except her instinct. Through the maze of doors, they walked as quietly as they could, stopping now and then to listen. It took some time before they finally reached an area where Esmeralda felt her intuition heighten.

"Here?" Cesare asked silently, moving only his lips as he pointed to the door.

In response, he saw her nod.

"On the other side of the corridor this door leads to," she said.

They remained still, listening in the hope of hearing either set of parents on the other side. There was only silence.

CHAPTER 54

"Come, Elder Rhys," Isabella said when she and Trent reached the bed-chamber of the ancient. "We must move you."

Elder Rhys looked at the young woman he'd grown to regard so highly. While he appreciated that she and Trent had shown up to help him, he was not scared of whatever was to come. He didn't know why the couple was in his room with him, but he could sense the intense fear in both of them. Although he was prepared to pass and move on in his next journey, he would make no effort to deny their help in getting him to safety.

"What is it?" he asked as he stood.

"I do not know, but you are not safe," Isabella replied as Trent helped Elder Rhys prepare to leave the room. "It is coming for you now."

Elder Rhys nodded. No more explanation needed to be given. It was likely the entity again, even though the circumstances were not the same as previously. The system might have changed. He suspected the desired result had not. While Isabella had seemed to be the target on the previous two occasions, everything about her words and actions told him that he was the target of the present moment.

The three left his bed-chamber and walked through the corridors, intent on entering any of the hidden rooms that only ancients could see the door to and enter. It was a fair plan. It should have worked. It didn't.

"Step aside, Isabella," Kat's voice rung out down the corridor toward the large open space Isabella, Trent, and Elder Rhys had reached. "My time with you will come. First, I must remove someone else."

Isabella and Trent moved to stand in front of Elder Rhys. For a fleeting moment, Trent wondered why it was that he, with his limited abilities, had been trained to fight such a being as was in Kat, when the most powerful ancient was right beside him but needed Isabella's protection. Acknowledging it was a ridiculous question to consider at that moment, he pushed the wonder of it aside and focused on his hands instead.

Isabella watched Kat's movements. She'd seen them twice before. No matter how long had passed since the last battle between them, the movements were exactly the same. Isabella was pleased. It would make it far easier to anticipate Kat's attempts at hurting her.

As she watched, she saw Kat raise one hand and summon a blue ball of flame. What surprised Isabella most of all was that it was only one. In the training that she and Trent had been undertaking, they'd made sure they worked toward being able to summon two flaming orbs at a time and combine them to increase their strength. Isabella wondered if Kat had even thought about some form of training to grow her battle efforts since the previous time. She suspected not.

Looking at Kat's face, Isabella could see the difference between what Kat had looked like only a week before and what she looked like at that moment. The exterior was the same, but the expression and movement were quite different.

"You are not Kat," Isabella said as she brought up both hands and instantly summoned two flames.

Maintaining eye contact with Kat, Isabella saw the surprise on the younger woman's face. It was Kat's face, but not Kat inside. Whatever it was, it hadn't seemed to anticipate that Isabella might have been training and waiting for that moment to happen and history to repeat.

Kat watched, mesmerized by the two golden orbs of flame jumping on Isabella's hands. She watched further as Isabella moved one onto the other, making one double in size. That was surprising enough. It was a further surprise when Kat watched Isabella summon yet another orb of golden flame onto her palm again. The process repeated. With another movement, the double-sized orb grew into the size of three. Although she should have been worried about what she was seeing, Kat was hypnotized.

Trent watched from beside Isabella. He could see the way Isabella's hand movements and tricks with the orbs were affecting Kat. She was clearly in some kind of trance, holding her ball of blue flame over her hand but not moving to use it in any way. Remaining so still made no sense to Trent. She didn't seem to register that more orbs were being produced by Isabella, and they were getting bigger. If Kat wanted to attack, she was not doing herself any favors by waiting and allowing her enemy to build a larger and stronger weapon.

Seeing the level at which Kat was unmoving, Trent focused further on his hands to summon two golden orbs of flame himself. He was relieved that they emerged easily. He didn't think they would be needed, given the contrast between Kat's spoken desire to hurt Elder Rhys, but her equally obvious lack of ability to move.

Out of the corner of his eye, he saw movement. From the shadow of the corridor, he watched as Antonio moved into the area. Seeing him, Trent raised his hands in anticipation. Kat being there with only one orb was one thing. Trent had seen the speed with which Antonio had summoned blue flames previously. He hadn't seen Antonio produce more of them like Trent and Isabella had practiced doing, but that didn't mean he couldn't.

Trent watched Antonio as he took his place next to Kat. He saw Antonio look at her with only a sliver of recognition on his face about who she was or how they were supposed to work together. It was just one more way that things were different from the previous occasion they'd come together in the temple. Back then, Antonio had pleaded with Kat to help him, seeming to know who she was and how they should work together toward a common cause. The two people in front of Trent did not seem anywhere near as connected as they had previously.

Antonio was still vague about what he was doing, but his body kept moving him forward to do things he felt hardly in control of. The young woman beside him was familiar, but his mind couldn't hold onto any particular thought or memory. He wondered briefly if his mind had been injured. Nothing made sense in his thoughts. Even less made sense in how his body was doing things without him feeling like he wanted it to.

From a distance, the entity monitored all that was happening. Things had begun, but they were not going exactly to plan. The entity kept losing connection with Antonio. That was a problem. It had wanted to use Antonio's bodily strength to kill Elder Rhys. If the connection wasn't there, that wouldn't happen. It was also going to make it much harder to get him to work with Kat, especially if the connection was broken at the wrong moment. At least with Kat, the entity could be satisfied. She was doing what she was meant to, albeit much slower than she should be.

In a moment of clarity, the entity also experienced a moment of hindsight. It could see through the eyes of Kat and Antonio that Isabella and Trent had both improved their skills greatly since the last time they'd all come together in such a way. The entity was angered by that. In never sensing they had been training or even thinking about expecting another attack, it had assumed they would be taken by surprise. With that belief, it had never thought to try and get Antonio or Kat more skilled in their attack moves. It was a stupid error for the entity to have made, but it could do nothing about that at that moment. It had one more play left.

Nobody in the room knew it was hosted primarily inside a person that they all trusted. Seeing the odds stacked against its two sub-hosts, the entity took over Elder Scott's body and mind completely.

As the body of Elder Scott walked out of the elder's bed-chamber and embarked on the journey along the maze of corridors, it continued to monitor what was happening in the minds of its sub-hosts. No joy came from that. Both were stuck, unmoving. Kat had one blue flame poised and ready to strike, yet she didn't use it. Instead, she still stood watching Isabella create orb after orb and combine them to build their strength. Just as useless was Antonio. With his mind connecting to then disconnecting from the influence of the entity, he was just a man standing still. He was waiting for something, but he had no idea what he was waiting *for*.

Overall, the entity was frustrated. It had felt that way increasingly in recent times, but its frustration had risen to an entirely new level over the previous few minutes. It was sure the path it was on was what was meant to be for itself, for the village, and for the entire population who resided in it. It could not accept that things were destined to be any way other than what it saw as the perfect life for itself.

When it was close to where it felt the five people were, it stopped the body it was in and waited. More players were approaching. One was the golden child of Isabella. The other was its own offspring.

To itself, the entity smiled. Although Esmeralda had closed her mind off, the entity was confident she would help it when she realized she'd been created from it, and it needed her help.

Isabella waited for Kat to strike. She didn't. Whatever was happening in Kat's mind, Isabella could see that it was leaving her inactive at that moment. It was an odd thing to see, given how forthright the entity had been inside Kat on previous occasions.

Uncertain what to do, Isabella waited, maintaining focus on the power she held within her hands. While waiting, she moved her sight back and forth from Kat to Antonio. There was no mistaking that something wasn't right with him either. On the previous occasion, Antonio had shown strength and power. If he still had either of those inside of him, Isabella couldn't see it.

Under the guise of Elder Scott, the entity walked into the large area. It took its time to enter. It took its time to walk around. It pushed itself to remain calm and be patient. One stupid move and its plan could be ruined. It had happened twice. The entity wasn't going to let it happen a third time.

As it began to walk toward Elder Rhys, pretending to be an elder who would support the ancient, the entity became aware of the final two players entering the area. Slowly the body of Elder Scott turned to watch them enter. One it was not interested in. The golden boy was a future ancient, but as yet held no powers. He could provide emotional support to his mother and father, but nothing else.

The entity turned its focus to Esmeralda - its own offspring. It had never been so close to her before, having only seen her through its mind. As it resumed its journey to where the ancient stood, it found it difficult to pull its sight away from the presence of its child.

"Esmeralda," the mouth of Elder Scott said out loud.

The tone of the voice caused all in the room to turn and look. The glances were dismissed as the entity resumed its walk toward the first person it wanted dead.

Esmeralda and Cesare both stopped still when they saw all who were in the room. It looked odd enough seeing Cesare's mother and father facing Kat and the man beside her. Of most note, though, was what they saw on the hands of Kat, Trent, and Isabella.

Cesare turned and looked at Esmeralda. She wore the same look of surprise that he suspected he had on his face. They'd always thought they were the only two in the village who could do such a thing. To see their own parents possessing the orbs left them speechless.

"What is happening here?" Cesare called out when he found his voice.

"You must leave, Cesare," Trent said, regretful that he and Isabella obviously hadn't been quiet enough when they'd left their home. "This does not concern you, and it is not safe."

His father's words instilled in Cesare the understanding that while he and Esmeralda had used similar orbs to play their childish game, what was happening in the room was not the same thing.

"Safe?" he asked for clarification.

"Leave!" he heard his mother call out.

Usually, Cesare was a person who did as either of his parents asked or directed. As he moved forward and saw the faces of Esmeralda's mother and the man who stood beside her, Cesare made the decision to not follow the instructions he'd been given by his parents.

"I will not," he said as he raised both palms. "If you are not safe, you can use my help."

Isabella and Trent watched their son do as they'd both done. Before their eyes, two golden flames appeared over his hands. He played with them, just as he had hundreds of times during his evenings with Esmeralda.

While Isabella was surprised, she maintained her focus on Kat. As yet, Antonio hadn't summoned anything. With his hands hanging by his sides, he didn't even look like he knew how. Isabella chose to keep an eye on him also, allowing for the possibility that his lack of action was just a ruse.

Esmeralda watched everything and everyone. Whatever the people in the room were preparing for, she, too, believed it was not for play.

She understood why when she watched Cesare naturally move close to his father. When he found his place, she saw him summon his golden orbs of flame, then turn to look at her.

At that moment, both realized something had to happen. Cesare and his family were facing Esmeralda's mother. Kat was also poised as if ready to strike at Isabella. It seemed an impossible situation for Esmeralda to be in. She had no regard for her mother at all, but taking a side to fight against Kat didn't seem right.

While Isabella mostly focused on Kat, she monitored what else was happening in the room. It had been a surprise that her son could do what he'd done, but she could process that news at a later time. Of more importance was her awareness that Elder Scott was slowly edging around towards the area behind Isabella and Trent. He was subtle, but she could tell he was intending to go to where Elder Rhys stood.

Her recent suspicions about Elder Scott made her wary. Was he currently himself, moving to provide strength and protection to the ancient? Was he currently under the influence of the entity, with the full intention of causing Elder Rhys harm?

Each of those questions, she knew she had to find the answers to - quickly.

CHAPTER 56

Sensing the uncertainty in its offspring as Esmeralda looked at the others in the room, the entity pushed harder into the minds of Kat and Antonio. The connection with Antonio was reinforced, resulting in him raising one hand and summoning a blue orb of flame into his palm.

"Come to us, Child," the voice of Antonio said under the influence of the entity. "Your mother needs you. *I* need you."

Esmeralda looked at the man as he spoke. If she'd ever seen him previously, she had no recollection of it.

"I do not know you," she said, glancing from him to her mother.

As always, her mother showed no emotion. It was yet another example of the contrast between Kat and the parents of Cesare, who had both appeared genuinely concerned for him and eager to see him safely out of the area and away from any threat of danger.

"You do not," Antonio said, enjoying the cool that had engulfed his hand. "You have not met me in this form, but you are special to me."

Esmeralda looked at Kat again, hoping for some guidance or clarity. While her mother's eyes looked in her direction, they held no emotion whatsoever.

"I am special to only one," Esmeralda said out loud.

"Yes," Kat's voice finally said. "Your father."

Esmeralda was confused. The words, she would have easily accepted if she'd thought Kat meant Adrian. As Kat had spoken, it was obvious to all in the room who she meant as her finger clearly pointed to Antonio.

CHAPTER 57

Adrian remained where he was. For quite some time, he'd been outside the area, looking in from the darkness a side corridor provided. He'd listened to all that was happening. He'd seen his child enter the room with Cesare by her side. The surprise of everything he saw and heard had been enough to hold him where he was.

Although it had been so long since the previous battles, he could still summon the memory of when Kat had pushed pain into him. He could also remember that he'd served no purpose from being in the room with the people who held the skills he'd seen. They were all fighters with the ability to cause pain in one another. He had no skills in any aspect of previous battles. He assumed he also had no skills that would prove useful for what was presently happening.

What he saw as he looked at all people in the room made him feel the same level of inadequacy that he had previously. It seemed to him that all in the room had the same ability, except for the ancient, the elder, and Esmeralda.

As Adrian watched his daughter, he saw the interaction between her and Antonio. He also heard the words that came from Kat's mouth. On hearing them, he wanted to run into the large space and drag his daughter away. Had Kat known what she'd implied, or was it some kind of play by whatever was driving her to do and say the things she was?

Adrian cast his mind back two decades. He didn't want to, but he couldn't help it. He'd been unhappy enough with being paired with Kat. He was the one who had agreed to that. In that, he could blame nobody. He'd accepted his choice in the pairing and had devoted himself to playing the role. It had been important to him as a father to his daughter.

His daughter. Was she his daughter? The words Kat had said, and the way she'd pointed at Antonio as she'd said them, made Adrian question that. He'd always thought so, but had he helped to create her at all?

As quickly as he found himself asking that question, he argued with himself. In the silence of his mind, he remembered all of the eighteen years that he'd supported Esmeralda as she'd grown. Throughout that time, Kat had played little role in teaching Esmeralda how to do the simple things of life. It had been Adrian who had helped Esmeralda take her first step, taste her first food, and dress herself for the first time.

When she'd been young, he had been the one who had cuddled her, encouraging her to talk about her day, and trying to make her believe that he truly wanted to hear whatever she ever wanted to say.

While he could concede that in recent years their relationship had changed, Adrian would not accept anyone saying that she was not his daughter or that he was not her father.

Without any further thought for the pain he knew he might bring to himself by doing so, Adrian stepped into the open space, bringing the attention of all to himself as he walked up to the young woman that *was* his daughter.

CHAPTER 58

As Isabella watched Adrian enter the room, her heart ached for him. She'd heard what Kat had just implied. While she conceded that it could have been a trick of the entity, making Kat think that when it was untrue, Isabella suspected that it wasn't an untruth at all. During their previous battle, she'd seen the closeness of Antonio to Kat before both had broken out of their trances. She'd also seen the two of them in their visions of the night much earlier than that, conspiring to meet late at night with determination to not let anyone else know.

Despite what he must have just heard, the look on Adrian's face was one that Isabella knew represented determination. She watched as he moved to stand next to Esmeralda, hold his chin up high, and speak.

"Esmeralda is my daughter, Kat," he said.

Through Kat as its sub-host, the entity projected every move she made and every word she spoke.

"She is not of your seed," Kat's voice said. "There is no part of you in her."

When Adrian looked at Esmeralda, he saw the confusion in her eyes. Usually not one to want to upset her in any way, he took a step toward her and placed his arm around her shoulders. He knew she might not want that, but he didn't care. He was going to fight for her, no matter the outcome.

"Inside of her is my *heart*," he said. "Even if what you say is true, she *is* my daughter. She has my heart, and she has my love … forever."

Esmeralda heard the passion in her father's voice. She could see tears threatening in his eyes, and she could sense the fear running through him. She could also feel the pride emanating off him when he'd spoken about her. It had been a rare speech to hear from either of her parents, even though the content didn't surprise her, coming from him. While she knew she might have to face what her mother was saying, Esmeralda resolved that she equally would only accept Adrian as her father, not the stranger who was standing next to Kat.

Through Antonio's eyes, the entity fumed. Its primary existence still rested and waited inside Elder Scott, but it didn't hold back from making Antonio's hand raise, the blue orb of flame ready to strike.

Seeing what was about to happen, Esmeralda moved in front of

Adrian. With remarkable speed, she raised both hands and summoned cold blue flames into her palms. As she did so, the entity realized it had made yet another mistake.

"Come to me, Esmeralda," Kat's voice said. "You are my daughter - my flesh and blood. You see that you have the same ability as your father and me," she continued as she once again pointed at Antonio. "We share the same skill, and we are a family. Walk to me, Daughter."

Esmeralda didn't know her mother as well as she'd often wished she did, but she knew Kat well enough to understand that something was seriously wrong with her thinking. Seeing it, Esmeralda remained where she was with the full intention of protecting the only man she had ever considered her father.

CHAPTER 59

As Cesare watched the strange interactions between Esmeralda, Adrian, Kat, and the odd man in the room that Cesare had never seen, he felt torn. He wanted to run to her and remind her that if she needed him to, he would protect her. It was a fruitless idea. From their many years of their childish play, he knew she was far more skilled in the use of the flaming orbs than he was.

Seeing her huddle close to Adrian, standing up for him as her father, pleased Cesare. He'd heard her talk about her parents a great many times, but rarely in a positive way. He'd often tried to make her see that Adrian was a good man. It had been a difficult effort and one that she'd seemed, at times, to reject with the full amount of her stubbornness. It was nice to see her stand up for Adrian in the strange situation they'd found themselves in at that moment.

Looking to his left, he glanced briefly at his father and then at his mother. He could see the two orbs his father held dancing over his palms. Beyond that, the much larger orbs of flame his mother held steady impressed him. He'd never heard either of his parents talk about having the ability to do such a thing. Seeing the harshness of them both doing it at the same time, particularly to the degree that his mother was, both surprised him and stirred him with the pride he felt at being their son.

Watching the interactions between everyone, the entity increased its hold on its sub-hosts as it moved within its host towards its primary target. As amusing as it was, watching how the humans in the room were talking to one another and looking at each other, it had one job it wanted done then and there.

Thinking that Elder Scott's presence had been forgotten by all, the entity moved closer to where Elder Rhys stood. It was annoyed by how things had played out so far. As far as it was concerned, everyone who held a flaming orb at that time should have already let it fly.

It knew that it was time to let the fight between cold and hot begin. Previous attempts had proven that neither side would ultimately be hurt to the point that the entity wished they would be. What it could serve perfectly well as at that moment was a distraction. The strongest fighters in the room were poised and ready. They were just waiting for one to make the initial strike. As soon as that happened, they would all be distracted for at least a few minutes. That was all it would take for the entity to use Elder Scott's mind and body to move to Elder Rhys and end the ancient's life for good.

It played out possible scenarios as it moved closer still. It had no weaponry. If it summoned a flame like Antonio and Kat had, everyone would see that Elder Scott wasn't Elder Scott at all at that moment. The disguise would be over, and the entity's main host would be revealed. No, a better play would be to wait for the orbs to fly and then make sure that Elder Rhys was right in their path. The combination of multiple hot orbs simultaneously connecting with multiple cold orbs would cause an explosion sure to kill the ancient.

So absorbed with its plan to use the elder's body to facilitate the death of the ancient, the entity didn't notice the degree to which Isabella's attention was on it.

It also didn't have any idea that another player was entering the space, and that player was not one that it could ever recruit to be on its side.

CHAPTER 60

Trent watched as Kat and Antonio simultaneously raised their hands, guiding the orbs of blue flame in preparation for an obvious strike aimed directly at Isabella and Cesare. It was a pointless move that made no sense to him. Antonio and Kat held one orb each. They were facing three people with two orbs each, including the one that Isabella had worked on to increase its size and power. There was no way those with the blue flames could win, no matter how good they were at hitting their targets.

When Esmeralda saw her mother move to strike, once again she felt like she had been put in an impossible situation. She didn't want to fight her mother. If she stood with Cesare, she would have to. Similarly, she couldn't move to her mother's side and attack Cesare and his family. They weren't her family, but they had always treated her with kindness and tried to help her feel welcome in their home. To hurt them would also mean to hurt her closest friend. That was something she couldn't do.

Behind her, she knew Adrian still stood. She didn't perceive any form of power inside of him. He was utterly helpless if anyone was to attack him. That was her determining factor in remaining where she was. She was ready to defend, but she would not attack anyone. Although her loyalty did lie with Cesare, she was on neither side completely.

"Stay behind me," she said to Adrian as she quickly looked behind her to where he stood.

Adrian nodded. He wished he'd stayed where he had been earlier. While he cared nothing for the possibility of getting hurt - or worse - he knew his presence in the area made things more difficult for his daughter. He'd forced upon her the need to protect him. That wasn't the way things were supposed to be between parent and child. He wanted to protect *her*, not have her protect him.

As regretful as he was that he'd put himself and others in the position, he also knew he couldn't move. To do so could interrupt everyone's concentration. He couldn't allow that. He'd made enough of a mistake going into the area. There was no choice but to remain still and wait for whatever was happening to be over with. When he'd witnessed similar events previously, everyone involved had survived. He held onto the hope that all would again.

CHAPTER 61

The entity knew it had to time everything perfectly. Its consciousness was well familiar with being split between multiple bodies and minds. That aspect didn't need too much concentration. It was as easy as flicking a switch, making its host and sub-hosts do what they had to at the precise moment that was best. The difficulty came from accurately anticipating where the orbs were going to fly and timing the most likely point of impact when it pushed Elder Rhys right into it. It was a sound plan, but it used heavy resources of the entity's mind to look and assess everything so that it happened with precision.

It continued to take its time working around the outside of the large area in its effort to get to Elder Rhys. The ancient glanced at him now and then but, for the most part, was more focused on what was about to happen with everyone else in the room. The entity was glad. For a moment, it quietly sang its own praises in the calm of Elder Scott's mind, thinking it was about to see the first stage of its overall plan successfully happen.

While Isabella maintained focus on the blue orbs pointed straight at her and her son, she continued to monitor how close Elder Scott was getting. He'd moved behind her visual line of sight, but she could heavily sense his presence as he moved. To him or anyone else, she wouldn't look like she was aware of his movements, but she certainly was.

As the entity moved the body across the last space between it and the ancient, it heard a screech of a magnitude it had never conceived could exist.

CHAPTER 62

As had been the intention of the entity, everything happened at once. Kat and Antonio used all their force to throw the blue orbs of flame they'd been holding onto. At the same time, Isabella, Trent, and Cesare did the same with their golden orbs.

In perfect synchronization with the orbs meeting, the screech of the highest volume and pitch was heard. It was nothing like the entity had ever experienced. Its intended movement toward Elder Rhys was instantly halted, interrupted by the tiniest sliver of time as the mind-piercing sound became unbearable.

For all in the room, it felt like time stopped. The light filling the room from the orbs striking one another, combined with the high pitch that all could hear, halted both sides in anything they might have been planning to do next. It was almost deafening, pushing all to quickly raise their hands to cover their ears.

"You!" Elder Scott's voice rang out as the entity saw who was making the unbearable screeching sound.

The sound of him yelling forced Isabella, Trent, and Cesare to all turn around to face him. When they did, they saw Elder Scott lunging forward in an attempt to stop the creation of the noise. As they heard the end of the mind-drilling scream, they saw it was coming from Alessia.

Isabella's natural instinct was to run to her daughter, fearful of what was happening to her. Before Isabella could move forward, she was restrained by Trent's hand forcefully grabbing and holding her wrist. When she looked at him, she read his silent request to wait for just a moment to see what was going to happen. The conflict was intense, wanting to save her daughter from whatever was happening, but also trusting that when Trent stopped her from acting, he was usually right to do so.

While Isabella reluctantly followed his lead, she remained where she stood while focusing power into her hands again, just in case another strike would be necessary. It had already been suspected by her that Elder Scott had been taken over by the entity that had for so long been intent on hurting people in the village. Seeing the way his body had just moved in an attempt to lunge at Alessia secured that suspicion in Isabella's mind. She'd never seen the elderly man move so quickly or forcefully. She knew he never would if it was truly himself in that body.

It was an instant in time, but Isabella saw so much. Questions flowed over her mind. Why was Alessia there? What had she been doing, screeching as she had - and why?

Resolved that it was a moment when she did have to wait and watch to see what was about to unfold, Isabella prepared to strike. She also prepared to learn. Her daughter was doing something. She hadn't accidentally stumbled upon the area or the people within it. She seemed to be needed for a role in whatever was playing out. Isabella watched the young woman who, with the same red hair as her own, was so much like her.

Feeling Trent move his hand to take hers in his, she looked at him. He was by her side as they watched whatever was about to happen to their youngest child. He was there, and he was ready to strike too. Isabella had to find strength in that.

CHAPTER 63

Inside her head, Alessia had seen and heard every action taken, every idea considered, and every word spoken by every person in the battle area long before she'd set foot in it. For as long as she could remember, she'd been listening to everything that everyone in the village had ever said or thought. It had almost driven her crazy at times before she'd taught herself to block out the unimportant and hear only the important.

She'd often wondered why it was that she could hear and sense so much. She'd wondered if everyone could do it, but she'd never heard anyone talk about it. In her heart, she'd always considered she might be the only one even though she had no idea why.

As she stood in front of the body of Elder Scott, she understood. What she was currently about to do was her absolute destiny. It was what she'd been created for, why she was who she was, and why she could do what she could do. At that moment, so many questions she'd always had about herself were finally answered.

Although she knew that part of the entity was spread over the minds and bodies of Kat and Antonio, she equally perceived that the head of it was in Elder Scott. That was where she focused, knowing the entity could easily jump around from one person to the next. She knew it could happen. She also knew she couldn't let it.

Ignoring every other person in the room, she walked closer to where Elder Scott stood and looked closely into his eyes. They were blank. The thing that was inside of the elder was preventing any piece of the man from being present at that moment.

Knowing exactly what needed to be done, purely through intuition, Alessia maintained her gaze with the elder's eyes. Standing still, she opened her mouth to speak. The voice that came out surprised everyone. It was not the voice of Alessia at all.

CHAPTER 64

Isabella wanted to be ready for another strike. Even she found it difficult to think about such preparation as she watched her daughter move and then open her mouth to speak. When the words finally came out, Isabella wondered just who her daughter actually was.

"Reveal yourself," Alessia said, her voice loud and confident. She repeated the words once, twice, then a third time. The fourth time, she shouted them as she raised her hands high as if reaching out to the ceiling of the vast area. "*Reveal yourself!*" she screamed at the outer shell of Elder Scott.

As all watched, light of a form similar to lightning extended out from each of Alessia's fingertips. To Trent, it was how he imagined electricity would sound. To others, they'd never seen or heard anything like it. As Alessia's mouth opened, another screech came out of it. Her face contorted, revealing the level of concentration and physical change she was going through.

Isabella felt Trent's hand squeeze hers to the point where it was painful. Despite how much the sight before them was obviously affecting him as well, he didn't act in any way. Both looked at their youngest child, watching the effort on her face and the great light that was flowing from her fingers and her body.

With one more screech and command from Alessia, a lit orb moved from Elder Scott's body. Upward it moved, out of and then away from the host it had resided in. As all watched, the elder crumpled to the floor without saying a word or showing any sign of life. At the very same time, the same thing happened to Kat and Antonio.

It was at that moment that Elder Rhys finally moved. Minutes earlier, he'd wondered about Elder Scott being possessed. Sensing the entity had moved out of the elder, leaving the empty shell on the ground, Elder Rhys rushed to the crumpled man and knelt beside him. When he felt the side of Elder Scott's neck, Elder Rhys was relieved. The elder was alive. For that moment, the ancient knew there was nothing that could be done for Elder Scott. He would be fine with a little time to pass.

At the precise moment that Elder Rhys had moved toward the elder, Esmeralda had rushed forward to her mother with Adrian right behind her. Both knelt beside Kat, attempting to revive her. There was no response.

Elder Rhys stood and moved to where they were. Reaching down, he found Kat's pulse.

"She will be well," he said, reassuring them. He moved to Antonio and repeated the inspection. "As will Antonio."

Standing tall again, Elder Rhys directed his attention to the people nearby. All people in the area who were awake became focused on only one specific point.

As all saw Alessia move, surrounded by the purest of golden light, their eyes followed her trail. She was mesmerizing, making them feel powerful and helpless all at the same time.

Nobody else moved as she walked to the center and stood midway between Isabella's family and where Esmeralda and Adrian remained beside Kat and Antonio. Once Alessia had stopped walking, all watched as the golden image of her looked upwards.

With what had just happened, nobody had again thought about the light explosion of blue flame meeting gold. When they all looked to see what Alessia was looking at, they saw it.

Hovering above them all was the broad-sized light. It was acting as a magnet, pulling toward it the orb of light that had left Elder Scott's body. Before everyone, the small light connected with the larger one, sinking into it and becoming one with it.

"Reveal yourself," Alessia said again, directing her words at the hovering light. "It is time for this to end. You must reveal yourself to me. You must take your true form. It is time for this to end."

All saw the light begin to move downwards. Nobody made a sound as it slowly changed. The more it descended, the more it took on a form that was identifiable to the people in the room.

They continued to watch. Despite how bright the light had been, nobody could look away. Not one had seen such a thing before, including Elder Rhys. Until that moment, he'd thought he'd seen and experienced everything that could be seen or experienced. He had not.

The light slowly descended further until it approached the level at which everyone stood. All continued to watch as if they were hypnotized by it.

What had looked like a golden cloud altered in shape to eventually reveal a man.

CHAPTER 65

Downwards still, the bright golden shape moved, progressing in its development until it reached the ground. As its feet touched the surface, the golden light fell away. All gasped at what they saw.

Alessia watched the man evolve from the light. She already knew who it was. That didn't stop her from feeling intrigued by him. She'd always known he was coming. It was a part of who she was.

Stepping up to him, she looked closely at his face. It was aged, almost as much as the face of Elder Rhys. Yes, it was aged, as was the body, but there was no mistaking who the eyes belonged to - or the golden hair.

Isabella thought she might faint. She saw the face. Even in its aged state, she knew it well. Briefly looking at Trent, she saw his surprise too before they both turned and looked at their oldest son.

Even though all eyes turned toward him, Cesare was the only person who couldn't see what they all could. With no such thing as a mirror in the ancient village, he was the only one who had no comprehension that who he was looking at - was actually himself.

Isabella looked back at the old man. He was old, but he was her son - her golden boy. As she watched the older version of Cesare, she saw him look at himself, lifting one hand then the other, studying them. She then saw him move his hands to his face and his hair. The confusion in his expression was obvious, and it was immense.

"I..." he began to say, his voice like Cesare's but so much older. "I do not understand."

Elder Rhys looked at the man. He knew him. He knew him not as the young son of Isabella, but as his friend who had left the village a great many decades earlier. He walked forward, slowly approaching the man as he studied his face, needing to be sure. It made no sense, but he could not deny what was before him. When young Cesare had been an infant, he'd held the old soul of Elder Rhys's friend for a short time. The ancient had thought they were two separate beings. He now realized that they weren't. They were the same person, just of different stages of their life.

"Cesare," Elder Rhys said as he approached the man he was sure was his old friend.

The elderly man looked at the ancient, then whispered, his shock evident.

"Rhys," he said. "I am confused. Why am I here? What has happened?"

"You have not completed your journey," Alessia said, answering the questions that all had. "You should never have come back here. It was wrong. In doing so, you returned as something you never were. You have been to the future. You have been to the past. Your soul has moved through love, through greed, and through immense anger. The pain you have felt, you have pushed onto others. You have forgotten the happiness you once lived. In your loss of direction, you changed. Now you must be sent on your way. It is long past your time to complete your journey … Cesare."

At the declaration of the old man's name, Esmeralda looked at her close friend. She could see the intense confusion on his face. With a glance to her father to ensure Adrian remained with Kat, Esmeralda moved to her close friend, stood by his side, and took his hand in hers. After looking at him in such a way to assure him she was there for him, she looked forward again.

The old man looked at Esmeralda, looked back at the ancient, and then finally seemed to notice others in the room. Seeing the golden hair of Isabella's son, he walked toward him. For a long while, they studied each other, both with the knowing that they were the same person, just many years apart. They needed no use of words. They looked at one another before the old man moved to stand in front of Esmeralda.

For a long while, he studied her, still saying nothing. There was something she needed to know, that he had to tell her, but at that moment, the words evaded him.

He moved further still until he stood before Isabella and Trent. Glancing first at Trent, his eyes then fixed on Isabella's. The emotion that flowed over him was nothing like he ever remembered having experienced. His entire life before was absent from his mind, but there was something he knew without any doubt. The feeling of familiarity sunk into him as he studied Isabella's face further.

"Mother," he said quietly.

Isabella couldn't hold back the sob. So often, when others were confused about anything, she had the insight to help because she *knew* the answers to so many things. Seeing her golden son in front of her, as an old man, was difficult enough. Seeing him as a young man to the left of her at the same time was just too much. She sobbed for her son as he was in his elderly state. Too many emotions flowed through her for her to be able to handle.

Seeing his mother's distress, the elderly man turned away. He let his eyes rest on his father's once more, but neither said anything. The look of comprehension that flowed between them was enough.

The man was drawn back to Esmeralda. She moved hardly at all as he stood in front of her, studying her eyes, the structure of her face, and the blue-black color of her hair. When the full comprehension hit him, he took one step forward. He made no move to touch her or get any closer. He only had one thing to say to her before he would have to leave.

"Part of my soul resides in you," the elderly version of Cesare said. "I see it. I feel it. I do not remember why, but you are a part of me."

Without waiting for any response from her, he moved back to the center of the area, toward where Alessia waited.

"It is time, Brother," she said to him before repeating what she'd already said to him. "You should never have returned to us. In doing so, time has been changed. It has become confused. You must go on your journey forwards, not backward. Where you are going, you are welcome. You must reach it. When you do, the things you have done here in the past will cease to be remembered, for you and for all of us. Prepare to go. The journey will bring you happiness, and it will bring us peace once again."

The man nodded and waited for whatever was to come. Although he searched his mind for memories from his life before, he found little. He didn't remember having lived with the few people in the room, and yet he knew who they were to him. Beyond that, he knew nothing.

Without having received any ancient training, Alessia began to speak, maintaining full control of the interior space and the people in it. She knew that in his elderly state, her brother had done unspeakable things. She knew that in recent years, his pained soul had contributed to the death of Isabella's father - his own grandfather. She knew that his pained soul had passed back in time and been a childhood friend of Elder Rhys's, even though Alessia could tell that the ancient hadn't made that connection. She also knew that in the distant future, the pained soul of Cesare had traveled with greed and hatred and destroyed the entire village and all who lived within it.

Alessia could see all of the destruction and pain that had been delivered by the lost soul of her oldest brother. She could see everything. Nobody else could. She was glad. No good could have come from any of them seeing or learning about all that had transpired as the pained soul had moved through time, confused, and in need of direction.

The things she knew, she would never share. The things that had passed, she would make sure nobody knew about. Anything that they *did* know, would soon be removed from their memories.

Despite all that she knew about her brother, Alessia knew what had to be done. With him, the usual forward path of their people had not been followed. His soul had veered off its intended path, and people had suffered because of it. Things had to be put right, and only she could make that happen.

"Join hands, one and all, as we prepare to farewell this man, Cesare," she called out. "He lived a great life. He was a great man. He did not complete his journey. Now he must," she said, watching as everyone joined hands.

Even though they'd so soon before wanted to fight one another, the desire for it had disappeared. It was replaced by a simple understanding that at that moment, all needed to join together.

When the circle of hands was complete with all standing in a ring around the elderly man, Alessia continued.

"Cesare," she said to him. "Brother. It is time for you to now continue on the journey you began many years ago. We thank you for coming back to us and the joy that your life provided during your time of living. Do not be afraid. Your new journey still waits for you. Go now, our friend, son, and brother. It is time."

Isabella watched, unable to stop her sobbing. Before her, was her son. He was older, but he was there. What was about to happen felt like the same as when she'd had to say goodbye to her father, Tomas, many years earlier. It took all her will, and the force with which Trent was holding one hand and her current Cesare was holding the other, to refrain from breaking the chain and rushing forwards.

"Please, everyone," Alessia said. "Bow your heads and give thought to the gratitude." After a few minutes, she saw the process begin. She'd never lived through a passing, being only fifteen years of age, but she knew what to do and what was happening. Her head was full of knowledge, even though she'd never studied to gain it. "It has begun," she called out. "Maintain silence, continue to hold hands, but raise your eyes and watch as we see and encourage Cesare to once again begin his journey to the happiness beyond."

As all in the room watched, those who had seen such a thing before recognized the process. The golden glow that emanated from Cesare's body was great, but it was able to be watched without discomfort. Before their eyes, the human form of Cesare was replaced with a small, perfectly formed, golden glow. It moved, first to Isabella, then Trent, and then Esmeralda. There it hovered briefly before moving back to just in front of Alessia's face.

"You have leave of us, Cesare. Go forth on your journey. Find the path you should have been on long ago. Move only forward. You have our blessing," she said to the golden glow in front of her.

The golden glow grew brighter, then smaller, and then disappeared altogether. When it did, Isabella fell to the ground, unable to hold back the heavy sobbing anymore.

Trent moved with her, unable to comprehend anything that he'd just seen and heard. His son had appeared before him as an old man. His son was also standing nearby as a young man. If he'd accurately interpreted everything, it had been the old version of his son that had caused every pain since he'd arrived, in every person in the room. The idea of Cesare doing that when he was such a good person was the hardest thing for Trent to accept.

As he crouched and held Isabella in his arms, he couldn't help but look up at his son. He could see Esmeralda holding Cesare tightly. There was another aspect to consider that seemed unbelievable.

At that moment, he knew he couldn't present any questions. The previous minutes had been hard enough for him and Isabella. How Cesare must have felt at that moment, with what he'd seen, heard, and learned, was far more important.

Although Trent didn't want to pull away from Isabella as she felt the pain her sobbing showed, he knew that his son was going to need his support and his love more than ever. He'd always loved being a father. He resolved at that moment to be the best father he could ever be, once the current moment was all over with.

CHAPTER 66

Alessia hung her head. She felt drained from the experience she'd just been through, but she also felt empowered. The feelings that had flowed through her as she'd taken all through the experience had been immense. They'd also been how she knew she'd always worked towards being.

She watched her mother and father console each other with what they'd just seen and heard. Turning from them, she saw her brother with Esmeralda's arms around him. Alessia could read that neither had fully comprehended what they'd just been told. She would explain, but she would give them some time first.

Turning further still, she saw Kat and Antonio wake. Moving forward, she helped Antonio stand just as Adrian helped Kat to do the same. When they were both on their feet, she addressed them one at a time.

Moving to face Antonio, she looked into his eyes and placed a hand on his shoulder.

"For much time, you have not been yourself," she said, seeing his eyes focus on hers. "You may have confusion inside of you, but know that your thoughts, your actions, and your feelings will always be yours from this moment forwards. Your love for Ariana is real. Your love for your children is real." When she said those words, she saw his head automatically turn toward Esmeralda. Through his mind, Alessia knew it wasn't a conscious thought that had made him look at her. She smiled at him. "You did not make her. She is not your daughter. Your children are those you made out of your love with Ariana. They are your offspring." Moving her hand to his head, she was happy to see his calmness and lack of desire to move away from her. "Your mind is free of memories that were never yours. Go home to Ariana. She is your love. She is waiting for you. After this night, nothing of this will be remembered by you." She smiled at him one more time before whispering her final words to him. "Go home, Antonio."

With a renewed feeling of alertness, and a great desire to see his Ariana, Antonio silently turned and walked out.

When he was out of sight, Alessia moved to stand in front of Kat. Once again, she raised a hand and placed it on the shoulder of the person before her.

"You were once your own person," she said. "You have not been that person for many years. You were robbed of who you truly are. Now you can be that person." She paused as she looked at Adrian and raised her hand in a silent request for him to place his in hers. When he had, she looked back at Kat. "You have been paired for many years. During that time, you have never truly seen the man you are paired with, just as he has never truly seen you." After she moved her hands to bring one of Kat's to join with Adrian's, Alessia placed her hand on Kat's heart. All watched as a golden light began to emanate from the point of impact over Kat's chest. "All that has prevented you from feeling, will be removed. It should never have been as it has been. You will feel and experience love. That love, you will share with this man, Adrian, and your daughter, Esmeralda. It has not been easy for you. Now it shall be." Alessia moved her hand to Kat's head. "What should never have been, will now never have existed. Time is mending. Your life will be as it always should have been."

Seeing what she thought was the very first smile on Kat's face that she'd ever witnessed, Alessia stepped back before turning to her brother.

As Cesare saw his sister approach him, he felt so many emotions that he almost felt none. Feeling Esmeralda hold and squeeze his hand was a comfort to him, but it was also a source of confusion.

Alessia studied the faces of Cesare and the young woman beside him.

"You know that the man you just met … was yourself," she said to Cesare. "He is not who you are. He is not who he was at the age that he passed. The man you just met was a confused and lost soul. Through his long journey of misplacement, he caused hurt and pain to the people of our village. In the distant future, he caused the *destruction* of our village and our people. That is not who you are, Cesare. You are not him. You are good, you are loved, and you are important to all of us, exactly as the person you are now. You will not become that person. You will not cause pain."

She saw the look of confusion and hurt on Cesare's face but moved her sight as she took one step sideways. Looking at Esmeralda, Alessia could see and feel every emotion flowing through the young woman.

"You love him, but you are confused," she said. "Do not be. The lost soul tried to create you. It did not know that it was not successful. You are the daughter of Kat and Adrian. This is true by your soul and the seed your father gave to your mother. Do not doubt who is your true father. You see him here," Alessia continued, pointing at Adrian. "The soul did not lie, because it did not know. I know. I see, hear, and feel everything. There is no mistake. In here," she said, placing her hand on Esmeralda's heart. "You were only made by two - Kat and Adrian. Rest easy. All is well."

Moving back to Cesare, she sensed the relief that flowed through his mind and body.

"You are destined to be together, to pair, to raise a family, and to live a long life together," she said. "There is no hurry for this. You will know when the time is right for you to move through the pairing process. There shall be no pressure. There does not need to be. You do not feel it yet. When you do, it will happen."

Cesare turned his head away from his sister and looked at the woman beside him. He could see that a partial transformation had already begun. He knew Esmeralda's body language and facial expressions well. Whatever Alessia had done when she'd touched Esmeralda had affected her deeply.

Alessia moved to where her mother and father had risen from their previous place on the ground. She smiled at both of them.

"It was your son - my brother - but it was only his lost soul," she said. "Cesare is here with us, as he should be. What his lost soul did is of no importance now. You have your oldest son with the brilliance of golden hair. He is here, before you, and the person he always will be. Do not grieve for what you just saw. It is time to forget," she continued before she raised both hands and placed one on each head of Trent and Isabella. "Forget what must be forgotten. Remember only what must be remembered."

Pulling away from Trent and Isabella, Alessia turned to look at Elder Rhys. As she did so, he moved forward.

"You are an ancient," he said to her as he looked into her eyes.

Alessia smiled and nodded.

"Yes," she said. "My mother will become an ancient in the distant future. That is the way of our people, but it will not be *my* way, because I am already one, Elder Rhys."

Elder Rhys nodded at her. He'd never heard of such a thing before, but he knew it to be true.

"Yes," he said simply before moving back from her.

As she watched him, she acknowledged all that she knew about his wishes and thoughts.

"You have long wanted to be on your next journey," she said and saw him nod. "You could not go before. You were needed. You are not needed now for that purpose."

As Isabella heard the words, she accurately interpreted them and was horrified. Stepping forward to where Elder Rhys stood, she yelled out.

"No!" she exclaimed. "Alessia, what are you saying? Do not speak of such things!"

Alessia smiled at Isabella.

"You love Elder Rhys," she said. "It is how it was always meant to be, that you would lean on him and learn from him. He has needed you as much as you have needed him. He wishes to begin his next journey. It is not for you or I to decide when that will happen. When it does, we shall all embrace it and celebrate the great man that you are, and always have been," she said as she faced Elder Rhys once again.

Elder Rhys nodded. He felt relieved of a great many years of responsibility. When it was his time to leave them all, he knew he could do so without having to worry about them. He turned to Isabella, moved to her, and took her hand in his.

"It is not my time yet, but it does draw near," he said. "I have felt this for many years. When the time does arrive, you will know and understand how important you have become to me, and how important you will become to our people. Your daughter is true in her words and her love for you and all of us. Together, the two of you will keep our village alive, well, happy, and thriving for many years to come."

Isabella felt Trent move up behind her before his arm wrapped around her shoulders. She didn't argue with what Elder Rhys had just said. Instead, she accepted it.

Alessia moved to where Elder Scott still lay. Placing a hand on him, he became animated once more.

"You have not been yourself," she said, helping him to stand. "Now you are. Go home. You must rest."

CHAPTER 67

Adrian felt overwhelmed by all that he'd seen and heard. He'd felt that way on the previous two occasions that he'd seen Kat try to attack Isabella. While he considered the knowledge he'd gained while in the space with those close to him, he fought to understand it.

Something had been trying to hurt the village for decades. Now it was known that it was an ancient soul of Cesare that had been doing everything all along. Turning to look at the golden-haired son of his closest friend, Adrian wondered if he would ever look at Cesare the same again.

As he wondered that, he felt Kat's hands on his arm.

"Let us go, Adrian," she said to him, her voice calm.

He nodded in response before shifting his sight to Esmeralda. As if sensing him looking at her, he saw her move toward where he and Kat stood. When she reached them, she hugged her mother. Adrian was pleased to see Kat remove her hands from his arm and instead place them around their daughter. It was something he'd never seen before. Witnessing it forced his eyes to threaten to water.

"Father," Esmeralda said.

Before that evening, she'd only ever considered him to be. During the evening, she'd been forced to wonder if he had been at all. She was glad that he was. He'd always shown her kindness and more attention than she'd ever accepted. She found no difficulty in wrapping her arms around him and holding him close, knowing it would be much easier to be a daughter to both of her parents from that moment forward.

"Will you come with us, Esmeralda?" Kat asked, her voice revealing a level of sincerity that was new for all of them to hear.

Esmeralda turned and looked at Cesare briefly before turning back to her parents.

"No," she said. "Cesare needs me now. I shall stay with him and return when I know he is well."

Kat nodded before she and Adrian turned and walked away from the crowd. She felt renewed in many ways, but mostly she felt a closeness toward Adrian that she wasn't sure she'd ever felt.

Adrian looked back once at Isabella but knew at that moment that she wasn't the woman who needed to be his focus. That woman was beside him with her hands wrapped around his arm. He smiled at Kat and saw her smile in return. They'd lost so much time. He hoped they wouldn't lose any more.

Esmeralda moved back to Cesare at the same moment that Isabella moved toward him.

"My son," Isabella said as she enclosed him in her arms.

"I am well, Mother," Cesare said.

He'd felt confused. As minutes were passing, his confusion was dissipating, leaving his mind clear and at rest.

"Go with Father," he said to her. "I shall spend time with Esmeralda for the moment."

Isabella nodded and allowed Trent to guide her out of the area. She, too, found her mind clearing and taking on a new level of calm as she walked away.

Briefly, she turned and looked at Alessia.

"I will walk with you," Alessia said, knowing her job was done, and it was done well.

CHAPTER 68

"I feel different," Esmeralda said when she and Cesare were alone. "I cannot explain the sensation within me. I am unfamiliar with it."

Cesare smiled at her as he raised a hand and pushed aside her hair from her cheek.

"Perhaps it is happiness, Esmeralda," he suggested.

She smiled and nodded. His suggestion could have been true. She wasn't sure she'd ever felt truly happy in her entire eighteen years of life.

"Perhaps it is," she said. "I … I am starting to feel uncertain about what has happened."

Cesare nodded.

"I feel the same," he said. "It is of no worry. We know that we are safe and well."

"Yes," Esmeralda agreed. It was the first time she'd ever truly felt that she *was* well.

As they relaxed with no desire to move, they remained silent until a noticeable lightness began to flow over them.

"The sun is rising," Cesare said as he watched it.

"I do not think I have seen it rise before," Esmeralda whispered.

Cesare looked at her.

"Nor I," he said. "It is like magic, how it rises in the sky as it does. Something so big - how does it do that?"

Esmeralda rested her head on his shoulder as she sighed and continued to watch the miracle.

"I do not know," she said. "I do not *need* to know. I am here with you … and I am happy."

CHAPTER 69

As Kat and Adrian returned to their home, Adrian was hesitant to say or do anything. He'd seen Kat flow in and out of moods and approachability many times throughout their years being paired. He didn't know if anything would have changed between them, regardless of what Alessia had said.

"I am tired," Kat said, moving toward where they slept. "I will not go to the mill this morning, Adrian."

Adrian nodded, feeling weary himself. The thought of going back to bed was a pleasurable one. Regardless, he dared not try to invade Kat's space if she was not welcoming. She'd already been through enough.

Resolved that he would remain awake and then go to dine for the morning meal when the sun was fully up, he was surprised when he heard her voice call to him.

"Will you sleep also?"

Still uncertain, he walked to where she stood beside their bed. As he watched, she moved under the cover but held one side open, indicating for him to join her.

Once in their bed, he lay on his back. Further surprise came when he felt her move to him so that her head lay on his shoulder. When he turned to look at her, their lips met. For the first time in almost two decades, Adrian felt comfortable enough to at least try and approach her. Moving his lips gently on hers, he felt the difference in her. She responded with the same hunger that he had.

Adrian seized the moment. Kissing her, he could feel her lips and tongue were as eager as his own were.

"I do not know," Kat started to say as she pulled away slightly.

Adrian pulled back further, aware that she'd likely be about to reject him. When she spoke again, he was reminded of all that Alessia had said - that Kat had never been her true self at any time during their time of pairing.

"I do not … know what to do," she said.

Adrian smiled in relief.

"Let us just start with this," he said, tentatively placing his lips on hers.

"Yes," Kat mumbled quietly between kisses. "Please."

Taken into a world that she had no idea she'd ever been in before, Kat enjoyed the sensations she experienced. In her memories were many joyful moments but the closeness to Adrian was something missing. As he kissed her and then began touching different areas of her body, she made a firm decision to herself. She didn't know why they had never been close, and it didn't matter. What did matter was that she appreciated who he was as a person, and she showed him that she could love him.

After a long while, she welcomed him inside of her, enjoying the feelings it evoked in her as if she were a virgin and had never felt them before.

Adrian felt his heart begin to mend as he moved inside of her. He suspected it might take a long time for him to forget everything, but he would try.

Shortly after that thought, his memory finished its mending. The negative was removed. Only positive remained. As his first orgasm in many years struck him with its full power, Adrian kissed Kat passionately. It was a new beginning for the two of them, in so many ways.

CHAPTER 70

Isabella was sad and openly displayed it. Her dear friend of so many years was gone. On the fourth morning after the events of that night, an elder had found Elder Rhys eternally asleep in his bed-chamber. The ancient hadn't looked like he'd been in any distress when it had happened. The look on his face as he lay in his bed had been one of serenity, like he'd welcomed the end of his very long life.

At the onset of the news, Isabella had sobbed. She knew Elder Rhys wouldn't have wanted her to. He'd told her many times that he'd lived a long and wonderful life. He'd never expressed any unhappiness or regret about anything that had ever happened to him. Regardless, Isabella had been distraught and continued to feel the grief that came from knowing she'd never again see the elderly man who'd become such a good friend.

Trent watched her and monitored her. Years earlier, he'd seen her experience grief of a sort when she'd thought the golden glow that had been appearing over her belly had been a child. It hadn't been, but she'd grieved for it as if it had been. That had been difficult for him to watch. It was equally difficult for him to watch her following the news of the death of Elder Rhys.

"Do not worry for me so," she said to him one morning after the ancient's passing. "I am sad, but I know he wants me to be happy, and I shall be."

Trent tightened his hold around her and kissed her forehead.

"I know," he said. "He was a great man and always supported us."

"Yes," Isabella said as she raised her head and looked at him. "He liked you."

Trent smiled sadly.

"That was fortunate," he said, remembering his uncertainty about everything when he'd first arrived in the village and met Isabella.

"I like you also," he heard Isabella say, her voice containing a healthy blend of teasing, happiness, and suggestion.

Trent laughed out loud.

"That is fortunate also," he said.

"It is?" Isabella asked. "How so?"

Trent shifted his body, forcing her onto her back before kissing her gently.

"Because I also like you," he said, grinning.

"You do?" she asked, enjoying their teasing banter.

"I do," Trent replied before placing his lips on hers and letting flow all the passion that he felt for her.

It was a passion that he'd felt since he'd dreamed about her before they'd even met. It was a passion that had never lessened. Every day that he'd had her in his life, he'd looked at her with desire and need. Every day, he'd been happy knowing he was spending the rest of his life with her.

She was his future and his destiny. She always had been. Something powerful had brought them together, binding them in a world and a life that was so different from the one Trent had started out in.

A different life. A happier life. A more fulfilling life. A *better* life.

A long time later, as he plunged inside of her, Trent knew he was complete.

~~~~~~~~~~~~~~~~~~~

The End
~~~~~~~~~~~~~~~~~~~